Acclaim

"A spellbinding tale where grief births magic and stories become reality. Heartfelt, imaginative, and brimming with danger—a must-read for fans of grounded magic and unforgettable heroines."

—MORGAN SHAMY, bestselling author of *The Stricken*

"This is one adventure that is not to be missed! For anyone who has ever dealt with the pain of anxiety and dreamed of meeting their imaginary friends in real life...this book is for you."

—AJ SKELLY, bestselling author of *Of Flame & Frost* and The Wolves of Rock Falls series

"*Flameheart* takes the dreams and imaginings of every person who has ever wished their story-worlds alive and weaves a tale of breathless possibilities and fantastical lore. With high-stakes danger and beautiful first-love, *Flameheart* is an impressive coming-of-age story that you will not soon forget."

—AMANDA WRIGHT, bestselling author of *Darkfell*

FLAMEHEART

FLAMEHEART

Quill & Flame
PUBLISHING HOUSE

DALTON BEQUETTE
& EMILY BEQUETTE

To our sons—
run toward the roar, little lions.

PRONUNCIATION GUIDE

CHARACTERS

Aurelia: Ah-rail-ee-ya (Lia: Leah)

Kacerion: Kah-seer-ion (Kayce: Kay-see)

Jace: J-ace

Terranth: T-air-anth

Fiducia: Fi-do-see-ah

PLACES

Emperium: Em-pear-ee-um

Somnium: Some-knee-um

Exterreri: Ex-tair-air-ee

Silvae: Sill-vay

Montes: Mont-es

Litores: Li-tor-es

Inferis: In-fear-is

OTHER

Volatequis: vol-ate-quis

Initiis: Eh-knee-tis

CHAPTER ONE

S hifts could be subtle. A missed bus. A surprise box to unpack. Chinese take-out for dinner instead of leftovers. However, some shifts rioted, tearing a life asunder in a breath. The average teenager could be melodramatic about it.

Lia didn't have that luxury. Except for when it came to this.

Papers covered in chicken-scratch handwriting were spread on the patio table with Lia's journal. It sat open before her grandfather, his eyes darting across the page. Back and forth. She tried to count, to gauge where he was in her story. That dreaded red pen was poised over the paper, a knife already dripping with her heart's blood—

Melodramatic. But writing was the exception. The only time she could afford it. Funny how it had only taken a week to develop this routine. It was the first thing Lia treasured since moving to Seattle. Not the bigger bedroom. Not the proximity to a forested park. But being walking distance from him instead of thousands of miles away. Even with the writing critiques—and even now, when it doubled as "keeping an eye on him", which her mom liked to remind her to do. Not that Lia needed reminding.

But each text asking how he was doing today, if he seemed *present*, made Lia's escape into the pages harder. After years of throwing herself into fiction, reality was demanding to be seen. She'd rather not. Not when this was all she allowed herself to begin with.

"Honestly, Aurelia. You've got to give this captain more *pizazz*." Her grandfather waved his wrinkled hands in encouragement, dropping the pen as he finally looked up at her. Sunlight caught the stubborn streaks of red in his silver hair.

Lia fought a smile. He was the only one who could get away with her full name. Papa privileges. "A villain needs pizazz?"

"He's a captain-turned-pirate!" His boisterous tone rose. "You can't just make him evil for evil's sake."

"Aren't villains supposed to be evil?" Lia asked.

Papa peered over his tortoise-shell glasses, but a grin tugged at his mouth. "You read plenty. Which villains do you find most compelling: the ones that are evil just because, or the ones that do evil acts with a sympathetic motive?"

Easy for him to say. Old man was retired, but to the world he was still Julian Corvine, author of the Floating Kingdom series starring Kayce Weatherstone—which, to be fair, had been *her* idea. Kayce, her childhood imaginary friend who, now age eighteen, was stuck with a thieving member of his court in her own stories.

She chewed on her pencil, staring at her journal. Papa had a point. Lia could think of several books where the villain's story was nearly as compelling as the hero's. Sometimes more so. A captain in a kingdom's navy needed a reason to turn to piracy, but she wasn't about to admit it. At least, not so readily. Writer's pride and all.

Her papa's eyes narrowed as she thought. "Let it come to you. These characters, we don't tell them what to do—"

"—they reveal themselves to us," Lia finished.

"Exactly. Norenth has always been yours," he said. "But you've always been theirs."

Theirs. The floating kingdom's, the Weatherstone court's, and Kayce's. Like Lia belonged with them. It had comforted her as a child when she first imagined this fantasy world, but as a teenager, the idea no longer settled her. It felt like a puzzle piece forced into the wrong hole. Close, but not quite. And *not quite* was turning painful, the cross-country move making her want to push in some-where, to fit in—

Lia picked the surrounding skin of her stubbed fingernails. It took a moment to recognize the action, to pull her cardigan sleeves over her fists. But her knee jerked, a rhythmic bounce under the table. Shifting in the patio chair, she looked out to the garden. Big mistake. She clenched her jaw, chest tightening. It was like the tangle of roses hadn't changed. She didn't know if she wanted to rip those roses from the ground or seek shelter amidst the thorns.

Breathe. Focus. Breathe—

"Aurelia," Papa pried softly. "You with me?"

"Fine." She plastered on a smile.

He assessed her with river-stone gray eyes, like her own. Her brother's. Mom's. Unlike her father's green. A green she hadn't seen—

"Has he contacted you yet?" he asked.

Lia bit back a groan. Sometimes she hated how well her papa read her. But even with him, she had to fix her face. Her father hadn't bothered to reach out beyond the obligatory birthday card. The fact didn't stop her from checking the mailbox every day, nearly ten years later.

"You think sharing a time zone would make him remember he has two kids?" She managed a laugh, but even to her it sounded forced.

"Your dad—" Papa started, then cleared his throat to begin again. "When your dad left, there was a great deal going on. More than you realize."

He wouldn't dare give her father a sympathetic motive for ditching. Those were a lot easier to figure out in fiction. In reality, people sucked. Some didn't need any reason to be the bad guy. Which was why she had to be there, to fix the wreckage.

Her nails dug half-moons into her palms, but Lia gave a simple shrug of her shoulders, disguising the unfurling of her tense knuckles with a stretch. "It's been ten years, Papa. It doesn't matter. We came back for you. To be close to you. Besides, you and I finally get to write without Mom griping at us."

He chuckled across the table, looking out at the yard and those darned roses. "You have a knack for seeking out the good."

A classic Papa euphemism, but a more genuine grin tugged at Lia's lips. "Care to elaborate?"

"Your eighth birthday here. Right after he left. When Kayce entered your life."

Even now he spoke like her fictional prince was real. Back then, her papa had caught her talking to thin air in this garden. Perfectly normal behavior for an eight-year-old, if you'd asked her. And creating her own guest while waiting for friends to show was better than ripping off her freshly painted nails, one pink shard at a time.

In her mind's eye, it was nothing beyond what a lonely little girl could conjure. She'd watched *Prince Caspian* a time too many. As a boy about her height, Kayce's dark brown hair had been ruffled from a trip, with several leaves clinging to his light blue tunic and beige breeches.

"He was teaching me to use a sword," she recalled with a chuckle. "For a fourth-born prince, he was pretty demanding."

"You had said he hated the reminder, but I'd never been one to forget nobility." Her papa laughed with her. Back then, he'd taken a stick for a sword to swing at the air. He couldn't see Kayce, but Lia had known with child-like certainty that Kayce's amber eyes lit with the calculation of his next move as he parried with a wooden sword.

Her imagination was as clear of a memory as any. If only Kayce were as real. Loneliness was a bitter aftertaste when their laughter died. Escaping into her stories didn't soothe as readily as it did before the move. Even with these new afternoons with her papa, with the journal laid open before her. If only Lia could stay inside her stories, maybe everything would be better. People would make more sense. But that wasn't an option.

Wings flapped in the looming cherry tree. Lia glanced at the owl nesting there, partially hidden by the leaves. She frowned. *A bit early for owls to be out.*

The barred owl watched. Sunken rings extended from its eyes, a mottled mixture of black and gray.

Lia did a double-take. The owl had six eyes. And stared right at her.

Pulling off her black-framed glasses, she rubbed her face. "I think my prescription needs upgrading. For a split second, that owl had three pairs of eyes." Lia laughed it off, but it was strained. She had to get a grip. Rein it in.

Papa stiffened and looked at the tree. But then he relaxed, reaching for his pocket. "Trick of the light. Be a dear and get your old man a new pen? Mine's dried out."

Shrugging, Lia shoved her glasses back on before heading into the house. Papa had been jumpy all week, so this sudden shift in demeanor was nothing new. It had to be the shift in their familial dynamic. Lia had done well to display that she had it all together. Her family could depend on her that way. They always had. But sometimes she wished her fantasy world was more reality than this place.

Selfish.

Lia stiffened before she could brush the thought away. Maybe she *was* selfish, and seeing things was the repercussion. Stupid birds with multiple eyeballs were something from a horror film. Not that she could stomach any of those. At least Norenth didn't have creepy birds of prey.

In the kitchen, Lia combed through several drawers, finding loose change, chip clips, take-out menus, pen caps—everything but an *actual* pen. How could a darned author not have a single pen in any of these junk drawers? Her copper curls tumbled loose from the velvet tie atop her head; she didn't know why she bothered trying to tame them. Lia blew an errant curl from her face, glancing aghast out the window that hung over the farmhouse sink.

There was Papa, waving a stick around like she was eight years old again and he not seventy-five! Her heart lurched with her startled yelp. This was not what Mom meant when she said Lia could visit Papa after school. He wasn't ten years younger! There was no imaginary friend to engage. She'd grown out of those. Hadn't he?

Says the girl still pining over the boy who could never talk back.

Lia grabbed the pen she'd missed in a pile of letters and made for the door. A flash sparked outside the window, quick as a struck match. Gone in a breath before Lia could really look. Another trick of the light?

"Papa," she warned when she made it outside. "What are you doing?"

"Admiring this tree! It's gotten so full." The stick was gone, his hands in his pockets.

The owl had disappeared. A faint scent of burning paper lingered in the air. The way her papa spoke a touch louder than necessary...something felt off. An itching in her mind, like she'd forgotten something. Missed something. She couldn't miss anything—

Papa swayed, knees popping as he turned toward her.

Not again.

Her heart faltered. Lia rushed to catch his elbow. Steady him. Scents of burning parchment intensified on his clothes. *This* was why Mom nagged her so much. Any annoyance she'd felt earlier about it evaporated.

"You sure you're all right?" Lia asked as they headed to the table. Her phone glared, reflecting sunlight. Mom would want to know. But her papa waved her off.

"Fine, just fine, when everything's back where they belong." He frowned, deepening the wrinkles carving his face. "To be frank, Aurelia, I'm worried about *you*."

Concern gave way to fear, and shame closed Lia's throat. She had to focus. Everything was under control.

"A new school can't be easy," he continued, "nor being so close to your dad again—even if he doesn't return any of Cordelia's calls, the insufferable—" He cut off, mumbling more to himself before turning to her. "Have you had any headaches? Feeling feverish? What about your sleep—"

"Papa, I'm managing. School's never been an issue, and neither has Dad. Don't go thinking I'm losing it. That owl was nothing, remember?" Lia shoved the journal into her backpack. She had to forget her father, to manage her tics. She had to tuck stories and oddities away. Reality was plenty to contend with. But putting stories aside was like holding her breath, being forced underwater.

"I have to get home. Dinner's on me tonight." Her brother Marcus wouldn't be eating out of foam containers again if she could help it. And her papa's stare made her skin prickle.

He sighed, gathering his papers. "It doesn't always have to be on you, little lion."

Lia stilled. The Norenthian nickname loosened something in her, as it always did. A role she didn't have to force herself into. But if she didn't return home like the responsible seventeen-year-old she was, she knew it would be another spin at the take-out menu roulette. Besides, Lia had gotten pretty good at cooking. The ordered steps, the measured ingredients, it all soothed her. Steadied her hands. She always had a plate ready for when Mom got home. Whenever that would be.

Lia shouldered the backpack. "How does tomorrow night sound?"

His assessing gaze softened, then skipped to his papers. He chewed his lip before a gleam lit his eye. "Perhaps I can show you what I've been working on."

"New book?" she asked, heading for the path winding around his Victorian home.

"Of a sort. Bit of a family tale."

"Is this the secret research you've been doing all week? Your mysterious social calls?"

"What? Because someone's over seventy, they aren't allowed a social life?"

Lia laughed at his dramatics. It broke apart the lingering tension like the sun over morning dew. "Party away, Papa, but be home at a reasonable hour. Sleep's important, they say."

"*They* know nothing about how important it is."

Sometimes his odd musings never seemed to make sense. In the moment, at least. Lia noted the taut pull of his shoulders as he walked her to the front of the house. He cut their writing time short several times this week; whatever project he'd been working on had put him on edge. Why would a family tale do that?

Unless...unless it had to do with her father. A *Corvine* family tale. Lia squashed the thought and swallowed the bile that came with it. Everything was *fine*.

Kissing his leathery cheek, Lia left him in the driveway. Walking home, she popped in her earbuds, escaping in daydreaming where her writing had left off. Allowing her to drop the mask and fake smiles. She stuffed her hands deeper into her pockets and walked on.

Neither Corvine noticed the second owl swoop into the hedges across the street. Its wings flapped once, twice. Six eyes blinked.

And it settled on the shoulder of a figure, watching the pair from the shadows.

A shift in the making.

CHAPTER TWO

For the entire forty-minute walk, Lia allowed her imagination to run wild. The brine of Norenth's salted air lingered in her mouth when she rounded the corner to her street. Blinking hard, it was like she had torn her focus from a television screen too fast, ghosts of images overlapping. Flying ships and oceanic clouds over suburbia.

Imagination over reality.

Maybe *she* should be more concerned about sleep than her papa. Maybe then she'd stop seeing things. But the allure of her fictional world and what it allowed her was hard to ignore.

It was a quick work of muscle memory to get settled once home: dumping her backpack, pulling out the needed ingredients from the pantry and fridge. Each sound echoed through the house, its walls still bare. Too empty. She needed something to fill the silence until Marcus came home.

Advanced trigonometry homework could wait another hour. No one was here to see.

Lia's shoulders relaxed a fraction, and she pulled out her journal. While water boiled for dinner, she bulleted notes about her sea captain's motives until the front door banged open. She dropped her pen with a start, whirling around to see Marcus nearly putting a hole in the wall before slamming the door shut.

Marcus didn't notice she was a fictional world away. Red-faced, he stormed like a twelve-year-old tornado across the kitchen to the staircase, tennis shoes pounding earthquakes to the foundation. A second slam shuddered through the house.

That was not the hello Lia was expecting. Nor the near heart attack. Norenth had to wait.

Turning off the stove, she made for his bedroom.

Marcus was face down on his bed, picking at a loose string that threatened to unravel the quilt. Granted, the old thing was in a sorry state. Clearly Marcus was, too. Upending one's life did that to a person. No matter how much they had claimed not to mind.

"I hate it here," he grumbled.

"Keep that tone and your voice will crack." Lia leaned in his doorway, but her teasing missed its mark. He didn't roll his eyes or snap back. The smirk disappeared from Lia's lips. She pushed off the frame to sit beside him. "What happened?"

He shrugged. "Nothing. It's just different."

There was something in his flat tone. What didn't he want to tell her? The again, what preteen *wanted* to open up his older sister? Regardless, Lia needed to try again. Humor was one of many coping mechanisms that helped him out of these funks.

"Higher altitude, for one," Lia said. "Ohio was pretty flat. Lots of corn."

"Maybe that's why everyone here acts like they've got something shoved up their—"

"Not another word!" Drowning him out, she lobbed a pillow at his head. "This city has already ruined your mouth!"

Marcus ducked before surging back, flicking russet curls from his eyes. "These guys are jerks! Are they any better in high school?"

"I wouldn't know. You're supposedly the social butterfly."

Despite my best efforts. But what high school senior wants to hang with the weird girl who prefers friends on paper? The intrusive thought sent a shudder down Lia's frame, an impulse to pick at the fragile skin around her stubbed nails. She focused on Marcus, fisting her hands into the pillow like she had evidence to hide.

Which she did.

"Clip my wings, I'm done with people," he sighed. "Can I get a story?"

Lia relaxed, his petulant demeanor vanished—*thanks, raging hormones?*—but the request threw her. The merciless weasel had requested so many stories since the move. A creature of comfort, that one. Well, namely a creature. Though, thankfully, he *had* at least discovered deodorant. The air happily lacked the perfume of moldy laundry. Not that they had been there long enough to accumulate it.

Lia shook herself from her brother's emotional whiplash and her own mental tangent. "Aren't you getting old for those? Besides, I have dinner to work on." She cringed. It sounded more like Mom than she'd intended.

It doesn't always have to be on you, little lion.

Well, no one else was here. Shaking off her papa's words, she looked around the room. "What about your books?"

"In boxes."

"How does this even allow you to relax?" Lia crinkled her nose at a precarious tower of cardboard.

Marcus picked at the quilt again. "It's just in case."

"In case what?"

"Dad calls."

Those two words were stones sinking inside Lia's chest. Marcus was still holding out—after all she'd done to make this as smooth as possible for him? For their mom?

"He's never visited," she said, forcing her tone to stay even.

"So? We haven't lived here since they split. Maybe he's been busy on a business trip. Can't get Mom's calls."

Did she dare tell him that those calls went straight to voicemail each time she'd eavesdropped? No, that would only devastate him. And she wasn't about to make the poor kid feel worse. Not when she could help it.

"It's possible," Lia reassured, grin in place. Even when it bottomed out her stomach. "But we're here for Papa. Mom needs to be close to him, and she needs us to be close to her. And I've got to be close to you."

"But who helps you?"

She blinked hard. Dug her nails in harder. Plastered on her more convincing smile. "Papa's helping me flesh out Norenth beyond his books. With my writing, I'm fine."

Liar.

Marcus didn't look entirely convinced either.

Unable to keep her face smooth and hold his gaze, she looked at the speckled stars emitting a soft glow across the ceiling. How did her brother manage to put up those but not unpack the rest? It was distracting. She hadn't been in here a full five minutes and her hands were itching to do something, anything, that might get things *perfectly* ordered.

"Tell you what," Lia bartered. "Let's unpack a bit, then I'll read from my journal." She couldn't waste time thinking about people who didn't matter. And honestly, neither should Marcus. Maybe if she settled him in enough, he wouldn't wish their father would appear. Because that would be nothing short of a magic trick.

To that end, after dinner Lia helped fill Marcus's dresser and closet with clothes. She even organized his astronomy textbooks. Plopping onto a vibrant orange bean bag, she opened her journal. "I wrote another plan to ruin some pirate schemes. Papa said this sea captain needed more *pizazz*."

"He would know all about that," Marcus sighed. "I wish I was like Kayce: a prince battling rogue captains, saving stolen animals and goods. Very Robin Hood. No wonder the fandoms love him."

"If he knew, it'd only go to his head." Lia looked at the clock. Mom had been gone for a twelve-hour shift at the hospital. It was now overtime. Unsurprising.

Forcing her jaw to unclench, Lia focused on the journal's warm leather cover. An anchor of the softest velvet. Opening to the first page, her papa's instructions were in his cramped script:

Write your stories, and they will become real.
Bring Kayce's kingdom to life.

The chicken scratch prompted a genuine smile. Papa had always encouraged her imaginings. And though she was to help him in his old age, Lia felt grounded. With him, she really didn't have to try so hard to keep everyone happy. Maybe she should be a little more honest with him. He actually *tried*, his worry knotting her throat.

Maybe she really didn't have to pick up the pieces alone.

Lia paged through her journal, half-full of snippets detailing the wayward prince. Writing about Kayce grounded her too, even when he was content to be wherever the skies took him.

Sensing Marcus's eyes on her, she read aloud. Here, she could give Marcus a glimpse of her secret self. They were stories, after all, and at least on paper she didn't risk anything. Unbound, ironically, since there she was free to be bolder, braver. What she wished she could be. Marcus may have wished to be Kayce, but all Lia ever wanted was to be the truest version of herself, unbeholden to anyone save the skies and seas. Sometimes, she didn't know who was fictional: Lia, devoted daughter and sister, or Aurelia, the Norenthian character she'd fashioned alongside Kayce.

Deep in reading, Lia and Marcus didn't notice their mom's return.

"You guys still awake?" Mom stood in the doorway, nursing scrubs wrinkled. Typical Seattle, with rain drops glistening in her copper hair. But she stood rigid, holding herself at the elbows. Lia frowned. It was more than tension from a long day.

But Marcus was already talking. "Lia was reading about smugglings. Turns out some captains are secretly pirates."

"It's not a secret, exactly," Lia couldn't help but correct. "Kayce knows."

"But the court doesn't! Not the king and queen, his brothers—"

"Guys!" Mom snapped. "Leave the fantasy alone. There are more important things to worry about."

Lia clenched her fists under the journal.

Their mom wasn't a storyteller. She avoided stories like a plague no disinfectant could stave off. It stung how she never asked about Norenth. But Mom worked so hard for them. Especially after their father left. Lia didn't want to add more strain, even if it killed an intrinsic piece of her.

But this was different, Mom's tone harsher than the sibling banter warranted. Even Marcus held himself so still, as if fearing his next breath could set her off.

"Sorry, Mom, we're finished," Lia said, shutting the journal. Her knuckles remained white around the binding. "Is everything okay?"

Mom's thin smile pulled the fine lines cupping her mouth. Her lip tremored. She opened her mouth. Closed it. Then she started talking.

And with those words, Lia's blood was an ocean, its roar deafening in her ears. It nearly drowned out their mom's muffled words. Nearly.

A shift. And then an anchor breaking. Leaving Lia unmoored.

She wouldn't have dared to write this plot twist.

CHAPTER THREE

With her careful perch by the fireplace, sandwiched between her mom and brother, Lia was an encapsulated sea, oceans stuck in a body. Only moments from bursting. One moment was really all it took. The space between one heartbeat and the next.

Or the last.

Papa's antiquated home was full of old and unfamiliar faces, but all wore black. Only one face was missing. It'd been a week, and her father had just sent a bouquet of lilies. It squatted on the coffee table like a noxious mushroom, oozing toxin in the form of *sympathies*.

The sickening sweetness burned Lia's nose, despite turning her cheek at the display.

Keep it together. Be strong for them.

Ashy depths were rising, pulling like tar. Her skin itched with it, too tight to hold the rising flood filling the space between her bones. No matter how hard she pushed, it kept coming.

She wanted to scoff—like anyone could stop the sea from rising. But she had to.

Breathe. Paddle. Swim. Thank them for condolences.

Papa's face stared out from an easel by the door—his professional author's headshot. Black and white. His hair combed, glasses perched low on his large nose. Smile wide, engaging. Warm.

He wouldn't smile anymore.

Take a breath. Tread water. Think of something. Anything.

According to the internet, drowning was a type of suffocation through the submersion of the mouth and nose in a liquid. Most instances of fatal drowning occurred alone or in situations where others present were either unaware of the victim's situation or unable to offer help.

While Lia's search history may be questionable—to be fair, she *was* a writer—the fact of the matter stood. It wasn't necessarily the water that killed. It was the overwhelming volume within a capacity never designed to hold it.

Grief was like that.

The human heart was never meant to withstand it. But there it was, consuming every inch of her. She could hardly breathe, an aching and mind-numbing pain washing over her like a rising tide on the beach.

He was her mentor, her best friend. The glue that kept them together, who helped her understand and connect with her mom. Staring at his portrait, Lia could almost hear him.

Run toward the roar, little lion.

Whenever she was afraid or withdrawn, Papa would always tell her to embrace the lion within. That the lion would roar in the face of any danger, any obstacle. And that she should run head-first into that roar to surpass anything that tried to keep her down.

But he was gone; the glue dissolving under grief's tidal wave.

Looking over at Mom and Marcus, Lia watched numbly as they greeted more guests. She noted the tight set of her mom's shoulders, the slouched back of her brother. How he kept looking at the lilies—then to the door. Lia glanced at the fireplace. Was October too soon for a fire in Seattle? Flowers made excellent kindling.

She picked at a loose piece of skin on her pinky. A small bead of blood bloomed. Marcus shifted beside her. He hadn't seen it, right? She fisted her hands, but the anxiety retreated only to her leg, a small bounce.

Marcus put his hand on her knee.

Her chest cracked. Forcing herself still, Lia wrapped an arm around Marcus's shoulders. No one could see her flail. Sniffing inconspicuously, Lia dug deeper. If their papa wasn't here to be the glue, she had to be. She needed to get her grieving family ashore. Toss them a life raft. Even though she felt like that poor guy from *Titanic*, someone else shoving her down in order to stay afloat.

You'll be alone in your room soon. Just paddle a little more.

Voices bled together. People spoke to her.

Yes, he was a great man.

Yes, he will be dearly missed.

What if she had stayed? Brought Marcus over for dinner? Maybe—

She couldn't go there. She couldn't let that thought, that imagining, torture her. It would drown her. Though she was barely treading water, she couldn't succumb, not yet.

"Do the police have any leads?" some nondescript cousin asked her mom, patting her shoulder. "Kids these days, always texting and driving."

We don't even know it was a kid. But Lia bit her tongue. Hard. Saying it wouldn't be helpful.

Mom stiffened. "The police are doing all they can."

Not like vehicular manslaughter was high on their list of priorities, even though it happened right outside the house. Apparently, Papa had been on his way somewhere, another one of his social calls. Except this time, he wasn't looking at the road when he headed out. On foot. Late in the evening.

A hiccup sounded from Lia's right, hardly diffusing the tension.

"If you would excuse me, I think my son and I need something to drink," her mom said.

The cousin pursed her lips, withdrawing her hand with another nod as a group of three approached the couch. Mom and Marcus had been standing, but now Mom stiffened, her bloodshot eyes a fraction wider.

An elderly man with weathered, sepia skin spoke first. "Cordelia, we are so...sorry."

"I appreciate that." She managed a faint smile. "It's good to see you again."

"It's been too long, and I wish it were under better circumstances." A middle-aged woman wrung her hands. "Julian will be so missed, I still cannot believe he—" Choking on tears, her upturned eyes blinked hard, like she was a grieving daughter herself.

Mom's face crumpled before she embraced the strange woman.

"Do we know you?" Lia's brow furrowed. There were plenty of faces she didn't recognize here—but these people seemed close to her mom, who hadn't lived here in almost ten years.

Mom righted herself. "I've known them for a long time. Friends of Papa's."

"From the bingo league!" the second man—a scrawny guy with bottle-thick glasses—interjected, drawing the attention of several others in the parlor. He shifted under the scrutiny, the other man glaring especially hard, causing Lia to lift her brow. Downright squirrelly, that one.

"I didn't know bingo had a league," Marcus muttered.

Lia bumped his shoulder in agreement. Who joined a bingo league? And since when did their papa like bingo? The questions jostled in the tide, a buoy to grapple for. Lia turned to her mom. "When did you and Papa pick up bingo?"

"Really, it was more of a writing group. I dabbled a bit when I was pregnant with you." She looked away with a smile that didn't fit her face.

Lia's jaw almost dropped. Mom *hated* stories. Well, severely disliked them. Definitely had never mentioned writing before.

The corner of the eldest man's mouth quirked up. "It's a little-known thing, but Julian was one of the best. At the writing *and* the bingo."

"Isn't it all luck?" Marcus asked. Lia wasn't buying a word of this, either.

"Not entirely. It's all in the wrist," the man continued. "I'm Leonard, though Leo is fine. I've known your papa since Cordelia was Lia's age."

Lia stared at Leo's outstretched hand. Bingo, writing groups, lifelong friends? All things she didn't know. Were they the reason behind her papa's social calls? His absentmindedness?

Finally, her mom elbowed her side, causing Lia to stumble toward Leo's hand. It was a firm shake, and he introduced the woman as Mirel and the squirrel—really, his gaze kept darting about and his hands never stopped moving—as Adrian. His tics were worse than her own.

After a few more forced pleasantries, her mom put a hand on Marcus's shoulder and ushered him to the kitchen. Lia was left behind with the bingo league, but it was good that Marcus was out of this room. Maybe she could "accidentally" dump the lilies while they were gone. She hardly ever stumbled, so maybe she could get the squirrelly guy to bump into the table? No, that wouldn't be right.

Lia adjusted her glasses and summoned a smile. It cracked like an unbroken book spine. "You knew Papa for a while?"

"He was a great man—heart on fire for the game, you could say!" Adrian practically shouted with a strained chuckle.

What was Papa doing, being friends with *this* guy? Leo, she could see. But this one was too odd. Maybe Lia should reconsider using him to get rid of the lilies.

Leo shot Adrian a glare before looking back at Lia, his gaze softening. "He spoke of you often. You and Kayce both."

She stiffened, all flower-foiling plans evaporating. "Kayce?"

"You still write about him, right?"

It was none of his business, but a defensive urge prompted Lia's tongue. "Papa liked that I never really gave him up."

Adrian clapped his hands together. "I'm sure you inherited Julian's talents."

"Adrian," Mirel cut in, "this isn't the time."

Heat burned Lia's cheeks, her gaze dropping to the faded ornate rug. Didn't this guy know this was a funeral? She crossed her arms. Those conversations with her papa had been *private*—her heart lurched. Her throat tightened.

Waves rose.

That writing session was the last time she saw her papa alive. Which wasn't this *bingo league's* business, either. Writing club. Whatever.

Her silence left a gaping hole, but Adrian seemed intent on filling it. "We often find the best of friends in a book, don't you think? They stay with us forever, through it all. Especially when we have to do things like move across the country. Julian mentioned that not many back east have stayed in contact—oof!"

Leo's elbow to Adrian's rib expelled his last word in a gust of air. "Enough."

Lia wanted the floor to crack open and devour her. To drown in the sea she'd become. Instead, she bent down and straightened the memorial pamphlets. Considering how she'd stayed busy, Lia hadn't really noticed the social quiet. At least, that's what she'd told herself—because they were right. No one had bothered to stay in touch. A few text messages, but ultimately, nothing. And now that her mom and Marcus needed even more from her, making friends here had dropped to the bottom of her priorities.

Which was fine. She could do this. She had to do this.

The din of conversation faded. Her chest constricted further, lungs compressing as if without a single ounce of air. She clamped her lips shut, fighting the burn. It pressed against the back of her eyes, threatening to spill over. She looked out the bay window. To the street.

Would there still be a stain on the pavement after another week? She tore her gaze away.

The waves crested. Bloomed into an ache between her brows.

She wasn't fine.

"Excuse me," Lia managed and hurried for the central staircase.

Murmurs followed, but they were a distant rumble. She didn't care. Once at the top of the landing, Lia ran to the end of the hall, yanking open the door for the attic staircase. The steps creaked, light filtering through windows set between the eaves. Trunks littered the small space, a side table and armchair relatively clean. Lia plunged into the faded green fabric as if it could hold her, papers scattering from the armrest.

Grief dragged Lia into murky depths. She gasped, air rushing through her shriveled lungs. Her chest painfully tight, the dam she had built to hold it all in, threatened to crack. The cushions still held her papa's bergamot scent. An anchor, pushing her back to the surface.

Breathe. Tread water. Hold on.

Lia counted her breaths until the tension in her chest eased, and her eyes burned less.

Not a drop had fallen. No one had seen. She was fine again. Almost.

An ache pulsed along her forehead. Ignoring it, Lia eyed the nearest trunk. Dust fell from the lid as she pushed it open, revealing paper curled and browned with age. On top was a crayon drawing: a young boy rode a horse with wings. A watery smile pulled at her lips. Afternoons in this attic had included scribbling away with her papa, building her kingdom. Another anchor.

Fishing through the trunk, she freed a stack of lined paper with edges frayed from where it'd ripped free from a notebook's spine. Lia skimmed the first few lines of a short story she had written when she was roughly thirteen. A fourteen-year-old Kayce was teaching her how to fly a volatequis, the kingdom's breed of winged horses. Well, trying to. But he goaded her petrified self into doing it anyway. Like he always did.

A lump threatened to return to her throat. Her nail caught on the loose skin of her thumb. Pulled. She needed to escape, if only for a few moments. Maybe that would get rid of her headache. Settling back into the armchair, Lia looked out the window to the cherry tree's swaying boughs. Something fluttered in the leaves, a dark shadow, some bird—

Focus. Breathe. Tread water. No optical illusions of creepy birds.

Her eyes grew heavy. She could shut them. Just for a few minutes. Then rejoin Marcus and Mom after finding a trash bag for those lilies. Maybe she'd blame it on Adrian, after all. Least he could do after the embarrassment he'd put her through. Even if he didn't know it.

Behind her closed lids, each breath was ebbing and flowing, the push and pull of the tide. However, Lia didn't feel the tar-like sea rising inside. Bergamot faded. Sea salt and pine replaced it, crisp and clean. Nostalgic. Her head pulsed again.

Then, she wasn't Lia at all.

CHAPTER FOUR

"You're certain he has them?" Aurelia, ranger to the kingdom of Norenth, called over the wind. Her abundance of curls remained tucked into a wrap around her head, and she fixed the black mask concealing half her face. Another gust tore through the sky. The volatequis she rode, Seagrove, angled her broad, smoky wings to ride it out.

Even after years of this, she had to remember not to look down. Nothing between her and those thousands of feet to the ground but a muscled equine with bird feathers. *Lovely.*

"Captain Luddeck is transporting a new cache of flitterbirds from the Western Isles," Kayce drawled from his mount, Storm. "My contact assured me the captain would be using the mist as cover for the hand-off."

She scoffed. "Were your contact's pockets empty this time?"

"That was *one* time, Aurelia, *one!*"

And that one-time sell-out had nearly cost them their identities. They'd been tracking smugglers and their illegal operations for three years, but that *one time* a couple months back had nearly tossed all their hard work to the trenches. "We cannot risk the

Ranger's Guild, let alone your parents, finding out we're the ones sailors like Luddeck complain about—"

"—all the while filling his own coffers," Kayce grumbled.

Aurelia bit her tongue, the sharp barb right there about what *they* did on the side. But she wasn't about to announce their own hypocrisy. Even if it was in the name of justice. With only the teeniest, tiniest bit of profit.

"Which is why we're here, doing what your parent's council won't and the Rangers' cannot," she said. "But we risk it all if we aren't careful."

"Must you always be the voice of reason?"

She smirked.

The answering smirk he gave sent a traitorous flip through her stomach. Definitely the heights. It had nothing to do with the similar mask framing his tanned face, amber eyes glinting like polished stones of mischief. His tousled hair was tied back at the nape of his neck, but several dark strands freed themselves as the wind pulled at the black tunic he wore.

Aurelia swallowed. Heights. Had to be the heights. Even after all these years of flying...despite now finding the thrill in it. Regardless, it was definitely the source of unease.

But when did this outfit make him look so...*roguish*? Aurelia shook her head. Focus. They had a job to do.

While mist almost perpetually shrouded the kingdom below, the Skyward Seas above were an explosion of color. Robin's-egg-blue painted the sky, shifting to deep indigo in the falling dusk. Pinpricks of light peered through the firmament, stars blinking in the darker distance. The clouds above the mist were buoyant and housed the seas to Norenth's land below. Some were the blue-gray of stormy waters, waves erupting around the edges so its spray added to the mist below. Others offered much more tranquil seas.

Kayce eyed one particular ship that had set anchor on such a sea, a kelp-strewn chain swinging from cloud to starboard bow. Men and women were hauling in a net full of silver-dollar cod, their scales sparkling in the setting sun to be sold to the Forge Guild for armor plating and their meat to the fisheries of the Market Guild. Captain Luddeck's was one of the few remaining ships, others having long since shifted their sails to make port on Fealtek, the largest peak in the skyline.

Kayce shot her a lopsided smirk. "Ready to liberate their bounty?"

Anticipation thrummed in her veins. "Race you there."

The pair urged their volatequises forward. Their powerful wings were nearly silent as the brine-filled mist cloaked them. Under the ship's hull they flew, giving the ocean the crew fished from a wide berth.

With a gloved hand, Kayce motioned above the rudder. The gabled windows of the captain's cabin shone with lamplight. Hopefully dear Luddy wasn't in residence.

Brass spyglass raised, Aurelia peered through the fogged window. No shadows moved within—apart from the steel cage filled with iridescent birds no bigger than her fist. Perhaps she would be back in her quarters to enjoy the next chapter of her book before too long...with a big box of the chocolatier's pure goodness.

Aurelia pocketed the spyglass. She slipped her leather boots from the stirrups, drawing her knees to balance precariously on the saddle. Years of tightening her core—and learning not to look down—steadied her. "Be ready to take off, all right?"

"I'll provide cover while you get to the eastern side of the Coral Sea."

Acquisition was Aurelia's domain. Her nimble form and light feet made her nearly undetectable. Kayce, on the other hand, used his natural talents of troublemaking to clear the way for escape when plans didn't go their way. Which was often. She had to nag him about that more. It was far too coincidental.

Aurelia wrapped her fist in a band of cloth before punching a hole through the bottom windowpane. Glass shattered, cascading in sparkles of captured sunset to the churning waters below. She leapt through and rolled down the ledge to the floorboards. Soundless, she sprang up and wasted no time moving to the cage. An early night and chocolate beckoned.

The birds twittered in greeting, small wings struggling to open.

"Shh, it's okay," she whispered, giving the cage a quick once-over before grabbing the handle. "You're not going to be boiled down into lantern fuel tonight."

Aurelia lifted the cage, but a thin line of tension snapped. Metal ricocheted through the table, dropping something that shattered. Clutching the cage to her chest, Aurelia gasped as the object ignited. Flames leapt up the table legs, several catching her pants. Heat burned her thighs. Yelping, she juggled the cage, batting the flames, wincing at her scalding palms. The fire spread.

Not good. Definitely not good. She shouldn't have missed that.

I can't miss anything—

"Aurel—*Harpy*!" Kayce yelled, catching himself before using her smuggling name.

Her heart stuttered at the hitch in his voice, shaking the fears from her mind. But another bellow shook the cabin as footsteps thundered from the galley.

"Wolfe! Get down there before the vermin escape!"

Skies and seas. This was bad.

Scrambling, Aurelia made for the busted window and tossed the cage through the hole. Kayce caught it before flames leapt between them, cutting off her escape. The door crashed open, revealing a heavy-set man with a familiar sneer.

Even in the panic, she had to bite back a groan.

"You're losing your touch," Wolfe shouted over the crackling heat, drawing a long, sinister blade.

So much for her night of peace. Maybe she deserved it for missing the trip wire. But Kayce's contact should have known about the trap. They were dead men walking. Aurelia drew her sword with a hiss of metal.

"Get to the deck!" Kayce hollered, taking her volatequis's reins and surging out of sight.

"Let's keep this quick, Wolfe," she ground out. "I've got places to be. Chocolate to eat."

Wolfe was already poised to strike. "But our last visit was so rudely interrupted."

"Am I supposed to apologize for setting your vats of illegal rukwhale oil on fire?"

"It would be the mannerly thing to do."

Aurelia shrugged, fighting to appear unfazed despite the searing sting on her hands and thighs. She hid pain well. "Manners? Seem to have left those at home."

The older man lunged. Metal clashed as she raised her sword to meet him, blow for blow. Their feet wove patterns across the floor until flames licked at Wolfe's legs. Adrenaline warmed her muscles, welcoming the action. Emptying her mind.

"I think you need these little sparring sessions more than you care to admit," she mocked, spinning on her heel to land her foot squarely against his chest.

He cursed, tumbling. Served him right. Aurelia darted for the door, more curses of outrage following her to the main deck.

Chaos greeted her. Sailors clamored to reattach a sail dangling by a rope, to douse another fire on the port-side. Others rushed to the railing, trying to salvage one of the horizontal sails to keep the vessel from sailing too high into the darkening sky. Kayce's doing. She'd bet her latest book that he'd been elated when their plan went wayside. Crew members lunged as Aurelia darted around casks of salted meat and fish, coils of rope, various sacks.

She glanced up through the rigging for any sign of Kayce, and her breath stilled.

An owl watched from its perch beside the mast. Mottled gray and ringed eyes, too far to see details. But familiar. *What in the skies and seas—*

A sailor leapt for her legs. Heart in her throat, Aurelia sprinted across the deck, sheathing her sword before vaulting over the railing. *Don't look down, don't look down, don't look—*

Arms flailing, she landed stomach-first on Seagrove's saddle. Kayce snatched her collar. She gasped for air once hoisted upright.

"'Run for the deck?'" she repeated in a croak.

Kayce shrugged with a laugh. "You needed the practice."

Now *he* was a dead man walking. "Next time you make me 'practice', sleep with one eye open."

They veered away, but Captain Luddeck was ready. "Fire!"

Kayce dove left as a volley of cannon fire rained upon them. Silver gelatinous spheres flung through the air. Wind ripped Aurelia's hair wrap free as Seagrove flew hard and fast, taking her away from him. Aurelia cursed, trying to wrangle her curls into her shirt one-handed. Her copper tresses, streaked with auburn and blonde, weren't exactly inconspicuous.

A flutter of wings, too small to be Storm's, drew her attention.

There was a whisper on the wind, between the bursts of Luddeck's cannon-fire.

The hairs on the back of her neck prickled. She strained to listen, to hear the rustle of a smaller wingspan. She scanned the sky. A dark shadow flitted in the corner of her eye.

Lia—

Aurelia jerked, stomach bottoming out. That wasn't her name. She didn't go by that.

Another flutter. Closer. The whisper came louder.

Lia, wake up—

Twisting in her saddle, Aurelia caught sight of the shadow, those ringed eyes tracking her, before water hit her from behind. Seagrove whinnied sharply. Wings drenched, she plummeted.

Taking Aurelia with her.

"Lia? You—are you all right?"

Groaning, Lia rubbed her eyes open to see Adrian standing over her. What was he doing up here? She stretched her legs, muscles protesting from curling into her papa's armchair. "I think it's better to ask what *you're* doing here. No offense."

Adrian flushed with embarrassment, fixing his glasses. "I-I thought this was the bathroom."

Right—the funeral. Guests. Her family. This nap was supposed to be a short reprieve. Not a whole fantasy adventure. But strangely, sea water coated her tongue. Even her hands tingled like she'd been sitting on them for too long. At least they weren't burned.

Vision blurred, she smudged her glasses while rubbing her eyesight back to normal. A perk of imagining herself as Norenthian Aurelia—no glasses. But not even her hair seemed to cooperate. Nor her fruitless feelings for a guy who didn't exist. She had enough to worry about besides stupid, hormonal crushes. Especially on fictional characters.

But she couldn't worry about that right now. She'd had her moment alone.

"Okay, maybe I lied about the bathroom." Adrian fidgeted. "I was looking for you. I'm sorry. For pushing earlier. About Kayce and all."

Just hearing his name aloud summoned his laughter, an echo in her ears. Lia bit the inside of her lip, looking out the window. No shadows in the trees, though she half-expected another six-eyed owl to make an appearance.

"Don't worry about it," she said. "Funerals make people weird."

"Oh, I'm just terrible with people."

A startled laugh burst from her at his candor. "Aren't all writers?"

"It would seem so." He smiled, crooked but sincere. His gaze wandered over the trunks, catching on the drawings of Norenth before her. "If only they were real, hm?"

That inner sea surged, her loneliness echoing. Kayce's smile flicked across her mind. He was her best friend, a nap away. A world away. For all her pining, today was the most real he'd ever seemed.

Pathetic.

Lia bit back a wince at the intrusive thought. But it was true—Kayce *was* her best friend. And, well, that likely *was* pathetic. Not that her papa ever admonished her for it. He was the only one she trusted not to.

But he was gone.

Lia feigned a smile. "Bathroom's next door."

"Quite right." Adrian chewed his lip like he was internally debating, turning before deciding to face her again. He smoothed the argyle sweater that no mid-thirties man had business wearing. "Julian, he—he loved you. Very much. His death...I'm sorry for it."

It was too easy to force her smile a little wider, even as the sincerity choked her when he left. Here was the thing—everyone was sorry. But there was nothing they could do.

Her head throbbed sharply. Lia winced.

She wanted—needed—to get lost in Norenth again. She'd take another water cannonball to the back. Dozens of them. Maybe tonight she could trick her mind into continuing where she'd left off. It'd felt so real. She *needed* it to be real.

Digging through the attic, Lia found a cardboard box to fill with those records of stories and dreams, hoping it would build a raft.

CHAPTER FIVE

ourners had trickled out, and the remaining Corvines were more than ready to head back to their own home. Lia had managed to dump the lilies while no one was looking. She hadn't blamed Adrian for their demise.

Down the hall from her brother's room, Lia's room was pristine. It had been since the moving van left. Her endless book horde had found a home in a white wall of shelves. She hadn't decided whether to keep the spines arranged by color, a gentle rainbow gradient from row to row, or if her obsessive compulsiveness would kick in and demand to reorganize them by genre and author.

For the third time since her mom gave them the news.

When she shut her bedroom door after the funeral, Lia spent the first twenty minutes making sure the spines of her books were in precise alignment before changing. Her black dress returned to its hanger in favor of cotton sweatpants and an oversized T-shirt, Lia scratched the ear of a purring Fiore. The long-haired, black and white cat lounged on the journal Lia had left open on her bed. The box of Norenthian treasures waited next to her.

"You, my dear, are not a bookmark," she muttered, scooping up the cat. Lia kissed the black heart of her nose. The feline, likely sensing the emotional drainage of the day, hardly protested against settling in her lap.

Peering into the box, another drawing caught her eye. What a miracle she had stayed inside the lines. The continent floated in midair, the kingdom atop an enormous expanse of trees with limbs upraised. A central mountain pierced the mist that forever clung just above the forest's canopy, flanked on either side with smaller ridges capped in white. Rivers flowed over the edges of the land, falling in blue lines down past the cragged earth at the base. But her favorite part was the seas: bordered in wavy lines, the clouds were filled with all the blues the one-hundred-and-eighty-count crayon box had provided. Fish stickers dotted their surface.

Quite the artistry. She snorted, causing Fiore to leap down. Flipping the page over, Lia's breath hitched at the familiar scrawl.

Honor, courage, truth, and justice. These were the virtues Lion Magnar and Lioness Silva—the king and queen of Norenth—strove to instill in their sons. They impressed upon the four brothers that family was everything. They molded their sons to be the pillars on which the kingdom would rest, for each of them played an important role in helping Norenth thrive. Jace may be the next crowned Lion, but Kristof, Terranth, and Kacerion would help their brother rule.

She could still hear Papa asking endless questions about Kayce and his family. At the time, she'd found them annoying. She had wanted to play. Now, she would give anything for one of their world-building discussions.

Putting the drawing to the side, Lia riffled through the other pieces of Norenth snagged from the attic. Such layers had developed when the young prince aligned with the Rangers, known for their scouting and emissary missions. Yet the Weatherstone family was ever-present, trade equitable within Norenth's guild economy. Not to say underhanded dealings and mischief didn't happen. Politics had evolved—grown up.

But Kayce was still finding his place. Still getting into trouble. Stuck. Like her.

Lia was lost to the scattered dreams encased in paper. A strain soon pulled across her shoulder blades as she hunched over her various relics, a crick forming in her low back. She couldn't clear the lump that had grown to the size of a tennis ball wedged between her windpipe and esophagus. Her headache surged, that persistent pain sharpening.

She needed more escape. And something more than smuggling heists.

Turning to her journal, she opened it and wrote.

Kayce, Aurelia knew, loathed the inauguration ball for the Lion's Guild Council. Having reached what was considered adulthood, one would think he would have an actual say in the matter of his attendance.

Not likely. But at least he wouldn't have to suffer alone.

"I would owe you for the rest of our lives, Aurelia," the prince pleaded, having tracked Aurelia down at the Ranger's Guild stables. "Just please don't leave me alone to socialize with these people tomorrow night."

There were eleven guilds across Norenth, each holding a seat on the Lion's council. Each guild's respective members voted on who held those seats, the democratic process valued by all, especially the floating kingdom's rulers. A ball accompanied the ceremony, recognizing the new office holders charged with evaluating Norenth's progress and any halts to it.

Naturally, Kayce had learned to do well in a crowd.

Aurelia rolled her eyes, brushing out Seagrove's tangles from their last covert flight. Sea salt crusted her mane. Unfortunately, the same could be said about Aurelia's curls. Of course, Kayce was perfectly dry. Even windswept, his hair was annoyingly perfect.

"I don't do dances," Aurelia retorted after letting him sweat for several quiet moments. "I don't even know how, apart from the handful of lessons your mother wrangled us into."

"I swear she likes you better than me. Though, you were far more successful at evasion tactics than I." Kayce rubbed his chin before brightening. "I could teach you."

"Like you taught me how to use a sword and ride? I didn't know you could actually teach me something ladylike."

His eyes narrowed. Words seemed to have left him, leaving Aurelia to wonder if the joke had been misplaced. Her stomach tightened under his assessment.

"You know, I think this whole unity thing, knowing what we know, is a farce, but...it's important to my parents. And I want to show up for once." He looked to the ground, raking a hand through his long, unbound hair. "Just not alone."

Guess the family still berated him for the last two balls he had missed for some misadventure or another. Granted, she had been with him for both. But perhaps dresses and dancing instead of breeches and smuggling would be a good change.

Biting her lip, Aurelia caught his gaze and became rooted to the floor. How could she refuse? And it wasn't like her life would be at stake this time. Just her reputation in court.

And perhaps her sanity.

Lia's eyes burned. Her pen trembled, rereading the scene. But all she could think of was her papa. Of words he would never read, never critique. Not even saving Kayce from civilized society was enough to forget it.

That dream in the attic. She needed to see him. Like he was right in front of her.

Pain flared between her brows. It forced her to grit her teeth. The words blurred, pulsed with each beat of her heart. She screwed her eyes shut.

Breathe. Tread water.

Her head *hurt*.

Lia groaned, clutching her temples. Her fingers tangled in her hair.

She hated it. The move. The loss. The stupid flowers from her father. The way Marcus had looked at the door, hoping he would waltz back into their lives. The way Mom removed herself, leaving Lia to deal with everyone else while she—she was drowning.

The pain split her mind open. Shattered the mask she wore.

Lia's face twisted into a snarl, the pain radiating down her temples, along her cheekbones. She had to get it out, but she couldn't cry, no matter how much it *hurt*—

Turning, she punched the pillow. Over and over, she struck until her shoulder burned more than her dry eyes. Each punch helped with the pain. Gave it somewhere else to go. Gasping for breath, Lia slumped into the bed. An aching exhaustion dragged her to sleep.

Reaching for the other person she could never have.

CHAPTER SIX

When Lia opened her eyes again, she was nose-to-nose with Storm the volatequis. He snorted, causing several suspicious drops to land in her mouth.

"Blech! Seriously?" she cried, scrubbing her face. Where was the mouthwash when she needed it? The winged horse nickered, going back to his meal of hay and apples. Another volatequis snorted in the neighboring paddock, the sounds of their mockery echoing in the Ranger's Guild stables. "You're lucky Fiore isn't here, or I would sick her claws on you."

The steed didn't deign a response, munching away. Seagrove whinnied from the next stall. Lia waved them off, stalking toward the open stable doors. Then she blinked, halting mid-step. And blinked again. How did she get here? Her mind was drawing a blank, like it had been wiped clean. Something was different.

Each leaf held an overly defined crispness, like Lia had upgraded her glasses too much. Not that she needed them *here*. Along the packed dirt road that wove into the ravine housing the capital city, the trees and shrubs glowed with sunburst orange and scarlet hues. They swayed in their constant upward lift to the mist, mist that kissed her cheeks with cool tendrils and dampened the fine curls framing her bare face. The evergreens wore their needles, the crisp scent of pine clearing her nostrils to the point her eyes watered.

It was as though every moment for the past ten years had been in low resolution, and Norenth had just discovered high-definition. She'd never been so aware in her dreams before. Was this what lucid dreaming was all about? She could get the hype.

"Are you seriously still here?"

Lia jolted, whirling toward the voice of Mara. A senior ranger, the elderly blonde sauntered around the pens like it was her own kingdom. With one hand on her well-rounded hip and the other gripping a pitchfork, it might as well have been.

"P-pardon?" Lia stammered, not understanding what the other ranger meant.

"Aurelia, should you not be getting ready for the ball?"

"Cinderella's?"

"Who?" Mara studied her like a second head sprouted from her shoulders.

Lia shook her head, bringing a hand to her temple. Of course, Mara wouldn't know the reference. She was losing the separation, the distinction between Aurelia and Lia, Norenth and—

No.

One thought of reality sent a wave of revulsion through her, her mind rearing like the idea was a flame ready to scorch her to the bone. The pain was an echo, a spark between her brows. All she'd need to do was blow for it to erupt and consume.

She decided right then to take this lucid dream for all it was worth. Lia shoved her grief, her pain, her doubts deep inside that ocean her mind had become. Drowned them all so that Aurelia could breathe.

Stories became memories. Fiction turned into fact.

Her clenched hands unfurled. Her shoulders rolled back. Her chin lifted a notch. Aurelia's grin fell into place on Lia's lips. That was all the prompting she needed to shove Lia aside and step into Aurelia—completely.

"The Council's inauguration," Aurelia gathered. So much for Kayce's lessons.

"There she is, skies and seas!" Mara said in a rush. "Honestly, Aurelia, I thought you might have taken another tumble."

Aurelia forced a smile. Guess it was tonight, post-flitterbird-debacle. Not that Mara would know that.

"Apologies, Mara. I'm a bit out of sorts today." Maybe that fall with Seagrove had been harder than she thought.

"Ease up on those extra training sessions. Now, off you get—and take a brush to those ragged curls, why don't ya!" Mara jabbed her pitchfork mockingly to get her moving. Aurelia didn't need to be told again.

From the outskirts owned by the Ranger's Guild, Aurelia headed toward the capital of Norenth. Protruding from the mountain itself, Highguard sprawled before Castle Finerda's granite towers. Ravine walls rose on either side, creating a natural protection around the city. Stone bridges connected the sides of the ravines and stretched toward the castle. Smooth from wear, the arched coverings of the upper-level bridges were especially helpful during the rainy spring seasons. Pulleys and hoists protruded from platforms, ready to move cargo and even horse-drawn carriages from one level to the next. From the melting snow at Mount Fealtek's peak, small rivers converged to form a mighty waterfall that flowed to the west of the castle. It cut through Highguard like a mighty sea serpent of myth, weaving through man-made canals and past lumber and grain mills before continuing into smaller streams to the villages beyond.

At mist-level, closest to the sunlight, the tops of the ravines were flattened into several tiers like stairs built for giants. The Grain Guild owned the top of the western ravine, the vast fields shifting from emerald to gold throughout the year. Each tier held a different crop, and wide, sloped paths lay on either side of the fields to help the wagons and plows traverse easily. The tiers had been hollowed out beneath the crops, and large sliding doors installed to make barns and granaries with the next tier of fields as roofs. The barns and storehouses were lit with the soft, amber light from crystalline veins that had been molded into them. In the storehouses, large chutes had been carved through the ravine to the grain mills below.

The other side housed the shipyards of the Sea Guild. Similar to the western ravine, the upper levels held the merchant and naval docks. Tall towers stood in a line like proud sentries standing guard over the city. Each tower had several docks wrapping around for ships to dock between them. Mooring lines kept the ships firmly locked on either side when not out on the Skyward Seas. On the lower tiers, several vessels in various stages of construction were strapped to similar towers. Others were tied down to large platforms for ease during repairs. Hangers had been carved into the outer wall of the ravine, mainly used to store ships during storms, though several were used for extra docking.

The city—despite the verdant slopes of the ravines, cascading waterfalls, and a network of bridges—was open, airy, and filled Aurelia with warmth. The smiling faces of Norenthians bustling toward their own celebrations, a mirror to the inaugural ball, settled her further.

Perhaps everything was fine. She was home, memory gaps aside.

Packed earth gave way to cobblestones. Aurelia arrived at the Belhaven Bookshop in the Market Guild, a district closer to the castle. Going there during frequent rainy afternoons had become such a tradition over the years that the bookkeeper was more than honored to offer the youngest prince's best friend a room upstairs.

She had refused several times before relenting. Namely because Kayce had finally convinced her that he couldn't keep hoarding her things.

It wasn't much: a small bed pushed to the side, an armoire across from it and two cushioned chairs they would occupy while reading and plotting. It didn't take much to discern who was doing the former, who the latter.

Aurelia shed her sky-blue tunic—why couldn't she remember anything after her fall yesterday? While it nagged at the corner of her mind, it was like a distant knock on the door to a room on an entirely different floor.

Kayce hadn't said much when he asked her to come to the ball. He'd likely finished the flitterbird plot without her, maybe assumed she'd shook Luddeck off their tail. She could gripe at him later for his lack of concern, though he likely needed to get ready as quickly as she did. Especially knowing his mother. They really needed to work on margin.

Aurelia donned the gown she had purchased with nearly every coin from their teeniest bit of profit. Her half, anyway. Dark blue chiffon clung to her curves, the color lightening as it cascaded to the floor. Sleeveless, so her freckled arms were bare. The blue panels over her chest met a gray leather strap that encircled her neck. Similar leather bands crossed over the bodice in various patterns, accentuating her form. The final piece, pinned to the strap over her shoulder, was the bronze emblem bearing the sigil of the Ranger's Guild: a crossed quill and sword.

Looking in the armoire's mirror, Aurelia fidgeted with the straps. Would Kayce laugh? Tell her she should have spent her earnings on something more practical? Maybe she should have.

She picked at the skin around her thumb, then fisted her hands against the alien action. The urge still made her fidget.

She should've taken more of Lioness Silva's dance lessons when she was a kid. Kayce's earlier offer? Way overdue.

Maybe no one would mind her two left feet if she could tame the bird's nest she called hair. It took longer than she would have liked to wrangle her curls into submission, but thankfully the lavender-scented oils did their job. Soon, soft ringlets flowed down her back.

Not a moment *too* soon. A knock came at her door. "My lady, are you ready?"

Aurelia snorted, recognizing Kayce's voice instantly. "Since when is it *my lady*?"

"Since the occasion calls for it." A pause. "And I know how much you hate it."

Catching a final glimpse in the mirror, she faltered. Why did her heart want to burst from her chest? Instantly, she regretted her choice for the gown instead of a nicely-embroidered tunic and slacks. Not like the queen would have allowed it, but at least the outfit wouldn't have been too far from her usual attire.

She mentally shook herself. "Last I checked, I'm a ranger like you."

His soft chuckle came from the other side of the door. "My mother and brothers have lectured me for half the day that tonight is to be a completely formal event."

Aurelia lifted a brow, managing a carefree air that she was desperate to make genuine.

Be normal. Pretend this is a meeting at the stables. Fancy clothing shouldn't make this difficult.

Kayce was her best friend—

When she opened the door, that carefree air evaporated to the mist above the kingdom. A bronze tunic embroidered with sapphires and copper cut close to Kayce's chest. The lion pommel of his family sword rested at his hip, and his hair was held back with a leather tie. Two emblems shone on his chest: a bronze medal with the Ranger's Guild sigil and a golden one bearing the Weatherstone seal of a longsword flanked by roaring lions and cresting waves. A single, dark strand of hair fell forward into his eyes, their amber irises dark. Her fingers itched to tuck it back.

Gone was the rogue smuggler. He was every inch royalty personified.

And your best friend, she had to remind herself.

But the humor drained from Kayce's face the longer she stared. His eyes held hers. Dipped. Lingered. After an unbearably long moment, Kayce finally dragged his gaze back to her own. He opened his mouth, but no words left until he finally managed, "You look...beautiful."

Aurelia's cheeks heated, but she ignored the sensation and fixed her skirts. Snark would disguise the wobble fluttering in her stomach. Maybe it was indigestion. "That's the infamous charm I've heard so much about?"

His chuckle, a low rasp of waves over the shore, didn't help. "You need to learn to take a compliment, *Lady* Aurelia."

That did the trick. She glowered at the title. She really did hate it. Both of them had taken to the Rangers because they wanted to elude the propriety of court. For Aurelia, it was namely because of a pervading sense of imposter syndrome she couldn't seem to shake.

On a night like tonight, she was sure he would use it any chance he could. Good.

"Thank you, *Your Highness*." She curtsied low to add insult to injury. "I must say, you clean up rather well yourself." It was the understatement of the year, but he didn't need to know that.

Kayce brushed an invisible speck from his chest. "Well, I'm glad you find my attire suitable. I spent two entire days at the mercy of that ornery seamstress. She threatened that if I didn't remain still, she would make a pincushion out of me."

"After you hightailed it out of Luddeck's attack?" She still was a bit annoyed he wasn't more concerned about the water cannon she took to the back.

"Seagrove got you to cover just fine." He frowned, taking a step closer. "I'd never abandon you, Aurelia. Smuggling innocent creatures or not."

Aurelia swallowed as he towered over her. He was right. It wasn't his fault her memory was faulty. Pieces missing. An ache flared in her head. She brought a hand to her temple. "I think I may have taken the hit harder than we thought. My mind's foggy."

Concern shadowed Kayce's tanned face. He reached for her temple, fingers gently prodding, mindful of her curls. He watched her eyes closely—for signs of a concussion, *obviously*. She chewed her lip. He held her gaze a beat longer. "Maybe a little off, but no signs of harm."

"I'm sure it's nothing." Heat flamed her cheeks. Several strands of her hair slipped through his fingers as she took a step back to ease the distance between them.

His nearness hadn't affected her like this before. She had to get it together. Maybe she *was* concussed.

Kayce coughed, his neck reddening. "Allow me to fill in the blanks. The flitterbirds made it safely to our contact. Had to pay the gate guard double the normal fee to pass. Seems the inauguration may cause some inflation for bribes, at least for a few days. Harder to let contraband slip by unseen when every eye is out but…" He fished out a small pouch from his belt and handed it to her. "Here's your half."

Taking the payment, she tossed it into her drawer for safe keeping. His words clicked the pieces together, easing her frazzled mind. "The dwarves below Fealtek will treat them well until we can get them back on a ship to the Southern Isles. *That* much I remember." It was her favorite part of the smuggling—the liberation of new and exotic creatures from nefarious hands.

"I hope the captain is on his best behavior tonight," Kayce said as Aurelia stepped around him for the stairwell.

"I doubt he would recognize us, but it may be time to adjust our disguises soon. We've been using the same ones for over a year now."

Kayce watched her, his brow furrowed. "Are you certain you're all right?"

Am I? She gathered her bearings before nodding. "I'm fine. Now, shall we go make a mockery of those we swindle from under your parents' noses?" Even saying it with a warm smile in place, she couldn't help the gnawing sensation—that ache growing at the back of her mind—that she was missing something.

Something important.

CHAPTER SEVEN

Their carriage wove over the various bridges that arched over falling waters from Fealtek's mountain face. Castle Finerda shone, its towers puncturing the cloud of mist with copper turrets, its ridges a muted green. Banners bearing the Lion sigil flapped in the wind, the rushing waters on either side of the central courtyard doing little to dull the roar of citizens arriving in all their finery.

Veins of luminescent crystalline splintered through the ravine walls, casting a white glow over all in the twilight. Torches flickered throughout the courtyard, filled with the same material mined from Fealtek's mighty deposit at its summit. The pureness of the light always stole Aurelia's breath.

"It's so bright here," said a soft voice outside the carriage. "Garrett told me it was like a cave, the city buried into the mountain."

"Your brother thinks all city dwellers are cavemen," answered a deep baritone.

"Are they not? Feels fairly tight to me," said another.

Peeking out of the window, Aurelia watched an older man and a young woman step down from one of the larger carriages. Several others emerged, dressed in pine greens and browns of the richest soil, each with a bronze sigil pinned to their breast. Aurelia didn't have to peer closer to know they bore the cloven volatequis hoof of the Fauna Guild. The murlik, a stout breed of oxen with antlers bowing outwards like ancient limbs, snorted heavily with relief to have the journey done with. No wonder the poor beast was tired—the Fauna Guild was several days' ride over land.

Typical. Their members never liked the city, far preferring their ranches, stables, and hunting parties. She tried not to take offense, considering that they helped feed the kingdom.

The party of dwarves exiting the carriage beside them couldn't say the same.

"Just who do you think you're calling cavemen, eh?" hollered the tallest, though by human standards the difference didn't account for much. "Who do you think is responsible for the light around here?"

Aurelia's gaze cut to Kayce, who was already watching the scene with far too much glee. She rolled her eyes as the steward ushered their carriage closer to the castle entrance, leaving the Fauna and Miner's Guilds to sort out their differences. Again.

Many newcomers expected the ravines and the city to be unforgivably dark with all the clouds and jagged stone walls. The light was thanks to the strong friendship Highguard kept with the dwarves who dwelled deep under the mountain. Fealtek was home to the largest crystalline deposit in the floating kingdom. A special mineral, it was similar to a rocky crystal, with one major difference: it grew from a central point at the peak of the mountain like the root system of a tree. When sunlight shone straight onto the crystalline, the minerals carried the sunlight along the roots that spread throughout the entire mountain, illuminating even the deepest dwarven cities. Along the walls of the city, even in the structures themselves, the crystalline roots were exposed and carved to keep the entire city lit and warm with a soft glow. Highguard remained lit well into the night, when the light finally winked out.

It was no wonder that the Miner's Guild was held in such high esteem, which most others had resented. However, it was discovered some decades ago that the crystalline-imbued waters feeding the trees was what made their limbs float toward the sky, enabling the construction of ships that soared. Then the Builder's Guild became the one to envy.

"Think Darrow will make an appearance?" Aurelia asked once they pulled to a stop, the steward coming round to open the door.

Their friend—a dwarf content with his feet so firmly on the ground he was almost always in the tunnels below the capital—was never keen on their schemes. The smuggling he was happy with. The acquiring...not so much.

Kayce snorted. "Not if he can help it. Darrow hates these gatherings more than I do. He'd rather mine crystalline for a week."

She chuckled, taking his hand when he it offered to help her out of the carriage. "You aren't wrong, but don't forget his uncle was voted to represent the Miner's Guild. His presence could very well have been strong-armed like ours."

He arched his brow.

"Oh, you *know* you roped me into this. You're no better than your mother."

"I recall a couple of children, best friends really, that vowed to remain together no matter the danger." A teasing smirk warmed Kayce's face. "Or are you backing out, admitting there are some things that scare you?"

The incident he'd referred to had been a small matter compared to the hijinks they got into these days—a scuffle with a council member's son, who'd called Aurelia a carrot-headed crown-kisser. Young Kayce had punched him in the nose. Running away was the obvious choice to avoid the Lioness's wrath, and they'd stolen Kayce's eldest brother's horse to do it. The next thing Aurelia knew, Kayce had a dagger and swore his allegiance to her. To them.

And he was near impossible to say no to. Not that she had wanted to.

"I would never break a blood oath and you know it." She forced her gaze ahead, despite the perfect scar that seemed to tingle over her right palm. "Admit it, cutting across the hand was stupid. All those nerve endings? My hand throbbed for a week."

Kayce shrugged. "We were kids. Stupid is part of the territory. Next time, I'll be sure to mention the forearm instead."

"Much more practical."

"Just not as poetic."

Aurelia bit back a laugh.

Roughly hewn stone rose several feet above their heads before shifting into smooth, beige limestone as they entered the castle. Their heels echoed against the marbled floors veined with copper, the high arched hall guiding them toward the ballroom. Veins of crystalline ran through the carved inlets of the doorway, glinting off sigil pins of various guild members. Whispers swirled over the string music of a small orchestra.

"The Ranger prince is here. Hard to believe he made an appearance."

"Ah, and he's got his sidekick in tow. Think she corrupted him, or the other way around?"

"You know the youngest Weatherstone—he's certainly to blame."

Aurelia's stomach turned. The bodice of her gown constricted like a snake coiled around her belly, turning her breath shallow. The minor ache in her head radiated with a persistent hum.

Water would help. And air. And maybe some food.

As they passed by one particularly loud group of whisperers, Kayce leaned in to catch their attention. "By definition, spreading rumors constitutes a form of corruption. So it stands to reason that I'm safe among friends." His response was polite, yet it carried the bite of truthfulness as he winked at the now-horrified group.

Aurelia bit her lip at their affronted faces.

One man in a rich navy tunic—the loudest of the bunch—stammered, "Of course, of course! My prince, you are never short of friends here—"

Kayce wasn't finished. "You know, it's considered rude to speak ill of your hosts within the confines of their home." Spying an uneaten apple in the man's hand, Kayce plucked it and took a bite. The man gaped, utterly speechless, as pink ruddied his tan cheeks and Kayce gave him a mirthful scowl. "Don't bite the hand that provides for you, good sir. It's bad form."

The group flushed, looking anywhere but at the pair.

Aurelia was going to die from second-hand embarrassment. "You're incorrigible," she finally managed once they were out of earshot. However, the tension had eased from her shoulders. He could do that, her Kayce. Dissipate the anxiety, quell her fears. Make her laugh, even while mortified. Not that she would ever admit it.

"What can I say; I've never been able to bite my tongue," he said with a shrug, slipping his free hand to the small of her back. Her heart pounded at the touch. It never bothered her so much when they were shoving each other off tree limbs or curled up by a fire after a long day of training. Yet every brush of his hand now sent shivers down her spine.

Aurelia glanced back toward the entrance—and the exit. "The queen hasn't spotted us yet. We could make a dash for the bookshop, or better yet, take Storm and make for the skies."

Kayce assessed her, taking a bite of his questionable apple. "I know these large gatherings cause discomfort, but you seem much more anxious than usual. Are you certain you're all right?"

Aurelia closed her eyes, taking a slow breath in on a count of five before exhaling the same.

Breathe. Hold. Tread water—

What? That was a strange thought.

Rolling her bare shoulders, she looked up at Kayce again with a smile. "Just a headache. Some food would do me good, but maybe acquired more politely."

"Well, *somebody* had to teach them etiquette. Besides, I'd rather have them talk about me than you—hey!" His mouth hung open as she snatched the apple from him and took a bite.

"Thank you, *Your Highness*. See, manners matter." She winked at him. "This apple is far sweeter than I'm sure it was a moment ago."

He sputtered when Aurelia laughed and took his hand to lead them to the buffet. Balls like these seldom had a formal dinner, instead being a time for mingling, dancing, and gossiping. Trays overflowed with ripe fruit, artfully displayed tarts with flaky crust, and various meats roasted to golden perfection.

And there was chocolate. *Praise the skies and seas.*

They ate, the food barely taking the edge off Aurelia's headache. It was a rising pressure, intent on finding every crevice of her mind.

A pressure she resolutely ignored.

Across the expanse of the great hall, a navy carpet ran up nine steps to a dais. Behind it, a triple fireplace roared with the Weatherstone royal crest carved at the top, the lions gazing down on all who passed under them. Marbled columns splintered with the same shimmering copper framed two ornate thrones, upon which sat the king and queen of the floating kingdom, formally known as the "Lions of Norenth."

Dark of hair, their skin had weathered gracefully with age and was a shade lighter than their skyward son. Lion Magnar's boisterous laugh filled the space beside his wife, Lioness Silva, who smiled in a more reserved manner. Her shrewd gaze surveyed the crowd, fingers idly tracing the necklace holding four small pearls against the hollow of her throat.

Aurelia knew Silva was looking for them. Washing down the last bit of food, she nodded to Kayce before gripping her skirts to head their way.

Kayce caught her wrist. A crooked smile emerged. "You have—" He motioned to his mouth, then chuckled at her blank expression. His hand came up to her jaw and gently brushed some crumbs from her mouth. Their gazes caught. His thumb hovered just under her bottom lip.

Why wasn't he moving? Aurelia didn't dare breathe, anticipation building inside of her. But for what—

"There." Lowering his hand after another heartbeat, he directed them to the dais. Red flushed his throat, his jaw working as he focused on his parents. She might've imagined how his gaze flickered back to her face, lingered on her mouth a moment longer than was necessary.

But there was no imagining how every fiber of her being burned from his touch.

Aurelia used each step to ignore the foreign longing in her chest. As well as the overwhelming urge she'd had to lean into him further.

CHAPTER EIGHT

Several onlookers glanced their way, plates and glasses in hand. Thankfully, the festivities continued without much fanfare to accompany their presentation. Maybe no one had seen that moment between them, felt how it'd stretched into eternity between one heartbeat and the next. Or maybe Aurelia was over-analyzing it.

Friends didn't let friends walk around with food on their face.

"Your Majesties," Kayce declared. "Prince Kacerion Weatherstone escorting Lady Aurelia Corvine, Rangers to Norenth."

Pain flared behind her smile. Why did those titles suddenly feel like a lie?

A look of satisfaction spread across Lioness Silva's face as she released her grip on her necklace. "Prince Kacerion, your presence as a representative of the guild is most appreciated, and your presence as a member of the presiding family bolsters our strength. Lady Aurelia, you have our gratitude for your support of the Crown. It is an honor to have a member of the Corvines present."

The plural of her family name snagged something in Aurelia's gut. Family. Her family—

Lion Magnar's warmth chased the otherworldly thought behind the door in her mind. "Norenth stands strong having the four brothers united in securing our future."

Kayce inclined his head, but Aurelia knew the tightening of his jaw. She saw the king's comment for what it was: he wanted Kayce home more, ranger duties aside.

Since the royal family had four sons, it was no surprise that the youngest would join the Ranger's Guild. Kayce utilized the guild's full repertoire for their personal smuggling affairs, unbeknownst to the Crown, of course. Watching the king's subtle raise of a brow, Aurelia wondered if he knew what they were up to. They bowed low as duty commanded, before the Lions waved them off.

Kayce's three older brothers stood nearby. It soothed Aurelia's frayed nerves to see them, all of them. Dressed in similar bronze tunics as befitting their station, they were roughly all the same height—each half a head taller than Kayce, much to his distaste.

Jace, the eldest and crown prince, had always made sure she wasn't pestered too much. Growing up, he was the buffer. Sometimes, she wished he'd see she wasn't a kid anymore. She knew she certainly didn't look like one tonight.

Kristof, though, he knew she could handle herself. More politically minded, he preferred to observe. His quiet bearing had comforted her during more than one social event, and he wasn't afraid to engage her on the academic level she thrived on.

Terranth? She bit back a groan. He was already digging an elbow into Kristof's side, motioning to a cluster of ladies across the dance floor. He was only a year older than Kayce, but Aurelia swore he was far more insufferable. He rivaled Kayce for the position of primary instigator—probably why he did so well in his military position.

Jace's eyes met hers when they approached, a warm amber similar to Kayce's. His rich chestnut-brown hair curled slightly from under a golden crown, simpler than what his father wore. Aurelia couldn't imagine having to wear it. It likely wouldn't fit over her hair. Besides, he was far better suited for it, anyway. She had no desire for such a responsibility, not that being a daughter of minor nobility offered much. Papa's position as an advisor to the crown carried enough burden.

"Kacerion, thank you for coming. You'd have cracked Ma's pearl if you were another moment late." Jace shot a tight smile toward the dais. "Do we have Aurelia to thank for the prompt arrival?"

She frowned. Now she hoped the crown was tight.

"Hilarious, Jace," Kayce countered. "Where's Fallon?"

Aurelia was also looking for the tawny wolf-dog that seemed permanently fixed to the crown prince's side.

Jace smothered a chuckle. "He seemed intent on remaining by the fire. He *did* assist in the hunt for this feast, after all."

"Of course, you would seek out the dog for company," said Terranth, his own eyes the dark blue of stormy seas gifted from their father. A precisely groomed scruff framed his angular jaw. Aurelia couldn't help but admire the new growth, wondering for an instant how that would look on Kayce. The sudden image did nothing to ease her current discomfort, and her nail caught on the skin of her thumb.

Kayce snorted, forcing her out of the foreign tic. Since when was picking at her nails a habit she couldn't control?

Terranth's gaze, deep enough to drown his military opponents in, flicked to her. "Lady Aurelia. Who knew a dress would be so becoming on one insistent to run amok in the clouds?"

Arrogant dunderhead. She crossed her arms. "Honestly, Terranth, if you even knew what we were up to with the rangers, you wouldn't seem so pleased with yourself."

He shrugged, smirking. "I still don't quite understand why you wanted to join them. Perhaps to add some beauty? Skies and seas know they needed it with Kayce's ugly mug."

Jace frowned, elbowing him while Kristof narrowed his lighter blue eyes shrewdly before asking, "Captain Luddeck certainly came in full steam. Wouldn't know anything about that?"

Well-played. Soft-spoken, though the words were sharp as any sword. Aurelia always wondered if the second-eldest knew more than he let on about their illicit activities—even if they *were* for the greater good. She refused to look at her partner-in-crime. "Who knows what gets the esteemed captain's sails in a knot these days?"

"It would not surprise me if his friendliness with pirates had something to do with it," Kayce remarked.

"Kacerion!" Kristof snapped in almost a whisper. "Allegations like that are serious. You can't accuse a captain of conspiring with pirates without any legally acquired proof. Especially one about to take a seat for the Sea Guild."

"Emphasis on *legally*," Terranth added.

Mirth danced in Kayce's eyes. "Who's accusing?"

Kristof folded his arms across his leaner chest, while Terranth muttered under his breath, causing all brothers to turn a glare at him. He ignored them, focusing on Aurelia. "Would you care for a turn around the dance floor?" A dimple appeared as he extended a hand. "Leave the captain's concerns with these gents. I, for one, would truly enjoy a chance to keep your feet on the ground."

He wanted to dance—with her? Now? Did he not just insult her? Then again, Terranth was always one to pull her pigtails, so to speak.

Aurelia glanced at Kayce. Best friend aside, she had technically come with him. He stared at his older brother, brow furrowed like he was trying to work out a move in a game of chivet.

During winters where the western wind blew hard around Mount Fealtek to cloak the capital city in snow, chivet occupied hours of her and the princes' time, bitterness flowing freely as they stole each other's coin. Their pieces maneuvered around a miniature Norenth, the game floating above any tabletop as the actual continent did. Players tried to make a fictional living by traversing from the outer reaches to Mount Fealtek's peak while avoiding tithe payments or going to prison. Skies forbid someone drew a minstrel card, occupying one's piece for several rounds as one was forcibly serenaded by the draw-er...which coincidentally always seemed to be Terranth. Kayce was so competitive, he often let a single game stretch on into the next day, not that the winter storms would allow them leave otherwise.

Several revelers paused their neighboring conversations to watch the princes, for Kayce looked at Terranth as though he had stolen every coin—and Kayce wanted them back.

Aurelia couldn't say no, not with onlookers gawking at Terranth's offer. So why did her hand suddenly feel like a dead weight at her side? Shaking it off, Aurelia managed a half-grin in return as she took his hand. "Fair warning, you may lose some toes."

As Terranth led her away, Aurelia couldn't help but notice Kayce's jaw drop open. Jace reached over and promptly shut it on his brother's behalf with a chuckle.

The strings of violins and cellos trickled over piano keys. Aurelia placed her other hand on Terranth's shoulder, feeling the sturdiness of muscle beneath his brocade jacket. "Seems like all Weatherstone boys have a penchant for over-training," she observed.

"And those in Weatherstone company, it would seem." He squeezed her hand, their calluses matching. As he guided her in a waltz, his other hand pulled her waist closer. They turned in slow circles, weaving around couples bedecked in various jewel tones. Gratefully, he was skilled enough to avoid much toe-stepping.

He looked over her shoulder. "The lion cub doesn't look too pleased."

Aurelia's brow creased, but in their next turn, she saw what he meant. Kayce's gloved hand flexed over the pommel of his sword as he tracked their dance. Jace whispered in Kayce's ear. Whatever the words, they caused his jaw to clench. He caught her stare, even when several dancers flitted between them.

"I don't blame him," Terranth continued, "I would certainly keep you all to myself if I could."

She blew a stray curl from her eyes, ignoring the burn Kayce's gaze ignited and focusing on her dance partner. "He wouldn't know me any differently if I was covered in mud or half-tangled in sails. Nothing's changed."

And it hadn't. Right?

But even as Terranth held her, she couldn't shake the ghost of Kayce's thumb under her lip. Her skirts swayed around her legs as they danced, and Aurelia's traitorous eyes gravitated back to Kayce. Perhaps it was only the finery and the candlelight that made the planes of his face more intriguing. Besides, all would go back to normal once they were bickering in the stables tomorrow morning.

Surely it would. Right?

A throb pulsed in Aurelia's head. A rise in the sea of pressure.

"Are you well?" Terranth frowned.

"Just a headache." She focused on the steps instead. "You shouldn't goad Kayce. It makes the whining I'll have to deal with worse."

Terranth chuckled. "He *is* my brother. It is my job to be the resistance he needs to grow as a man. Only with friction is a blade sharpened into a weapon. I would do a disservice to Kayce if I were I to let him go unchecked."

Unchecked in what? She couldn't see how dancing with his brother could help.

"I must admit. It wasn't to rib Kayce that I asked you to dance." Terranth's gaze, suddenly filling with warmth, traced over her.

Oh. *Oh*.

Her breath caught in her throat, a flush building in her cheeks. "What other motive could you possibly have? I'm the same as I've always been. A dress changes nothing."

"You're correct." Terranth held her stare. "It doesn't."

He was always one for jokes, but this sudden seriousness stole her breath. The intensity of it distracted her from the headache, from the certainty that something wasn't right—

She pried her tongue off of the roof of her mouth. "Terranth—"

A throat cleared behind her. "May I step in?"

Stopping, Aurelia turned to find Kayce staring down at her before slanting a loaded glare at his brother. Terranth looked between them with a smile Aurelia had seen when they'd played war games growing up. Like his tactic had just succeeded. But how was Kayce stepping into victory?

"Brother, be mindful of the lady's toes." Terranth winked before releasing her with a deep bow. He clapped Kayce's shoulder roughly before heading toward their brothers.

Some of the flush Terranth caused had eased from her cheeks. Kayce took her hand, the scars from their blood oath aligned. Then heat rekindled as he placed his other hand possessively on the swell of her hip, pulling her close.

"You certainly waited long enough," she managed. "It took nearly all of my concentration not to maim your brother." Though he had done a good job of distracting her in other ways.

Kayce stared over her shoulder, his jaw working. "Well, I'm glad you didn't. Would have killed the mood of the party."

She quirked a brow at his verbal flailing. He normally had a barb for everything. Why did he cut in if he couldn't bother to look her in the eye and behave as himself? His arms had wound around her so easily, but they stiffened the longer they danced.

However, the pain in Aurelia's head increased to where she hardly noticed Kayce's odd silence. The candlelight in the room was steadily heating everything in sight, herself included. The spinning didn't help. *Were the candelabras revolving?* Wincing, Aurelia tried to grit her teeth through the headache that was quickly overwhelming her senses.

Kayce's throat bobbed when he finally looked at her. She tried an encouraging smile but felt its strain. Pressure rose in her chest, her skull. Lingering glances and infuriating young men were forgotten.

Frowning, Kayce brought a hand to her temple, his tension wavering. "You're flushed."

Of course, he saw right into her. Gripping his shoulder, Aurelia glanced at the glass doors that led to the gardens. No longer could she ignore the pain that had become a steady staccato beat in her temples. "Would you hate it if we went outside? I-I think I need some air."

He exhaled a sigh that loosened his shoulders. "Not in the slightest. But should I send for the carriage?"

"Don't mother hen me. I'll be fine."

Liar.

She stiffened at the thought. But the council hadn't been presented yet, and Aurelia didn't want to incur the Lioness's wrath by departing early. Everything was fine. Her pain didn't matter.

On their way out the door, Kayce snatched a glass of water from a nearby serving tray and passed it to her. Taking it, she drank quickly as they stepped outside. Filled with the gentle symphony of crickets and distant music, the cool night air kissed her overheated skin. A copper frame extended over the terrace. Draping willow branches wove through the muted green railings and swung gently in the breeze. Aurelia shivered as she crossed the flagstone to the farthest point, away from the noise and the people. She stared at the twisted bark of the thin willow trees, forcing her breath to steady, willing the pain to recede.

"Distract me," she urged. "Do you think Kristof knows *we're* the smugglers going after Luddeck? Or was it a lucky guess?" She held the chilled glass to her neck while sitting on a marble bench that was surrounded by moonrose bushes, their pale petals shimmering like they were carved from their namesake's stone.

Roses. Like in a garden. A stick for a sword—

"Well, I'm uncertain." Kayce rubbed the back of his neck before sitting beside her. "Kristof knows me well. It's possible he suspects and hoped to force an admission. He's used that trick before. If he *knew* it was us, I think he would have been blunt about it. Either way, I'm not concerned."

She nodded, the pain pulsing. Focus, she had to focus.

Breathe. Hold. Breathe.

The crickets quieted as Kayce rubbed his gloved palm. "Aurelia...tomorrow, I want you to meet me at the alcove." A tilt of his lips brought out his normal smirk. "I have something I think you'll like."

His gentleness threw her, the soft rasp of his voice reaching beyond the pain in her skull. She watched his hands, knowing their shared scar was beneath the glove. He'd never mindlessly traced it before. But he stretched his hands out too quickly for her to ask if it pained him, and reached for a moonrose instead. His fingers ensnared her attention. That delicate trace of a petal captivated her, reminded her of something...no, not *something*.

Someone.

A hand, beginning to gnarl with age and decades of use, brushed against a white rose petal. "Quite beautiful this time of year, don't you think, Aurelia?"

She shrugged, coloring a similar flower in her sketchbook. "Kayce likes fall best."

A laugh. "Of course he does. You do as well. Doesn't mean those flowers cannot bloom whenever you wish."

"We're not the same person, Papa."

"But he certainly shares a great deal with you." The elderly man cleaned his glasses with his shirt before sitting beside her. "Are those rainbow petals?"

She shook her head, ringlets flying. "Nope. Moonstone. Mom had this necklace with one in it, and I liked the colors. Thought it would be a pretty flower."

"It would be indeed. Perhaps the Lioness's favorite?"

"Definitely."

An ocean of grief swelled. Her mind fractured, flooding with it. Dragging Aurelia to the dark depths of reality. In the distance, an owl hooted.

She dropped the glass. It shattered at her feet, and she clutched her head.

Kayce lurched for her, gripping her shoulders. Concern choked his voice. "Aurelia, what is it? Talk to me."

She couldn't answer him. Pain made her double over; the crack ricocheted down to her heart where it felt like a furnace ignited. Scorching pain and chilling grief warred inside her. It burned. It drowned.

It *hurt*.

"It's—it's Papa—" A broken whimper escaped. She crumpled, her body limp, pain undulating in waves through her skull. Strong hands gripped her arms, then held her face. She heard something, but murky waters filled her ears. It left no part, no crevice of her untouched.

Maybe it was her name. *That* name again.

Papa privileges, she thought, before darkness consumed everything.

CHAPTER NINE

In her Seattle bedroom, Lia woke covered in sweat with a pounding headache. She supposed there were worse ways to wake up in the morning. Until, after wrenching herself free from the tangled sheets, she found a lovely gift from Fiore beside the bed. The hairball squelched between her toes.

Gross. Thanks, whiny-baby.

Lia groaned, fumbling for her glasses. The journal fell with a thud, but it was beyond her noticing. Her vision blurred as she blinked hard. Perfect. Just what she needed—worsening vision. Still, she could make out the papers strewn about from last night's jaunt down memory lane.

Her dream rushed in and sent her swaying. That was the thing with escaping to Norenth. It wasn't real, no matter how surreal these dreams were lately. And she hated it. A soft snarl curled her lips. But Lia didn't have time to deal with the rising tide inside her. Not with her family rustling about downstairs, awake and grinding on with daily life. Her eyes burned. Taking her glasses off, she blinked hard before storming to the bathroom to shower.

Under the water's hot spray, her body remained clammy.

What on earth did she eat yesterday to encourage such vivid dreams? Maybe the funeral catering had been bad. Or those lilies really did ooze toxin.

Normally the dream's edges would blur, details fading before she could even get pen to paper. But now, as the water did little to dull the ache beating between her brows, she could remember the inaugural ball with startling clarity. Almost as clear as the funeral.

Grief's raging sea stole her breath, nearly driving Lia to her knees. She had to be fine. She couldn't give in. Not a tear fell, even as dry sobs heaved through her. Her hands itched. Her eyes burned. Lia held herself tighter, a sudden roughness against her arms. She lowered her hands, watching droplets trickle along a bed of raised calluses over her palms.

Lia was hardly one for manual labor—let alone working overnight. Frowning, she traced the calluses before looking at her right hand. Her breath caught.

A scarred, silver line cut through her palm.

In her dream, she and Kayce had just reminisced on it. But that was in Norenth, a world Lia had imagined entirely. So, why was it on her hand *now* when she was in Washington state, having never set a physical foot in her world of fiction?

She had to be sick. Crazy. Sleeping too much. Not sleeping enough. Coming down with something. A fever dream. That had to be it, her body shivering when she left the water's warmth. Fumbling through the medicine cabinet, Lia found some Tylenol and took two.

But upon closing the door, the reflection made her pause. Lia wiped the condensation away. Her pale skin was wane, freckles stark with dark circles under her eyes.

Figures. Sleep was complicated these days.

She touched her hair. Was it darker? Lighter? Maybe it was just wet, but it looked different. Lia continued her assessment, hands wandering over her shoulders, down her arms to her torso and legs. She was generous in the curve department, but not overly so considering that her walking habits balanced her penchant for statue-like immobilization when reading. Not to mention a ravenous sweet tooth.

But underneath the gentle swells of her body, there was a hardness that she didn't recall. Not a bad thing, but she didn't think puberty made muscles. Moreso just redistributed fat. She wasn't that lucky. But that wasn't the most startling piece of her assessment.

On her thighs, pink splotches remained like healing burns. Like from fires, courtesy of a pirate's snare.

"Lia! It's time for school," her mom called from the foot of the stairs.

She rubbed her eyes. Her mind was playing tricks.

Education didn't pause for grieving periods. At least, her history teacher didn't, jerk that he was. Her email likely had yet another reminder that she had plenty of work to turn in. But where the inner motivation to excel, to perform to the height of what everyone expected of her was, only an empty void remained. Something had sucked all her energy elsewhere.

This fever was wreaking havoc on her entire being.

Shrugging on a pair of leggings and a sweater, Lia emerged from the bathroom. She must have been a sight, because her mom was upstairs in an instant. Her gray eyes bounced over Lia from head to toe, mouth pinched. "Did you dye your hair? Something looks different. Have you been sleeping?" she questioned, bringing a cool hand to her daughter's forehead. "You're burning up."

"It's just a fever, Mom. It's been going around school. All the stress, everything going on...my body couldn't be bothered. So, no. No dye job." She tried to smile, but her joke fell flat.

Mom's frown deepened. "A fever?"

"And a killer headache. Some lucid dreams."

No one would want to get pulled into your mess. Suck it up.

"Dreams?" Mom pressed further, her eyes a fraction wider. What was with her?

Lia nodded with clamped lips, padding back to her room for her glasses. Slipping them only made the blurred vision worse. She threw them onto the bed with a sigh. "And not even my glasses are working right."

Overnight workout, hair appointment, and vision correction. Totally signs of a second wave of puberty. Grief-induced, to be certain. Lia rubbed her face, hating the look of wary concern from her mom. Where was Nurse Mom to the rescue? Jumping into action, knowing exactly what to do?

She just looked lost. Unprepared. Losing Papa must have rocked her worse than Lia feared.

"Lia—" Mom began.

"I'll be fine, I just need a day." Lia took one look at the rumpled sheets and scrunched her nose. "I can stay home, right?"

Her mom bit her lip, looking like she needed to question more before letting the issue drop with a nod. Gathering the tangled sheets from the bed, Mom headed back downstairs with Lia trailing behind. Marcus sat at the kitchen table, a fluorescent yellow cereal box with an elderly sailor smiling in uniform before him.

Captain Luddeck would *never* smile over breakfast like that, especially after the last time she saw him. His tanned cheeks had reddened to the point that Lia thought the blood vessels in his eyes would burst—

Lia stopped short. That was a random mental tangent. Since when did she reminisce about her fictional adventures like they'd happened yesterday? She needed to get her head on straight.

"There's more casserole in the fridge, chicken and broccoli, I think? There's a couple frozen ones, too. Mirel brought a lasagna." Their mom was bustling around the kitchen, her blue scrubs crisp.

"What is it about funerals that make people want to give casseroles?" Lia muttered, brushing off her wayward memories and taking the laundry from Mom to toss into the washer.

"It's a thoughtful gesture. People don't want to cook when they're grieving. Or after giving birth, ironically."

"What a grim combination," Lia said.

The television was on in the next room, the news anchor's voice filtering in. *"In other breaking news, a rabid animal escaped from a local research facility. The public is asked to remain alert, and if anyone sees an animal exhibiting signs of rabies, please call the animal control hotline."*

Their mom paused. She headed for the living room, abandoning her morning routine.

Lia hardly paid attention, peering into the freezer. "Nice of the bingo league to give us some food. Think it'll take long to defrost?"

"In market news, the stock market shares for ImaginX have doubled since last week as their newest product, the MemoryBank, hits the shelves just in time for the pre-holiday—"

The television cut off.

"Mom, can I get a MemoryBank?" Marcus asked, putting his bowl in the sink.

She came back into the kitchen and snatched her bag from the counter. "Absolutely not."

"Aw, come on! Everyone will be getting one soon."

"What does it even do?" Lia asked, fixing herself a bowl of cereal.

Marcus bounced on his toes as he shouldered his backpack. "It's like a tablet, but instead of games and stuff, you can record your dreams."

"So it's like a diary?"

His face scrunched. "Kind of. Apparently it can sense emotions while you sleep, so it'll help you remember them. *Then* you can write them down and use the MemoryBank to turn them into a movie—"

"That's enough." Mom's tone sharpened. "I'm not having any ImaginX nonsense in this house. Especially not one that watches you sleep."

"I'm with Mom on this one. Sounds creepy to me." Even as Lia said it, the prospect tickled the corner of her mind that held onto Norenth so vividly. "Though, if I'm going to be a hot mess, it might not be bad to escape into dreams of pirate heists and dragons."

"Are there even dragons in Norenth?" Marcus piped in.

"No, it's got more of a coastal vibe."

Their mom pulled open the door. "Lia, these tales you weave—" She chewed her lip, and her shoulders turned inward before dropping with a sigh. "Just focus on catching up with school. Let *that* be the escape."

Everything and everyone else comes first.

The thoughts crept in as they always did for Lia, low and quiet, like a serpent slithering through tall grasses. Unseen until right under her.

Lia nodded, a false smile slipping into place as the door closed on Marcus and her mom's heels. Her head still ached and felt overly warm, but thankfully, the medicine had done its job. Or, some of it.

Glancing down at her palm, Lia frowned at the new scar there.

It was a small mercy that a pharmacy was about a mile away. Lia knew a walk would do her good after a day of nothing but casserole eating, reading, and ignoring schoolwork she'd have to make up.

Granted, those activities seemed to do wonders for her body, the headache gone and her temperature back to normal.

Well, relatively back to normal. Additional heat emanated from her chest, residual bits of whatever virus had tried to wreak havoc on her immune system. Hence the walk to the pharmacy, for more Tylenol and Gatorade.

Her sneakers scattered leaves across the path as music thumped in her earbuds. She was grateful for the sweater against the damp October chill that had overcome their small suburb. Their home was only a few blocks from a downtown area where various small businesses displayed their fall sale signs. In the few short weeks since their relocation there, Lia had memorized the various routes to take around town.

But her mind was lost.

Not exactly *lost*, but replaying waltzes with Terranth and Kayce to music similar to what she listened to now. She could envision every step, as though her body had truly made them. See their faces above her own, recall the looks in both of their eyes. Feel the warmth where they'd held her.

She had never had such a dream. Not even the one of the smuggling heist and pirate ship felt this real. Of that, she was grateful, since it kept Papa's loss at arm's length, though the clarity still startled her. It wasn't even hard to remember the tarts she'd eaten, the flaky crust as easily recalled as the fruity crunch of the cereal she'd had that morning for breakfast.

Did grief do this to a person?

She was old enough to vaguely recall when her father had left. Those memories were quarantined in her mind; she tried not to dwell on them too often. But she remembered her sullen silence, the avoidance of crowds and keeping everyone away.

The dark waters that had welled in her then seemed like a puddle compared to what filled her now. But that was when Kayce first came to her mind. He was the only friend she'd had then, the only one she'd needed. Perhaps there was a connection.

Turning a corner, Lia took a shortcut down an alley. Brick buildings rose several stories above her head, a cool wind making her burrow deeper into her sweater. A few trash cans overflowed from the weekend. She was almost to them when something banged from within one, loud enough to be heard over the swelling music in her ears.

Lia stopped. Removing her earbuds, she listened and eyed the cans warily.

Probably some stray cat or raccoon, but skies and seas knew she wasn't in the mood to fend off some scrappy animal.

Skies and seas?

With a shake of her head, Lia continued. But another rattle echoed inside a can. This time, a low growl accompanied it.

She froze again. All she needed to do was get past the trash cans. She wouldn't be discouraged by some rodent. But what if the rodent had rabies? What if it was that animal from the news?

Stupid. She had to get it together.

Lia hadn't taken but two steps when a can tipped, metal clanging throughout the alley. She yelped, jumping back as moist to-go bags, crumpled paper, and other waste tumbled to the asphalt along with the culprit.

It wasn't a stray cat. Nor was it a raccoon.

It didn't remotely resemble either.

The creature was larger than a cat, shaking a bat-like head with large ears that fanned to the sides. Its scrunched nose scented the air, eyes that shimmered like gasoline in water squinting despite the cloudy day. Leathery gray skin stretched over its limbs, each one tipped with talons that clicked against the ground.

The fever was making her hallucinate. There was no way that creature was real. Lia didn't dare breathe. But her shoe scuffed the pavement, betraying her retreat.

The gremlin's head snapped toward her, baring a mouth full of small, needle-like teeth.

She shrieked, booking it for the street. Lia had to get home, had to get out of here—

Another shriek tore the air as the gremlin gave chase. Hot air chomped at her heels, and the gremlin snatched her ankle, tripping her. Asphalt bit into her hands and knees on impact. Pain barked in her body.

Definitely real.

The gremlin dug its claws into her skin. Snapping out her leg, Lia kicked the vile thing off before rolling onto her knees. No way was this fight fair. She scoured the ground for something, anything. A busted table leg lay nearby, the wood splintered at the end.

The gremlin launched at her again.

Lia rolled out of the way, popping up with a speed her body should not have known before grabbing the table leg. She wielded her instrument like a sword, thrusting the jagged edge toward the gremlin as it skittered closer. It hissed, narrowly missing the wood before swiping its claws.

The table leg broke in half.

Lia chucked her remaining piece at the gremlin, landing a hit on its head. The gremlin growled, shook its head, and lunged for her.

Grabbing a bottle from the debris, Lia whacked it on the side of the dumpster. Glass shattered, and she lunged with her new weapon. Shards sunk into flesh. The gremlin screeched, blood coating her fingers before Lia leapt back. It slumped, twitching once before settling.

Her heart raced, breath coming in short pants. Where on *earth* did that thing come from? Certainly nowhere natural. She forced herself to breathe in and out in equal measure, but her heart continued to pound like a hammer against the anvil of her ribcage.

Had she killed it?

Her nose scrunched as she looked at the black blood coating her hands. Maybe it'd come from some lab, an experiment gone wrong. Terribly wrong, in this situation. It was the only rational explanation, even though something deep inside told her that was not the answer—even if she wanted it to be.

Blood welled where the creature's claws had sunk into her ankle. Grabbing her sweater, she wiped most off, revealing a lattice of five shallow cuts. Thankfully, the blood was already slowing.

She rid her trembling hands of the noxious fluid, wiping her palms on her jeans, her skin breaking out into gooseflesh when the scent tickled her gag reflex. This was too much, far more than she was equipped to deal with. Lia wrinkled her nose at the sight of her blood *and* the gremlin's, smeared like a line written across the pavement.

Should she call the police? Animal control? This was so beyond her wheelhouse—

The gremlin's body glowed like a flame before snuffing out of existence. Taking all traces of the creature with it, including the black muck spattered on her sleeves and jeans.

Lia whirled, turning left, right. No sign of the creature. As if she had just...fought herself. Her breath came in quick gasps. Had she lost her mind? Had grief ravaged her so entirely that she could no longer cling to reality?

No, she wasn't losing it. She couldn't be.

Lia turned, dashing from the alley. And crashed into a pedestrian.

"Oh—Lia!" Mirel's eyes widened as she steadied Lia, nearly dropping a sleek briefcase. Even with the surprise, she barely seemed ruffled as she let go to dust an imaginary speck from a close-cut pantsuit.

"I'm so—I'm sorry! I didn't see you," Lia stammered, whipping around to see if another creature had appeared from thin air. They could multiply like mice for all she knew—if it had been real at all. The second thought nearly cracked her chest in two.

"Is everything all right?" Mirel frowned and smoothed the black sheet of her hair, looking beyond Lia to the alley. "I can walk you home—"

"No!" Lia half-shouted, stealing a breath to lower her tone. "No, there's no need."

"Truly, I wouldn't mind—"

Lia bolted.

Ignoring Mirel's calls, Lia ran as fast as she could. Ironically, the only thing that comforted her was the sight of her bloodied sleeve and the pain that twinged from her ankle.

Pain was truth. And if her mind wasn't playing cruel, grief-stricken tricks on her, could there be more of those things?

Thoroughly shaken and doubtful of every traitorous thought, Lia didn't pause to consider where her quick reflexes had come from, nor how she used the resources around her to defeat the creature so easily. Like a blade she had never touched on this earth.

Her only focus was her racing heart and the safety of her house. Dread dogged her steps, a fear that Lia couldn't be as brave as Aurelia.

CHAPTER TEN

Once home, Lia slumped against the inside of the front door, chest heaving. Every rattle of a windowpane made her jump. Her chest began to tighten, the familiar feeling of a screw being torqued down inside her, each gasp constricting her lungs further. Her fingernails dug into the rug. Lia tried to focus, to suck in deep breaths while she squeezed her eyes shut to block out the world around her.

More of those wretched things could lurk outside. If she wasn't totally crazy.

Her mind spun, overloaded. Meanwhile, Lia's heart raced so fast the blood rushed to form yet another headache that pulsed behind her eyes.

She was losing it. There was no other way to describe it.

Her head slammed against the door, her eyes flew open, wide and wild with fear. She finally lost her mind. She was seeing things—creatures that didn't even exist.

She'd been stretched to the ripping point even *before* Papa's accident.

And now?

Lia's laugh escaped in a fit of hysteria, severely misplaced in the empty house. Clamping a hand over her mouth, she banged her head against the bolted door once more. If that gremlin was real and the city was crawling with them, maybe it would be better if they ate her up. At least then her problems would go away.

No! It was a cat, it had to have been. A hairless cat with rabies, like the news had said.

Anxiety, bereavement, and now hallucinations. Perhaps that was why she was going crazy and thought she saw a gremlin. The human mind could only take so much. Maybe she needed to check into a mental hospital. Was that where she belonged?

Why wouldn't you be losing your mind? What do you think happens when you try to be perpetually perfect and noninvasive?

No. She had to dam it all up.

Just breathe, tread water.

Even though she was on the cusp of adulthood, Lia wanted nothing more than to crawl into the embrace of her papa, the one place where she felt safe outside of her pages. Found comfort in the scent of old leather and...something spicy? Woody? It was harder to recall, her memory of him already fading—

And that did it.

The dam broke. Water swelled. Leaked from her eyes and didn't stop until it was a torrent. Lia allowed herself to drown. She didn't even care if anyone heard. Her shoulders shuddered with the sobs, hot tears gushed down her cheeks. She was unable to curl tight enough, cries convulsing in her chest.

The waves washed over her, suffocating. Consuming. Drowning.

Everything ached as she let it all out. Snot and tears ran freely down her face. Her body shook with the grief, the pressure, the expectations. The sobs crescendoed. Kept coming. They wouldn't stop even if she tried to force them. Her breath hitched, leaving her gasping for air.

The waves crashed over her, drowning her. She was tossed around in their turbulent grip. Darkness crept in on her. Unable to stop the waves now threatening to carry her into the depths of her despair. She was that little girl again, watching her father leave and wanting nothing to do with her. Who would? She couldn't even hold it together without *seeing* things. No one wanted a broken person.

Kayce would.

The thought came unbidden, but promised a tether. A lifeline to hold on to.

Her eyes ached as the tears finally slowed. Maybe she'd run dry. Numbness pulsed in her chest, her knees cracking as she straightened them.

Duty nagged her until she stood up, joints popping, and checked the time. Her family would be home soon. They couldn't exactly find her huddled against the door, in sneakers coated with blood. Even if the gremlin guts were gone, she was a disturbing sight.

She had to suck the waters into herself. Seal up the holes. Keep the floodwaters in. She couldn't drown in front of her family.

Her second shower of the day was so hot it burned.

Every part of her body ached as she finally dragged herself out of the bathroom and into clean clothes. Her mind was a fog thicker than the mist rolling across Highguard. Perhaps she was truly losing it, she wondered as she stared at the scar on her palm. It would explain why she thought of her imaginary world as real as her present one.

But it was an anchor in the storm.

She padded on unsteady feet to the box she'd filled after the funeral. Flipping through it, Lia paused. Halfway deep was a page she had never seen before. But the script haunted her. Frowning, she pulled it free.

Wait—she *had* seen it before. Over a week ago, on Papa's back patio.

His new project. *Bit of a family tale,* he'd called it.

How had it gotten in the stuff she'd grabbed from the attic? Lia didn't know he still wrote up there. But it would seem, according to the *bingo league,* that she didn't know a few things about him. Bile burned in her throat as she rose to get into bed and read.

It has been said the stories we treasure most live within us. Truthfully, those stories have lived far longer than that, and will live beyond the last mind to recall them. However, there once was a time where no stories existed.

No stories? Lia frowned, reading on.

Darkness flooded all there was, until all that is came to be. Nothing existed apart from the breath that began the story of us. Alone in the darkness, words and life were breathed into the very essence of everything, until the universe as we know it was born. Stars spun around planets, and those planets whirled around stars so bright they burned for eons. There was potential on these planets, vibrant life flowing in an array of patterns.

Lia pressed a hand to her chest. Marcus would have loved this one, and it stung that he would never hear their papa tell it.

On one planet, Man was crafted from earth. Both men and women sought to fulfill the creative call on their souls to its fullest potential, cultivating the world before them. But unlike the mere animals that thrived in the soil, air, and waters, they had a yearning for more: someone to dream with.

And so, between the molecules of the world that could not be touched as one could hold a stone within their palm, from that breath was fabricated a place—a dreamscape of realms wrought of the wonder and joy threaded through the ever-evolving universe. The humans of Earth, as it became to be known, were given access to this place through their imagination, namely in sleep.

It sounded like a creation story for the imagination. Papa had written this? He was sword fights and heists. Not...fairy dust. But these words—his *last* words—she needed to understand.

But when dreams came, so did nightmares. Darkness drew humans from sleep, plaguing their waking hours with conflict, jealousy, and hatred. Even fears of the unknown in the world around them. The predatory noises that rose in the dark, made more sinister under the cloak of ambiguity. Therefore, another realm was formed to work through those insecurities. But humans needed aid, those spheres in the realms needed observation once the human imagina-

tion breathed life into them. And so the guardians, guides of a sort, birthed from stars and the darkness between them, assisted humans to face their woes and to preserve their tales.

Was this the research Papa had seemed so concerned about? She knew various mythologies, but this was entirely original. Questions rose the waters inside Lia, but she couldn't stop herself from flipping the page.

Imagination took on a life of its own. Humans crafted stories, wove dreams, and fought nightmares—each one birthing a world as real as Earth, but separate. Until there was one guardian who no longer wished to be an observer, but instead desired to birth a world of his own. However, guardians were not designed to create, and it was all wrong.

Something was missing. In this sphere, a filmy haze ruled over the days and a piercing blackness won at night. Warmth hovered on a cusp, a bitterness of winter promised in the air. And in the eyes of its denizens, a hollowness looked back like the windows of a home standing vacant for far too long—the glass fogged and shattered.

His world was a farce; his intentions useless. Bitter with rage and pain, he became the Devourer: the ending to all stories. He consumed that which he could only covet: a dreamer's world. It was so violent a rendering, it not only broke the dreamer's mind—it tore a rift between Earth and the realms. Imagination bled into reality.

Ink smudged over the last word, like a droplet of water had ruined it. There was nothing left. Julian Corvine's last story, unfinished.

Lia sat frozen. Creatures that did not belong in the physical realm.

This realm where imagination existed like it was living, breathing—*real*?

A family tale. There was no way this was real. And yet, how else would it explain her vivid dreams? That monster—no, that *nightmare* she'd barely escaped? Her mind raced, thumb absently tracing the scar on her palm. She already thought she was borderline insane. Why not try to prove it?

Looking up at the ceiling, Lia spoke to nothing but herself. "If this is real, bring him here." Her voice tremored, but she pushed harder. "Give me Kayce."

She didn't expect an answer. It was likely just another fantasy. A story from an old man past his prime. Disappointment pricked in Lia's eyes, several tears slipping down her temples as she laid down. Her damp curls soaked the pillow as Fiore hopped to join her. Lia had nothing left to give, her body—and mind—worn out. Her eyelids grew heavier, drifting shut.

At least no gremlins existed in Norenth. At least there she wasn't losing her mind.

CHAPTER ELEVEN

The crisp linens were not her own. Not only that, but Fiore was no longer purring against her, the absence leaving Lia cold. But male voices trickled in as she fought the fog that sleep had pulled over her senses. She caught several words, but none made sense.

"I've tried, Jace, I tried last night. It's just..."

"If you do nothing..."

"...I don't want..."

A third voice, not as deep as the second but higher than the first. "Nothing in life is guaranteed... You need to have courage now..."

Kristof. That's who spoke, Lia realized.

"Like Father always says, 'Courage is having the strength to push through your fear'," said Jace.

Both brothers were speaking to Kayce. Did *they* know why she fell ill?

Did they know she was losing her grip on everything?

Because unlike her last dream, Lia couldn't don Aurelia's mask. All her memories were there, even her body ached from that—

No. Not here.

Again, that recoil. That revulsion from what reality held. But Lia was still...*Lia*. Groaning, she shifted under the sheet, raising her hand against the light. "Kayce?"

Footsteps, then a hand in hers. "I'm here."

Their faces came into focus, sharpening on the relief evident there. Lia touched her own face, realizing she didn't have her glasses. Not that she ever needed them in Norenth. She dropped her hand. Why would it be any different while dreaming? Her mental wires kept crossing, not exactly a comforting sign.

Her dream had resumed where her rude awakening left off. But since that was the case, why did she feel so...aware? Not that she minded—she just wanted to keep the horror of her waking world behind the dam in her mind.

Maybe she could try to be Aurelia, Norenthian ranger. Not Lia, prone to debilitating headaches and imaginary gremlin attacks while mourning the loss of the most important figure in her life. That person—and his last story—were far too complicated. More unknowable than she thought. Yet she couldn't shake the fact that the headache during the inaugural ball had followed her to the waking world—

No. Lia wasn't going to focus on that. Not when she was here. Safe. Free. Even if she couldn't step into Aurelia's name. *Imposter.*

Looking around the marble columns and latticed windows framing a view of Highguard's arched bridges, Lia licked her cracked lips. "Where am I?"

"You're in the palace infirmary," Kayce answered, his taut shoulders sagging. "It seemed you came down with a fever. I brought you in not long after."

Last thing she needed was being the laughingstock of court. She winced, sitting up against the headboard. Kayce still held her hand, and she gave it a squeeze before he caught his eldest brother's look and dropped her hand to rake his own through his hair. The tie was gone, but he still wore his fine clothes, the jacket slung over the back of his chair.

Skies, had he been with her all this time?

Lia cleared her throat, ignoring the lingering warmth in her palm. "Please tell me I didn't cause a fuss."

Jace seemed to swallow his smile. "*You* didn't, but Kayce sure sounded the alarm."

"Between him and Terranth, the whole infirmary came running and could have tended to the entire ball," Kristof added.

"I wasn't sure what had happened," Kayce snapped, low. "I was concerned she had a concussion or was bleeding internally."

Kristof snorted. "A tad dramatic, don't you think?"

"He acts like a mother hen where I'm concerned. Though, I recall distinctly asking you *not* to." Lia rubbed her face, grateful for being spared that mortification, even if it was due to Kayce's mother-hen-ing. "I'm not worth this much fuss. Please tell me the inauguration ceremony happened." She cut a glance at Kayce. "Much to your dismay, I'm sure."

He turned his glower on her, though it lacked teeth.

Jace spoke. "It did. Once you were here, there wasn't much else we could do."

"It was an effort to pull Kayce back to the ceremony, however. He had no desire to leave your side," Kristof said.

"Anyhow!" Kayce shot another glare at his brothers, both sharing an amused glance, before Kayce truly softened. "How are you feeling? You've been asleep a long time."

She watched the exchange with a suppressed smirk. "I'm all right, truly. But...skies and seas, that came out of nowhere—"

Papa!

Lia winced, the memory and sorrow that came with it thumping against the dam. Time to distract herself.

Despite the aches in her body, Lia pushed the covers back and swung bare feet to the floor. "Can I break out now? After giving my sincerest thanks to your parents, of course." Lia rushed to ease the concerned looks on their faces, unwilling to deal with...everything. The mess she was hardly able to contain.

Only *she* needed to drown. She couldn't drag anyone with her. Lia was determined to leave her grief—and likely, her insanity—for the waking world. She hadn't been conscious of this dichotomy before, and now it unsettled her.

The brothers shared a glance, as if they could sense the pressure teasing against Lia's grasp on reality.

"Please?" she insisted. "I fear I've overstayed far too much already."

There must have been something in her voice. A strain even she couldn't hide. Kayce's eyes narrowed before looking at his older brother.

"You're practically family, Aurelia," Jace responded. "You're not intruding. I'll go get the healer." A jerk of his head caught Kristof's eye, who also excused himself.

Kayce watched them leave before turning back to her with a shrewd glare. "Are you sure you're all right? And don't even think about calling a fine specimen of a man such as myself a 'mother hen' again, or so help me..."

"If someone asks me one more time—" She exhaled her frustration before relenting. Genuine concern scrunched his brow, despite his attempt at humor. It touched her, a gentle prod that made her want to open up. To release the waters just a little. "Physically, I *am* fine."

"Physically?" He paused, picking up on the omission. "Before you passed out, you called out for your grandfather. You sounded distressed."

Her throat constricted at the question. Grief sloshed in her overflowing soul. Lia didn't want to ruin this dream, not yet. But his amber eyes were dark with such concern, looking at her as if he could see something rising in her, consuming her...

As if he wanted to jump in after her.

And she knew, fairy tale or not, Kayce deserved the truth she couldn't out-swim, no matter her desperation.

"Ask me again later, please? I'll tell you, but not here. Not yet."

A muscle flexed in his jaw as he looked away. It wouldn't be hard to imagine the reason behind her plea, the heaviness which she had carried lately. He knew she'd been off. When he met her gaze again, concern remained, with softness alongside. "Know that I will. Some fresh air would do some good, don't you think?"

"We can still go to the alcove, like you wanted. I remember that before my grand exit."

"And here I thought I was the one with a penchant for dramatics."

A healer arrived and checked Lia over, declaring her healthy if a bit dehydrated. Another generous gift from the queen was delivered: a fresh sage green tunic with brown slacks. Lia smiled at the embroidered lions on the collar, donning the clothes quickly behind a privacy curtain before tying her curls back.

She almost missed the cuts encircling her ankle. Lia's stomach revolted at the sight, but she shoved her boots on over them nonetheless. She could only focus on one world at a time. Try to, at least. Why was it so hard? Was it that story? Because she'd let the dam slip?

Fresh air *could* do her some good.

As Kayce straightened to head out with her, the Lioness of Norenth herself breezed through the infirmary. Both of them dipped into a bow for the queen, who was resplendent in a fitted dress of burnt orange that highlighted the copper hues of her eyes like flecks of metal.

"Kacerion," she said, as she bid them both to rise.

Kayce inclined his head, unsuccessfully trying to smooth his furrowed brow. "Mother."

Lia watched the two with interest. What could the Lioness possibly want? Perhaps now was the best time to give her thanks. With the hectic schedule of royalty, who knew if Lia would get another chance soon, but even that reminder made the Lioness's appearance now all the stranger.

Those reserved eyes slid to her. "Aurelia, how are you feeling? I was glad to hear your fever broke." She took Lia's hand and felt her forehead at the same time.

Lia straightened at the maternal gesture. At the latest inquiry to her health, she caught Kayce smothering a chuckle. Oh, he'd pay for that mirth later. "I'm well. Thank you, Your Majesty."

"Your mother must be sick with worry," Lioness Silva added.

Kayce frowned as Lia did. While the queen was never unkind, the sudden emotional interest in Lia's welfare was disquieting. So much so that Lia blurted out the first words that came to mind. "My mom isn't the overly worried type these days, I'm afraid. At least where I'm concerned." She chewed the inside of her cheek. While she wasn't one to belittle what her mom did to keep their family afloat, to criticize her so openly shook Lia from her discomfort. Besides, it wasn't like Lia allowed Mom to see her struggle to tread water.

"What I mean to say is she's so busy with her own work," she tried again. Having only ever written herself and her papa into Norenth, she didn't give much thought to the remainder of her family. All the Weatherstones knew was they were from another part of the continent, her papa knighted as "Sir Julian" with advisement to the king and queen. Lia—*Aurelia's*—mother was content to leave her daughter under her papa's care in Highguard. "She knows I can take care of myself. Even if I'm under the weather." She could fend for herself in dreams and waking well enough.

The Lioness hummed in acknowledgement. Then, she glanced toward her son: a look of dismissal. No. He wouldn't. He seldom listened to what he was told, and *now* he was going—

Kayce inclined his head to them both. "Forgive me, I must tend to my duties." He looked at Lia. "See you shortly?"

Traitor. She glanced from him to the queen, fighting the urge to fidget. Panic fluttered like a caged bird inside her, but she nodded. Of course, he had no choice. The Lioness was his mother; she was the *queen*.

"Storm is in the royal stables. I brought him up earlier this morning." Kayce gave her that withered look he always did when she needed to take a breath and relax.

His mother had seen Lia through all the awkward growth spurts and social fumbling. Besides, Lia and her papa had *created* this world of her dreaming. Surely, she shouldn't be this intimidated.

Lia watched as the Lioness gave her son a small smile on his way out before turning to her. Silence reigned. This time, Lia did fidget, brushing another errant curl behind her ear. Better than picking at her nails—which, come to find out, looked as stubbed here as they did in reality. Her other world. Now *that* was just cruel.

She forced her hands into fists and smiled, though it felt weak. "I appreciate you taking the time to look in on me, but, truly, I'm getting on fine. Everyone has been very...thoughtful."

The Lioness laced her fingers before her. There was a way in which she studied Lia, like a puzzle box she would open but couldn't quite figure out how. Eventually, she nodded to herself. "As a queen, my people turn to me for leadership. For strength, particularly in times of turmoil. My sons, we raised them to be strong, to learn how to work through their emotions. They cannot get overwhelmed, not when so much depends upon their choices."

Lia held her breath. Where was she going with this?

Lioness Silva assessed her, a tightness to her mouth. "I thought I had displayed a similar lesson to you."

The words rocked her.

Lia cleared her throat. "I don't know what you mean, Your Majesty."

"You do, though," the queen chided. "While I have taught my sons to master themselves, I did *not* instruct them to shove their emotions away to rot and darken, or swell in a manner that damages those around them. And you, my dear, are perilously close to one of the two."

The dark sea in Lia surged. Whirlpools churned.

This wasn't a crack to her dam; it was a threat to demolish it.

The queen *saw* her.

Lia couldn't let that happen. She straightened her shoulders, summoned that bemused smile Aurelia would wear when Kayce went off on something asinine. "Your Majesty, I don't know what you're—"

"Sir Julian has died." The Lioness's voice was gentler, and a sadness lingered in her eyes—a transparency Lia had never known in her. It was gone in a blink.

But the bluntness of her words cracked the dam inside Lia.

"How—how could you know Papa's gone? He was an advisor to you all, gone on a—" She struggled for the memory of how she had left her papa's influence on the page of her journal. "An emissary mission to the dwarven cities. I haven't told anyone that he—that he is—" She couldn't say the words. Tears welled, and she clawed at each drop to remain where they were. She couldn't cry again.

Breathe. Tread water.

Blubbering before the queen was *not* how this dream was supposed to go.

The Lioness placed a hand on Lia's shoulder. Her grip was strong, anchoring. "Everybody breaks," she said. "Everybody bleeds. But when you hide it, you will bleed on those who never cut you. And I know you well enough to understand that is the last thing you want."

Lia closed her eyes. The queen didn't mince words. But to be strong, didn't she have to soldier on alone?

"How?" Lia's voice was barely above a whisper. She cleared her throat, her voice strengthening. "How do I...deal with this?"

"Dear girl," Lioness Silva sighed, that tenderness resurfacing. "Sharing our griefs with others seldom burdens them. Seeing you drown from the inside would be far worse." Her tone deepened, the queen's gaze flicking to the door.

Guilt snatched what little breath Lia had left. Never did she want to hurt Kayce. She wanted to keep this pain from him, knowing there was little he could do... But perhaps more could be saved, even healed, in sharing than Lia understood.

"You need the strength for what is to come." The queen continued, her voice full of stern, maternal authority. "And for that, you must tell Kayce."

Lia's head jerked up. The queen's last few words were an anchor of their own, one linked with questions. What was to come beyond grief? She couldn't see an inkling of anything. Not a single letter or a hint of foreshadowing. Her pages were blank, empty, and she was afraid to fill them without Papa.

Before Lia could ask more on what she meant, a steward came for the queen. Lioness Silva inclined her head to him, gown sweeping the floor behind her. She paused in the doorway, turning her profile to Lia. "Allowing others to see you is not a chore, Aurelia." Her smile was soft. "You are not a burden."

CHAPTER TWELVE

S he wasn't a burden.

The queen's words haunted Lia as she rode Storm through the mist toward the Skyward Seas. She breathed in the brine-filled air with a sigh, the salt steadying her. The threat of drowning had receded, at least for now. However, she knew it would surge again. She knew what she had to do.

Kayce and Lia's favorite spot was an alcove in the side of Mount Fealtek about twenty feet above the mist. It housed a small meadow, large enough for several winged horses to land and graze with tall pines and oaks set a little further back. The cliff's walls peered from between the floating tree limbs, the crawling vines boasting violet mistcup blooms every spring. A waterfall fed into a creek before it spilled over the cliff's edge and evaporated into the clouds. Between the vines and waterfall, the outpost was well hidden.

Spotting Kayce's profile in the tree line, Lia waved as Storm's hooves bit into the earth to slow on touch-down. He was busy whittling, crafting an arrow from one of the many fallen branches that littered the ground. Several more were piled on the stone beside him.

"Whatever happened to training in style?" Lia teased. She knew he had a whole cache nearby of the best arrows the Forge Guild could craft.

"Training never stops." He flicked the hair from his face as he glared. "You had to go to a ball to get a taste of the finer side of life I've tried to open your eyes to?"

She scoffed, turning for the waterfall. "If you think that's the case, then I hope delicacies from the other night are inside."

"You would doubt me?" Kayce dropped the arrow he was working on. He darted across the creek, using several stones worn smooth by the water and years of booted feet. Lia was right behind him, weaving between the trees. Even with the coloring canopy and dancing leaves, the floating limbs kept them hidden. The water was a gentle roar, no louder than rainfall, and it covered a path large enough to allow a volatequis and its rider to slip behind the waterfall.

Kayce slid his hand across a smooth stone, triggering the doors. Engraved with the royal crest and preserving all within, double stone doors slid open to either side. From the dust and critters upon discovery, it had been long forgotten, but Lia knew it had started as one of the first outposts of the realm, hewn from the mountain face itself.

The main room could have been found in the castle. The long, rectangular room was split in two by a simple wooden wall, one section housing paddocks for winged horses while the other held common tables, chairs, and a small cooking area. The studded stone walls on either side of the doors housed the armory. Kayce had an eloquent collection of weaponry that now resided there, arrows included. The opposite side of the door was the stable, wide enough to allow the volatequises passage. All around them, centuries of carvings covered the walls from the different watches stationed there.

Depictions of ships flew through crashing waves. Sea monsters attacked several vessels. Roaring lions prowled the bottom of the walls. A stone staircase carved in the back of the room spiraled up to the next floor. With the stairs worn smooth from centuries of use, the wall winding up the staircase depicted dwarves tunneling the mountain and battling the mountain wyrms.

It was fitting that Kayce and Aurelia should have rediscovered this place, even before they joined the Ranger's Guild. Over the years, they had outfitted it for their needs as Trident and Harpy, but of course, Aurelia made sure the finest cushions and crystalline lamps their coin could purchase made their way amidst Kayce's shipping maps and daggers. She had loved it upon first sight, the history and quietness of it. The veins of amber crystalline splintering through the walls and ceiling, like strings of lanterns overhead, only amplified that this was a place where the world could disappear.

Kayce headed over to the table, the amber glow of the jeweled lamp casting leftovers from the inaugural ball in a filigree of shadows. For the first time in over a week, hunger ravaged Lia's stomach. Hunger had never claimed her stomach so fiercely in a dream before. She had eaten, knowing she needed to, but genuine hunger had evaporated the instant that Mom had told them the news. "I could eat as much as you on a good day."

Instead of rising to the jab, Kayce studied her with a slight smile before nodding. "I nearly lost my head trying to wrangle this out of the kitchen, so please savor the fruits of my labor."

"You'll be lucky to get a bite for once."

"Ravenous thing!" He snatched a tart before sitting at the table. Crumbs scattered over their latest maps of the Skyward Seas.

"Sweet Chef Rosalind was in a mood today?" Lia snorted before tearing into a roll filled with cheese, roasted pine nuts, and tart jam. She groaned as the various flavors burst on her tongue.

Kayce huffed, suddenly finding a speck of dirt on the table captivating. "Perhaps Captain Luddeck should hire her to guard his black market goods like she does the kitchen. It would certainly make our jobs of stealing it back much harder."

"She has far too much time on her hands," Lia mumbled.

"Her throwing arm? She nearly took my head out. She could hit a sparrow mid-flight in a hurricane while standing on a rocking ship."

Lia reached out to pat his head. "Poor, helpless ranger, chased away by a frying pan."

He swatted her hand, sending her into peals of laughter. It was the lightest she had felt in days. Perhaps deciding to tell Kayce was the right decision after all. But she didn't want to chase this lightness away yet. How did one find the right time to emotionally vomit all over someone?

Kayce continued on about the chef's violent tendencies. She had tuned him out as she struggled with how to open up, how to broach the subject—

"Maybe that's why Terranth hasn't asked to court you yet. He knows how good you are with a blade," Kayce muttered, throwing an apple core at the waterfall. It whizzed through the air with suspicious force, a loud splash echoing off the stone.

Lia choked on her food.

Terranth court her? As in—*dating*? She hadn't written about that, hadn't even hinted at it. And while she nearly always preferred books to people, Lia guessed what a man with certain intentions looked like. And Terranth had that look. But then he'd let Kayce step in so easily, looking almost victorious at the intrusion.

Face a wash of scarlet, Lia stuttered. "He speaks so prettily to anything in a dress. And that was the first time he's seen me wear one in...well, a long time." She tore off another bite and talked around it. "Not all of us were playing with knives while we were teething. If I didn't know for a fact you were born to royalty, I'd have called you a heathen."

Kayce inclined his head in a bow. "I think that's the best compliment you've ever given me. And I believe my family would agree with you."

Lia hardly registered the words, reeling at Kayce's implication. But also, the sheer impossibility of it. Her dreams had often taken on a life of their own, but for a member of the royal family to appear interested in *her*?

She was a nobody, sequestered in a bedroom outside Seattle. They didn't know that, but maybe that was why "Lady" was a title Lia always shrank away from. Even as Aurelia. Imposter syndrome at its finest.

"Regardless," Kayce prattled on, "he was with you half the night—"

With a look, he was silenced. Lia almost felt guilty with the way his cheeks flushed, his mind finally caught up with his mouth.

"For the death of the matter, *no one* is getting romanced—" A loud whinny cut Lia off. Then, a scraping of earth as if something pawed at the ground. Like something had landed just outside the waterfall.

"What was that?" Lia stood, hand going right to the long dagger sheathed at her hip. But noting Kayce's ease, her eyes narrowed. "What did you do?"

Because of *course* he'd done something.

A roguish smile curved his lips, tension disappearing. "Why don't you go find out?"

Please don't be something gross, please don't be something nasty.

Both of them exited their outpost, hopping back over the creek where Storm couldn't be bothered from his meal. Much to her relief, what she saw was neither gross nor nasty.

A stunning white volatequis ate peacefully. The winged horse lifted her head with a cheerful nicker in greeting.

"She's yours," Kayce said from behind. "Not that Storm or I don't enjoy your company, but since you're a full-fledged ranger, it's about time you had your own mount."

A slight tremor took hold of her hands when Lia reached for the volatequis's muzzle. "Kayce…"

"She's a two-year-old purebred, her parents both from strong bloodlines—some of the best. Seagrove's sister, actually. She's fearless, like you. Strong, light on her feet, gentle yet battle hardened." He paused. "And unmatched in beauty."

Fearless. Oh, how she wished.

Lia had hardly heard the way Kayce's voice softened. The other words he had said. Her throat closed, the volatequis leaning in to examine her. Not for the first time did Lia wish that this—Norenth, Kayce, and everything else that came with this world—was her normal.

Papa's story was a cruel joke.

Closing her eyes against the familiar burn and the rising waves inside, she leaned her forehead against the side of the horse's face. Not yet. Not in this beautiful moment.

"I…I don't deserve her." Her voice was hoarse, hardly over a whisper. "I'm not fearless."

She hadn't shed a tear in front of her family. She hid away in her books and writing instead of facing the stressors in her life. Retreated to a world in which she hadn't had to acknowledge her papa's passing, until that morning, when clearly her subconscious prompted the Lioness.

No, she was not fearless. She was a pretender, pushing off her pain until it bent even her waking world by conjuring monsters she had no choice but to deal with.

"You are, Aurelia," Kayce said dismissively, unaware of the battle waging inside her. "The qualities of fearlessness are courage and boldness. You show these every day."

If he only knew. The intrusive thought was bitter.

He stepped closer. She could feel his warmth against her back, but she refused to turn around. "Slipping onto naval ships to look for contraband. Sabotaging and attacking pirates. Tracking and exposing smugglers of the nefarious sort. I've seen you fight four men at once. I've seen you scared, but push through that fear." His voice dropped lower. "What is that if not courage?"

Pulling back from the volatequis, Lia held both hands to her chest. Hearing Kayce list such feats only made her clench those hands tighter. All those things were *Aurelia*; Lia was an imposter. She barely knew how to swim in this flood of her own making.

But maybe...just maybe, he could help her tread to shore.

"It is the courage within dreaming," she whispered, the breeze taking the words. Lia turned to face him. His nearness rocked her, the words tumbling from her lips. "I have done nothing but hide lately."

"From what?" His gaze didn't waver.

Blinking rapidly, she looked from Kayce to the seas in the sky and knew this was what the queen had pressed for earlier. It was now or never.

She took a breath. "My papa... I called out to him at the ball because I couldn't hide from it anymore"—her voice hitched, eyes burning—"and I've been so scared of drowning in this pain that if I start crying, I fear I might never stop. And then your mother—"

Several tears slipped free as Lia caught her breath. "She told me to confront what I've been trying so hard to keep away. But it's like the air is sucked from my lungs and I still can't stand to feel anything. And I have to hold it all in so no one else will drown when I finally let go."

Kayce listened, the furrow in his brow smoothing out. Realization dawned.

"And that grief..." she continued. "Kayce, I'm terrified that this grieving is making me lose my mind." She couldn't look at him. Couldn't bear to disappoint him, for him to see how broken she was inside. The five slashes around her ankle burned like a brand. There was nowhere she could run from any of it. Lia bit her lip so hard she tasted copper. "Papa's dead, and now... How can I be fearless when I don't even know what's real anymore?"

Kayce drew her into him, enveloped her. She clung to his arms; her eyes squeezed shut. Held him so tight that she trembled like a buoy in the storm. Tears slipped down her cheeks. She was so tired. Tired of paddling in this tar-like sea.

Tired of doing this alone.

"This is real." Kayce's breath shuddered in her ear. "I've got you."

Her heart lurched into her throat, and that tight embrace she knew him for shifted as it went on longer than the boundaries of childhood friendship. She couldn't ignore the lingering glances, how he'd stared at her during the inauguration ball. How she had, somewhere along the line, stopped seeing him as that gangly teen ready to take on the crooked captains the Ranger's Guild could not. How he was now a young man—taller, stronger, his very presence consuming her senses—and how she longed for even more amidst the tempest raging inside.

Here, now, each breath whispering against her ear as he tucked her head into his shoulder, made her realize how perfectly she fit into him.

Even though he had been there in her imaginings, through it all—her father leaving, the trials of growing up, moving somewhere new—this embrace was stronger, warmer, and *solid*. Real. It was an embrace Lia could sink into. Depend on in a way she never had before.

Kayce didn't move an inch, not even when tears stained his tunic. He just smoothed her curls, his other arm braced around her back.

He tamed the tempest.

Floodwaters receded. The pain was there, but Lia no longer needed the dam. It coexisted with everything else inside her. But like a relentless pest, darkness swarmed again. Flashes of oily eyes and talons shredded through Lia's mind, making her shiver.

"I wish you could go where I go," Lia mumbled into his shoulder. "I don't want to face this by myself."

He rested his chin on her head, stroking her hair. "My mother once told me that a flower is bright and warm in the sun. Yet in the storm, its petals sag. Maybe a couple fall off when thrashed by the wind, but it's still a flower. Perhaps not as vibrant as it was, but it will be again."

"Are you trying to say that this will pass?" She pulled back to look at him. "You may not enjoy the trappings of court, but you can't seem to let go of those pretty metaphors. Jace would be proud."

A soft chuckle parted his lips. "What I'm trying to say is you may not feel strong or brave right now, but that doesn't make it so."

She hummed in acknowledgement, soaking up the solid warmth of him. The lightness he brought to her chest. The full breath of air to her lungs.

"I think she likes you." The white volatequis had brushed her velvet muzzle against the back of Lia's neck.

She shivered at the touch, turning partway in Kayce's arms to reach out to the beautiful creature. "She's such a beauty... I can't thank you enough," she said and swallowed the lump that threatened to choke her again. "I cannot imagine what she cost you."

"I may be a royal and have the privileges of one, but I want to make my own way." A grin spread over his face when she quirked a brow at him. "That's why I take extra missions on commission."

Of course he didn't take a single coin from the royal coffers.

Circling the volatequis, Lia ran her hand over her mane, marveling at the swan-white feathers of her wings, the delicate cloven hoofs made for the mountain range. She hauled herself into the saddle. "What am I gonna call you?" Lia whispered, urging the volatequis through the trees.

Kayce ran toward Storm. He threw himself over the saddle before urging his mount into a run, straight off the cliff. "Race you to Corinth's Peak!"

All Lia could do was laugh and follow. Flicking the reins, she whooped before she, too, charged through the alcove. The volatequis's hooves churned the earth until she leapt off the edge. Wings caught the wind when they snapped out, banking hard and fast.

Uninhibited by fear, pain, or sorrow, Lia flung her arms as wide as the volatequis's wings. She flew past Kayce toward the far side of the mountain. Closing her eyes, the dying sun warmed her face. It all melted away from her, knowing she was no longer fighting this dark sea alone. Someone had her. One that wasn't going anywhere. At least in her dreams.

A word came to her suddenly.

"Paxia," Lia murmured, lowering her arms to hug her neck. "That's your name, my fierce girl."

She whinnied in reply, the sound echoing off the snow-kissed peaks.

The sky, once painted in broad sunset strokes, had faded into deepest indigo when they returned to the alcove. They had raced to Corinth's Peak, a smaller sister to Fealtek, and Lia insisted she won. Nothing left her feeling freer than being in the clouds. Every qualm and heartache was on the ground, and once in the skies with her best friend, nothing could touch her. The steadiness followed her as they went to relax up in the outpost's look out, leaving their mounts drinking from the creek.

The second floor held two rooms, the sleeping quarters and the study. The study boasted floor to ceiling bookshelves, desks with journals and documents dating back hundreds of years. Aurelia had been quick to adopt the room as her own, and now only a single desk sat in a corner near a neatly made bed piled with folded blankets on the footboard. The bookshelves were filled with her own collection of books she'd acquired over the years, more even than her apartment over the Belhaven Bookshop in the city. The sleeping quarters had become Kayce's domain; a single bed off to one side, a desk piled high with all sorts of sharpening stones, a hunting blade, new arrowheads, fletching feathers, maps, and a single book.

Following the stairs up, the last floor opened into an area allowing observation through the waterfall to the skies above. It was a small space illuminated by crystalline carvings, now emitting the soft luminance of the moon's glow instead of the sun's rays. Lions prowled where the walls met the floor and waves crashed around the border to the observation window, water falling beyond like a curtain. The crystalline's glow was enough to read by, a small horde of novels shelved in the stone wall.

None of them called to Lia tonight as she dropped into the pile of cushions in the corner, the muscles in her thighs quivering from the ride.

"The two of you are definitely more agile than Storm and myself." Kayce dropped a fur blanket on the cushions. "For now."

"Just wait till I've had half as long to bond with her." Lia smirked. "Then we can race again. You know I won't settle for such a close tie."

"Always the competitive one," he sighed as he settled beside her. A small distance rested between them, something she was all too aware of since he'd held her so close.

She smiled, not bothering to deny it—the competitiveness, she reminded herself. Looking out the window and beyond the water, the stars were brighter than anywhere on Earth. A cosmic sea in and of itself. A sense of familiarity settled over Lia, a memory of her waking world stirring.

"My papa took me camping once," she murmured. "He said sleeping under the stars was the second closest thing to feeling part of the universe's grand design."

"Your grandfather was a wise and honest man." Tearing the last stuffed roll in half, Kayce handed her the bigger piece. "I wonder what the first one was."

"He never said."

Leaning against the stone wall, Kayce ate thoughtfully. "Looking at the stars, one can imagine whole other worlds out there. I've always sensed a peace lying underneath them." From the corner of her eye, she watched as he faced her. Studied her. Then, his hand brushed her arm and he uttered softly, "Tell me more about him."

Lia watched the stars, wondering what to delve for: truth or imagination. She reached for what she thought would honor Papa best. "He was a writer, loved to tell stories. He always needed a cup of tea in the afternoon or else he became grouchy." Her eyes filled.

But she didn't fight it. "He was one of those odd people who put ketch—ah, tomato sauce on his eggs." Despite several tears sliding into her wind-swept hair, she chuckled at her Earth-lingo slip.

Kayce laughed with her. "Tomatoes on eggs? Sounds like a bold, unapologetic man who knew who he was."

"Bold was certainly the word for him." Lia rubbed her nose. With any luck, the waterfall would hide the tears she tried to hold.

But she was short of luck as of late.

Kayce opened his arms to her, and she couldn't fight the need to melt into him. She scooted over, closing the few inches of distance between them. Such a distance had never felt so big before, and to cross it didn't feel easy. A new thrum of tension hummed between them. Still, her heart was too heavy to ignore his warmth as she used his thigh for a pillow, gazing at the glowing ships carved across the ceiling.

A gentle tug pulled at her curls, slow and methodical. That, coupled with the weight of his arm over her shoulders, made Lia's eyes heavy. "He would never correct the wait staff if a restaurant—uh, tavern got his order wrong," she continued. "Then he'd say it was the most delicious meal he ever ate."

"Bold and kind, a powerful combination," Kayce hummed, watching her while her eyes drooped closed more and longer. He continued running his fingers through her hair, gently teasing out the wind-snarled knots. "Like someone else I know."

Lia fought her blush as he continued the uncharacteristic yet tender gesture, offering pieces of Julian Corvine as he was on Earth until her voice grew hoarse. Kayce listened, his hand never stopping. Held her like she was his best girl. She certainly felt it.

The lull of sleep grew harder to ignore, Kayce's body warm against hers under the furs. The waterfall rushed, droplets occasionally floating upward as greetings to the seas and constellations above. Lia tracked them to the stars her papa loved.

Sometimes, she swore those stars stared back.

CHAPTER THIRTEEN

S parrows twittered outside Lia's window, disturbing her peaceful slumber. Growling at the obnoxious banter, her eyes cracked enough to see the dark sky fighting dawn. Her next glance was at the clock on her nightstand.

How obscene.

"Shut up," she croaked. "It's not even six thirty."

Fiore's warmth radiated against her back, leaving her chest cool—the feline's usual spot. Eyes shut, Lia's brow scrunched. "What did I do to tick you off, prissy thing?"

She rolled over to pull the cat close. And froze. Her hands didn't meet soft fur. They found hard muscles. Too big to be her brother, way too muscular to be her mom.

Skies and seas, what the—

Jerking back, Lia flailed for something to swing. The scrambling in the dark pushed her off the bed and onto her backside. Pain shot up her tailbone, but she was already moving. Panicked, she surged off the floor with a pillow. Not heavy, but it'd do.

Lia swung at the stranger curled into her bed. His snore cut off in a choke as he jerked awake under her assault.

"*GET OUT!*" she shrieked, hitting him again and again. More words tumbled out, but she was too scared out of her mind to give this guy any room to—

He jolted upright, wrenching the pillow from her. "Aurelia!"

Oh. Oh, *no.*

"How do you know my name?" Lia rushed, stumbling back against the bookshelves. Her weapon was gone. A cheap motion-light in the outlet kicked on, illuminating the intruder.

"W-why are you dressed like that?"

Blood rushed in her ears as she assessed him in more detail, the embroidered tunic and slacks so reminiscent of...Norenthian fashion? This was too weird. No good at all.

"Where—what is this place?" The young man—she could guess he wasn't too old, though that was still not entirely comforting—looked about in confusion, tripping out of the sheets. "What in the skies and seas is going on?"

Skies and seas? Didn't I just think that—

Her mind scrambled to make sense of this craziness and she gripped her forehead. There had to be a logical explanation. "Listen, I don't know what the boundaries were for my papa, but I don't appreciate cosplayers showing up in my bedroom!" She pushed the tumbleweed of hair from her face and squinted to see. "Even if you share a scary resemblance to Kacerion—you're taking the Floating Kingdom obsession to a whole new level!"

Admittedly, she was mildly impressed. From the little she could make out, the resemblance was pretty spot on.

He gaped at her. "Cosplay? Obsession? What are you—Aurelia, it's me!" He enunciated each word slowly. "Kayce, I *am* Kacerion."

"I'm half blind, not deaf!" She needed her glasses. Or maybe she didn't. Light flooded the room as she flipped on the lamp, leaving them both wincing. Once her eyes adjusted, she looked.

Looked.

And looked *again*.

This wasn't possible. None of this made sense. She must be dreaming.

But a pinch to her arm only made her flinch.

"Did you smoke seaweed last night?" The Kayce-fan grumbled at her gaping silence, shaking his head before looking around the bedroom. "Were we drugged?"

If he was a cosplayer, he was a believable actor. And that voice—it sent a shiver down her spine, a rumble that had pitched low like rolling thunder.

"*You* took something, to think it's perfectly fine to end up in a girl's bedroom!" Lia snapped before realizing she knew exactly what he was talking about.

"What the—" He looked down with wide eyes as Fiore rubbed against his leg. The motion drew Lia's attention to the *flipping sword sheathed at his hip*. That's it. She was done for. Lia needed to get rid of this problem—hadn't her screaming alerted *anyone*?

She held out her hands. "Listen pal, I don't want any trouble, just don't hurt—"

"Aurelia, stop—"

Lia feigned right to rush around the bed, but then bolted over the mattress. Legs tangled in the sheets, she nearly fell off the bed when his arm wrapped around her camisole-clad midsection like a vise.

"Let me go!"

"Not until you calm down!"

A volley of swats and smacks landed anywhere she could find. Several made it to his head. How could her brother down the hall sleep through *this*? He'd always been a heavy sleeper, but this was next-level. And curse Mom's workaholic tendencies!

"Listen!" The pure authority of his command seized her. He let her go, a heavy sigh flared his nose while he brushed his hair back into place. An *alarmingly* familiar gesture. "I don't know where we are or why you're dressed in such ridiculous garb. We went to the alcove last night. Ate delicious leftovers from the boring ball, then you met Paxia. We went for a race. Fell asleep in the outpost's bird's nest." Seeing her blank look, how she held herself like she was about to break apart, he softened his tone. "Come on. Focus. Breathe."

Lia's eyes widened.

Breathe. Focus. Breathe.

He watched her, exaggerating each breath until she couldn't help but mimic him. It forced her blood to slow, the coping mechanism settling her anxiety. How did he know to do that? And he'd detailed her dream with such accuracy. Her shoulders curved inward as if she could hide from a window left open at night.

A beacon blazing into the dark void. Into the very essence of her.

Tearing her gaze from him, Lia found her papa's page on the floor by his boot. That story, where imagination came alive. Where nightmares came into the physical world.

And dreams.

Give me Kayce, she'd demanded last night.

She shook her head. It simply wasn't possible. Lia started to push past him.

Defensive, he held out his hands to stop her, palms up.

And her pounding heart stopped. A scar carved through the calluses—a scar that was never mentioned in Papa's books. That scar was private, an oath made between children a long time ago in a dream. The twin to the one that had appeared on her own only yesterday, from a world and a time in fiction.

Slowly, she raised her own palm and stared at it. Her memory flooded with the moment they swore to protect each other. It felt as real then as this did now.

"This is insane," she murmured to herself. "There's no way."

She aligned her palm with his; the scars faced one another. Lia dragged her gaze up his body, really *seeing* him this time. Adrenaline came crashing down.

Not a dream. Not some illusion of insanity, some coping mechanism come to life.

"Kayce..." she mouthed. "*My* Kayce?"

"Your Kayce." He sagged, holding onto her hand. "I've been trying to tell you, but I was busy being assaulted."

"*You* were busy—" Her brows shot up, still not believing what was clearly in front of her. Touching her. "How is this happening right now?"

"Do you mind telling me why you're acting so strangely?" He heaved a sigh, releasing her to run both hands through his hair once more as his gaze bounded around the room. "And please tell me where in the skies and seas we are?"

Lia dragged both hands down her cheeks. A character she wrote stories about now stood in her room. Did she bring him here? Her papa didn't explain how this all worked.

Kayce snapped his fingers in her face. Right, focus.

She cleared her throat with a shake of her head. "Ah, well, this is my bedroom. And I'm acting like me? Well, the *me* that's awake."

"Then why are you acting like you don't know who I am?"

His face scrunched in confusion as she poked his chest. She jumped slightly at his heartbeat before snatching her hand back. His question, already forgotten. He was *here*. Her best friend. And it didn't really matter how it was possible.

She flung her arms around him.

Kayce stumbled. He stiffened in her embrace before softening. A heartbeat passed before his body bowed over her own. "Are you all right?" he murmured.

She shook her head with a wet laugh. "I'm losing my mind. But I don't care right now."

Not when he was here. This hug made every impossibility since she'd awoken yesterday seem bearable. Like it could all actually be happening. Pine and sea-salt clung to his hair as she buried her face in his neck. Skies, he was *warm* and solid and real—

Her knees wobbled. She would've sunk to the floor were it not for the voice at the door.

"Uh, Lia?" Marcus called out, head poking into her room. Of course. Of *course*, he would check in now and not when she was screaming.

"Don't you knock?" She leapt from Kayce, voice skipping an octave.

Her brother glanced between the two of them. "Who is that?"

She blinked, relief allowing her a full breath. If Marcus could see him, that final bit of doubt could be forgotten.

"'Lia'?" Kayce questioned with a frown. Fiore took that moment to emerge from under the bed. Her purring was a small motor as she twinned around Kayce's legs. He jumped, taking a step from the cat to look at Marcus again. "Who are *you*?"

"Um, Marcus. Lia's brother. What's going—"

"Why do you call her Lia?" Kayce jabbed a finger in her direction. "This is *Aurelia*."

Marcus fidgeted with the doorknob. "Uh, I don't know how to handle this. We haven't learned about this in health class yet—"

"Ick, Marcus, no! This isn't like that *at all*." Closing her eyes, Lia rubbed her pinched brow. "Marcus, Kayce. Kayce, Marcus. And I go by Lia here."

Marcus gasped. "Wait, Kayce? As in *the* Kayce? From Papa's books?"

"Apparently," Lia mumbled. Maybe she needed therapy.

Relinquishing the doorknob, Marcus walked in. "Can you really fly a volatequis backward and upside down without falling off?"

Kayce flashed a strained smile.

"Marcus, that's your biggest concern?" Lia blurted. "Besides the fact that he's here, in the flesh?" She'd expected more freaking out from a middle schooler.

"The most basic part of scientific research is a study of the five senses," he said. "Considering Kayce is right where I can see and hear him, and you were just all over him—"

"No, I wasn't!"

"—then he's obviously here." Marcus frowned, tilting his head. "But how, I got nothing. Wait." He pointed to the ground, the paper beside the box of Norenth materials. "What about that story?"

Lia knelt for the paper. Their papa's tale of imagination, a realm of dreams. A guardian that tore it all to pieces. "He's...a story brought into our world," she said. "Papa was working on this the day he died, acting all shifty—wait, how did you know about this?"

"Well, I read it."

Lia blinked. "*When* did you read this?"

"While you were getting ready the other day," he said. "I needed a pencil, and I saw it."

She couldn't berate him for the total disregard of sibling boundaries. Not when Kayce cleared his throat, stepping between the two of them.

"What do you mean? I'm not a story," Kayce insisted. It forced Lia's attention back to him. She hadn't meant to shut him out. But he looked utterly lost as he whipped between the siblings, trying to keep up. Guilt brought heat to Lia's cheeks. Clearing his throat, in a much calmer tone, Kayce continued, "Can somebody *please* explain to me what is happening?"

Lia's throat closed. She went to a bookshelf and snatched a thin, dusty-red book. "*This* is what we're talking about."

Kayce studied the cover—an illustration of a young boy on a flying gray horse, a ghostly ship rising from the mist behind him—before flipping it open. "The Floating Kingdom series?"

"Last night, when I said my papa was a writer," she explained, her mouth dry like parchment. "He wrote that book. Three more, too. About you, Norenth, all of it." She glanced at Marcus, who studied Kayce like some star he could barely make out through his telescope. How was she supposed to tell someone they were a fictional character when they clearly no longer were?

Licking her lips, Lia continued, "But what inspired him was me. Because I—well, I kind of created you to be—" Flame engulfed her face, her tone dropping to a mutter. "My imaginary friend."

Kayce's brow arched, fixing her with a peculiar look of puzzlement and disbelief. "An imaginary friend?"

"Yeah. Yes." She found a brown knot in the flooring. It looked like a twisted grin slashed into the wood. Maybe if she stared at it long enough, she wouldn't have to confront the way the worlds had split open and vomited before her. Nerves got the better of her as she started picking at her nails.

The silence was heavier than a downpour.

Why wasn't he saying anything? She felt like she'd told him a dirty secret. She didn't lift her gaze, and the knot sneered at her while she waited for him to speak.

"So, you somehow came to my world?" Kayce finally reasoned. "Then, you told your grandfather about our adventures, about my family, all of our conversations?" Paper fluttered like a flock of geese as he turned more pages.

Lia wrung her hands. "Well, partially, but he helped me bring Norenth to life. All of our adventures, they were real to me when I—when I needed them most. He knew that and helped me by writing—"

"An imaginary friend to be *like* me? Aurelia, I have memories from my childhood long before I met you. And you're trying to tell me I'm made up?"

Her head jerked at the agitation in his tone, which had never been directed at her before. She knew the confusion, but there was a blank expression on his face, features carved from stone, his lips pressed in a pale, firm line.

"Do I look made up to you?" he pushed.

She flinched. "No, Kayce, but you—you *are* him. Yes, you're made up, but not like that—"

"No, because I'm real," he spat, thrusting a finger out for silence. Red inched up his throat. "I don't know what game you're playing at, but you need to stop. This isn't funny."

The blood drained from her face. This was all going so wrong.

"You're my best friend, Kayce. I don't understand how this is happening, but—" she faltered, looking at her brother who seemed as lost as she felt.

As they all felt.

Kayce took a step back, keeping Lia away with an arm raised. He shook his head, his face twisted with confusion, dark brows pinched. "Stop this nonsense. Whatever trick this is, it's not funny. People can't make up other people."

Tears burned as her voice hitched. "Now *you* quit. This isn't a trick! Do I look like I know what's going on any more than you do?" Maybe this had to still be a dream, some twisted nightmare stuck between waking and sleeping.

But Kayce pulled away again as she moved closer, the motion a visceral pull in her stomach. One too real to ignore. "No, you're doing something." Kayce ran his hands through his hair, holding his head. "Or this must be a dream."

The irony wasn't lost on Lia.

Before Marcus or Lia could react, a bewildered Kayce rushed out the door.

"Kayce!" Lia rushed after him.

Marcus caught her arm. "Lia, wait—"

"I can't just let him go! He could get lost or—" *Hit by a car.* The fear rose like a tsunami, made her shove against Marcus. She couldn't lose Kayce. Not when that secret, selfish wish had just come true.

Marcus held firm, blocking the doorway. "I know he makes your stomach feel all kinds of butterflies, but Kayce's a ranger. Until you get into some better clothes, he'll be all right."

"How do you know that?" Her gaze narrowed. She never read *that* part to him, but the revelation diverted her fears. For the moment.

Marcus shrugged. "You don't exactly keep your journal hidden."

Lia opened her mouth but closed it with a shake of her head and went into the closet. "You're getting too smart for your own good."

"Thanks, and don't worry about Mom," he called. "She's already at the hospital."

Figures. She doesn't need the extra burden, anyway.

Lia's shoulders struggled to remain upright while she changed into blue jeans and threw on a cardigan. She knew their mom had a lot to deal with. Losing their papa impacted her the most. And while she noticed Lia was sick yesterday, there was a disconnect. Like Mom was holding back. Did she know about this family tale of Papa's? The bingo league even mentioned she was a writer, once upon a time. But Lia couldn't bother her with this. Not until she had answers of her own.

And Kayce came first. Frustrated tears burned in the back of her throat. Lia swallowed them before emerging from the closet. "Not a word about this."

"Of course not! Like she'd believe me," Marcus mumbled. "*I'm not sure I believe me.*"

Lia grunted in agreement, but a thought nagged at her. Why were nightmares and dreams coming true *now*? It didn't make sense. But one thing did. Papa knew. And she was going to get to the bottom of this family tale he started. Even if she had to finish it herself.

"Get dressed," she said, heading for the stairwell. "You need to go to school."

"School seems kinda anticlimactic."

She whirled around to demand it again, needing to do *something* right that morning, but drew short. She could see every inch of Marcus's pained expression, her glasses a phantom limb. And she hadn't needed them yesterday, either.

"Just—get to school." Throwing the door open, Lia hit the sidewalk at a run.

CHAPTER FOURTEEN

Instinct led Lia to the park. It was the closest, thickest grouping of trees, away from all the noise. She remembered the countless times she had found Kayce, tucked way up in the nearest tree, anytime the pressures of the court were too much to bear.

Now, she was the cause.

It made her want to empty her already hollow stomach right there on the sidewalk. Instead, she ran faster. Pain was the last thing she wanted to give her—suddenly real—best friend. But she would find him, as she always had. Just as he always found her.

Relief soothed her burning lungs like a balm when Lia saw Kayce cradled by the nook of a sturdy oak. Her shoulders dropped, slowing her pace to a walk so she wasn't sucking wind. It was a comfort she knew him, even here. But his brow furrowed, casting a shadow over his eyes as he stared out at her world. His body was so stiff, like he had become one with the tree. Even though he knew her footsteps well.

"Hey," she tried lamely, stopping below him.

He didn't reply.

Lia toed the ground. She'd earned that. Didn't make it sting any less. Like when he'd lost his pendent bearing the family seal. Each Weatherstone brother had one. It had been only a week after he'd gotten it on his tenth birthday. He and Lia—*Aurelia*—had pilfered the royal kitchens, taking treats the chefs spent *days* working on for that year's inaugural ball. Didn't matter that his pendent was left at the scene of the crime. She'd still snitched on him when the Lioness cornered them, faces dusted with sugar and hands sticky. He didn't talk to her for four whole hours. And that, for a nine-year-old, was a *long* time. She'd never snitched again.

But this wasn't stolen sweets. And they weren't kids anymore. So, Lia waited.

Eventually, Kayce let out a forceful breath. "You really are not from Norenth," he said as if trying to convince himself.

Following his gaze, dawn had painted the clouds—here, in this world, fluffed as cotton candy—a soft pink. The prospect that his world—no, *their* world—was as alive as this one made a tingling surge from her chest, spreading outward like the sun inching over the horizon. It was a warmth that enveloped her, chasing away every dark thought.

But even the sun created shadows. And doubt made that sensation in her chest restrict with each breath she took.

"No." The soft response hung between them a moment. Lia swung herself to straddle the limb as she would onto the back of Paxia. Settling into the spot next to Kayce, her gaze followed his once more. Uncertain of what to say, she waited. But the silence was unbearable. Pulling the sleeves over her hands, Lia stared at the tree bark. "I don't have answers, Kayce. And for that, I'm sorry. But that doesn't mean we can't figure this out together, like we always have."

"You mean like *you* always have," he said, unblinking, but the muscles in his forearms twitched.

Lia clamped her mouth shut. Shame heated her neck. Silence ticked on, a robin twittering overhead. Suddenly, Kayce surged forward, causing Lia to jump. "It's true, isn't it?" Jaw ticking as he clenched his teeth, Kayce returned his focus to the horizon. "You made me up. My family, the kingdom, the seas. None of it is real—"

"It is to me!" she insisted. "It's always been real to me. I've always felt more at home there. Yes, they were stories, but they were mine. They were ours. And I...adore them with every fiber of my being. You, your brothers, the people." She sighed, almost tasting the salty, Norenthian air. "You've *always* been real to me."

But Kayce pushed on as though he hadn't heard her—or hadn't cared to. "It somehow lives in your mind, and I'm just an imaginary friend along for the ride." Red splotched his cheeks in contrast to the paleness of his lips. But his eyes...they didn't rove calm and confident over the trees and clouds beyond. They were chips of amber, glinting like cold stones.

Lia's throat itched with bile. It filled her mouth, roiling her stomach. She forced a swallow, closing her burning eyes. But she couldn't hide from this. She couldn't sequester herself away to her room, her books, her journal.

No escaping this time.

"Kayce, there's no 'just' about it." She bit her lip. When she opened her eyes, she found one scarlet leaf hanging below the rest. "When my parents separated, my father didn't call on my birthday. Only sent cards. He didn't even come when Marcus kept having night terrors."

She grimaced. That was a particularly dark period for Mom. Lia hated how she had twitched every time the phone rang, the constant meetings with the school for their whistleblowing concerns. Older now, she could see the validity of it: any unexplained bruising on a child would do that. Still, it had been a harrowing few months. And her father couldn't be bothered. Maybe she shouldn't have been surprised when he stood up the funeral.

"No one wants to be friends with a kid dealing with that stuff. I didn't get invited for sleepovers anymore. And when I turned eight, only four people ate the giant cake my mom bought."

Kayce's shoulders curved toward her. Silent, distant, but listening. It pushed Lia to continue. To help him understand.

"Even though I thought my stomach would burst with icing, I felt like I ate nothing at all," she whispered, watching the leaf tumble on a breeze. "That gnawing was always there."

That empty, aching void inside. A loneliness that left her hollow. That had tried to swallow her, drown her completely, since Papa died.

Kayce's eyes slid over her, flickering like a beacon in the dark. His voice was hoarse. "You wore a green dress."

Lia blinked back the tears that threatened, the corner of her mouth lifting. "I did."

They stared at each other.

"Papa's garden was the best place for the party, before my mom decided to move us. When no one showed, I tucked myself into the rose bushes."

He cleared his throat. "You never minded the thorns."

"No one looks there." She tilted her head. "Except you."

"I needed somewhere to practice without my brothers mocking every move I made for once." Kayce soured, uncrossing his arms to drop his hands to his lap. "Besides, I didn't think you would want to sit on that rock and watch all day."

Her smile opened up. "But you said it would do you no good to have an utterly defenseless partner."

"Which is why I had to teach you."

"To feel better about yourself?"

"Absolutely. A boy's pride is no small thing."

They both chuckled, their reminiscing proof of the past. The truth it held.

"I had no choice." He sobered. "Though you were nearly a lost cause."

"Now you know why!" She pushed his foot off the tree with a grin that faded like mist. Because he filled the void in ways he would never understand. "Since then, I have always seen you. And my papa, he coaxed you out of me. Asked about our adventures, your kingdom and family. My answers always came easily, and I never once doubted from where. In fact, you seemed to tell your own story. I was only the recorder."

It was her papa's best writing advice. It was like Kayce was living inside her all of that time, waiting for her to open the door to find him.

He nudged her knee with his foot. "I'm sorry for leaving like that, I just—" Kayce looked back over her world with a heavy breath, shaking his head. "It's a lot."

"I know the feeling," she mumbled, leaning her chin on a fisted hand. "It's not every day your stories come to life."

"Or discover *you're* a story."

"Touché."

He cracked a grin. She wanted to capture that uniquely Kayce smile, hold it in her palm to savor so she never had to see his desolation again. But her mind was a vicious creature, intent on reveling in the questions while ravenous for answers.

"Kayce." Her voice pitched with urgency to get her friend to understand. "I didn't make you up, not really. You came to me when I needed you the most. That made so much difference, that was real."

The young ranger smiled softly, turning to her with a reassuring nod. Nothing more needed to be said. But as they sat in silence, a thought built in Lia's mind. "What if that story Papa wrote really was true?"

"Is this your way of telling me I was actually right for once?" She pushed his pesky leg off again as he insisted, "Well, I feel alive! And to me, Norenth felt real, like this place."

"Norenth felt real to me too, but even more so lately." She looked down at her newly scarred palm, despite her nailbeds still being a mess. "My hands didn't always look like this. The blood oath we took was in Norenth, not here. But yesterday, I woke up with the scar and my hands were worn like I'd been working with them for years."

"Because you *have*. I have a bad knee to prove it."

"Here, the only calluses I had were where I held my pen." A shudder raced down her spine. "And then there was the gremlin."

"The what?" Kayce frowned, a hand to his belt for his sword. Thankfully he hadn't run into any police on his way into hiding.

Quickly, Lia detailed what had happened: how her dream of the inaugural ball felt clearer than ever before, how she woke with a splitting headache and fever, how that horrific creature attacked her. How she'd called for him. It was a relief to speak it aloud, to reflect with someone. It made it real. And it had been, all along. She hadn't been losing her mind.

"Have you ever fought here before that attack? In this world, I mean. Because in Norenth, I'm pretty sure Wolfe is still nursing his pride." Kayce scooted closer. She could see the small scar through his eyebrow, her finger itching to touch it. His coldness had melted, but muted smiles and scant glances shuttered Kayce's usual warmth.

Lia ached for it. But she focused on his question. "Skies and seas, no," she said. "Huh. I've been saying that here more lately, too. But I could defend myself like I had really trained with you at the guild. Like it was all—" Lia stopped herself. Kayce was there in front of her, so she would not continue to rub "reality" in his face when the basic understanding of what that was had gone out the window.

Obviously, he'll be disappointed. His best friend's been traded in for the prototype model with only a few begrudging upgrades.

Lia chewed her lip. "Anyway, I hadn't seen anything like that in my life. It was like something from a—"

"Nightmare?" he offered.

She nodded, tapping her knee to hide another shudder that worked up her spine.

Noticing the nervous tic, Kayce took her hand and flipped her palm up. Showcasing what they shared. "You know everything from my world. How to fight, how we speak. You have scars and calluses you never got in this world." His gaze snagged hers. "I'm here. And that gremlin thing too, but I'm better looking."

She rolled her eyes but paused, biting her lip. Lia hopped off the branch, turning to face Kayce while tucking a flyaway curl behind her ear. "We need to go to my papa's house. Maybe he wrote something else that I missed."

Landing nimbly beside her, Kayce readjusted the cuffs of his tunic. He flipped his hair back before he met her gaze with a determined smile. "I'm with you, Aurelia."

Her stupid heart flipped as they stared at each other, his lips softening. He really shouldn't be calling her that—especially not here. He was going to see how unlike the Aurelia he knew Lia really was.

But she didn't have the heart to correct him. Not yet.

CHAPTER FIFTEEN

The park was only a mile from her papa's home. As they walked, Lia gave Kayce a better summary of the new story her papa had written. Other than the fact that he wrote it, she couldn't figure out what he meant by the notion of a family tale. That nagged her almost as much as the foreignness of Kayce walking the streets beside her. Had it only been a couple weeks ago that she had listened to music, longing for Norenth to be real as she left Papa's?

She wrung her hands, trying not to fidget too bad. The Victorian house soon loomed over Kayce and Lia, withered rose bushes climbing the front porch railing.

Lia paused before the front door. "We need to fix you. You can't run around with a sword anymore."

She was delaying.

She hadn't been back here since the funeral. And while voicing her struggles to Kayce in their alcove had eased the grief, she knew this wouldn't be painless. Not with the way her chest tightened, her eyes pricking at the sight of letters with his name sticking out from the mailbox. Her nail caught on the loose skin around her pinky.

Kayce frowned, hand tight on his sword. "You cannot fix perfection—"

"Remember, I wrote you," she warned, a wry smile emerging. "And I recall exactly how far from perfect you are."

He held a hand to his chest. "You wound me, *my lady*."

"Just wait till you see what they have at the mall, which we will need to go to eventually. Then you'll really think I enjoy your suffering, *Your Highness*."

Reluctantly, Kayce propped the sword beside a planter.

Their banter had always eased her anxiety, but when Lia opened the door, whatever peace Kayce's teasing provided was stolen by vacuous silence. The air was stagnant, the windows sealed as if to hold in the last vestiges of bergamot that only lingered in the farthest corners of the room. Blood pulsed in Lia's ears as they walked into the foyer. A tissue box remained on the coffee table from the funeral. The easel where her papa's portrait had dominated the room was empty.

Lia stopped, unwilling to trespass further into the tomb it had become.

She tore her gaze from the easel but remained frozen. The emptiness, the sneaking around to get here, it set her teeth on edge, cemented her feet. She knew that if she took those stairs, a different person would come back down. Whatever they found, there would be no forgetting it. And suddenly, Lia wasn't sure if she could face that yet.

A warm hand settled on her shoulder. "No matter what we find, your grandfather cared for you," Kayce said, his voice calm. "He's still here. You knew he would have answers. Painful, perhaps. Difficult. But necessary." Taking a step past Lia, he broke the invisible barrier keeping her in the foyer, then shifted on his heel to look back at her. "He would help you if he could."

Lia managed a half-hearted tilt of her lips, uprooting herself. He always knew what was raging inside her head. Granted, he came from there. But, a thought gnawed at her as she led him upstairs. "If he would have helped now, why not tell me before?" she mused. "Why the convoluted story he didn't even finish?"

It had circled her mind like a restless stray while they walked, hoping they might find the answers, yet dreading the implications. But the truth had to come out. Stories just didn't come to life in your bedroom. Nightmares didn't just chase you down alleyways.

The door to her papa's study was open, but nothing could have prepared them for what they found inside. It was ransacked.

Frozen once more, Lia gaped at the drawers pulled open, papers strewn everywhere. The coffee-brown shelves paneling the walls should have been lined with novels. Instead, most of them scattered across the floor, splayed open like broken birds. An older laptop sat open on the desk, a sea of papers and notes smothering the keyboard.

"My mom wouldn't have done this," Lia breathed.

Kayce held out a hand. He spied the fireplace, twin to the one in the sitting room below, and grabbed a poker. "Stay here."

"Like skies I am." She moved to grab the other one.

They divided the house, making quick work of canvassing the study and the rest of the second floor before doing the same downstairs. All they found was the back door open, but no one else was there. Lia only loosened her breath when they returned to the study.

"Who would break in to trash Papa's office?" she wondered aloud.

"Someone looking for something," Kayce gathered. "Maybe what we are hoping to find."

Lia didn't exactly find that comforting. She started for the desk, pushing aside the leather chair before rifling through the papers. Broken glass clinked when she pulled a picture frame free from the mess. The four of them, last Christmas. Lia's hand shook.

Her first thought was to call her mom and then the police, but this was one more piece to this evolving puzzle. What business was Papa entangled with? She needed to figure this out before calling anyone. Even Mom. The imagination story was too fantastical for someone to come in here searching for it, let alone believing it to be true without proof. But crazier things had happened in the last forty-eight hours.

Chewing her lip, Lia looked out the window. From here, she could see right out to the front yard. The driveway where she had kissed her papa goodbye. The street it led to, right where the police reports say he was struck by that car—

Lia squinted her eyes, focusing on the street. A driver would slam on the brakes to avoid hitting something in the road, even if they were distracted. It was instinct. Lia knew that from her driver's ed classes.

So why were there no skid marks where Papa was hit? Or any *at all* on the road before his house?

"What if it wasn't an accident?" Lia whispered.

She felt Kayce's warmth behind her, his hand on the small of her back. He stood next to her, looking down at the street. "Sir Julian's death?"

Lia blinked hard. He wouldn't understand the mechanics of a car accident. She tried to explain it in the plainest terms possible. "The police said he was found there in the street, like he'd gone for a walk. Neighbors said they heard a crash, like a car hit something. It was filed as an accident, but the person who hit him fled the scene."

Kayce rubbed his jaw. "So no one really saw what happened."

"No. So what if he was killed on purpose? Or what if he was attacked by a gremlin too, but the police didn't know how to explain it so they made up the car accident story?"

"But what about the neighbor who heard the crash?" he asked gently. "Did his body look like it'd been attacked by a monster?"

Lia had tried not to think about the funeral. It'd been a closed casket affair, but Mom had arrived on the scene with the ambulance when she heard the call at work. She'd identified the body. A small kernel of relief eased Lia's mind. She would never want to consider a monster had killed her papa, and it seemed like she wouldn't have to.

But the study remained destroyed around them.

Lia shook her head. "Something from Earth killed him, like a car. But if the driver didn't try to stop..." She started to turn back to face the room. "I don't think they wanted to."

Kayce's hand slid over her hip, pulling her into his side. She wanted to lean into him, like she had in the alcove. But they had answers to find. Now more than ever.

Digging deep, Lia focused on the task ahead. "Look for anything about the guardians that helped humans navigate their dreams and nightmares—"

"And stories being unleashed on Earth?" Kayce pulled away to begin flipping through folders.

It sounded too fantastical to be real, and yet, there they were, searching for it. For something like Kayce, or something like the gremlin. Something not of Earth. Part of her, the one enamored with stories, felt like a child searching for Christmas presents in her parents' closet. The bigger part held her breath like she was opening the lid to a box that was best left alone. They worked quietly, each lost in their task of finding anything to do with the imagination story. Lia had better luck deciphering her papa's handwriting, but Kayce was a quick study. It wasn't as though she devised a whole language system for Norenth. She was no Tolkien.

Looking back to the wall of bookshelves, Lia saw Kayce's fingers pause in their search. "Everything in this world is so strange," he said.

"Boring, if you ask me," Lia commented. "So far, I'm coming up with nothing but old manuscripts and Norenth histories."

"Then think like this is Luddeck's quarters. Where would he hide the goods?"

"I feel conflicted using skills from our smuggling pastime in my papa's house."

"Our intentions were pure!"

Unable to help herself, Lia prodded, "I wouldn't exactly call your schemes pure of heart."

"That's a matter of perspective," he shot back, matching her smirk. "Besides, I didn't see anyone hold a knife to your throat and force you to join me."

Lia hummed in thought, recalling those escapades like she could remember her first day of freshman year or the time she went to writing camp last summer. A true memory. Not a mere recollection of some dream or story written long ago.

A muscle feathered in her jaw, that earlier smile slipping like sand through her fingers. How could she have acted so dauntlessly there and be this trembling mess of a girl here? A reader, cloistered away with a cat for preferred company.

"I did those things in my dreams, my writing," she reminded Kayce—and herself—a touch louder than needed for the small study. "I doubt I could find the guts in this world to leap off a ship thousands of feet in the air onto a flying horse's back."

"*I* didn't dream it," Kayce muttered under his breath, shoving another book back. They continued their search quietly, but nothing availed itself.

"Remember when we thought we raided the wrong ship?" Kayce reminisced a few minutes later. "One of Luddeck's men had hidden the crystalline in a private hold beneath his quarters. We searched that room for almost an hour before your foot caught the rug and revealed the trap door."

Lia dropped a notebook. "It was hidden in plain sight the whole time." She went for the rug situated before the desk. "Kayce, that's brilliant—"

Flipping it back, the wooden floor beneath was utterly bare.

"What did you expect? If a trap door was there, it would fall right into the sitting room," Kayce said, turning to the bookshelves.

Flushing, Lia whipped the rug down. "You have a better idea?"

"No, a different perspective." Kayce pulled the random books remaining out of the shelves, tilting them two at a time as he made his way from the bottom shelf upward.

"A book to a secret room? Isn't that a bit on the nose?" she asked, walking to the shelf next to him. "Whoever was here clearly tried that."

"Beats flipping over rugs."

She refused to rise to his bait. They rifled through the bookcase, ultimately to no avail. Lia paused, a small bust of Shakespeare catching her attention. Once nudged, it didn't open anything. She frowned, scanning the shelves and cupboards beneath. Papa must have more on that story somewhere. There had to be something they were missing. Some latch, a hole, a false door.

All that remained were old board games her papa always beat Lia and Marcus in. The cupboard closest to the desk held several boxes of family favorites. And there, propped on its side, was a bingo box.

"No way." Lia tugged on it.

Only it didn't come out, merely tilted forward. The motion unlocked a latch, the entire bookshelf popping before it swung open.

"That's a lot bigger than a cabinet," Kayce said, jaw slack.

Lia whistled low. "Way to go, bingo league."

"What's a bingo league?"

"Some incredibly weird people that came to Papa's..." She let the last part die in her throat. Weird people, indeed. Could they be related to this strange story, somehow? Why else would the *bingo box*, of all things, open a secret room?

With Papa, nothing was accidental. This was likely no exception.

Kayce pulled the bookshelf back even more to reveal a shadowed space the size of a large walk-in closet. Lia grappled along the wall until she hit a light switch.

Inside was like the study, but all was in order. Whoever broke in hadn't found this room. More bookshelves lined the walls, one of which was bare apart from a corkboard. Illustrations, notes, and newspaper clippings were pinned to its surface. More rabid animals escaped from testing sites, but these weren't only stories from Washington. They were all over the country. Lia's fears about more gremlins running amok tripled. She leaned in to read another clipping. It was a cryptid article on...Bigfoot? Mothman? Papa was no conspiracy theorist, but even his notes scrawled on post-it notes made little to no sense. Lia squinted to read her papa's tight handwriting.

"Aurelia, come look," Kayce said from the central table.

She turned, standing beside him to study the sketches illustrated in varying pencil shades. Her body stilled in shock. Each sketch was a region, a realm filled with stars and worlds, a name scribbled on the top corners.

Realm of Exterreri... Realm of Silvae... Realm of Litores...

But that naming convention was where the commonalities ended.

Within each realm, the illustrations shifted from utter darkness to towering forests to surging oceans. Some held cities like ones from ancient history books, while others looked like ones set in a science-fiction film. It was like a vast collection of snow globes, spheres with entire worlds and lives encased within.

Then Lia lifted them to reveal what dominated the table underneath.

At first, it seemed to be a hand-drawn astronomical map of the stars. But on further inspection, it was the realms mapped accordingly, smaller renderings of the sketches they had looked through. Far too elaborate for Lia to delude herself into thinking this was worldbuilding for some new novel.

Wherever this place was, it was massive with countless spheres, some more detailed than others. The largest regions, the Realms of Somnium and Exterreri, were to the left, neighboring each other. With spheres of varying lightness and effervescent clouds, the former realm only heightened the darkness brewing in Exterreri, several worlds encased in claws and teeth. Along the center of the map were the Realms of Montes, Litores, and Inferis: spheres of verdant forests and mountains shifting down to worlds of ocean, finally darkening to the muted, spectral gray of Inferis. Tempus, Moderni, and Futurum bordered the right, their spheres marked by cogs and gears, other elements of the modern world or a world not yet achieved. And surrounding it all, illustrations of various creatures and dragons took shape in the stars.

Lia knew that like any map, creatures often meant the unknown: terrain to be explored, to be cautioned.

This place was limitless.

Kayce braced his hands on the table, amber eyes roving over the terrain before him like it was a ship he meant to rifle through. "Wait a minute," he started, brows creasing as he read the map and snatched a handful of sketches to flip through them. He finally paused, pulling a page free that shivered in his hand.

Lia looked over his shoulder to the sphere filled with a familiar rise of towers that disappeared into a fog, bridges crossing a mighty ravine. The Skyward Seas. As Lia pressed into his side, Kayce cleared his throat. The unspoken agreement between them heavy with expectation and unvoiced longings.

"It's..." Lia whispered.

"Home," Kayce choked. With searching eyes, he consulted the map. His finger traced until he found the circle that matched. "This sphere right here"—Kayce tapped where the realms Litores and Montes bordered, a small sphere bearing the floating continent—"it's Norenth. And then you have these other spheres. It's a map of worlds. Which means—"

"It's all true," Lia finished, looking at the different parchments. "This place where the imagination of *all* mankind is real." With trembling fingers, she took the map from him.

The world of Norenth looked just like her drawing, minus the fish stickers and vastly more complex. A far more detailed version, stuck in that snow globe-like sphere. She could scarcely manage a full breath. Some last hope for normalcy, for sanity, evaporated like mist. The only balm to such vulnerability was the sheer relief radiating from Kayce, who leaned heavily against the table. He wasn't *just* a figment of her imagination, after all.

Relief expanded in her chest like a breath of the cleanest air from the Washington mountains. She wasn't losing her mind. But the longer she stared at the maps, the more she realized how familiar something was.

"It's my papa's handwriting." Lia realized, picking up another map. The realm depicted spheres filled with clouds, each leading to a doorway under a pirouette of revolving stars. "Realm of Somnium" was written in the corner, framed by the peaceful forms of dreamers cushioned in the clouds.

"Do you think he traveled to these places?" Kayce hedged. "Like you did, with Norenth?"

"In his sleep?" She followed his gaze, looking to the others as emotion clogged her throat. Another sketch on the table held darkness, shadows of jagged mountains and pits sketched in gray shades, full of eyes and teeth. "The Realm of Inferis doesn't seem like a holiday destination."

"It certainly isn't," said a deep voice behind them.

CHAPTER SIXTEEN

The earlier intruder had returned.

Lia froze. Instant regret lurched in her empty stomach for forcing Kayce to leave his sword. Perhaps it was a good thing they'd been so consumed by the impossible that breakfast had not even been a thought. But then Kayce was moving, stepping between her and whoever was behind her. She spun around, gripping Kayce's arm to move beside him even as he tried to block her from view.

Her papa's bingo league partner Leo faced them. His gaze settled on Kayce. Tilting his head, he gave the young prince a once-over.

"You aren't supposed to be here," Leo intoned softly before shifting his dark eyes back to Lia. "What are you doing?"

"And who might you be, to so boldly inquire?" Kayce demanded, his hands deceptively lax at his sides. "Considering you've come back to the scene of the crime."

Lia crossed her arms. "He's Papa's friend. Supposedly."

Her mind was a jumbled mess. Leo was *relaxed*. Concerned, but not like he'd been the one to destroy the study. More puzzle pieces added to the growing pile, yet no signs of answers. Leo didn't look surprised at the secret room, the maps it held, the implications of it all.

Only displeased at their presence.

Lia shook her head. "Considering it's my papa's house, I think you should explain first."

"Your grandfather and I had an ongoing agreement. Should anything happen to either of us, that is." He gave them a wry smile that deepened the wrinkles in his dark brown skin, lifting a house key hooked to a ring with several others. Leo rubbed the back of his head, covered in closely-cropped gray hair. "When you get to my age, one starts counting the years and making preparations."

"Preparations?" Lia inquired. Seeing the look on the old man's face, realization hit, and she flushed.

Leo chuckled at her embarrassment. "I got an alarm on my phone that someone was here. Considering your mother is at work and you are supposed to be at school, I came to make sure all was well." Amusement faded from his face as he looked back at the study. "Clearly, it isn't."

Understatement of the century.

"Who would do this?" Lia pressed. Beside her, Kayce had relaxed slightly, as if he also realized that Leo likely wasn't a threat.

Leo shook his head. "Someone for the authorities to deal with. Considering your discovery, I'd imagine you have more pressing questions."

Only one thing would prompt more urgency than her papa's house getting broken into. And she didn't trust the authorities much if her papa's accident was more than it appeared. Even she'd noticed the lack of skid marks. Still, she'd only just met Leo, and there was clearly more to the bingo league than social calls.

"What is all this?" Lia gestured to the room, a drawing flapping in her grip.

Leo gave her a knowing look. "Cordelia told you, didn't she?"

"Mom said nothing. I found a page of Papa's. He wrote about stories being real. Being allowed—well, *unleashed*—on Earth." Maybe if she didn't look too closely at Kayce, Leo wouldn't notice a story brought to life. Not that his notably *not* average clothes didn't give it away. But she could hope, right?

Disappointment flickered over Leo's face. "He found a way to tell you on his own."

"You do know about this," Lia confirmed, picking at the edge of her fingernail. She really needed to break the habit. Needing something else to do with her hands, she gripped the map of Norenth with both of them.

"As you no doubt already deduced, your grandfather and I—our 'league', so to speak—do more than play bingo and write together."

"I still don't know what bingo is," Kayce muttered, crossing his arms.

"That's not exactly important right now," Lia hissed.

"Seems to be. Is it a guild he joined where dueling is involved?"

"Can you please—"

"Listen?" Leo interrupted. "There doesn't seem to be a lot of that going on, I fear." He strolled toward the corkboard. Studying the scribbled notes and string attached to various pins, Leo frowned at one note in particular, its edges crisp.

"If you guys aren't really in a bingo league, what are you?" Lia narrowed her eyes. "Are you...guardians?" It was the only part of her papa's story that could make sense. Maybe he, along with Leo, was a guide, one of better morality she hoped. That's why he needed all of these maps. Lia liked to think she'd know if her papa was some cosmic guardian of fiction.

Leo's bark of a laugh quickly dispelled that theory. "No, not at *all*. Did that story of Julian's not explain how the First Rift was dealt with?"

Lia and Kayce shook their heads.

"It was chaos," Leo sighed, walking around the table so that Lia and Kayce were closest to the open door. Kayce relaxed further, and it loosened some of the tightness in Lia's chest. Leo continued, "Men and women suffered under terrible beasts. Some took to magics of the darkest sort. But others rose in the face of such wild fantasy, prepared to defend the land that had become theirs to nurture. For they also sought to protect the dreams and pure creatures that had come through the torn barriers."

"What was done to the nightmares?"

"Certain brave souls were gifted an ember, fed by the breath we all came from," Leo said, pointing to the table strewn with maps. "These humans, Flamehearts, gained unlimited access to these other worlds for a singular purpose: to put back those creatures that escaped."

"Even the good ones?" Lia dared to hope that the precious creatures could remain. It would add some interesting perks to her own mundane life. What better excuse was there than saying a fire fairy burned her homework? Or even claiming that one was too busy swimming with mermaids and fighting off pirates to think about the assigned reading? Not that she would dare forget the reading. Though, a girl could wonder. But thinking back to those cryptid newspaper clippings behind her, Lia's hesitancy returned.

Leo shook his head. "Flamehearts were tasked to return everything that did not belong in the physical realm of Man. This was for protection. It was the Flamehearts' stories that housed the creatures and folk of the Emperium. Such stories, woven first as songs and poems, became written words."

The Emperium—where fiction had a life of its own.

"And those stories, as Flamehearts captured them, are the ones that live today," Lia surmised. Her pulse fluttered in her throat. All of this was so new and difficult to grasp. Despite the many pinches over the last few hours, she wasn't fully convinced this all wasn't a dream. Her gaze drifted back to the destroyed study.

Or a nightmare.

Maybe throwing up would help. Or maybe she needed the breakfast she'd skipped.

Leo studied her. "The older you are, the easier it becomes to accept that life isn't as straightforward as we think."

Lia was wrong before: *that* was the understatement of the century. And easier said than done.

"Apologies, sir, but Aurelia has a faster wit than you give credit for," Kayce interceded. "Just a little slow on the draw." He patted the hip where his scabbard should have been with a smirk directed her way.

She scowled, wishing *she* had his sword. How could he joke around right now? How was he so calm about this? Maybe the fact that this all validated his existence had smoothed any lingering tension from that morning. But he often hid his fears under banter. She had never cursed that fault more—even if she shared it.

"Kacerion Weatherstone." Leo turned toward Kayce and extended his hand. "I had my suspicions, considering the clothes. And the sword out front. But your commentary proves it."

"I don't know whether to take offense or accept the compliment." Kayce chuckled, shaking Leo's hand.

"Can we focus, please? The Emperium exists, but what does a Flameheart do now?" Lia ground her teeth. Something didn't add up.

"Well, we—Flamehearts past, I mean to say—have written many of the stories back, but we can still traverse the various realms. See the creatures and worlds like the reality they are. Live a little, as they say."

"Like what, exactly?" Lia pressed. She wasn't sure what to expect; she braced herself on the map table.

"Where do you think myths and legends come from?" Leo allowed a small smile. "Dragons large as castles. Creatures that were half man and half beast. Little folk that could lure you to a glen of nothing but revelry. Sea monsters that could cleave a ship in two. And I happen to know an ogre who's a pretty good cook."

Lia shuddered at the thought, thinking about all the stories out there, about the seas and the terrors they held. Even Norenth's aquatic clouds were relatively tame, a kraken or two notwithstanding. Yet delight held sway too, that fantasy was real.

To think, a time where all that the human mind could imagine was here. And those things still were, just locked in a plane apart from them. The urge to turn around and scour the maps itched at Lia, but she forced her focus to remain on Leo. Even as her heart leapt at the wonder. But that logical part of her brain kicked in. Should she mention that little demons with pointy teeth were here in Seattle? The words were there, but she wanted more answers.

Lia's eyes narrowed, assessing Leo. "What did Papa do?"

His smile turned pained. "He made it his mission to build all this." The complicated web of notes and clippings, maps and sketches attested to that fact.

"How did he get there?" Kayce asked, looking back at the table. "It must have taken him years to make."

"Yes, his special project. Generations of Flamehearts have worked tirelessly to map the Emperium, as it is ever-evolving. This is just your grandfather's portion." Leo walked to the table, dark eyes bounding over the celestial sea of spheres. "Think of it like two dimensions: reality, which holds Earth and our universe as we know it, and imagination, which holds the various spheres birthed from stories, organized into realms—just as a library's books are shelved by genre. Your papa was hoping to finish mapping all the realms, or at least most of it. It's easiest to access in dreams—that's where everyone can reach it—but Flamehearts can actually *go* to spheres first-hand. We can navigate between spheres while normal humans can only go to ones they have made themselves, though they are not conscious of it. Yet, there are billions of humans—"

"—so there are billions of spheres," Lia finished.

"One would stand to reason."

Lia wished Marcus was here, learning about this too. He would no doubt be itching for his telescope to witness the swirling stars above, even though she guessed it would be a weak comparison. Her throat tightened. He would have to be told.

"No one person has ever visited them all," Leo continued. "Julian aspired to be the first. One person can create hundreds of spheres, surviving beyond their death and involving different worlds and stories. Making it so every story ever told spawned a world as real as our own."

"Like Norenth," Kayce said, thumbing the sketch that Lia had set down.

"Papa spent his whole life exploring this plane, the other realms, where all stories exist, in order to map it out?" Lia leveled her stare at Leo, seeking confirmation for the thought that had needled her since that morning. "He knew Norenth wasn't just in my head, but an actual place?"

Leo simply stared at her.

Papa, he'd known. All this time, he knew her fantasy stories were real. Real people, in a real place. While Norenth had always been hers, her papa helped write it. A stab of pain pulsed inside her.

How could Papa not tell her? All they did, creating this world. All the pain Lia went through in her childhood, and he'd said nothing. Keeping the Emperium secret. His job.

The awe and wonder she had begun to allow herself to feel winked out under the shadow of doubt. "He knew what I had made and never told me?" she choked.

"Because it wasn't his place," Leo said softly, sadness reflected on his face. "You must know that he wanted to tell you. Several times, in fact, he came close. But he respected your mother's wishes."

Her head snapped up. "Mom's *wishes*?"

Leo paused, staring at the wall in front of him with eyes darting like he could find the right words there. "There is much more going on, so many elements in this. I was your papa's best friend, his confidant. We often shared our frustrations with each other. But I respect your family too much to divulge what isn't mine to share. You need to speak with your mother. Only she can provide the answers." His gaze returned to Lia's. "All I will say is this: she did what she thought was best for you and Marcus."

More questions popped into Lia's head like popcorn in the microwave. Only, her head was the bag, and it was ready to burst. She opened her mouth to inquire further, yet the resolve on Leo's face made it clear that particular subject was no longer open for discussion.

Forcing her shoulders to relax, she did her best to push those questions off. "Why is all this happening now? Why—*how* is Kayce here?"

"Well…" Leo now looked uncertain. "He was brought through. Likely, by you."

"It's my fault?" Her voice jumped an octave.

"You say that like it's a bad thing," Kayce soured.

"No, no, it's not," Lia reassured in a rush. "But that means that I'm—"

Regaining his composure, Leo nodded. "You and your brother are Flamehearts. Like your mother, like her father. The ember, given to the first Order, passes down through families."

A family tale, indeed. *Give me Kayce.* She hadn't been serious. But the piece of her that mattered had been.

The world rocked.

Knees buckling, Lia would have dropped to the threadbare rug were it not for Kayce's firm grip on her elbow. The burning she had felt in her chest, the pounding headaches, the increasing realism of her dreams. All because she had this inherent ability to walk between worlds.

The sting of betrayal clawed at her. It would be so easy to grab it, lash out with it. What gave her mom the right to dictate what she could and couldn't know? Lia clenched her teeth. She couldn't go there, not when her conversation with Lioness Silva was so fresh in her mind. The warmth of the dream returned to her then, like the sun breaking through clouds. She allowed it to melt away the sting, though it needled at her.

Wringing her hands, Lia fought to keep her voice controlled. "How did I not know I could do this?"

"Your ember has just Sparked, as we call it. Powerful emotions can Spark the ember once you come of age, awakening your Flameheart abilities." Leo pulled a chair out from the table. Sighing, he sat. "Grief included."

The word rang in the hollowness carved into Lia's heart. The echo of it clogged her throat. Kayce helped her take a seat. He had zeroed in on her, his features slightly pinched, worry that one could easily miss. But she knew him as well as she knew herself.

Though apparently, she didn't even know herself that well.

"Flamehearts cannot bring creations here." Leo rubbed his face, clearly uncomfortable with Lia's silence. "The barriers between the Emperium and Earth were mended to a degree after the First Rift. New creations occasionally come through, but...it's possible the veil is more tenuous than any of us believed."

"Clearly that's true," Kayce said, pulling over the last chair. "I'm not over the lack of horseflesh here."

The group shared a chuckle at Kayce's meager attempt at lifting their spirits. Kayce, though, didn't let his gaze stray from Lia's face. Not until she rolled her eyes with a small smirk that he mirrored.

Leo watched the prince. "Aurelia—"

"It's Lia," she grumbled softly.

"So, it's not just me," Kayce quipped, earning a soft blow to the stomach.

Leo cleared his throat, calling their attention. "The passing of your grandfather—who always used your full name—caused this emotional power surge. None can blame you for that. Now, with Kayce coming through to Earth..." The older man trailed off, considering Kayce. Analyzing him as though something about him was not quite what Leo expected. "Have you seen anything else peculiar or out of place lately?"

Lia slumped, relieved to hear his words. She already felt so lost and responsible, somehow. Like she should have been able to keep it all together. It took some of the burden off her shoulders. Time to 'fess up about the little demon friend. But could she? Already she'd done something other Flamehearts—at least to Leo's knowledge—hadn't, by dragging Kayce here.

And the matter of Papa's death haunted her choices. Who to trust? For all she knew, the gremlin could have slipped detection since the First Rift centuries ago. No, that didn't make sense. Especially if the fiend was digging around Seattle's garbage.

"No," she lied. "I've been sick the last few days, then I woke up to Kayce this morning."

With a heavy sigh, Leo gazed at them for a moment. "There is so much beauty and wonder in creation, but darkness exists in all the spheres. Nightmares work through a person's fears, anger, and other such emotions. They are necessary. But the Emperium is now shifting in a way that was never intended. If Kayce was brought through, I fear more monstrous creatures could appear behind him. There are some who would use it to their advantage."

Lia sucked on her lip. Kayce stared at her, a small frown marring his brow. He knew she'd lied, but he'd never call her out. Not until he knew why. She didn't know if she deserved that trust, given everything he was learning about her. Granted, she hadn't known about half of it herself.

But if the gremlin was somehow brought here on purpose, who could possibly benefit from it? It'd attacked her, right as she was Sparking. And the waters around her papa—his life *and* his death—were so murky. He never believed in coincidences. Neither did she. Like the fact that Mirel, another member of the bingo league, had found her right after it'd disappeared. She was likely a Flameheart. But if she was coming to send the gremlin back to the spheres, Leo would have known about it. Based on his question, he had no idea.

Lia wrung her hands. For an ancient order, they seemed to keep a lot of secrets from each other. It wasn't exactly a comforting realization.

"So what does that mean for us?" she asked.

"These are extraordinary times," Leo heaved into the silence, examining the corkboard. "If these unstable barriers are left unaddressed, it could be disastrous for both the Emperium and our world. It's why we were given these gifts to begin with."

Lia fisted her hands where they pressed into the tops of her thighs. Who was she, really, in all of this? A Flameheart, one who saved the realms?

Kayce reached over and gripped her fist. His gaze held her own as she looked up, like he saw exactly who she was. Not the little girl hiding in the rose bushes. Not the young woman curled up in a secret study. But something more. Something Lia possibly began to see, too. Even here.

Leo noticed the silent exchange, bracing his knees to lean toward Lia in earnest. "This is not your fault. You brought Kayce here when you needed him most," he said gently. "You have this miraculous gift, Aurelia. To be a Flameheart has its hazards and unknowns but…it's a gift, nonetheless."

"A gift?" she echoed, training overly bright eyes to Leo. Deep emotion gripped her, smothering her senses. "I have no idea what to feel. This is the best and the worst moment of my life—Norenth is real, Kayce is here, but Papa is *gone*. Everything I knew about the way this world works has been a lie! And to top it all off, it sounds like the apocalypse could be coming."

"Let's not get ahead of ourselves." Leo rubbed his temple before taking her hand. "Please, trust me when I say none of this was intentional. New Flamehearts are brought in far more gently. On the Order's behalf, I apologize for the crash-course entry."

The unexpected apology knocked her off-kilter. "You don't have to," Lia stuttered, her composure fraying. The sting of betrayal flared. "I can't believe my mom kept all of this from me."

Leo squeezed her hand and for a brief second, she could almost believe it was her papa comforting her. "I know you feel overwhelmed and hurt, Aurelia—you have every right to be. It's confusing and hard. But I do know your mother only did what she thought was best for you and Marcus. You must talk to her. Tell her everything."

Lia's attention wandered about the table, absorbing what Leo had to say. Her gaze drifted to one of her papa's drawings. She spied the serenity of Norenth—the seas floating above Fealtek and the castle she navigated throughout her youth. A home she knew as well as the one left behind in Ohio. And just as real. A gift she'd longed for since she was a little girl, alone in the garden on her birthday.

Glancing up, she caught Kayce watching her. The small smirk he gave encouraged Lia to relax a fraction and return it. She tore her gaze away from him to the hand Leo still held. Stared until the moisture dried in her eyes.

"I want to know more. Everything about this gift. How to use it. How to help keep the dangers at bay." Lia swallowed. "But, you're right—I need to talk to my mom."

Kayce whistled low. "Someone mark the day and time. Aurelia Corvine just admitted someone else was right."

CHAPTER SEVENTEEN

When Lia and Kayce turned onto her street, her mom's car was already in the driveway. Lia had prayed she'd have more time.

They had been quiet on the walk, digesting the information from Leo in their own ways. He had offered to drive, but Lia had insisted they walk. It was the only thing, apart from writing, reading—*or flying*—that calmed her. She couldn't sit still, and there were no volatequises here.

Lia stole glances at Kayce whenever he wasn't looking. Every so often, his face would furrow, tension tightening his jaw. His hands were stuffed in his pockets, sword riding at his hip. He was hiding more than he let on. Lia wanted to ask, to see what she could do to help, to ease the discomfort this morning had wrought—

But Mom waited.

The school would've alerted Mom they hadn't arrived that morning—namely Marcus, who did *not* have an excuse. Why couldn't he just listen? But he'd seen Kayce, too and probably had burning questions. Like he said, school *was* a bit anticlimactic. Especially now.

"I would wait out here a few minutes if I were you," Lia told Kayce, heart hammering. She stared at the front door. "It won't be pretty."

Kayce touched her shoulder, his hand warm. "I can come if you wish. Just say the word."

Even after everything, he would still help however he could. Her lips twitched into a small smile, though her gaze never wavered. "Five minutes. Then by all means, come charging in."

"I'd like to think I'm a bit more regal than that."

"Hardly." She still hadn't moved.

Her mom knew everything. Leo had said it was to protect them. She must have known something was going on with Papa. Why else move back here after so long? It wasn't like his health was in terrible condition. He'd been distracted. Absentminded. More prone to worry. And if his death was no accident, he had every reason to be.

But what *was* the reason?

Lia wrung her hands. If Mom had ever intended to tell them their heritage, it should have been well before now. Her timing was trash. Lia didn't think she'd be able to hold back. Keep the smile in place. Stay complacent. Not after everything she'd discovered, the story her papa had left behind—somewhere he knew Lia would go if she ever needed to escape.

Tears stung her eyes, but she blinked hard against them. Only when Kayce squeezed her shoulder did she head inside.

Lia only made it four steps when Mom, still in nursing scrubs, whirled on her. Light copper locks fell from her hair clip with the force of the movement. "Do you have *any* idea how terrifying it is when the school calls to say your son isn't there?" she shrilled. "Not to mention what you found at Papa's. Reckless! What would you have done if *they* were there?"

Guess Leo had called her. But Lia would bet he'd left most of their interaction out. He earned a trustworthy point for giving Lia the chance to approach her mom. And she had every intention of doing so.

Marcus, still sitting by the window, winced at their mom's tone. "Mom, I'm sorry, it's just—"

"Just what, huh? What could be so important that you skip school and not even tell me?" She barreled on, "This isn't the slightest bit like *either* of you, and I—"

"You're disappointed?" Lia's lips flattened in a firm line. "That's rich."

Oh, the exquisite irony of it all, she thought bitterly.

Their mom's expression hardened. "Excuse me?"

At least Marcus hadn't let it slip about Kayce. The restraint almost made up for not going to school like she'd told him to. But she was about to implode his world even further. She didn't want to—wanted to ask him to leave, to wait for her to explain later—but there was no dancing around this. No protecting him from what was hard, as she had tried to do since their father left.

Not when their other parent had left them in the dark.

Nails biting into her palms, Lia crossed her arms. "How does it feel, Mom, not knowing what's going on? Kind of disorienting? Well, welcome to my day—no, the better part of my *week*. And it's only Tuesday!"

"Lia, I don't know what's going on, but—"

"No." She trembled, unable to contain herself. "You *do*. That's the entire point. There are whole worlds out there for us to explore—*us*, because we're *Flamehearts*. Papa was one. You're one. And we are too."

Mom's mouth fell open. She pressed a hand to her stomach while attempting to school her features, glancing at a confused Marcus. "Lia, I know the break-in was a shock, and you *have* been sick—"

"I found Papa's secret room off the study. The maps, the sketches of all these worlds created by stories. The Emperium. I saw *Norenth*, Mom!" Lia surged, a tidal wave to break levees. "This amazing, beautiful world that's mine is actually real...and you never told me." Frustration burned in her eyes, and she turned to hide how they shone. Hearing her mom's denial—it broke something inside Lia.

Even Marcus stared at his scuffed sneakers.

"I thought I had more time." Mom's voice had softened. Her fingers trembled when she gestured to the living room, but she fisted her hand as they all moved to the couch.

Lia kept her gaze trained on the door, silently commanding Kayce to come in. She needed his calming presence, the reliability of his strength. Evidently Flameheart powers didn't work that way, and the door remained shut.

"Mom, what's Lia talking about?" Marcus asked vaguely. Bless him, he didn't bring up Kayce, but Lia was sure he was trying to work out how her accusations fit with Kayce's sudden appearance.

Their mom took the armchair across the room. Even though she opened and closed her mouth several times, hesitating on how to start, she was blunt when she did. "Our family is descended from a line of Flamehearts, an order charged with protecting the balance between this world and those within the realms of the Emperium. Worlds birthed from the human imagination—all made real."

"Leo told me," Lia muttered, "at Papa's."

"I gathered as much," Mom said before growing unusually quiet, a fixed look of concentration on her face. "What exactly did he tell you?"

"More than you ever did."

Their mom sat straighter, back rigid. "With good reason."

"I would love to hear the good reason behind lying to your children," Lia fired back. No longer did she need to save face before a stranger. Her questions overcame the desire to be the good and obliging daughter. The burning need to understand engulfed everything.

Why couldn't Mom see? Lia had spent her entire life yearning for a world she never thought existed. It comforted her in the darkest moments. Her mom knew. How could she not, when Lia spent so much time in her room, when her friends were few? But Mom had also never seemed to understand Lia's relationship with

Papa. Now that Lia knew everything, such discomfort around stories made even less sense.

Mom studied her. "Flamehearts walk a delicate line between worlds. It's easy to get lost in them. Many of the stories have been written back, but there are those who seek to release them for power."

Lia knew with a sickening sense of dread she didn't mean something like a small gremlin. She recalled the guardian who'd unleashed it all from her papa's story. Was that the cause of Papa's distraction leading to his final afternoon?

"You mean like when the First Rift was first torn." Lia turned back to her, lines forming between her brows. She noticed Marcus about to speak, then closing his mouth. Guilt flashed through her, but he would have to wait.

"It happened once," their mom warned. "There are those who would see it happen again. Many want the power Malum brought here."

The name hovered in the air like a shadow.

"Are you saying there are people today who want to do what he did?"

"I'm glad to see Leo left at least this part to me." Their mom inhaled deeply through her nose and then exhaled through her mouth. "For shredding apart the boundaries, the Devourer was banished to the world he tried to make, but his actions had influence. Those who were not given an ember grew very jealous. They wanted more than the taste the First Rift offered them."

Lia frowned. "More than Flamehearts know about the Emperium?"

Her mom nodded. "A counterpart, but without noble motives. They passed down their version of events. Now they call themselves the Seekers, searching for that power once again."

"How could they even access it?" Marcus asked, always the quick study. "According to you, only Flamehearts can."

"They've sought us out over the centuries. Find creations that stumble through the patched tears. Thankfully, none have been successful. Neither of you showed signs of Sparking," their mom said, "and I believed if you didn't know, neither would they. I wanted to keep you safe."

Lia's throbbing ankle begged to differ, and she bent to rub it. "I'm not safe."

The color drained from Mom's face.

"Seekers aside—nightmares are here," Lia rushed to say, heat creeping up her neck and building behind her eyes. Her words were a rushing flood. "This...*gremlin* came out from a dumpster and attacked me yesterday, which is utterly terrifying when I have no idea what's going on, *and* when I can defend myself like my body has a mind of its own. I shouldn't have to find all this out through a stranger in a novel-worthy secret room I never knew that Papa had—"

"Lia, stop. Listen to me," Mom interrupted, leaning forward. Her voice dropped an octave, choked with restraint. "It's more dangerous than you know."

"*How?*" Lia begged. "Please, Mom. I need to know."

They regarded each other, both pushed to the brink.

"It's why we moved here," Mom finally said. "Papa kept telling me his suspicions about the thinning between veils, the First Rift's mending about to fail with more creations pouring in. I brought us back to help him. But then he died. And when you showed signs of Sparking, I—I wasn't ready to deal with it yet. Not without him. There is so much about this life, Lia, so much that you don't understand. And if everything about this is true, I'm afraid I don't have the time to teach you." She took a shuddering breath. "My fear put you in harm's way. That is my failing, and I am so sorry."

Lia knew about fear. About pushing things aside because she didn't want to deal with it. They both knew it was easier to focus on other problems rather than your own. Their mom never opened up like this; Lia never opened up like this. But it was a relief to tell someone else about the gremlin, someone she knew—despite the lies and omissions—she could trust. At least with this. Lia's smile wobbled, despite the sting she still felt. The words "it's okay" burned on her tongue, but she couldn't say them. Not this time.

Because none of this was okay. For anyone.

"I know, Mom," she said, her throat tight. "I know."

Their mom smiled tightly. It was a tenuous peace, like the calm before the rains came.

Marcus looked between them, bracing himself for the inevitable. He didn't have to wait long before their mom took a breath, meeting each of their gazes with eyes like hardened steel.

"In the spirit of honesty, there's something else you should know, sooner, rather than later. This cannot go beyond this room until I know more. Before his death, Papa called. Left a voicemail. He'd claimed to find the cause of these deteriorations. And now, with his study destroyed, it proves what I've feared." A breath steadied her. "Papa's death wasn't an accident. He'd meant to come here and share whatever he discovered. He was killed on his way here that night. I thought it was a horrid coincidence but..."

Papa would have told all of them there were no such things as coincidences.

Lia closed her eyes against the wave of pain that surged inside. Whatever he had found, it had put an expiration date on him. It solidified their theories. Made them fact.

Lia wiped damp palms on her jeans. "I didn't think it was an accident either. There're no skid marks on the road where he was hit. And if the police noted that, they'd be looking into this as a homicide." She couldn't help but swallow that last word. She didn't want to think of her papa murdered. It stole her breath, crumpled her heart. How could someone take a life, let alone from a man who embodied all that she knew to be good? Lia couldn't grasp it.

But she'd had more time to wrap her mind around the possibility than her brother.

Marcus's chin wobbled. "Why?"

Lia straightened her spine, locking it all down before wrapping an arm around him.

"I fully intend to find out," their mom said.

"Could it have been a Seeker?" Lia asked, mind skipping like a scratched disc. Images of the trashed study, that corkboard pinned together like he was connecting dots, kept replaying over and over. Lia gasped. The startling clarity of it was so obvious. "They're looking for whatever he discovered. They want to use it or—or maybe they already are, and Papa discovered what they're doing."

"I wouldn't put it past them." Mom's brow furrowed. "Regardless, you *must* leave this to me. You will not be getting into more danger if I have anything to say about it." Lia opened her mouth to argue, but her mom raised a finger. "So long as you live in my house, I have plenty to say about it."

Lia clenched her teeth, struggling to do as asked when the door opened.

Kayce, in his Norenthian attire, looked from her mom to Marcus before finding Lia. She clenched her hands, trembling with the effort to keep them still. All she wanted to do was rush to him, needing the warmth of his arms around her. Instead, she held Marcus tighter.

"I don't do waiting well," Kayce said, giving Lia a stiff smile before taking long strides to her side.

"Lia..." Her mom leaned forward, analyzing Kayce from head to toe. Lion's-head-pommel sword and all. "How is *he* here?"

"Thinning cosmic barriers, apparently."

Mom remained quiet, chewing the inside of her cheek. There was a critical light in her eyes, as if, like Leo, she was looking for something in Kayce that she found lacking. Her brow creased, but tension finally seeped out of her posture when she spoke. "The truth was never supposed to come out like this."

Lia's shoulders slumped. Despite how absent her mom had been lately, Lia knew that Mom loved her. Everything she did—every extra hour worked, every errand, every college tour—had been for her, for Marcus. But it hurt. It stung like a splinter embedded in her gut that she couldn't dig out—no matter how many explanations. No matter how justified.

And now, confirming that Papa was murdered, Lia didn't know what to pursue: evidence to avenge him or space to obey her mom. The pressure to do right by them both cracked at Lia's facade.

Silence stretched on until Mom rose, holding her elbows. "I need to call Leo back. Regardless of what I think about Papa's death, these new rifts must be addressed. An Order meeting called."

"Kayce being here isn't a good thing?" Marcus asked quietly.

"I don't mean that, but it isn't normal."

Lia stiffened, and Kayce shifted closer.

"I'm sure time will tell sooner rather than later," Kayce said. "Secrets don't stay buried for long."

Lia could scarcely breathe. Her mind was spinning. What would this meeting decide for them? The room felt inexplicably smaller than it was, like all the air was being sucked out of it for the others while she suffocated.

Thankfully, Marcus had leapt up, drawing everyone's attention. "I know I'm late to the party, but if every story is real, does that mean...*we* are all a story? We all only exist in some book, our lives written before us and someone is reading about us, and our actions are not really our own—"

"Take a deep breath." Lia commanded, standing to grip her brother's shoulders. She really needed to take her own advice, but throwing herself into helping others, being what they needed, was the best Band-Aid over her own problems. And this was separate from grieving. Even though Lioness Silva's words rang in her mind.

Kayce shot Marcus a sympathetic smile as he sighed, "Welcome to my day."

Lia closed her eyes. They had *all* had a day of it. "Think of the universe the same as you know it. You have the planets, the stars, the galaxies. The Emperium exists in a different plane. No one is going to turn the page on you."

Her brother sagged, nodding mutely. He gave her a grateful smile. She tried to offer one back, but could only manage a grimace. Because it felt like someone had dropped a whole library on Lia's chest.

CHAPTER EIGHTEEN

In the solace of her room, Lia curled on her bed. She pulled Fiore from where she had nestled on her pillow. The cat mewled in protest, but continued to purr. Her little motor eased the tension in Lia's chest, each breath becoming easier than the last.

Her mind struggled to wrap around everything.

She was a Flameheart. She had magic. *Book magic.*

Lia found herself drawn to every shadow in the room, squinting as if she could see into the cosmic realm sketched out in her papa's study. Norenth was real, a place she could actually travel to. How could she get there? Curiosity nagged at her, an itch to explore pulling at her bones. With all the secrets and exposures, she'd hardly had time to marvel at it all.

A place where readers could see their stories come alive. Could there be more of a wonder?

An intense longing for Norenth filled her more than it ever had before—until flits of doubts came and went like moths, flocking to the inflammation around that wound the secrets had pierced in her. But one stung more than the rest.

Papa was murdered. Killed on purpose. Taken. Stolen—

The sinister words kept circling in her mind. And Lia knew the oppressive thoughts wouldn't leave until she did something about it.

Setting Fiore beside her, Lia grabbed her notebook and pen, flipping to a page in the back, away from her stories. She made a list header:

The Murder of Julian Corvino

It sounded like the obscene title to a crime novel. Not in her wheelhouse at all. She bit her lip, her mom's words ringing in her ears. But this gave Lia a hole to shove the remnants of her grief into. It cataloged the pain in a way she could understand. Order soothed her, rounded up the vicious thoughts that swirled like carrion birds over her mind. She wrote them down:

How: Hit by a car in front
of his house
☒ *Where was he going?*
☒ *Who was he seeing?*
Who: Seekers
Why: Problematic veil —
more creations escaping
☒ *What did Papa find?*
☒ *Are the Seekers to blame*
or just taking advantage?

Lia huffed out a frustrated breath. She didn't even know what to look for. Though she'd always been the overachiever, and having only discovered the Emperium today left a lot of politics to learn. This grudge between the Order and Seekers being one of them. With rifts worsening, it seemed like a whole other mess her papa had found his way into. She was following right behind him. Maybe she really should let Mom handle it. She'd already been attacked once. But the gremlin attack and Seekers weren't exactly related. Right?

Ignoring the new headache, Lia flipped to the inside cover of the journal, Papa's familiar handwriting clenching her chest.

Write your stories, and they will become real. Bring Kayce's kingdom to life.

Lia blinked, then read it again.

Papa had tried to tell her what she was all along.

The door eased open, Kayce slipping in. Fiore leapt down and rubbed against his legs. The traitor purred louder as she wound around his calf. "Why me?" he groaned, stepping around the cat to sit on the bed.

Lia kept her gaze on Fiore, who was still obsessed with his leather boots. "I think when cats sense you dislike them, they're adamant to change your mind. It's all on their terms."

"Not going to happen."

Case in point to your realism. I would have made you a cat person.

She snorted, tapping the notebook and keeping the thought to herself. Her papa's note churned in her mind nearly as much as the fact that her Floating Kingdom book wasn't perfectly aligned with the other spines on her bookshelf. Ignoring the twitch, Lia showed Kayce the journal. He took it, bracing his forearms on his knees. Dark waves hung around his face as he glanced over the note. Her fingers itched to brush his hair back to better see his eyes.

"Julian wrote this?"

Lia nodded. "He did this a lot when I was a kid. Wrote little messages in journals and birthday cards that I later realized were bits of foreshadowing; things I didn't realize had any meaning at the time. I always thought it was just a writer's sense of humor."

"But?" Kayce prompted.

"What if he left more? What if he left these notes with double meaning, knowing I'd read them and realize it like I always have?" Her heart sped up. "Not just notes about the spheres. Ones about what he discovered with the Emperium." *What got him killed.* Lia wanted it to make sense, *needed* the senseless act of violence to have reason beyond taking one of the most precious people from her.

Kayce handed the journal back. "How would he, though? Not to doubt his confidence in you, but it's a bit of a stretch considering his death—"

"No, Papa was a meticulous planner, despite what his study looked like." Not that it was his fault. "He would've done it recently, as soon as he learned it. Just in case." She sat straighter. "What he found about the rifts or the Seekers is somewhere for me to find—I was his writing partner after all."

Kayce nodded, rubbing the scar on his palm. "He wouldn't trust such sensitive information for anyone to happen across. Where do we start?"

Lia deflated. "No idea."

There were countless places he could have hidden notes for her—most recently, a birthday card, but nothing tickled her memory. They could go back to his study, but she doubted her mom would let them go far from the house now.

"We've never solved a murder before," Kayce murmured, bumping her shoulder. She hadn't even realized she'd started picking at her nails, his motion freeing her hands. His gentle nudge didn't leave her feeling the normal wave of embarrassment as when her mom caught the habit.

"Smuggling was our speed, remember?" Lia nudged him back. "No bodily harm implied."

"Most of the time. Hazards have ramped up over the years."

Her lips twisted into a grim smile. "Consider the increased danger a hallmark of my teenage angst."

Kayce's grin didn't quite reach his eyes. Silence reigned until he spoke. "As much as I enjoy working around authority, I wonder if your mother is right. That we should leave Julian's death to her."

We. It was never "you". Not with them. It soothed the sting of his implication that they couldn't handle this.

Lia's grip tightened on the pen. "What makes you say that?"

"She loves you. And she knows that this whole Flameheart business is a lot to take in, without throwing a murder plot into the mix."

He was handling this far too well, which needled Lia. Couldn't he be more of a mess like her? Unless he really was—just far *better* at shoving it down. Her nails were close to bloodied ribbons at this point. Praise the skies and seas for long knitted sleeves.

"Sometimes the people who love us make stupid choices they think are for us, but really, are for their own sake," Lia said.

"You think your mother kept this all from you to make it easier on her?"

"No—yes—" Lia huffed a sigh. "I don't know. Maybe it was a relief for her, in a way, to pretend we were normal. I imagine raising two teenagers alone isn't ideal."

Kayce nodded. "It's a lot for anyone to handle."

Finally, a shred of what he was truly thinking. But Lia knew better than to push—she didn't want to make anything worse. She raked a hand through her curls, bunching them back into a loose ponytail. Once finished, she slumped against the pillows. "It feels so shifty," Lia managed. "Like she's dealing in half-truths."

"She seemed pretty straightforward about your grandfather. And the Seekers." He cracked a grin. "I may have been listening at the window the entire time."

She welcomed a genuine smile. "Typical."

He was right, not that she would ever let him hear her say it—not for a second time, anyway. Her mom had been blunt, even in her uncertainty, about the gremlin and Kayce's sudden presence in their world. Yet, there was something in how Mom had stiffened when Lia mentioned Leo had been more forthcoming at her papa's that made her chew her lip further. Leo hadn't known about her papa's rift theories. And he was supposedly his closest friend.

"There's something more she isn't saying," Lia mused.

"Besides the whole bit about looking into a murder?" Kayce turned to her. "What do you mean?"

She shrugged. "I get the sense that there's more. Something this big, there's often a couple of layers. Maybe she suspects Papa left clues, too."

Kayce nodded, studying his boots. "We've only toed the surface. And you have a sense for this. I haven't kept track of how many smugglings succeeded because of your knack for finding pirate hidey-holes."

"I *do* have a record," she said, jerking her chin toward the journal before returning it to her nightstand. "Considering I wrote where they go. Well, most of them."

"Of course you do." There was an edge to his tone before he cleared it away. "I'm happy to hear *some* things are beyond even your notice."

She rolled her eyes, but they returned to the journal. For the first time, a sense of dread pooled in her at the sight of it. Lia sat back up and scooted closer to Kayce. "You won't..." She trailed off, chewing on her lip. "You won't go away, right?"

His eyebrows drew together, dark gaze flying to her as he straightened. "Why would you even ask that?"

"Because what if this 'Order' decides you have to return to Norenth?" The thought alone hollowed out her stomach, making it hard to breathe again.

"Aurelia—" Kayce paused before putting a hand on her arm. "I was always there, right by your side. It's like what you said in the park this morning. That's not changing, no matter what this Order decides."

She nodded, her gaze burning the longer she stared at her hands. Then, the bed dipped beside her. Kayce's warmth pressed into her side.

Lia exhaled, turning into him and resting her cheek in the crook of his shoulder. After a beat, his arm wound around her, holding her close. It took a moment for him to soften. His hair tickled her nose, his breath fanning over her face as he leaned his cheek on her head. Pine and sea salt enveloped her. Cradled her. All she knew in this moment was him, his presence an anchor. Her heart thumped an extra beat, but she relaxed into his side. He hadn't held her like this since their alcove. It comforted her, yet felt like more. Probably because he was *here*. In her room. Sitting on her bed.

Don't think about that now. Lia forced her mind to empty, her heart to slow.

They stayed like that, only the sounds of their breathing and Fiore's purring at their feet breaking the silence.

"We will figure this out," Kayce said, his voice deepening. He took her hand and traced the scar on her palm that mirrored his own. "Whether it's here or in Norenth, I'm with you."

No matter what? But the question remained unspoken.

She nodded, but knew that when they found answers, nothing would ever be the same.

Even this.

CHAPTER NINETEEN

Malls in America were a dying breed, but the one closest to the Corvine home still pulsed with life, small businesses moving in as chain businesses moved online. Several department stores took over the far ends of the mall, the din of voices echoing through the central atrium.

Lia led Kayce toward Target.

At least, she tried to. She'd much rather go back home and continue last night's work of going through the feedback her papa had written on this year's Norenth stories. So far, nothing he wrote seemed to ring true to the Flameheart Order or the Seekers.

Just that one line in her journal.

"You mean to tell me that this one only sells hats?" Kayce was in awe, gravitating toward the window displaying tiers of hats. The rims were flat or curved, each portraying a different sports team.

Lia bit back a groan. "That's their schtick."

"'Schtick'," he copied, his tongue thick with the pronunciation. "I should like one, I think."

"Target will have plenty. That's where my mom expects us to be, anyway."

Guiding Kayce through the mall was like trying to net a butterfly. He bobbed and weaved through the crowd, thankfully sparse for a sunny morning. His Renaissance Faire-like garb garnered a few side glances, but mainly people paid him little attention.

A joy of the twenty-first century.

However, Lia was going to crack several molars if she had to remind him again that they had to go *this* way and that they didn't need *helmets* or *war paint*. The beauty shop was decidedly not on their list, once she'd explained the red paint was meant for lips.

"How does it intimidate their enemies in battle if it's on their mouths?" he asked as they finally approached their destination.

"Because it's not meant to intimidate!" Lia ground out. "It's meant to...well...be flirty."

"Flirty? How is a mouth so reddened it looks bloody appealing?"

She palmed her face. "I guess it depends on what you find attractive." Her lips tingled, recalling his touch at the ball. What *did* he find attractive? And why was she suddenly so curious about it?

He shuddered. "Please never wear it."

"What?" Her voice hit an octave higher. But Kayce was already heading toward the store.

The doors slid open automatically. He tracked the motion with a slow shake of his head. Lia smirked, pushing him through. When he took a moment to breathe and not ask asinine questions, his wonderment at Earth was endearing. She wanted to show him more, take him somewhere far grander than a mall, like an amuse-ment park or the aquarium.

On second thought, baby steps. She wasn't particularly eager to blow his mind even more. He *had* handled all of this Flameheart business far better than she had. Then again, he was always on to the next adventure. She envied him for that.

Her ribs squeezed tight with the thought.

Why couldn't *she* let go like he had, embrace all that this new world was? It was like every time she grasped the Emperium, the wonder of it all, it slipped through her fingers like sand, retreating from her conscious mind as if the rebellious, logical part couldn't bear to face it.

If only Papa were here.

She worked past the unexpected knot that tightened in her throat, focusing instead on Kayce's back as he meandered through the store.

"What's a MemoryBank?" Kayce pointed to a display bear-ing several tablets, each showcasing different movies. At least she thought so.

"My brother mentioned them the other day," she recalled, walk-ing to the table with him. "They can record your dreams." Both Marcus and her mom were over on the other side of the mall, thank the skies and seas. Lia frowned at the Norenthian turn of phrase so readily in her mind.

"Not quite, but we are hopeful. Tech is developing faster than we projected," said the man behind the table, an ImaginX rep-resentative by the look of his name tag. He was young, glasses perched squarely on his nose and an ill-fitting polo draping his thin frame.

Ironically, Lia missed her glasses. Mom had yet to explain why her calluses and scars appeared, why her eyesight improved. Another question, likely home to complicated answers.

"You guys looking for some gift ideas?" the man asked.

Lia smiled politely. "Clothes are on the agenda for today."

The man looked over at Kayce, tilting his head. "I thought the faire was long gone—"

"Well, we need to accessorize," she stammered. "For next year." She would milk this "Renaissance Faire" excuse for all it was worth.

He nodded, but his puzzled frown lingered.

Kayce widened his stance, notching his chin. "Seems meddlesome, prying into one's head." He was one to talk. Then again, so was she.

The man shrugged. "Or ingenious. Many people forget their dreams when waking up, and wish they could relive them."

Lia shifted uncomfortably. If he only knew. Her gaze snagged on the tablets, watching what seemed like a first-person shooter video game. One had the screen bounding through clouds of cotton candy. How original. In another, someone dreamed a dragon ride. She had to admit the scales on the dragon's back *did* look realistic in how they shone and shifted like a lizard's.

But the one of utter darkness gave her pause.

"That one isn't turned on." She pointed.

"Oh, no, it is." The ImaginX rep smiled. "Watch."

Kayce and Lia leaned in. Nothing but vaporous darkness shifted like liquid night. Then, in the center, two red eyes blinked open, a set of bone-white teeth grinning to match.

Lia started, jerking back into Kayce's chest.

He steadied her, frowning. "Some dreams are best not to be lived out a second time."

Considering her own harrowing experience with a real-life nightmare, Lia was more than inclined to agree.

"It makes for great creative fuel," the man pitched. "Think of how much more realistic horror films and haunted hayrides or mazes will be with this tech."

"At least they'll stay in the screen, or someone's head," Lia muttered, pulling Kayce along. She shot the man a weak smile. "Have a good day."

The man nodded, mouth pursing at the loss of a potential customer. Though his eyes roamed over Kayce's attire again, brow creasing.

"Kind of odd how that screen did what Flamehearts can," Kayce mused when they were a far enough distance away.

"Maybe someone at ImaginX is a Flameheart," she guessed, a fixed look of concentration on her face.

Kayce wandered into the nearby aisles. "All I see are satchels and eye protection!" he exclaimed, glaring at a small pink purse with a bow affixed to the front. "That cannot possibly hold any proper scouting equipment. The tailor erred greatly with this one."

Lia grabbed his arm. "Men's clothes are this way."

In the back of the store, the red walls and illuminated bulls-eye captured his attention more than the mannequins with jeans and plaid shirts.

"Can I practice my archery here?"

"*I* might," she muttered, pulling jeans at random, holding them to his waist with a squint. She handed him several pairs of dark-wash jeans and shirts before ushering him to the dressing room. With the door shut between them, it was a relief to lean back and close her eyes, rubbing the creases between her brows.

"When do you think the Order will call this meeting?"

And the premature worry-lines returned.

"I don't know," she exhaled, glancing about to ensure there were no other customers eavesdropping. "Mom said she'd hear from Leo tonight."

"What's wrong?"

"Nothing."

"Liar. You have that tone."

She huffed again, crossing her arms tightly. "I just... I hate walking into a room, being the stupidest one there."

"You aren't stupid, Aurelia," he admonished, clothing rustling from within the changing room. He muttered, almost beyond her hearing, "Why do these breeches have teeth?"

A smile wormed its way onto her lips. "It's a zipper. Pull the tab."

"The tab—" A quiet zip. "Ah, I see."

She listened to the shuffling before answering. "I know I'm not, but it's not a good feeling knowing there are people who know more about you than you know about yourself."

"Tell me about it," he said dryly. "Everyone reads about me in a book."

The door opened. Lia stared at him, her body stilling.

Kayce stood in blue jeans that flared wide enough to accommodate his boots. The shirt he wore was simple cotton, long-sleeved and dark green. The material pulled taut over his chest.

His toned, practically chiseled chest. When did *that* happen?

She licked her lips before a quick shake of her head. *Snap out of it.* "I-I think you need a bigger size."

He frowned, smoothing the shirt over his stomach. "It's comfortable enough."

"It looks a bit—" Her throat closed.

He glanced up through the hair that had tumbled into his face, and his infernal smile appeared. "A bit what?"

She glared, heat splotching over her cheeks. "Tight."

He hummed, glancing in the mirror in a movement that flicked the long hair from his eyes. Eyes that seemed even more amber against the shirt's pine-green hue.

A clerk entered to get more items to return to the racks. The dark-haired woman did a double take before turning on a smile. "Can I—"

"We're fine," Lia said through her teeth. A foreign irritation curled in her stomach while the woman continued to ogle Kayce.

Lia pointedly cleared her throat. The woman frowned, but backed off to resume her task. They were not getting out of this store alive.

Ignoring Kayce's raised brows, Lia ducked out to grab the next size up and kept her gaze trained on the floor when she thrust the garment at him. "Put this on."

"I think your cat took residence in your mouth," Kayce said before tugging the shirt over his head.

"You're disgusting to use such an analogy."

She thought he smiled wider, but she was too busy staring at his boots while he put on the new shirt. When she raised her gaze, the fluttering in her stomach had eased to a faint wobble. At least it was an improvement.

Kayce was quiet, still distracted by the newness of it all as they made their purchases and stuffed his Norenthian attire in the shopping bag. By then, clanging pots and pans echoed from the food court above. Kayce stopped in the middle of traffic, nose upraised.

"What in the skies and seas is that *smell*?" he asked, craning his neck to follow the scent.

Lia caught a faint whiff of teriyaki and sauteed vegetables, namely onions, that wafted down the nearby escalator. "Chinese."

"We must find it," he demanded.

Kayce led the way, his nose a guide while he almost tripped on the moving steps. He didn't seem to gather that they took him up, climbing until they reached the top. Kayce was so set on finding the source that he missed the way several teenage girls looked him over from head to toe, giggles muffled in their prissy hands.

His ignorance warmed Lia's chest as she followed close behind, a smile tugging at her lips—*stupid!* When did she care how other girls looked at him? Even in Norenth—no, there was *too* much going on. She couldn't analyze those implications with a ten-foot pole. Lia had plenty of other problems demanding her focus. *Priorities.*

With the leftover money, they ended up with two orders of chicken lo mein, pork fried rice, and Lia's personal favorite, General Tso's chicken. The high glass ceiling echoed dozens of conversations and various pans clanging from the food stalls. And yet over the clamor, Lia could hear Kayce's groan at the first bite of soy-infused goodness.

"This—" he tried to manage around a mouthful. "This needs to be on the next inaugural ball menu."

Lia chuckled, picking at a piece with her chopsticks. "I think you would be hard-pressed to find a chef in Norenth who knows how to work a wok."

"Many of them can walk. It's the cooking that needs attention!" he said into his food, eyelids fluttering with it. "Aurelia, let it be written, so then it shall be done, and I will not have to go back without the miracle that is this 'Chinese take-out'."

She huffed an errant curl from her face, leaning back in her chair. She didn't want to talk about him going back home. Not when he was here like she always dreamed.

Kayce reached for her hand and placed his on top of her own. "Humor me: what if there is a sphere where the world is entirely underwater? That there is a network of air bubbles with grand castles made of coral, and boats that work with the currents far faster than those of the air?"

"I hate to break it to you, but we call those submarines."

His mouth dropped open. "It's real here?"

"Not the coral castles, but the underwater boats are." He was still holding her hand. Fighting a blush, Lia pulled hers back.

Kayce cracked a grin, seeming ignorant of her blush. "You need to bring that majesty to Norenth. I always wanted to know what the inside of those sea clouds looked like."

Lia had wondered about doing that once, but she always got tied up in the mechanics of it. Her papa had also pondered the idea of a way to explore those seas in which sailors cast their nets. Perhaps in his various files he had written a way.

"I wonder if he put the proof there," Lia mused. "The proof that got him killed."

Kayce paused in his eating. "You mean he put the evidence somewhere in the spheres?"

"Where else would be safe from Seekers? They can't travel there." It made sense, considering anywhere here was fair game. Not even the roads were safe. "But he must have put it some-where we could find. Maybe it's in Norenth somewhere...but maybe it's here, especially if he didn't know if I would Spark."

Lia blinked rapidly, moisture gathering in her eyes. That was the thing with grief; it was always there, and sometimes, it could swallow you at the most unexpected times—just when you thought you were out of its grasp, when you have moved beyond it.

Kayce stared at her intently, evidently sensing the shift in her mood. He reached for her again.

A boom rumbled through the food court.

Kayce stood, hand automatically drawn to his bare hip as he assessed the room. "Get under the table."

"What are you talking about?"

"Don't argue, just—"

The food court's windowed ceiling shattered.

CHAPTER TWENTY

There was a collective pause, everyone sucking in a breath before screams filled the air. Kayce shoved Lia under the table before glass rained, piercing their food. Several patrons nearby cried out in pain as they struggled to find cover. Kayce grunted, a shard catching his leg. He covered Lia as best he could from the side.

"Kayce—"

"I'm fine!"

No, he wasn't, the liar. But from what Lia could see, the piece was small and would do better out than in at the moment. She pulled it free, despite Kayce's barked protest. It left a shallow cut, ruining his brand-new jeans.

Wind whistled through the gaping hole in the ceiling, the occasional shard clicking as it fell. A group of teenagers whimpered. A baby cried.

Kayce eased back and shook glittering dust from his hair. Scrambling for napkins that had fluttered to the ground, Lia caught several and shook them free of glass before covering the cut. "Keep pressure on it. It's not bad," she said.

He nodded, taking over. "Are you sure you're okay?"

"Only a little bruised." Lia's heart was in her throat.

Earthquakes weren't uncommon, being so close to the fault line in California. But this was the largest Lia had ever experienced. Were Mom and Marcus all right? Had the windows shattered across the whole mall?

Another boom reverberated through the food court, echoing in Lia's bones. Several screams rang out. Then another quake came. Closer. Each thudded like a giant had stepped onto the earth.

"That didn't feel like an earthquake," she said shakily. "But I can't think of anything else that caused this." It had to be. It was the only thing that made any sense. And she so desperately needed it to make sense.

Kayce shook his head, looking up. Then froze. "Aurelia, run when I say."

Her gaze dragged up the pillars to the metal shell of the ceiling.

And to the massive dragon peering at the food court, smoke curling from its nostrils.

A man screamed. The dragon's eyes, orbs of marbled flames, narrowed at the sound before its roar bellowed like a thousand cellos screeching out of tune. Lia's hands clamped over her ears, the sound deafening. This couldn't be real. There couldn't be a *dragon* in the mall right now—

Across the tables, a mother hunched over her bawling child, nearly smothering the poor boy to shush him.

"Run!" Kayce yelled, hauling her up.

The pair bolted around chairs and abandoned shopping bags, glass crunching underfoot. Lia's breath was quick and shallow. She pumped her arms beside Kayce, who kept one hand on her back to keep her moving.

The floor trembled. Rubble crashed from the ceiling. The dragon crawled in, gouging holes as it scuttled down the rafters with its wings tucked tight. Patrons screamed, several making a break for various smoothie counters and shops along the food court's perimeter.

Lia risked a glance over her shoulder.

From snout to tail, the dark red dragon stretched longer than a school bus. It landed on the scattered tables, crushing them like they were nothing more than underbrush in some faraway land. Because that was where this beast belonged—*not* a suburb outside of Seattle.

Lia prayed the dragon would vanish. That as she and Kayce ran down the corridor—littered with merchandise, glass from window displays, and collapsed sale signs—this was nothing more than some obscene bout of food poisoning.

The roar that sent her flailing proved otherwise.

Lia scrambled to her knees. The dragon's nails clicked against the tile floor—unsheathed claws, yellowed and ready to strike. Its armored tail sent chairs sailing across the food court as it turned.

Kayce bolted for a nearby antique store, darting around streams of people desperate for shelter. Glass shattered within, and he sprinted back to her side with two swords in hand.

"Not Norenthian quality, but they'll do," he said before tossing one to her.

Lia caught it deftly, her voice turned shrill. "Are you kidding me right now?"

When Lia had mentioned to her mom about fighting dragons if she was going to be an anxious mess, she had thought doing so *on paper* was a given.

The dragon swung its head, horns curling to the ceiling and catching the lights. Cables jerked. The lights flickered, but the beast veered toward her and Kayce: the only ones left in the open. Each step was a tremor. A potted plant tipped over and shattered beside them.

"Kayce, we need to hide!"

"Hiding won't send this beast back to where it belongs."

"But it will keep us safe!" she screeched, boots slipping as she scampered back for every advance the dragon made.

Kayce didn't move, a frown etching his face.

"What about them?" He pointed his blade at a mother dragging her young twins into the hat store. "Who will keep them safe?"

She shook her head, stammering, "Kayce, this isn't Norenth—"

"Why should that matter?" he snapped.

The dragon grumbled, rearing its serpentine head back, rusted-red scales coiling.

"Because I'm not who you think I am here—"

I'm a bookworm. A self-declared hermit. Tears filled her eyes. *A coward.*

"*You* decide who you are! Not what tries to break you or what this world demands of you!" he shouted.

The dragon roared, forcing the two to crouch against the hot, moist wind tunnel the beast created. An orange glow pulsed in the back of its gaping maw.

But Lia didn't move.

With a frustrated huff, Kayce ran toward the danger. His movements sharp and precise, he lunged with the antique sword as if he leapt from the ropes of a ship.

The dragon swung its tail.

Kayce rolled, narrowly ducking beneath it. Spikes lodged in the wall. Chunks of concrete tumbled to the ground as the dragon yanked its tail free. Kayce used the moment to stab at its belly. Shrieking, the dragon recoiled, then swung again.

Lia shivered. That wall could have been his head. She needed to get up. She needed to move. But her arms were leaden, trembling so much that the sword clattered against the tile.

As Kayce continued to distract the dragon, its claws casting sparks every time they met steel, Lia's panic mounted. How could he dive in to protect people, to protect a world he hardly knew? She had just found him—*really* found him—and she could lose him again.

Some things should stay in stories.

Lia's heart skipped a beat, body frozen in place. Kayce dodged a claw the size of his arm, one about to skewer him through.

But if she were in Norenth, what would she do?

She wouldn't be sitting on the sidelines as the damsel. No, she would be beside him, watching Kayce's back. Never would Aurelia let Kayce go against such a monstrous foe alone.

So how could Lia bear to sit still *now*?

She forced herself upright, knees almost giving out as she gripped the sword in sweaty palms. But her arms did not falter, its weight solid, familiar. She took a step.

But it was a step too late.

The dragon bellowed, claws raking down. Kayce jumped back, but two of those lethal daggers dragged over his chest, ripping flesh. He yelled, falling back against a wall. His sword remained poised, eyes glaring at the terror before him.

It was like ice doused over her whole being followed by a whiplash of heat.

She wouldn't lose him.

Lia moved.

It was like something clicked into place. Her body took over, that soft, timid piece of her shoved back into the wretched box that housed everything else she couldn't deal with. She bolted, swinging the sword with a familiarity she almost had no right to know.

The blade caught the beast's arm, slicing so deep that thick, steaming blood welled. Hissing in offense, those reptilian eyes narrowed—sliding from Kayce to her. The large maw opened to reveal a curtain of teeth intent on death.

Lia paled at the sight, her arms shaking, but she stood her ground in front of Kayce, who had pushed off the wall to join her.

"Nice to see you, Harpy." He smirked, face paling despite it. Blood covered his chest, already soaking the new pine-green shirt.

Lia focused on the dragon as she steadied herself with a deep breath. "Take the right."

The beast screeched, and the pair dove into action. Kayce bolted to the side, capturing the dragon's attention. It aimed another swipe, talons raised, but faltered as Lia took off to the left. One of its wings had stretched toward her, making it easy for her sword to slice through the leathery membrane like a scalpel slipping through parchment.

Screeches filled the air. The mighty reptile whirled on her.

"Lia!"

Up the escalator, her mom whipped around the corner with Leo not far behind. Lia took a second glance. Since when was *he* here?

"Mom, watch out!"

The dragon leered toward the two newcomers, blood trickling from various wounds.

Arms flailing, her mom almost tumbled to a skidding stop a dozen feet from the dragon. "Leo, do you have it?"

Leo huffed a sigh, rolling his eyes skyward. "I'm getting too old for this."

What could they possibly be discussing *now*?

Kayce grunted, a spasm of pain scrunching his face. He couldn't run on adrenaline and the heat of battle for much longer.

"Focus on me, beastie," Leo crooned, waving an arm as if calling for a friend from afar.

The dragon snarled, snaking its head while tracking the older man's movement. As Leo paced in a circle around it, he withdrew a wand from his coat pocket. At least, that's how it appeared, with an amethyst crystal at the tip and a long, silver base.

Lia frowned, realizing that what housed the crystal was a nib, like something found on an old fountain pen. "Now isn't the time to write something!"

Thick smoke billowed from the dragon's nostrils, growing darker by the second. Ash burned Lia's nose, making her eyes water.

"There's always time to write something, dear girl." Leo charged, and the dragon's infernal eyes dilated. It roared, dust and glass crashing as it thundered toward Leo.

A radiant purple light shone, bursting from the nib like a sword blade, and Leo wielded it much like Lia and Kayce had. He lunged for the dragon, but the beast was ready. Claws met amethyst, and sparks flew in a cascade of colors. The older man moved with a foreign fluidity, parrying left and right while the dragon grew more agitated.

"We need to get in there—" It was all Kayce could manage. The blood drained from his face, his legs giving out as he took a step to rejoin the fray. The sword clattered to the floor.

And Lia's heart stopped.

"MOM!" Her scream pierced the air as Lia rushed to him. Whipping off her sweater to press into the near-perfect cuts, she cried out again. "Mom, help me!"

Her mom fell to her knees beside them. "Keep the pressure on it," she instructed, tearing the cloth away to assess Kayce's chest.

Her hands worked quickly. "Stuff it in the wound. It's nothing stitches can't fix."

Kayce's lips were bloodless; his brow glistened with a cold sweat. Lia jerked a nod, opening her mouth to speak, but Leo's whistle captured their attention.

The dragon twisted, its barbed tail sailing through the air. Before it could knock Leo sideways, the pen flashed. Light morphed from the blade to form a rounded shield, under which Leo crouched as the spikes came hammering. Not one pierced the light, more sparks flying.

Far faster than reasonable for a man his age, he rolled to the side once the dragon let up, sprinting for its blood smeared across the tile. Skidding to his knees, Leo struck down with the shield that had shifted to a pen again, scribbling furiously with a tool that was now imbued with the blood of the dragon, using the tile as parchment.

The letters glowed, illuminating Leo's dark face. The dragon whirled on him. Jaws unhinged, the air smoldered, and embers spit forth as the dragon summoned fire.

Kayce's hand trembled, but he tugged Lia closer, struggling to sit.

Lia's pale face turned to his. Wasn't there a line in a poem on how some believed the world ended in fire and some in ice? This couldn't be that. She held his hand tighter, her mouth opening to speak, to say *something*—

Yet the heat never came.

"Look, you two," her mom breathed, her voice filled with restrained relief. "No one's dying today."

Lia turned to look. Flames *did* appear—but they enveloped the dragon. The fiery embrace scorched horn to wing to claw until not even ashes remained. Only the familiar, faint scent of burnt paper. Burnt parchment, like Papa had smelled of...

Leo grinned, the light evaporating. Other patrons peeked out from their shelters at the growing silence.

Marcus, gasping for breath, appeared at the top of the escalator. He threw his hands in the air. "What'd I miss this time?"

Lia pressed Kayce's knuckles to her cheek. He was safe. They were saved. He slumped against the floor, a flush on his cheeks and his gaze fixed on the ceiling. The words Lia had wanted to say evaporated. The relief, though, was short-lived.

"You were told to wait in the video store," her mom admonished when Marcus inched forward, his expression shifting from exasperation to concern.

"Is Kayce okay?"

"I need to get him to the hospital." She had that authoritative air about her, the nurse in her element. No room for argument.

"No," Leo said, wincing as he stood with knees popping. "He has no records, and there will be enough questions about what happened here today. The Order can only do so much damage control."

Her mom jerked a nod. "Fine. I have enough supplies at home to treat him."

"Mom, how did that dragon get here?" Lia asked, keeping hold of Kayce's hand as she pulled his arm over her shoulders to support him. Mom's calm yet firm gaze settled on her as she supported Kayce's other side. The tension in Lia loosened. She would make sure Kayce was all right.

"I take it those are not common," Kayce managed weakly, his steps wooden.

"They aren't," Lia answered as they rushed for the exit. Her mom and Leo exchanged a look. And it was clear to Lia they were equally as confused as she was.

"Aurelia, I'm fine." Kayce snapped, getting off the bed.

If he said that one more time, Lia would lose it. Patient or not.

"My mom said you shouldn't be moving around," she warned, blocking him as he made for her bedroom door. "Do you want to bleed all over *another* shirt?"

Why was he being such a stubborn mule about this?

He probably wishes I were Aurelia. She would never have wavered. Never had been so scared, frozen, useless. Helpless.

He wouldn't really think that—he was her best friend. Right? But ever since they got back, he'd been tense. More than his injuries would impose—even *after* receiving a liter of IV fluids in their living room.

He glowered at her. "I have so much padding on, I doubt it will be much of an issue." Beneath the white T-shirt he wore was a series of wraps, keeping at least an inch of gauze in place over newly stitched gashes.

She crossed her arms. "Then, please, be my guest and explain to her how you pulled your stitches a second time."

A muscle ticked in his jaw before he sank onto the edge of her bed.

Scooping Fiore, who had naturally refused to leave his side since limping in from the car, Lia sat beside him. It had taken her mom an hour, two rolls of gauze, a kitchen hand towel, and several dozen stitches to get the bleeding under control. Lia had followed every order, a soldier under Mom's command.

"You shouldn't be going anywhere," Lia admonished, scratching her cat behind the ear.

"If you think I'm staying here while you go to this Order meeting, you're severely mistaken."

There was that edge again.

He always was the worst patient. Then again, he had never quite had a wound this severe. He had collected minor cuts and abrasions from training with the rangers and his brothers. She thought Terranth gave him a black eye once, when he was sixteen.

But two gashes across his chest?

Lia barely suppressed a shudder. "You're lucky it wasn't your heart."

Kayce shrugged, tension holding him upright. "Lucky it wasn't your life."

"If we had ducked into a store—"

"What?" he asked. "We could have been fine until your mother and Leo came to the rescue?"

"It would have been the smart thing. Better than becoming barbeque."

"What about the others? Hiding isn't what we do. Not as Norenthians, not as smugglers from good-for-nothing pirates, not as rangers—"

"Kayce, this isn't a game!" At the mounting frustration in her tone, Fiore squirmed from her arms and darted under the bed. But Lia couldn't bring herself to care, hugging herself tighter under the guise of crossed arms. "How could you rush out there like this was the next adventure?" Lia pressed. "You're always jumping into things, but that was reckless."

"Because it's not about an 'adventure'." Kayce fisted his hands. "Joining the Ranger's Guild wasn't a frivolous matter to me. It wasn't about seeking a thrill. It was always about doing what was right, not what was *fun*. Together, we could have handled it. If you had trusted me—"

"Why didn't you trust *me*? You don't have plot armor here! You could've—" She cut herself off when his head snapped up, his gaze hard.

Lia wanted to melt into the floor and disappear as her words caught up to her.

"Could have what—died?" He sneered. "Yeah, because I can. Because I'm *real*."

"Who are you trying to prove that to?"

Kayce's stare burned right through her, his knuckles turning whiter. "Is that what Norenth is to you—a game? And me—am I merely a toy to you, a piece for you to play with and relax when you need to escape?" He leaned in close, his voice low. "You cannot corral me like the mother hen you claim me to be. I'm not an irresponsible boy you need to babysit. I'm not this caricature of a prince bent on reckless endangerment and heists."

Lia's breath hitched. This wasn't about the dragon anymore. Kayce's brows had drawn together the longer they stared at each other. Only several inches separated them, their breath and accusations filling the tense space.

"That's—that's not what I meant," she stammered, frozen.

"But it's what you said. We help people. It shouldn't matter where we are. It's what we do." Anger splotched life back to his face and throat as he pointed to himself. "It's what *I* do. I couldn't remain on the sidelines watching innocents suffer. It's why I started smuggling in the first place. You, of all people, should know this. There was always risk." He shook his head. "I'm not a story. What about you? If the Aurelia I knew isn't real," he muttered, "what does that mean about me?"

Shame engulfed her, stole her breath. Lia whirled toward the door, needing a moment to collect herself, to ease the pain at almost losing him before it made everything worse. Because it never had been a game to her. And it had never been about the adventure, either. It was always about them, about being the truest version of herself without the masks she donned.

But today, in the face of death, she stood to lose everything.

Kayce's reality wasn't the problem—it had stared her in the face through his blood on her hands. But in maintaining that Aurelia was fictional, that she wasn't her...she hated his point. Loathed it. As Lia, there were expectations here. But she had moved into action when his life was on the line. Could she be that way if she allowed herself to be?

"You're more to me than you could ever know." She angled her face away from him, eyes pricking. He didn't need her tears. "Rest, okay?" Her voice cracked. "You'll come to the meeting."

The bed creaked as Kayce stood behind her, but Lia was already gone.

There was truth to his words, that's probably why they stung so deeply. But facing what he said, facing him—how could she say she feared for his life more than her own right now? That meant dealing with feelings and emotions she wasn't ready to address yet. There was too much already, too much going on.

But she would have to decide who she was, in this body that had become both Lia of Earth and Aurelia of Norenth. Because when presented another opportunity, she knew she wouldn't have luck on her side again.

CHAPTER TWENTY-ONE

Leo and her mom had agreed to use Papa's home for the Order meeting; apparently headquarters for all things writing, bingo, and secret societies. As they pulled up, Lia noticed how red the leaves were as they twirled to the ground. Red like sunsets, similar to the one that illuminated the darkening sky. Like fire, crackling above abandoned tables and shopping bags.

Like blood staining tile floors. And her fingers.

Lia blinked, shoving yesterday's mall debacle away. But she could hear those roars, feel the bone-melting heat. From the front seat, she glanced up at the rearview mirror. Kayce was already staring at her, absently rubbing his palm. His cheeks were still pale, shoulders tense despite the hands loose in his lap as he listened to Marcus prattle on about some cosmic event forecasted in a couple months.

She looked away first. Fisted her hands, hiding the bitten nails, the scabbed nailbeds.

Since their fight yesterday, Kayce and Lia had hardly spoken, the silence fraught between them. It was the longest they had ever fought. She knew Kayce hated it as much as she did. He'd tried to catch her alone several times. But she couldn't face him, his disappointment. Not yet.

Coward. So much for Lioness Silva's pep-talk.

She claimed it was because she didn't want to "bleed" on him, as Norenth's queen had so eloquently put it. But this meeting could dictate that he needed to be sent back immediately. Life continued onward in the Emperium; had the queen noted Kayce's absence? Fight or no fight, noted absence or not, Lia couldn't see him go. She wouldn't. And she knew with how often she caught him staring at her, he felt the same.

Her mom parked the car. "Listen, you three."

Marcus groaned, but ceased at the raised finger their mom pointed.

"You are to listen, to learn. Speak only when spoken to," she warned. "Don't mention our suspicions about Papa's death. Am I clear?"

Lia frowned. Wouldn't she want the Order's help with this? Still, all they really had were suspicions. Dragons crashing into public buildings took priority.

Once she got a nod from everyone, the boys piled out. Kayce hesitated, the moment constricting Lia's chest before he left.

Mom put a hand on Lia's shoulder. "When you said a gremlin attacked you," she hedged, her hand warm. "What happened to it after you got away?"

"It was weird." Lia shifted, looking down at her lap. She bit her lip, but the earnestness in Mom's gaze, the way she leaned forward attentively, prompted Lia to continue. "There was this moment where my blood and its, well, *gunk* got smeared together under my hands. Kind of like what Leo did with that wand. That's when every trace burned away like it was never there." Lia suppressed a shudder, pulling her sleeves over her hands. While the tenderness in her ankle was gone, the scars would remain. At that moment, she was glad for them. For the proof.

"Leo mentioned you hadn't seen anything besides Kayce," her mom said.

"Because I didn't tell him."

Mom nodded to herself. "I told him about the gremlin, but you sending it back to its sphere needs to stay between us. At least for now."

Lia's brow furrowed. This was not the reaction she'd expected to her lie. "Why?"

Mom was no longer looking at Lia, but past her, her gaze distant. Blinking back to the present, she squeezed Lia's shoulder. "That tool Leo used on the dragon? That's the only way Flamehearts can get beings back into the Emperium. At least, that's what I had thought."

It took a minute. Then the implications settled into Lia like stones sinking to the bottom of the sea. Like she needed something else to prove she was different. Was that why she could see better? Why scars appeared on her hands, the muscles hard beneath her soft curves?

Mom was still talking. "Is there anything else you need to tell me?"

Lia stared out the window to the cherry trees peering around the house from the backyard. How could she have forgotten it? But with how much she'd been dealing with, maybe Lia needed to cut herself some slack.

"Before Papa died," she murmured, "there was this owl. I swore it had six eyes. Papa got all cagey, shooing me into the kitchen. I remember this flash of light, the smell of burning paper." Lia dragged her eyes from the tree to see her mom stiffen. "I don't think it belonged here."

It'd been on Captain Luddeck's ship, too. And she thought she'd heard an owl hoot in the castle gardens during the ball. Had it really been in Norenth—or was it her mind replaying what it had already seen?

"We'll figure it out, you and me. But that should also stay between us." Mom moved her hand to Lia's knee. Her nails were cut to the quick. "I know you don't understand. You are going through so much right now."

Lia pulled on a loose thread of her shirt. She wanted to say she understood. That she trusted her. But that new warmth in her chest burned, the heat worming up her throat to her cheeks. Blood pumped in her temples. She was tired of the secrets.

At Lia's silence, her mom pressed a kiss to her curls. Lia managed a strained smile that would have to be her answer. She didn't trust what would come out if she opened her mouth.

Exiting the car, they made their way to the porch where the boys were waiting. Unlike the other day, several cars parked in the driveway and on the street.

"How many are in the Order, exactly?" Marcus asked when they approached.

"I don't know the global numbers offhand. But when I was first inducted, seven representatives were in this chapter. We make up the West Coast, outside Canada. They have a couple of their own." Their mom opened the door, the foyer greeting them with warmth from the sitting room fireplace.

"But isn't the gift generational?" Marcus said.

Mom sighed through her nose. "Yes, but there is only one representative in the chapter per family. Papa was ours."

And will you be the next? Lia wanted to pry, but her mom strode for the sitting room.

Down the hall, voices echoed and the air carried the warm scent of tomatoes and cheese. Marcus inhaled deeply. "Smell that, Kayce?"

Kayce took a sniff. "Skies, Chef Rosalind makes a pie that smells like that—"

"Pizza, my friend." Marcus patted Kayce on the back. "It's pizza."

Lia smirked, her own stomach rumbling in response. Inside the sitting room, the fire crackled. Lia recognized Mirel, sitting in a designer pantsuit. She was glaring at Adrian, who was cleaning his glasses using the hem of his sweater. Leo nursed a cup of coffee, granting the three teens a smile as they paused in the doorway.

There were three strangers in the room.

Two stood beside the fire in intense conversation. One was a short, balding man. The woman's willowy figure trembled with barely suppressed emotion as she hissed in his face some remark Lia neither heard nor cared about. Only another woman seemed to pay the spat any mind, smirking from the corner closest to the foyer.

"Cordelia!" Mirel exclaimed, hopping from the bay window seat. "Thank heavens—I was about to lose my mind explaining to Adrian how much Washington's senator *doesn't* need to know about our 'gas leak' at the mall yesterday. I've been up to my eyeballs in paperwork."

"Gas leak?" Marcus questioned, glancing at the man lounging with his leg crossed over a bouncing knee.

Their mom sent a sharp look at Marcus after pulling from Mirel's embrace. He flushed.

Leo answered all the same. "All those startled people, they needed something that explained the shared hallucination. Gas leak ruptured by a terrible tremor. It helps that once creations are returned to the Emperium, the memories of ignorant humans fade like a dream."

Lia couldn't help but nod appreciatively at the man, earning her a conspiratorial wink. She had assumed as much before the dragon stuck its head through the ceiling.

"Though it would seem more are remembering them as fact." Adrian twitched on the far end of the sofa, adjusting his glasses. "I was merely inquiring that, well, perhaps a tale of an escape from the local zoo would also be prudent."

Mirel rolled her eyes. "No reptile is that big. Stick to your books and leave the damage control to me." Adrian opened his mouth, but before he could get another word in, Mirel cut him with a glare. "And all social media has been wiped. Gone are the days where the images would blur and they could be written off as a hoax. We don't need another Rio incident."

"Or Hammerfest, Norway," Leo tacked on with a groan.

The squirrel—Adrian still had that twitchiness like one—gave two nods in concession.

"What happened in Brazil and Norway?" Lia asked.

"Our senator isn't the first to use rabid animals as an excuse for the inexplicable. Not that he knows any different, just what Mirel tells him," Adrian said in a rush. "But people are more apt to believe it in a city than a small costal town where not much happens. Certainly not when someone caught a selkie transformation on their Ring camera, the woman then knocking and asking for shelter from the cold. Norway's Order chapter couldn't swipe that footage fast enough."

A throat cleared, and everyone eyed the new arrivals. The silence was heavy, full of secrets that were now being forced into the open. Gremlins in Seattle. Dragons in the mall. And now, selkies in Norway and skies knew whatever had happened in Rio.

Was this normal? Or were tears between the realms everywhere? Dread filled Lia's mouth with bile. Seekers were likely waiting for such a time as this.

Leo clapped, scattering Lia's thoughts. "Come, sit! Just in time, food's here. But, some introductions again." He glanced at Kayce and smiled as he and Lia sat in the chairs pulled up next to the couch. Marcus went to sit beside his mom near Mirel.

"Over there we have Veera. She handles our communications between Order chapters both here and internationally."

The woman with a caramel complexion and lustrous, dark hair smiled warmly. Lia couldn't help but return it, though she tore at her nails.

Ah, the cursed habit encroached again. Lovely. Lia moved to sit on her hands.

"Mirel is on the city council, plus acts as a liaison for higher officials. She helps manage public relations for us," Leo continued. "And the bickering twosome by the fire are Reynaldo and Mikayla. Don't mind them; they couldn't get plane tickets, so they've been stuck in a car together since Sacramento."

"What do you expect when every other ad on public radio is 'ImaginX' this or 'Stock Market Crash' that?" sneered Mikayla, who softened when she caught Marcus's wary assessment. "Don't mind me. Gluten and dairy make me cranky."

Leo gave Lia an apologetic grin. "They monitor Seeker activity for us. Now, Adrian here!" The man in question jolted at Leo's heavy-handed pat on his shoulder. "He's a bookstore owner downtown and our resident historian. Worked pretty close with your grandfather, actually. He has records on our origins, that of the spheres, and the guardians—"

"Guardians?" Marcus interjected, eyes alight with curiosity. "Have you seen one? The way Mom described them was kind of 'airy', so I've been wondering, do they have wings?"

"They *really* know nothing," Mikayla mused, a scathing glare aimed at their mom. "Honestly dear, the boy's an Ember, not having Sparked yet. *That's* understandable. But your eldest?" She scoffed. "From the way Julian went on, we should have inducted her when she was ten."

Mom showed all her teeth when she smiled at the middle-aged woman. "I've missed your unearned bluntness, Mikayla."

Mikayla huffed, adjusting the pearl necklace about her neck.

Leo smoothed the tension by introducing Lia and Marcus, saving Kayce for last.

"How did he get here?" Veera stepped closer, looking Kayce over as if he were pages and ink and not a flesh-and-blood person. "Doesn't look like he's missing anything, either."

Kayce flexed his hands under her assessment. "Should I be? No missing fingers or toes, though the dragon gave it a shot."

Lia glanced to the ceiling, wishing lightning would strike. None of them had done well at the 'seen and not heard' request. To be fair, she knew from the get-go Kayce wouldn't.

"Not much has come through from the spheres since the First Rift," Adrian said meekly. "It's quite hazardous for creations to do so. Unlike those initial creations, new arrivals—the far and few we come across, mind you—bear an injury as though burned by whatever tear they'd stumbled through—"

"And yet from the sound of it, you lot have been plenty busy," Kayce interrupted. Lia cleared her throat, but he ignored her. "Do you not believe the repairs to the First Rift are failing?"

Silence.

Leo steepled his fingers together. "It seems in recent weeks, other chapters are struggling more than in years past. And in the past few days, there have been three creations in our own region."

"Three?" Mirel questioned.

Leo explained Lia's attack downtown. Glancing over at her mom, Lia didn't miss the way her face softened, how her eyes flickered down as if in remorse. Lia felt the urge to stand and hug her, but she remained sitting. Instead, she studied Mirel, who refused to meet her gaze. She had been there when the gremlin attacked. Had she not seen it? Not put two and two together?

Veera spoke. "So this is more than leftover creatures from the First Rift? The chapter in Norway didn't seem all that concerned. Though, other chapters have whispered about the repairs to the First Rift failing. Some believe it was inevitable. None want to speak it into existence, you see."

"But this could be an isolated event," Adrian said. "Julian was a powerful Flameheart. Perhaps his death upset the cosmos, pulled a few things that needn't be here—"

"*After* he died? Tell me how that makes sense, Adrian," Mirel said. "Go on, indulge us."

The thin man frowned. "It was only a suggestion. A gremlin, a storybook character of his, a dragon. They all fit his studies."

His studies? He was a mapmaker for the Flamehearts. What could her papa be doing, looking into such dangerous beings like a gremlin and a dragon? Unless they had to do with the proof he was researching. Lia couldn't make sense of it. But maybe Adrian would know, having worked closest with him.

"I've been mulling this over," Leo said, his gaze turning to Lia with a soft twinkle in his eyes. "I believe the tears in the veil are reopening all over the world. But in Seattle's case, my theory is these creations were drawn like moths to a flame. A flame that was birthed from grief. Awakened, flaring and wild."

The room looked at Lia.

Her throat tightened. Her heart raced. Her hands numbed from sitting on them. She leveled her gaze on the coffee table, counted the number of crumbs on the nearest plate as the silence ticked on. Until a warm hand fell on her knee.

Tearing her gaze from the plate, she looked over at Kayce. He had pulled half of his hair back, securing it in a knot. It exposed the planes of his face far more clearly. He gave her a nod. The entire room faded away as his gaze held her, saw all of her. Their argument didn't seem to matter. It loosened something in Lia's chest, a tension she hadn't been able to release.

It would always be her and him against the world.

Inhaling through her nose, Lia returned the nod before looking around the room. "After Papa's funeral, I slept that night in a way I never had. My chest burned, my head ached. As the dream went on, both only got worse."

"Children born to a Flameheart line experience what we call the Spark," Reynaldo said, a thick Latin accent rolling in his words. "Typically in adolescence, they have the symptoms you experienced. The fever and lucid dreams are key signs to the parents that it's time for them to know the family trade."

Mikayla sent another glare to her mom, which the latter ignored.

"Will I go through that?" Marcus pressed.

"Likely, but it varies from child to child. Especially with the rifts coming back into play." Reynaldo frowned. "Though I hope a boy as young as yourself stays out of the fray for a while yet. It will get worse before it gets better."

"Fifty-six years ago is the last recorded Transcribing in Seattle, apart from Leonard's dragon." Adrian quipped, a notebook in hand. He chewed on the end of a pencil. "And no one has seemed to find Bigfoot yet, despite several sightings in our territory... The Flameheart who does, I don't envy."

"What, like *the* Bigfoot?" Marcus asked.

Adrian nodded with a small smile.

Marcus blinked. "Mind. Blown."

Lia didn't even know how to address *that* little tidbit. Though, she supposed even urban legends would need homes in the Emperium, too. It certainly explained the cryptid articles she'd found pinned in Papa's secret study.

"But the cities you mentioned earlier," Kayce interrupted, leaning forward with his forearms braced on his elbows. "They have seen creations. This city has seen three in but a week. You cannot bury your head in the sands and pray the storm passes over you."

Finally, the words seemed to register for Adrian, as he paled whiter than the pages of his notebook. Denial would only work for so long, Lia told herself. Perhaps that was why her papa kept his research into the rifts a secret. The Order, his partners, seemed more content to let the trouble pass beyond their notice. Until it was on their doorstep.

Leo sighed through his nose, garnering the room's attention. "The First Rift is reopening, but nothing with documented rift injuries had come Earth-side." Leo turned his attention to Lia. She wanted to shrink into her seat. "Aurelia is not to blame—you all know this. In her grief, she may have pierced what was already thin in search of comfort. Who better than her best friend? And as Veera said earlier, I suspect other chapters of the Order have been quiet about their own investigations. No one wants to stir a panic."

Lia looked at her mom, who frowned as she studied Leo. He'd seemed surprised in the study with Kayce's appearance. Well, his words were. His attitude had told a different story. But if he had already gone through some of her papa's work, what else did Leo know?

"Who—or what—is to blame, then? Surely you have a theory beyond the damage of time," Kayce demanded, his gaze narrow. It was a challenge: a dare to be explicitly clear. A line in the sand.

The grandfather clock in the foyer chimed the hour.

Her mom straightened. "Marcus, how about you head to the kitchen for some pizza? Veera brought her twin boys, and Mirel has her kids back there, too."

"You're kicking me out at the *good part*?"

"Marcus," their mom said firmly. "Now, please."

The boy huffed, shoes hitting the floor as he stormed for the kitchen. Mom followed, stopping to pull the pocket doors shut behind him.

"That won't stop me from telling him later," Lia said, freeing her hand to gesture where her brother had disappeared. Her hands pricked as blood rushed and feeling returned. But she was done with being shut out. For both her and Marcus's sake.

Her mom sighed. "I'm aware. But there are things he doesn't need to hear right now."

Not like you're the expert in that area, Lia thought.

"I'll cut right to it," Mikayla said. "After hearing all of this, I believe Seekers are to blame. I'll assume you at least know about them?"

Lia loathed the condescending glare the older woman sent to her mom. She may have had issues, but Lia wasn't about to let someone else belittle Mom like that. Lia wanted to smack the look right off her powder-pressed face. The suddenness of the urge was startling.

Lia ignored the impulse. "They want power, a greed that's generational like our gifts."

Mikayla nodded. "Only Flamehearts like us can access the spheres. From our research into known Seeker activity, they're trying to use modern technology to advance their agenda."

A connection clicked in Lia's mind, snagging on Mikayla's earlier reference to the tech company ImaginX. Her mom had adamantly refused to allow any of their products in the house only a few days ago—specifically, the MemoryBank. Lia's breath hitched. It could record dreams...a mockery of what Flamehearts had access to.

"ImaginX is Seeker-run," she blurted out.

Mikayla nodded. "Started up three years ago, pushing product this year without much success. Well, until now, given those infuriating advertisements they keep plastering all over the—"

"Wait a moment," Kayce cut in. "We passed by their display table in the mall."

Those tablets, the MemoryBanks, had displayed various scenes, dreams captured and recreated on film.

"He's right. One of the MemoryBanks showed a dragon." A shudder skittered down Lia's spine. Better that the dragon had appeared than whatever had hid in the darkness, baring only its teeth.

No one replied, the silence thickening and a grim heaviness pervading the air.

"When you were there," Mikayla finally said, her stare narrowing at Lia. "What a coincidence."

"What are you implying?" Her mom stood. "If you have something to accuse my daughter of, say it plainly."

"Ladies, let's focus on the Seekers and leave petty grievances aside," Reynaldo said as he stepped to block each other from view. "If they have finally figured out how to use technology to reach the Emperium, the situation is more dire than we realize."

Mirel toyed with her hair, her mouth twisted to the side. She didn't look entirely convinced. Neither did Adrian, still fidgeting with his notebook.

But the pieces of it aligned clearly for Lia. Seekers *had* waited for a time such as this, a time when creation was in the palm of their hand. The uptick in creations, the launch of the MemoryBank, Papa's death—it was all far too coincidental.

Her papa's death *was* Seeker related. Not that the Order knew that. To them, it was just a tragic accident. But what if the proof her papa found had to do with these MemoryBanks? What if the gremlin, the dragon, were the Seekers' fault—but also, what if they weren't the first creations the Seekers at ImaginX had let loose? A powerful company like that would definitely have the resources to take someone out.

Resolve filled her. She needed to find that evidence.

Lia looked between them all, now discussing—*arguing*—amongst themselves how the dragon from the MemoryBank had even gotten into the mall. For an Order honored with a gift to travel the human imagination and preserve its secrets, they didn't get along very well. But then again, what did you expect when you got a bunch of bookworms together? They weren't really known for their social skills. And it sounded like their true purpose had been dealt with by generations prior. Not to mention the odd tension between Mom and Mikayla. History had clearly soured between them.

No wonder Papa kept his research into the weakening rifts secret.

Leo cleared his throat. "We can speak of Seeker theories later, since those matters truly pertain to official Order members. As such, despite the issues that have risen, the sorrows we have endured, this is also a time of great joy." He beamed at Lia. "Aurelia Corvine has Sparked."

Melancholy swelled inside Lia, a living thing that ebbed and flowed like the tide. Papa would have wanted to see this. Longed for it, based off that note in her journal. Kayce's hand returned to her knee and anchored her. She finally moved to cover it with her own. Lia desperately wanted to make it right with him, and it seemed that he did, too.

Mirel took out a black leather folder. She passed Lia a document, causing Kayce to retract his hand. The gold-embossed sigil at the top of the page was a nib of an antique fountain pen surrounded by a sunburst.

Lia scanned the text, noting the empty lines at the bottom. "It's a contract?"

"Yes, but we like 'oath' much better. There's a certain level of discretion that this field requires. Especially considering the current political and economic climate riled up by the Seekers," Mirel explained.

Lia read the tenets, Kayce looking over her shoulder.

Since the Ember was bestowed upon the Order, Flamehearts across time have agreed upon the following precepts for the good of the Emperium and Earth, and all who dwell within:

> 1. *One shall assist the Order in a duty best aligned with the individual Flameheart. All duties serve the central goal of*

the Order as given to them.

2. *One shall Transcribe a being back to the spheres at the earliest opportunity and report the incident to their chapter's historian.*

3. *One shall not seek the Devourer, nor aid him in his aims for total destruction of the cosmos as we know it.*

4. *One shall not associate with or assist a known Seeker.*

5. *One shall not take a mortal lacking an Ember to the Emperium.*

6. *One shall not develop a relationship with a being from the Emperium past amiability.*

7. *One shall not spend more than one-half of the year cumulatively within the Emperium.*

The numbered items made sense, mostly. But a few snagged Lia's gut. "What happens when you spend more than half a year in the Emperium?" she asked.

"Studies show that humans spend more than a third of their lives sleeping," Veera explained, actively using her hands as she spoke. "When Flamehearts spend additional time in the spheres, it becomes harder to return to our true home."

While the words made sense, Lia couldn't fight the unease they prompted. Like something didn't quite fit. She looked back at the list. "How can one of us take a normal person to the Emperium?"

Veera shuddered. "Oh, it's horrific. *We* feel a bit of vertigo when we step through the portal. Then there's the motion sickness, but you get used to navigating with the pen after a while. Normal humans get violently ill. They can't take it."

"Must lack that spark of life," Reynaldo joked, earning several groans.

Lia raised a brow. "We make portals appear?"

"Not in a spinning wheel of sparklers kind of way," Mirel said. "Too Hollywood."

Leo pulled out the wand Lia had seen him use the other day. "Our pens, which we forge when we are initiated, not only allow us to Transcribe beings back into the spheres, but to draw open the door to access it ourselves." Leo grinned. "A bit like a Swiss-army knife for the literary-inclined."

"Handy," Lia mumbled, looking at the oath again.

Kayce spoke up. "Forgive me, but what's 'amiability' mean here?"

"Friendship, you ignorant sword-monger." Without thinking, Lia jabbed him in the side. But perhaps the quick barb would melt the residual tension. That it would forgo the conversation looming between them. Hopefully.

Unlikely.

"I have the tutelage of royalty, thank you very much!" He glared at her as he rubbed his chest. "A word or two may have escaped my notice." So much for that, his words holding a bit more aggression in his defense than normal. Granted, he was still injured, her memory lapsing. And her judgement.

Aggression hid her embarrassment. "Sure, when you weren't slipping out for some trouble or another."

"You say that like it's a bad thing." His eyes flashed, and she practically saw their earlier argument replay in them. *Like being the one who leaps into danger at the expense of others was wrong.*

"It is, according to the standard expectations for education." *And that of being realistic.*

"Who decided such standards?" *Where was the Aurelia I knew?*

"Well, everyone—" *Can you just drop it—*

Leo chuckled, his baritone laughter breaking off Lia's words.

Her mom cleared her throat for their attention. "This rule means no...romantic relations can happen between a Flameheart and a being from the Emperium. None. Friendship only."

Lia's mouth gaped open, cheeks flaming. "You don't—you're not implying that—" She darted a glance at Kayce, whose neck sported a shade of red. "We're just friends!"

He coughed, eyeing the floor. "Friends." Then, in a tone so quiet she almost didn't catch it, "If anything, it's Terranth you should worry about."

That dance in Castle Finerda flashed in her mind, but it didn't fill her with longing. It only tightened her throat, forcing her gaze anywhere and everywhere—but at Kayce.

"Need we explain why such a relation is forbidden?" Veera asked tactfully.

Both teens shook their heads.

"The first Order chapters had many mistakes to learn from," Adrian said, the tips of his ears reddening. "We follow their lead. Save us all a world of trouble."

"That'a boy, Adrian!" Reynaldo laughed, clapping the squirrel on the back so hard he nearly dropped his notebook. "You made a joke!"

The room mumbled groans and agreements. Her mom remained silent, watching them all as though outside the window. Separate. From the pieces Lia gathered, her mom had removed herself from the Order for some time. Why? Another puzzle with missing pieces. Maybe a separate one altogether.

Mikayla cleared her throat. "While the joking is all well and good, need I draw attention to the one precept dear Lia has so *conveniently* ignored?" She crossed her arms, voice brittle. "*One shall Transcribe a being back to the Emperium at the earliest opportunity.*"

Lia hadn't ignored it. No, as soon as she had read those words, they churned in her gut, burning from the inside. She clenched the paper tighter. She didn't reach for Kayce, not with the last tenet lingering in her rosy cheeks.

You have to be stable, dependable Lia. Couldn't she try to be—

Don't make waves, they might not like getting jostled. Let the Order see your value, that you can master this.

Leo rose. "Now, Mikayla. The dragon is gone, the gremlin disappeared. Kayce is here through no fault of Aurelia's."

"But the fact of the matter remains. He needs to go *back.*"

"The matter is a bit more complicated," Leo said.

"Do I not get a say in my autonomy?" Kayce crossed his arms, but winced as if remembering his stitches. "I would be hard pressed to leave unless Aurelia demanded it. And even then, that's questionable."

His declaration softened the tension in Lia's chest. How could he be frustrated with her one moment, then rise to her defense the next?

Mikayla's jaw twitched. "You don't belong here."

"I could say the same of you."

"What's *that* supposed to mean?"

The prince shrugged. "You're positively dour."

"Dour?" Mikayla huffed. "What is this, a Dickens novella?"

Her mom cracked a smile. "Lia was a fan of *A Christmas Carol*, even outside the holiday season. May have influenced Kayce a tad."

The room erupted into debate. All Lia could catch were fragments, those arguing for Kayce to be returned to Norenth drowning out those who demanded an exception.

It was all too much, and her heart had already decided.

"No," Lia stated with a quiet firmness. All eyes fell on her. She steeled herself, then stood, paper trembling. "He goes where I go while I figure this new life out." She looked at Mirel, lifting the oath. "I won't sign this without that accommodation. Please." Her words rang out, hesitant but clear. Kayce stood alongside her, and from the corner of her eye, she caught his appreciative stare. It wasn't her full strength—but it was enough. A gentle prodding.

Not enough to shame her mom, to upset the Order, but enough to voice what Lia needed.

Mirel and Leo shared a look before they turned to her mom. As if the decision rested with her. Words and feelings unspoken flowed between them.

"Kayce can remain with you, for now, if being a Flameheart is what you want," her mom said, her gaze intent. "You have always had a choice in this. I never meant to keep that from you, leave you in the dark for too long. This *is* your decision to make."

Her choice. To accept the gift, the life her papa so clearly had wanted for her. A life in which she could see Norenth, *truly* see it in a way she had always longed for. She bit her lip. There were dangers. Responsibilities. Oaths to keep.

Wiping her clammy palms on her jeans, Lia didn't have to look at Kayce to know he was already showcasing a slight smirk that spelled eagerness and trouble. She allowed a small one of her own. "I'm ready," she said. "I'll sign it."

All watched as her mom pulled out a pen similar in fashion to Leo's. Though where his was larger and plain, her mom's held swirls of stars and motes engraved along the sides. The small crystal embedded in the nib was a soft peridot, yellowish-green in transparency.

"You must use mine before you get your own. Another family thing." She crossed to her daughter, laying the paper on the table before taking her hand. "This will sting a bit."

It was all the warning she gave before pricking Lia's finger, light flaring and heat searing. Lia winced as blood welled. Precious drops clung to the tip of her mom's pen when she took it. Lia signed her name and handed the oath to Mirel. As she glanced down at her hand, the blood disappeared to leave behind a sunburst scar on her fingertip.

"Now what?"

"You need to see the Smith." Mirel's bubbly demeanor had returned. "It's something all Flamehearts who sign the oath must do, the irrevocable step in accepting their gift and the duties that come with it."

Taking a copper curl, Lia wound it around her fingers. "And where exactly is he?"

Everyone snickered at that, some with a few fond cringes. That didn't bode well.

Leo spoke. "That lovable fiend is in the Sphere of Malletor, home to the Forge. Many a powerful artifact has come from his flames and furnaces, including our pens."

A smile bloomed on Lia's lips as she looked to him, to her mom. "I'm going into the Emperium?"

Everyone nodded, and Lia's curiosity mounted. Finally, she could scour for some hint at what her papa was looking into. Whatever had scared Seekers and ImaginX enough to silence him. She could be another step closer to bringing him justice.

Since the ember was bestowed upon the Order, Flamehearts across time have agreed upon the following precepts for the good of the Emperium and Earth, and all who dwell within:

1. One shall assist the Order in a duty best aligned with the individual Flameheart. All duties serve the central goal of the Order as given to them.

2. One shall Transcribe a being back to the spheres at the earliest opportunity and report the incident to their chapter's historian.

3. One shall not seek the Devourer nor aid him in his aims for total destruction of the cosmos as we know it.

4. One shall not associate with or assist a known Seeker.

5. One shall not take a mortal lacking an ember to the Emperium.

6. One shall not develop a relationship with a being from the Emperium past amiability.

7. One shall not spend more than one-half of the year cumulatively within the Emperium.

CHAPTER TWENTY-TWO

After the meeting, everyone flocked to the back patio. Marcus was already chattering with the other Order children. It warmed Lia's chest to see it, but she hung back to observe.

Mirel ushered her mom forward, arm around her shoulder as the two reminisced of times gone by. *How long has it been since they spoke?* She couldn't understand the rigid posture her mom held, but her laughter was easy as Leo chatted from the table. Having naturally fallen into a host role, he outfitted a plate with several large slices for Reynaldo before working on Adrian's. He even served Kayce, whose eyes rolled back into his head at the first bite of cheesy goodness inundated with four types of meat. Lia couldn't hold back a chuckle as their gazes caught, several strings of cheese hanging from his mouth. His eyes crinkled at the sound.

The comradery brought Lia closer to the gathering, smiling at some poor joke Reynaldo made. They were all just people, Lia realized as the Order laughed together. All people, who loved stories, with hearts and dreams of their own.

It was a beautiful sight, even in the messiness of it.

Afterward, Lia and Kayce waited for her mom and Leo in the study. Books were back on their shelves, though with their spines out of alignment. The papers were stacked, the family picture righted without the frame's glass. The secret study's hidden door was shut. There were no leads from the police. There likely wouldn't be.

Lia recalled the corkboard full of snippets from newspapers, the notes. She was fairly certain ImaginX was on there. She wished they'd had more time to look around before Leo came. There could be another note, some clue meant for her to read and understand—

"So how long do you think we'll be gone?" Kayce asked, looking at the bookshelf like he also wanted to root around inside. "For all we know, weeks could have gone by for our days here."

Earlier over food, they had come to an unspoken agreement that they were good—as was their way. And they were, if a bit...off. A shift Lia couldn't linger on, not with what they were about to do.

Leaning against the back of an armchair, Lia pondered his question. "I don't think it does. Whenever I dreamed of Norenth, it seemed to move in step with time here. At least, the seasons did."

He nodded from his perch on top of her papa's desk. "Fair enough. But outside Norenth? I believe anything could be fair play."

"A wise deduction, Kacerion." Leo smiled from the doorway, coming in with her mom, who closed the door. Everyone else had remained downstairs. Marcus had pleaded to join, but since he hadn't Sparked yet, there was not much he would have been able to witness. Lia hoped his time would come soon. This was a marvel meant to be shared.

"Time in the Emperium itself, outside of the spheres, moves a bit differently, but not by much from what Flamehearts have gathered," Leo said. "It's hard for us to remain in that plane long, considering the side effects—not to mention the gravitational pull of different worlds."

Her mom nodded with a grimace. "Remember to breathe and to focus. Otherwise, you'll spiral."

Seemed simple enough. Then why the sudden tightness in Lia's chest? She wrung her hands. "Are you guys coming with us?"

Her mom shook her head. "This is typically a journey every Flameheart must make alone. It's very personal, what you craft with the Smith's help. A guardian close to your dreaming will guide you there, teach you the basics of how to use the pen."

Lia noted the paleness of her mom's skin, making the small smattering of freckles stand out on the bridge of her nose. They locked gazes before Lia motioned to Kayce—an unspoken request for his presence. Her mom sighed, but gave a subtle nod. Both of them were likely wondering the same thing: would Lia be able to navigate the Emperium without a pen, just as she had been able to Transcribe the gremlin with only her bare hands?

It was something only time would tell.

"Who's the guardian?" Lia looked around the room as though a guide would appear from between the shelves.

"There are scores of them," Leo informed her. "Each world has one. Then there are those who specifically monitor the humans who dream, us Flamehearts who travel." A smirk danced over his face. "You'll like her, I think. She volunteered. Quite adamant about it, too."

"She? I mean, she was?"

"Of course. She's one of the biggest fans of your work."

Lia blinked. "My work?"

"We're getting Norenth's guardian," Kayce deduced, hopping off the desk with a flourish. A dark lock slipped from its tie. "Glad to hear I have a fan."

And *there* was the urge to throttle him. "You can stay here, you know."

"And miss out on bestowing an autograph? Only Jace gets pestered for those. Not that I ever minded evading that nonsense. But now that the opportunity presents itself, I must admit, I *do* see the allure."

"Just when I thought your head couldn't get any bigger."

"It's the atmosphere here, fluffing my hair a bit. I'm at least *trying* to keep it in check." Kayce came over, bumping his shoulder against hers. But he didn't meet her gaze. "The hair, I mean. Not the ego."

"Never the ego," Lia replied.

Especially when you tie your agency to Aurelia's existence. Lia wanted to squander the bitter reminder. But even as their banter resumed, there was a force to it.

"It's time, Lia." Her mom, pen in hand, stood in the center of the study.

The teens watched her mom's eyes shut. She took several audible breaths, her brow pinched. An awkward minute ticked by. Lia and Kayce exchanged a glance. Didn't Mom know what to do?

Leo coughed. "Cordelia, I can—"

Hand raised and pen poised before her, her mom's pen's crystal tip began to glow in steady pulses. The light flared brighter, and Lia realized the steady thrums were in time with a heartbeat.

The pen's light surged white like a shooting star. And then her mom was drawing. She stooped to the carpeted floor, standing again to draw an arch. A white beam hung in the air like something a sparkler would cast in long-exposure photography. Lia could still see the desk through the arch until the air shimmered.

Pulsed.

A shift.

Spun like gossamer, a soft light filled the space.

"The guardian will meet you on the other side," Leo said. "None are allowed on Earth, though they can travel to other spheres."

Lia took a step forward, forcing her throat to work. "How will I get back?"

A comforting hand landed on her shoulder, turning Lia toward her mom. "When you're ready, you will do exactly as I did, but envision this room like it is now."

It was a good thing Lia had a penchant for details. She chewed her lip, apprehension seizing her. She didn't want to mess this up. Didn't want to fall flat on her face, be the laughing-stock of the

Order. Didn't want to disappoint Mom. Lia had already failed Kayce, even though he remained beside her. Supported her. She didn't deserve it.

Seeing her hesitation, her mom pulled Lia into a bone-crushing hug. "Run toward the roar, baby girl," she murmured in her daughter's ear. "Like Papa always said."

Lia smiled into her mom's shoulder, eyes brimming. The words anchored her. She stepped back, blinking her eyes clear. Lia mustered herself and looked over at Kayce. "Ready?" She held out her hand, scar facing upward.

"With you?" His answering smile finally lit the dark amber of his eyes as he grasped hold. "Always."

Her breath hitched. It was a reminder; it was a promise. An oath. Lia squeezed his hand tighter. That conversation about what this new reality made them was coming. But it would have to wait.

They approached the archway of shimmering light. Lia held her breath. Kayce squeezed her hand. Together, they took a step into the void. Lia turned at the last second to glimpse her mom's face.

It was pinched with fear.

Lia felt the lurch in her stomach. Hair lifted on her arms and the back of her neck. Spots of light and darkness danced behind eyelids screwed shut. Yes, she was a baby and had kept her eyes shut while stepping through the magical archway that likely disappeared mere seconds after she and Kayce passed through. It helped stave off the nausea rolling somersaults inside her. At least, that's what she told herself.

They walked several steps until she felt the warmth of the study dissipate and an atmospheric coolness take its place, clinging to her skin like static. The surrounding silence was *loud*. It filled her ears.

"Think we're there?" Kayce's voice was a pebble dropped into a cavern lake.

Lia's brows rose, but her eyes remained shut. "You mean your eyes are still closed?"

"I assume that means yours are, too."

She hummed in agreement. She didn't want to make noise, like their voices would disturb the hushed presence that seemed to fill the space around them. With her eyes closed, Lia wagered to guess she was in a room similar to a marbled atrium, walls bedecked with priceless art that spectators couldn't help but marvel at in silent awe, reverent. Or perhaps it was a granite cathedral, walls ensconced with stained glass and ceilings painted by hands long since deceased, sacred.

But something felt far more vast about this place, like the feeling of standing atop a ridge in the middle of a mountain range.

Lia took a deep breath. She opened her eyes.

And wished her brother were beside her. Marcus had dragged her out of bed on more than one occasion to observe some extra-terrestrial event through his telescope. For his last birthday, the Corvines had gone to the local science center to see a show in a planetarium that connected to the Hubble telescope and projected the Milky Way on white tarps all around. Lia had felt like she was enveloped by the universe itself.

This put that star show to shame.

Beads of light twinkled in a swirling sky of black and indigo. Thicker swirls puffed into clouds of grays and violets, like various rivers pooling into brighter bursts of lilac, some glowing white. It was endless, the magnitude of it stealing what little breath she had left.

But what dominated were the spheres.

Like glass marbles, they bobbed, suspended in the air by some cosmic force. In the spheres that orbited closer, Lia could see entire *worlds* within. Her papa's drawings had not done them justice. The spheres were like viewports to worlds she had never seen—never imagined before.

These were not like snow globes, showcasing a world in glass. No, the spheres, varying in size from one to the next, were gateways. The one closest, roughly the size of a two-story house, held a castle. Crags of earth pierced the mist as dragons swooped in from out of sight. Their mighty wings were soundless when they swerved behind the turrets.

Another sphere caught Lia's eye. She may have well been standing before Jupiter. Within was a desert, dunes of sand rolling as wind whipped around small domed houses. Two suns shone, a white and red orb both dipping into the horizon.

And no less beautiful in its intensity was a smaller sphere full of lush fields and a horse riding across, a singular horn on its head. A little girl clung to its white mane, peals of laughter unheard to the two viewers.

The spheres went on, an endless sea of dreams that stretched out before them, becoming the beads of light that Lia had believed to be stars in the distance. But, no. There were no stars here at all, rather the billions of stories and dreams spun since the moment humanity gained a heart. A soul.

The nightmares were there, but Lia refused to look at the realms with spheres of fire and shadow. She'd had enough nightmares for a while.

"Aurelia," Kayce whispered, his voice a strain between shock and awe. "Don't look down."

"What?" Lia mumbled, hardly enunciating the word before she unconsciously did what he explicitly told her not to. Her stomach bottomed out as she clambered for his arm, nails digging into the muscle.

"Breathe!" he choked. "Focus!"

She jerked a nod, staring beneath her.

They stood on nothing.

Well, nearly nothing.

A vaporous cloud of periwinkle had formed around their feet, but it was more likely to function as some comfort than a true platform. Beneath, the realms continued. More spheres moved below, the worlds continuing on within.

Lia's vision ebbed as the blood rushed from her head, sagging against Kayce. He held her tightly. "Come on, now. In and out." Kayce breathed in a steady rhythm.

She wrangled her thoughts, screwing her eyes shut so she could breathe with him. Eventually, the lightheadedness faded.

"Excellent coaching!" a disembodied voice called to them. "Flailing about first thing is *not* starting off on the right foot."

Opening her eyes, Lia witnessed a flash of light, a sunburst in its flaring intensity. Once it dimmed, a young woman appeared before them, the light pulling back into two arcs over her shoulders.

Wings, Lia thought. They were like twin cosmic clouds, a hazy prism of refracted colors known for their nurseries of young stars. The guardian was a year or two older in appearance than Lia, though she knew the celestial being had to be far older. Nearly as old as Time. Her skin was smooth ebony, her hair a shocking shade of silver, blues in varying shades curled throughout.

"Aurelia Corvine," the guardian said, smiling wide to showcase straight teeth. "An honor it is. What a mind you have! And you started working on the Norenth sphere at *eight*? I can't!"

Finally, something a bit more tethered to reality for Lia to focus on. Who was she kidding? They had left reality behind. *Far* behind. Might as well roll with it. She was done deluding herself into thinking she was crazy. With a shake of her head, Lia chuckled. "Thanks, but my papa helped a lot." Her cheeks reddened. "Which I'm sure you know."

The guardian sniffed, her hair a dandelion puff of shifting curls. "Here and there. You did most of the legwork."

"Considering I was the one running around most of the time," Kayce inserted, "I would argue that I did most of that."

Both Lia and the guardian leveled a gaze at him, staring until he looked back and forth between them. Finally, the guardian could no longer contain herself, rolling her star-filled eyes. "The boy spends a few days outside his sphere and he thinks the world revolves around him."

Lia opened her mouth to point out that in a sense it did, according to the Floating Kingdom series, at least. But the guardian glared at her, the smirk she wore lessening its intensity.

"Don't even try to deny it."

Kayce scoffed. "Unbelievable."

The humor anchored Lia further, her shoulders relaxing from where they jacked to her ears. Seeing Kayce's usual demeanor return was equally grounding.

"What's your name?" Lia asked.

The guardian smiled. "Fiducia. But you can call me Fee."

"Well, *Fee*," Kayce crossed his arms. "Aurelia needs her pen. The Order mentioned something about seeing a Smith."

Fee arched a pale brow. Those eyes—a cloudy haze mimicking the cosmic atmosphere—narrowed on the prince. "Obviously. I've been patiently waiting for the day Lia would arrive. I refused to miss more than the two minutes I did when you first got here." She waved a hand around her. "And *obviously*, you needed a moment. This is a lot to take in."

"No kidding," Lia said, but smiled. It didn't slip past her notice that Fee used the name she preferred on Earth. It was a small thing, but it made her feel...seen. Comfortable.

"Is it far?" she asked, her gaze darting back to the celestial maze around them. "The Sphere of Malletor?"

"Home to all things crafted and made. Gives the ugly brute Hephestus a run for his money, but don't tell him that." Fee smoothed her brows. "I just groomed these and have *no* desire to see them singed. Or to be blinded."

She held out her hands. Lia took one readily, Kayce a beat behind.

"Let me guess," he said dryly. "Hold fast, or dinner may revisit us?"

Mirth clung to the curve of Fee's mouth. "Absolutely."

And in that moment, Lia knew she never wanted to tick Fee off. Kayce was going to do plenty of that on his own, and Fee was likely one to know *exactly* how to make him pay for it.

Lia couldn't wait.

CHAPTER TWENTY-THREE

A lurch in Lia's stomach pulled her an extra step forward when they arrived in Malletor. She squeezed her eyes shut as the world continued to rush by, despite her standing still.

Whiplash warnings needed to be included in the Flameheart Order's contract.

Heat engulfed her, baking her skin with a discomfort more intense than what she'd ever experienced on Earth, even in the worst of summer. A trip to Arizona tickled her mind, remembering a July vacation spent in Phoenix where the sun was always cooking. That heat and the dizziness made it terribly hard to catch a full breath.

She was still working on breathing when Kayce said to Fee, "I thought you said we were going to see the Smith? How is this place even a forge?"

"Says the boy already sweating through his clothes. No offense, but that's disgusting."

"So guardians can regulate their body temperature as well as morph their clothing with their *fancy magic*?"

"Obviously."

Kayce was close as she opened her eyes, his own face disconcertingly pale and likely made worse since he was recovering from the dragon attack. Not that he would ever let on otherwise. Sweat shone on his brow, his tousled locks clinging to the back of his neck.

Fee crossed her arms. Her wings were gone, a pair of black-lensed goggles wrapped around her forehead, and her hair was braided close to her scalp. Similar leather gloves and coveralls were swapped from her ethereal attire.

Lucky girl. Her skin was perfectly dry.

"I know this is a blacksmith we're visiting and all," Lia said, breaking up their glaring contest. "But why is it so hot?" Never did she think fire could be so instantly suffocating. Lia didn't even see any flashes of red as she looked past them—

Because there were none. No flames whatsoever.

The trio stood on a vast field of what could have been lava rock. Black stone rippled and churned in petrified flows. The terrible heat source wound through the rock like rivers, lazily flowing and emitting steam. But the rivers were not the reds and oranges lava should have been. They shimmered, the molten rock an ever-changing swirl of golds, indigos and navy blues, glowing white from within.

"Stars burn hotter than any fire, volcanic or otherwise," Fee said. "It's what goes into every piece the Smith crafts."

They were on a planet of molten starlight.

Lia would have been impressed, awe-struck even, were she not so ridiculously hot. She wore jeans and a plaid button-down—attire more appropriate for fall. Not this place. She fanned herself, looking over the dark plain to iridescent rivers converging on an enormous dome. Steam billowed from the tapered peak, the entire structure hewn from stone yet polished like silver.

"Please tell me he has air conditioning," Lia whined.

"Don't worry. The structure's designed to keep cool despite the heat in the atmosphere." Fee came up alongside her, Kayce keeping stride. "The Smith has been here since the dawn of the Emperium. The sphere hasn't killed him."

Kayce tugged at his shirt collar. "Yet."

It didn't take long for them to reach the forge. Lia's hair was a frizzy mess, leaving her no choice but to wrangle it into a bun. Anything to keep its mass off her neck. It reminded her of all the girls in gym class who ran and played sports with their hair down. She never trusted them. It was far too uncomfortable, for beauty's sake or not.

But nothing seemed to bring her any relief from the blasted heat until the dome's doors slid open on their own.

"That never gets old." Fee let out a wistful sigh. The air steamed around them, coolness rushing to kiss their skin.

Kayce and Lia clamored inside, not waiting to be greeted. It was definitely one of those times to ask for forgiveness rather than permission. The doors slid shut, encasing them in cool, dimly lit air. It was like stepping into a walk-in refrigerator, the perspiration slowly drying on Lia's skin.

"Why couldn't you have zapped us in here?" she asked Fee.

Kayce nodded vehemently, running his fingers through his hair. "Certainly would have been safer. Aurelia almost tripped twice into those infernal rivers—"

"Yes, yes, I'm painfully aware," Lia cut him off in a rush of her own embarrassment. She couldn't help but smile when she caught his eye. "Thanks for catching me, though. Both times."

The corners of Kayce's mouth perked up, even as his eyes danced away. It didn't seem out of frustration or tension. In fact, during their walk, she had caught him staring more than once, a soft contemplation creasing his brow. Lia would have given anything to know what he was thinking.

The guardian moved ahead into a large chamber, where a set of stairs spiraled down. Steam rose from the center, its source hidden. Lia had little desire to follow, because Fee was headed *toward* the steam's source. A heat Lia was done with for a lifetime. Moving down south at any point in her future was out of the question. Period.

"I didn't 'zap' you in here because it's not polite. How would you like it if someone just appeared in your living room?" Fee waved for them to follow, but didn't wait to start the descent.

"I wouldn't." Lia soured when her eyes found Kayce's. She tried very hard not to remember the way his body had curled around hers, both of them blissfully ignorant in sleep.

It seemed like Kayce felt the same. He bolted after the guardian, smarting over his shoulder, "That wasn't *my* fault."

Lia rolled her eyes and followed, thankful he couldn't see how her cheeks had flushed even further.

The rhythmic hammering of iron pounding on metal echoed up the staircase, the walls narrowing with each pass around the circumference. Whooshes of expelled air accompanied the booms, the metal continuing to clamor afterward. They came upon a door, through which Fee led them down another, more direct set of stairs that opened to a spacious cavern. The steady pounding had stopped and the heat returned, though not as intense.

"Smithy!" Fee hollered. "Hope you're ready for some company!"

"At least you knocked this time, you bothersome sprite," came a responding bellow.

Fee glowered, muttering to Lia. "He knows I detest that insult. I might sacrifice my eyebrows if it teaches him a lesson."

"There was a time you didn't knock?" Kayce said, bemused. "What happened to not appearing in someone's living room, Guardian? Or is that a lesson you learned the hard way?"

A bark of laughter echoed. "Whoever that lad is, I like him already!"

Lia didn't doubt the murderous glint in the guardian's starry eyes. As apprehensive as Lia was, anticipation filled her. She wanted her pen. She wanted to learn her gifts, to master what she was born to be. It would bring her another step closer to figuring out what happened to her papa.

Kayce reached out for her arm. "Aurelia, let me—"

There was no hesitation this time. She was already out of his reach, entering the forge. A large anvil was closest, the metal worn smooth like polished glass from so much pounding. Not far was a tank filled with water, deep enough to immerse a longsword and broad enough to hold an axe like she had seen the Norenthian dwarves wielding while mining Fealtek. The cavern above acted as the hood and flue, extracting sparkling steam through a hole at the top of the dome. Lia tracked the steam to its source in the center: a gaping pit filled with molten starlight. The vat was massive, flecks of light swirling. It illuminated the room, a river of it running around the wall's circumference.

"Honestly, Fiducia, I've told you to give more warning when I need to host visitors. I would have made snacks."

A heavy clatter accompanied the gruff voice and drew Lia's attention. Various hammers and clamps covered the opposite wall, the table beneath strewn with more tools, fine picks, and other materials. Lia even thought she spotted a satchel full of gems sparkling in the starlight.

But it was the man—the *giant*, to be more fitting—that dominated her attention. She involuntarily took a step back.

Fee sighed through her nose, putting a gloved hand on her hip. "The last time I did that, you made me stand outside until the table was ready. It was only our weekly lunch appointment."

The large man turned, his long gray hair tied back and streaked with real strands of silver. It coiled through the braids of his beard, beads hanging over his barreled chest. He glowered at Fee, soot wrinkling his tanned skin. "It's all about the presentation. Seldom do I get to experience that. And you know I like the excuse to use the nice silverware—"

"It was tea cakes."

"But I *made* them! The silverware *and* the food!" he exclaimed, throwing up hands the size of small dinner plates. One eye focused on Lia. The other was covered by a diamond, carved as a monocle strapped to his face. It refracted like a kaleidoscope, his eye fragmenting as it zeroed in on her. "Do you have any idea how often I get to attend the presentation of my work? *Never*. Not Mjölnir, not Excalibur, not even the Elder—"

Fee cleared her throat. "We don't talk about that, Smithy."

Lia's mind went reeling, cataloging each item the Smith had ticked off. He'd made those things? And he was going to help *her*?

The Smith wasn't deterred, blinking hard with fists pressed to his leather smock. "I made them! I put blood, sweat, and tears into what would become the center of stories for generations—and does anyone invite the guy who made the sparkling thing? No, no one ever thinks about him. Or worse, they give the credit to someone else because their sphere demands it—"

"I know!" Fee interjected. She mastered herself with a breath, stepping toward the blacksmith. "I know, big guy. Presentation is important. Which is why I brought Lia."

Lia watched the Smith warily. He was clearly a passionate man, one who prided in his work. It was a shame he never got to see who got the results of his labors. Sympathy prompted Lia to speak. "I'm a Flameheart," she said, her voice cracking when the man looked down at her. "And I need a pen. So, you still get to do a presentation, right?"

The Smith studied Lia like she was a gem found in the rubble, analyzing her facets as if he could turn her about in the light. She fidgeted, that single eye making her feel exposed. Suddenly, her skin felt tight, the air restricted—

Kayce's hand brushed against hers. The simple touch loosened her chest.

The giant's face erupted into a grin. "Then this is a most excellent day. Any day is when you get to impart something on a life, no matter how small and ordinary it may seem. And Flameheart pens are the most special pieces that come from this forge."

Lia blinked, the simple statement stunning her into silence. He wasn't exactly wrong. It was always the small things, the random acts of kindness that moved people. Perhaps her moment of understanding did that for him. It warmed her chest further, her shoulders relaxing.

"Nothing in here seems small or ordinary," Kayce said, deeming it safe enough to leave Lia's side. He walked over to another wall, hands clasped behind his back to admire the display. "These are all no short of wondrous."

He was right. Swords fanned out to form a half circle, blades polished to reflect the starlight. Several pommels glinted with jewels, others were carved from different materials. Had the Smith crafted the Norenthian swords held by the royal family? Lia recalled how artfully done the lion heads were. She looked at the

Smith's hands, wanting to ask, but keeping silent when he moved to stand beside Kayce.

"You're too kind, good fellow. These are practice, but hopefully some will come to claim them in time."

Kayce's dark head tilted as he studied one sword in particular. It wasn't the largest. In fact, it was one of the smaller ones. "May I?" he asked, gesturing to the sword in question.

The Smith bowed. "I'd be honored."

"It is we who are honored, truly," Kayce argued gently before taking the sword down.

It shone just as the rest of them, the crossguard an elegant filigree of oak leaves. Acorns dotted the detail, so small only the wielder could note them. Supple brown leather wrapped the handle before ending at the pommel, simple but for a smooth stone, gray like a wisp of cloud trailing across a harvest moon.

Kayce's hand wrapped around the hilt with confidence and he took several practice swings. Lia watched him work, recognizing the sequence he often did for practice when they were in their alcove. This time, her gaze lingered, studying the muscles of his back moving like water.

An elbow dug into Lia's side, snapping her out of it. She glared at Fee, cheeks flaming, but the guardian only smirked.

"You wield it well." The Smith had been analyzing the prince's face.

Pausing in his strikes, Kayce's thumb brushed over the pommel. "It's well made. I know an excellent sword when I see it."

Fee rolled her eyes. "If they start gushing over metalwork, I'll fall asleep where I stand."

Kayce scowled, but before Lia could speak in his defense, the Smith whirled on Fee. "You wouldn't know a falchion from a cutlass—no, you wouldn't even know a longsword from a short-sword!"

"Yes, I would," she deadpanned, "those at least give it away in the name."

A vein pulsed in the Smith's temple. "Centuries, I have been trying to get you to see the art of what I do."

"Honestly, I'm just here for the food," she replied.

The two continued to banter back and forth, almost unaware of the others present. Kayce put the sword back on the wall before shrinking to Lia's side. He didn't take his eyes off the two celestial beings. "Are we this bad?" Kayce whispered to Lia out of the side of his mouth.

She shook her head, watching the guardian and the Smith go at it. The latter towered over Fee, but she didn't give him an inch in their verbal sparring. Her personality was more than enough presence. Lia needed to put a stop to this. It seemed amicable enough, but Fee *did* mention singed eyebrows...

Clearing her throat, Lia raised her hand. "So, how do we go about making my pen?"

The two looked at her, banter stopping mid-sentence. Lia lowered her hand, suddenly feeling silly. She wasn't in class or anything. Maybe she should trip again and fall into the star pit. That would save her from the mortification.

Kayce nodded toward the anvil, hands slipping into his jean pockets. "What ore do you even use? I don't see much steel lying around, but to be fair, pens are quite small." He caught Lia's eye, giving her a small smirk others may have missed. She answered it, embarrassment evaporating. But then Kayce's dimmed, his throat working.

The Smith clapped his hands together. Even Fee seemed less disgruntled, finding a seat atop the workbench.

"This will not take much time. I have several bases to choose from. Then comes the personalization, imbuing it with your essence and all. That's a bit of a rub, but for right now, you get to see why my forge is here." He took long strides to the vat, grinning as he pointed down. "Starlight, my friends. Every weapon, every tool of every story, is birthed from starlight. One of the core elements here in the Emperium."

Lia followed his gaze to the swirling mass. She struggled to understand, spying the sword Kayce just held. The blade looked like iron and steel, elements of the physical world she knew. Thinking back to Marcus's endless chattering about space, she remembered that stars were made of hot gas—mostly hydrogen and helium, which were the two *lightest* elements.

"How?" Lia asked. "Hydrogen and helium aren't even near each other on the periodic table—"

"She's a thinker. Chronic straight-A kid. And they say her brother is the science whiz." Fee shrugged, adjusting her goggles. "But, she created Norenth."

Lia balked. How did the guardian know her brother? How did she know about her *grades*?

The Smith huffed a laugh. "She's the one who crafted a fantasy world of floating ships and entire oceans in bubbles?"

Kayce choked on a gasp. "*Bubbles*?"

"Fine!" Lia waved her hands. "I'm not the one who should point out the impracticalities of defying physics."

Perhaps it was time for a little faith.

The Smith brought out a small tray holding various rods. They were bare, absent of any design or personal touches, roughly all the same length. Lia selected a silver one, slender and slightly longer than the length of her hand. He also brought over a pouch of stones, crystals carved to look like pen nibs.

"What calls to you?" he inquired, a sapphire lens flipping over his diamond monocle. "Feel it in your heart."

Lia frowned. Her heart? If anything, she felt a bit hungry. Not to mention she was in desperate need of a shower with all this hot and cold business. But she set her shoulders, focusing on the crystals. Several were clear quartz, a few soft pink. There were blue ones, citrine, some utterly black. None of them seemed to call her. What was she even waiting for? Something like indigestion?

She was about to give up when one caught her eye. It was faint—a small skip in her heartbeat. But Lia knew. That one was hers. "That quartz one," she breathed reverently, drawn to it like gravity. As she stared at it, the tiny crystal began to glow softly.

His eyes crinkled, selecting the point that shimmered with opalescence. "Yes, indeed." That sapphire lens snapped back, a pink one flicking into its place. The Smith turned the point over, studying it with awe. "A powerful stone, indeed. A light cutting through the mist. Your ember has called to it."

Once again the Smith's words left Lia a bit off-kilter as he brought the materials to the anvil. He grabbed a pipe, pulling a lever alongside it. Air hissed as the other end of the pipe descended into the vat of starlight.

"We don't need much. For this, several drops will do." The Smith waved her over, taking down a leather smock and a set of goggles similar to Fee's. He thrust both into Lia's hands. "But here's the rub I mentioned: *you* need to craft it."

Lia halted halfway through tying the smock. "Excuse me?" The Smith was grabbing a mallet, looking over at her with an analytical frown before putting it back to grab a smaller one. Clearly, she'd misheard him. "The Order told me *you* would—"

"No, Lia," Fee said in a stern, but gentle tone. "The Order said to see him. You need to make your own pen; all Flamehearts do. That's how it bonds to you."

CHAPTER TWENTY-FOUR

Lia clutched the goggles, unease settling into her stomach. Maybe if she didn't put them on, her hand wouldn't be forced. "Look, I appreciate the artistry, I really do, but I'm not exactly built for this kind of thing."

She was a self-proclaimed literary couch potato and proud of it. Then again, she had Aurelia's Norenthian skills now. Strange as it was.

Kayce's pointed stare felt like a brand. No one else broke the silence.

There was no getting out of this.

Lia was about to nod when she noticed the Smith twiddling his fingers, avoiding her direct gaze. Her pulse flattened. "There's more, isn't there?"

The Smith's mouth clamped into a firm line. "Yes. However, I've been told that it *is* worthwhile and therapeutic."

"Smithy," Fee interjected. This time, her tone was softer. "Just tell her."

His expression was solemn. "You need to give up something, pour it into the pen to solidify the bond to your ember."

"What?" Lia questioned, her chest clenching.

"A memory," the Smith said. "One pivotal to your being, fueled with emotion."

Her being? She struggled to understand. A memory of something. Something that happened to her, obviously. An event that impacted her. Made her who she was at this moment. There was so much that made Lia herself. And to be frank, she was unfinished, a clay sculpture partially formed. That was somewhat comforting, at least.

"What does the memory have to be of, exactly?" she asked.

"It has to be something you are willing to release. Something that no longer serves you. In the release of pain in our past, we can truly step into who we are meant to be," the Smith explained. "Who *you* are meant to be."

Silence filled the room as she contemplated, attempting to look inward. Kayce found a perch nearby, his gaze upon her as if willing her success.

A memory to let go of. Lia wished to forget many things. Adolescence had not been very kind. But it was deeper than that. What was she holding onto that was keeping her back?

Slowly, she approached the anvil, the silver rod and crystal waiting in a mold.

"Giving up this memory, creating this pen," the Smith warned. "It won't heal instantly. It will take time, processing. And that memory is likely tied to a string of behaviors that will have to be confronted. But it's a step in the right direction."

Lia felt a restlessness in her bones. She had been tired of standing still. Learning she was a Flameheart had been a shove, one she didn't realize she needed. Or how badly. Now she craved that momentum, something that would propel her to learn who'd murdered her papa, how Seekers were destroying the barriers between worlds.

Who she was meant to be.

Turning, Lia caught Kayce's eye. He stared back, starlight flickering over his features. He gave a slight nod, a thin smile tugging at the corners of his lips. Whether he realized it or not, Lia caught how his thumb rubbed into his open palm. Her own scar tingled as though in response. A small gesture, but it was enough—he was with her. As he'd always been.

The blood oath pulsed between them.

Fee watched the exchange with a twinkle in her eyes before she tossed a pair of goggles to Kayce. "You're going to want these."

Everyone put goggles on, black lenses tinting the room in shadow. The Smith handed Lia the hammer, the weight heavy. He then took hold of the lever, gesturing to the pipe overhead.

"When starlight fills the mold, you think of that memory. Bring it to the forefront of your mind. Let yourself feel it. Then swing—hard, fast like you are trying to punch through it." The Smith modeled the swing several times. "Expel it from you and into this instead."

Lia's hands turned clammy. She nearly stumbled on the first practice swing, but she found the more she tightened her core, the more control she had. It reminded her of sword-work with Kayce in Norenth.

The Smith didn't wait. At a pull of the lever, steam hissed. The vat bubbled and starlight was sucked out. Several fat drops came from the pipe, mercurial beads like mini galaxies falling into the mold. But the steam and heat such a small amount created was immense, an open furnace baking Lia's skin.

Now for a memory.

Lia thought they would have dispersed and scattered, and she'd be unable to grasp only one. She expected the funeral to surge in her mind, the grief manageable yet still hard to bear.

But as if her heart knew what it was about to do, one memory stayed. A small one, seemingly insignificant. Yet it echoed in her whole being—the pain pulsing with each beat of her heart.

Little Lia perched on her bed, clutching a stuffed lion to her chest while she watched her daddy. She could see him in his truck from her bedroom window. It had rained earlier that day. Drops clung to the windowpane, to his windshield. A bright red ember bloomed to life in front of his face before he took several puffs of a cigarette, flicking the ash out the window.

Look up, *Lia thought.* See me. See me sitting here, watching you. Get out of the truck.

She shifted to sit up on her knees. Held the lion tighter. Daddy, please. I need you.

But he didn't look up. Not once, as he pulled out of the driveway.

The memory scorched Lia's mind, burning in her chest, in the backs of her eyes, the pain resurfacing. On the day her father left, she'd sat staring out the window for hours. She didn't move until breakfast the next morning, her mom coming up to find her with tear-stained cheeks.

Lia hadn't wanted to risk it—miss seeing him come home. But he never did. It was like he'd disappeared, become a ghost to them. Even though he was very much alive, with a life that had a new wife and new children in a new town with a new job.

He'd left them. Abandoned her.

"Swing, Lia!" The Smith implored, gently squeezing her shoulder and breaking her from the memory's grip.

The hammer felt lighter when it collided with the anvil, the shock reverberating through her bones, into her marrow. Sparks flew about, pulling the pain out of her. Her eyes glassed over, hidden behind the goggles.

"Again, pour it into the metal!"

The burning cigarette filled her mind as Lia swung the hammer a second time, grunting with effort. He'd left her. The one person who was supposed to protect her. And he abandoned—

A sob hitched in her throat. Lia brought the hammer down again and again, each swing more powerful than the last.

"That moment does not define you, Aurelia," the Smith said, his gravelly voice stern. "It does not get to dictate your life."

The "but" clung to Lia's lips, and she hated it. She hated how she couldn't trust people to stay. How she always feared she would do something so embarrassing, shameful, or awful that people would turn their backs on her. Like he did.

Because who else cuts ties with their child?

Lia yelled her frustration, the hammer casting a meteor shower of sparks on the next swing. And the next. And again. Over and over, Lia swung until sweat trickled down her brow, her fiery curls tumbling free. Her muscles burned, but she relished in it, for it anchored her.

Was this the root, like the Smith said? The memory tied to her anxiety, her insecurities, her lack of desire to be around people or step outside her comfort zone? How she had nearly allowed herself to drown in her grief only to become her family's life raft?

She couldn't let her father's decision impact her own choices. Not anymore. He was gone; she was here. This was her life. Her future.

And that was her past.

With a final wail, Lia brought the hammer upon the anvil. Light burst forth, enveloping the room as the last bit of grief and rage and disappointment fled in the wake of relief and understanding. Of forgiveness, though not for her father. Maybe one day that would come. Today, it was for herself in clinging to this pain, this self-doubt that was never meant to be hers.

Light dimmed. Lia sagged, her frame trembling with the release. The hammer slipped from her grip.

"Hurry," the Smith urged, grabbing the flattened starlight with a pair of tongs. "We must mold it while it's still hot and the emotion fresh." The giant ushered her toward a work bench. In a whirl of activity, he pulled out a few tools and set about showing Lia how to shape the metal.

Time ticked by like an army marching toward war, yet it took no notice of the massive man and young woman. Slowly, they brought the pen to life, crafting each piece with the care of a mother tending to her infant. The Smith guided Lia, encouraging her to find what gave her peace and pour it into the engraving. At first it was just swirls wrapped around each other. But soon the engravings began to take shape. For hours they worked, focusing on nothing but the parts in front of them.

Fee and Kayce watched patiently from the background, waiting to see the final product as the pen was taken back to the forge. Reheated, worked more, than reheated once again.

Finally, it was finished.

Steam cleared from the room. The Smith gave the pen one last critical gaze while holding it to the light. His smile was gentle as he inspected the craftsmanship of Lia's heart.

"A fine pen, indeed. It will serve you well."

Lia was proud that her hand hardly trembled when he placed the pen in her palm. The hours of metalwork had been as therapeutic as the Smith had said. It was warm to the touch, the pen's body a swirl of cresting waves. Elegantly etched feathers swelled for a grip before flowing into a nib that housed the anandalite rainbow quartz.

Lia's heart fluttered, realizing how the pen's design reminded her of Paxia, the white volatequis Kayce had gifted her. A realization struck—that name, the one she'd chosen for her mount. She didn't understand at the time, the word foreign like the thought that summoned it that day, but she knew what it meant now.

It stood for peace.

CHAPTER TWENTY-FIVE

Heat lashed them once again as the three left the Forge. Lia twirled the pen between her fingers. The pain inside still pulsed. Like the Smith had warned, she had years since that moment to unpack. Perhaps, like her grief at losing her papa, the grief of her father's abandonment would always be there. She would just grow around it.

Why, of course, this all was rooted into your daddy issues—

Oh, she wished her thoughts to be quiet for *once*. Let her enjoy the win. And the money she'd saved, considering the cost of mental health care on Earth.

The Smith had been kind in the aftermath, offering them a small meal before they were sent onwards. Though something had nagged at Lia as the Smith escorted them out. Fee and Kayce had already been on their way, discussing the craftsmanship of battle axes, something Kayce found Fee sorely lacking in appreciation of. This had amused the Smith greatly, as he paused with Lia to watch them.

"Why do they call you the Smith?" she had asked him, one foot out the door.

His laughter sobered with a big shrug. "My name is far too lengthy, in a language long since deceased, for most tongues to comprehend."

"That shouldn't matter. It's your name." Lia frowned. "Names deserve to be spoken."

The Smith had looked at her then. His mouth tightened, that singular eye gleaming. "You really are like your mother."

Such a remark snatched Lia's breath, leaving confusion in its wake. But she didn't get to pry, to ask, for the gentle giant leaned down to whisper his name before bidding her farewell.

With the Forge a fair distance behind, Kayce turned to Fee. "Now that Lia has her fancy wand—"

"Pen!" the two girls corrected in unison.

"Besides the point—do we get to go exploring?" He rubbed his hands together, bringing some lightness to the situation—much needed, as far as Lia was concerned.

Fee rolled her eyes, taking the goggles off before chucking them into a ditch. They turned into mist before hitting the ground. "Not so fast. Some tutelage is needed first."

"Ever hear of trial and error?" Kayce questioned.

"Because that worked out *so* well trying to wrangle that mountain wyrm. Ever hear of better safe than sorry?"

Kayce's neck flushed. "Terranth swore he'd never breathe a word of that dare—"

"Norenth's guardian, remember?"

"Guys," Lia said warily, watching her pen pulse like a heating oven.

They didn't notice.

"Half the fun of exploration is figuring it out as you go," Kayce persisted. "The adrenaline alone helps establish memory."

"I'm pretty sure that's not right." Fee tossed her gloves next, wings arching out over her shoulders. "Many people suffer memory loss under high doses of stress."

"Who said adrenaline was stressful?"

"It's a fight-or-flight response; of course it's stressful."

Lia's voice cracked. "Guys, you're not helping—" As the two continued to argue, Lia's pen pulsed brighter, her anxiety flaring. She was emotionally raw, like a scab scratched open, blood beading. "Stop!" Lia shouted, but too late. The pen erupted, encasing her in light—

—and making her disappear.

Unable to focus on the Sphere of Malletor and get a grip on her spiraling emotions, Lia plunged through sphere after sphere, world after world. Her emotions had hijacked whatever made this new tool work. She was on emotional overload.

And tumbling through the Emperium wasn't helping.

Flipping over herself, she toppled and spun, arms windmilling for a semblance of control. But she only fell faster.

"How do you steer this thing?" she cried, the pen locked in her white-knuckled grip.

Still, she did not slow. Temperamental thing, apparently. It wasn't like the inanimate object could hear her. But Fee did. She and Kayce had left that fiery sphere behind, and Lia caught a glimpse of them standing on a nebulous cloud in the Emperium.

"Your anxiety is making it worse!" Fee called.

"You think?" Lia hollered back. "No thanks to—"

But she was gone.

She passed through a world of nothing but ocean, crested waves of white and salt consuming her lungs. Plummeted through a world of ash, ravines carved through cracked earth and jagged peaks—pure desolation. Lia balked, the wind snatching away a whimper as her pen flared—

Then, a sphere where ships with metal hubs of blinking lights whizzed through the air. Hundreds of them, crisscrossing in varying traffic patterns. Lia screamed when she almost collided with the windshield of one spacecraft, the cobalt-skinned people within returning her cry as she tried to barrel roll out of the way. Not without a few bangs to her arms and legs.

Gritting her teeth, she fought the current to raise her arm. The gem flickered, echoing the burn that flared in Lia's chest. Her ears popped. Then, she was back in the Emperium. Still falling.

"Breathe!" Kayce shouted through cupped hands. "Relax!"

"How do you relax in freefall?" Lia screamed.

She passed through a world where a cacophony of rainfall enveloped her. Passed over dense forests, verdant meadows, and grasses rolling like seas of their own. Only a single creature on a mountain rise—the body of a horse smoothed with feathers and the wings and head of an eagle—tracked her flight with a cock of its head.

Popping out the other side, Lia craned her neck to find her friends.

Fee waved her arms. "Find your peace!"

Peace? She was sopping wet and plummeting. Any inkling of that peace found after forging her pen was gone—

Think. She needed to focus, to think of something. What was peace but home?

The scent of brine and pine, mist-kissed breezes—

Another sphere gobbled her up, a dream world of clouds that rivaled the softest cotton candy. A castle in the sky—

Lia gritted her teeth. *Home.*

She passed through that sugary world without so much as a blip.

"You can do it, Aurelia!" Kayce called, his voice distant. "Focus!"

Through the Emperium she whirled, the heat in her heart burning in tandem with the gem of her pen. It pulsed brighter, brighter still—

Until she slowed, the boundaries of the next world easing her descent as it welcomed her. As if it had been waiting for her. But it wasn't the coastal forests of Seattle. Not even Ohio, where she'd spent most of her life.

A smile lit Lia's face, for it was mist that held her aloft, that ever-present mixture of river water and sea spray. The floating continent of Norenth. Fealtek and the mountains that accompany it dominated her view, piercing the mist and seas bobbing in the sky with ships transporting their daily goods.

A tentacle, thick as a tower and a similar orange shade of brick, flung from the nearest cloud's bounds to wrangle a passing skiff as she fell. The small boat sped away, sails shifting sharply to catch an upward breeze away from the particularly testy cloud.

Lia wanted to laugh—but she was falling. She should file a complaint about these hazardous work conditions. The Order didn't mention nearly falling to her death. Especially after getting bruised, drenched, and her eardrums ruptured from shifting pressure.

Kayce's idea of "exploring first" sucked.

Lia fought the current and whistled through her fingers. The sound pierced the air, searching, hoping, praying—

There!

The mist parted near Fealtek's summit, and Paxia raced toward her. Praise the skies and seas, the winged horse didn't think twice about her owner falling from nowhere as she hurtled toward Lia. Stuffing her pen in the waistband of her jeans, Lia grappled for the volatequis's reins, fumbling several times before finding her seat in the saddle.

"Good girl," she praised, her voice hoarse like it was several worlds behind. "Get to the balcony!"

Paxia snorted, wings pumping hard. The balcony selected was on the tallest turret of Castle Finerda, where a figure watched her descend. Terranth waved, the wind from Lia's landing ruffling his dark hair.

"Where have you been?" His features were tense as he helped her dismount, concern furrowing his brow.

Her knees buckled, feeling solid ground. She could kiss the cobblestones for hours were it not for Terranth gripping her waist.

"Aurelia, are you well?" He looked her over, cheeks coloring when he noticed how the modern shirt clung thanks to her world-tumbling. "And what in the skies and seas are you wearing?"

"Give me a minute before we play 'Twenty Questions'," she wheezed, putting a hand to his chest. She needed space. She needed to sit. If she could only figure out which way the ground was.

Paxia whinnied, wings kicking up dust. A flash of light burned to their right. Kayce and Fee appeared, the latter lacking wings and wearing a Norenthian gown of blue and copper.

Terranth jerked around, drawing his sword at the sudden intrusion before blinking. "Kacerion?" Metal hissed as he re-sheathed the weapon. "What are *you* wearing?"

"Jeans," Kayce replied, looking down at the slim-fit cut. "They do wonders for your backside."

As much as Lia wanted to scoff, she was trying to capture a full breath. Her knees finally gave out. Terranth whirled with a warrior's grace, catching her before she hit the floor.

"Someone has a great deal of explaining to do," Terranth muttered, lowering her to a chair. "But why am I not surprised?"

"I would be offended if you were," Kayce said, shouldering his way to Lia. His lightheartedness faded, taking in her wane complexion. "Brother, get her something to eat—"

"My stomach is somewhere in Candy Land," she groaned. It was the only descriptor for that sugary world she passed through, not that it made any sense to him. Her body was too unsettled, like her very bones were vibrating.

"You need to ground yourself," Fee said, sitting graciously in the opposite chair. "Food is mandatory after traveling."

Terranth eyed the guardian. "And you are?"

Her white teeth shone. "To you, an admirer."

His brows rose, causing Kayce to clear his throat. "Terranth, food. And get Jace."

CHAPTER TWENTY-SIX

The castle and sky stopped doing somersaults by the time the two brothers returned, provisions in hand. Fallon bounded toward Lia, sniffing her hand curiously as if he couldn't decide he knew her or not, despite several misadventures with her and Kayce when Jace had gone after them—pre-smuggling affairs, of course. After a weak pat, Fallon was content and returned to his master's side.

Under Fee's glare, Lia forced small bites before ravenous hunger took root. Looked like her stomach made the trek, after all—and then some. While hours had seemingly passed with the Smith, Norenth sported a twilight sky similar to what they left behind on Earth after the meeting. Fee pulled a pocket watch from the folds of her skirt, a delicate bronze compact embedded with a con-stellation of stones. Lia could only glimpse the face—several cogs churning with nearly half a dozen galaxies impressed upon clock faces, their ticking hands bearing tight, elegant script—before the guardian put it away with a nod to Lia's plate and a mention of second dinners being better than second breakfasts. Meanwhile, Kayce let Lia collect herself, explaining to his brothers everything that had transpired since he woke on Earth.

Gratitude filled her for his thoughtfulness. She was glad—relieved, even—when she figured out how to steer with her pen. But it unsettled her that emotions were so integral to this. Coping with anxiety had never been her strong suit. And this pen had a fine trigger.

Guess that's what she got when using a memory filled with...well, *that*.

She felt the Emperium pulling at her, a tingle along her skin, an itching in the back of her mind like she had forgotten something. But she settled in Norenth. A deep breath solidified the feeling.

Realization struck. Here she was, in Norenth, fully aware of what was happening. Lia *and* Aurelia. Both sides of her, coming together as they had on Earth when her blood oath scar appeared and her eyesight improved. It was different from the ball, even different from confiding to Kayce about her grief in their alcove later. In fact, she felt like a child stepping into her mom's heels. If she wasn't careful, she would fall flat on her face. People had expectations of her here.

As Kayce had already pointed out.

But he doesn't get it. He doesn't realize why it's so hard.

Pushing the empty plate aside, Lia watched the concern shift on Terranth's face. "These other worlds," he asked Fee. "Do you protect us from them?"

She pursed her lips. "I monitor the boundaries for Norenth. There are no threats to it."

"Yet," he said, arms crossing over his broad chest. "Boundaries are always tested."

Kayce snorted. "Between you and the Smith, we never have to worry about those again."

Fee shot him a look of annoyance.

Jace had remained unusually silent, leaning against the balcony's stone wall. A muscle feathered in his jaw as he gazed out at the kingdom. Fallon nudged his hand and Jace's fingers absentmindedly dove into the wolf-dog's scruff. He stared out at the lands and falling rivers beyond, the mist thin. Like he could look into the realm above itself.

"I knew of this," he murmured.

They all straightened.

"You knew?" Lia gaped, finally finding her voice. "How?"

"Ma and Da." He scratched at his face, where dark stubble shadowed his jaw. "They're getting ready to step down. We've been meeting to go over the castle's routines. More of the finer details."

Terranth and Kayce shared an affronted frown, but it wasn't to their brother's succession.

"I didn't know *everything*," Jace rushed to add. "I had no idea what Aurelia is, or about her grandfather's books. All they told me was that the world is part of a grander organization in the cosmos, one upheld by an order invested in making sure we thrive."

"That's sugar-coating things a bit," Kayce said. "They didn't tell you anything about these barriers thinning?"

Terranth nodded, his earlier point proven. But Jace shook his head.

"I'm not surprised," Fee sighed. "Rulers of spheres don't know much, only what Flamehearts and guardians tell them. Lia's grandfather gave us explicit orders not to interfere. Well, until now."

"Why now?" Lia asked. It struck her then that perhaps Fee knew more about her papa's research. A guardian would know about the barriers, and one to Norenth would know Papa.

"We didn't have many conversations." Fee wrung her hands, frowning in regret. "He was quite private, more so lately. But the last we spoke, he implored this of me, 'You may only make yourselves known to the Lions when Aurelia Sparks or when the darkness comes'."

"He meant the Seekers. He must have told the Lions enough so that when I did change, it wouldn't come as much of a shock." Lia's knee started to bounce slightly. She tried not to be disappointed at the vagueness in Fee's recollection. It was Papa's way. Infuriating man.

Lioness Silva's knowing gaze flashed before Lia's mind. Now, more than ever, she was certain the queen knew more than she had let on.

Terranth analyzed the kingdom, combing through valleys and rooflines, no doubt for their tactical advantages. "A darkness coming. Sir Julian made it seem inevitable."

The six-eyed owl. Was it really here?

Lia wanted the ground to swallow her up. Not her precious home. Not Norenth. Gremlins and dragons had no business disturbing their peaceful skies and lands. The owl hadn't appeared here as more than a flicker in the corner of her eye, a tickle to her ear—not enough to convince it was more than her mind playing tricks. Even though Papa believed a threat to Norenth was certain, she couldn't help but feel responsible for bringing this trouble to their doorstep. What would Aurelia do? What would she, a ranger of the floating kingdom, plan? She was in Norenth, after all. Her family wasn't here.

Find that proof.

"Did Papa—er, Sir Julian, meet with your parents recently?" Lia asked the brothers.

"The last we heard of him was that he'd gone on an emissary mission to the dwarven cities," Kayce said, eyes narrowed like he could peer into her head. "That was before he was announced—"

"But what if he wanted everyone to *think* that?"

Jace straightened. "You mean to say he told the Lions about these Seekers covertly? About what he found on them?"

Lia nodded. "I need to speak with them."

"That will be difficult," he said. "The council is holding their yearly meeting this week. Even *we* hardly see them."

"Then I'll just have to get to them the fun way." Lia couldn't help but grin. A grin that was all smuggling Harpy.

Kayce answered it with one of his own. Did his shoulders just loosen a fraction? "That's my girl." The endearment sent a traitorous flip through Lia's stomach. "We just need to make ourselves available for when the opportunity arises."

Jace sighed through his nose. "I know I should be concerned, but I fear for the realm far more than I do for my parents' sanity. They'll survive your trappings. Our world might not."

No, not if Seekers were set on deteriorating the boundaries to Earth and every world in the Emperium.

Kayce's face brightened. "Didn't your grandfather work closely with one of the other Flamehearts? The twitchy one?"

"Adrian?"

"Him! He's a bookkeeper of sorts. He might know what Julian was working on."

It was a solid lead. Whatever they found might give them some idea of where to start regarding the murderer, the Seekers' plan. Lia's knees no longer shook when she stood. "If darkness is already barging into Earth, we need to be prepared for the worst." She swallowed. "*I* need to be prepared. We'll pay him a visit while we wait on your parents."

The pen flared in agreement from her back pocket. Lia quirked a brow, pulling it free. The light burst, morphing into a blade seemingly hewn from a crystal sun catcher. Lia gasped, gripping it with both hands under the unfamiliar weight.

Everyone stood, staring at the weapon.

"Neat party trick," Kayce said.

Fee narrowed her eyes. "It's no trick. That pen will shift into anything she needs. It's connected not just to her emotions, but to her will."

"I didn't *will* a sword into being," Lia argued, watching the light shimmer in its transparency. She had no doubt it would cut like any other sword.

"No," Fee granted. "But it was your intent. You want to be ready. You want to train."

She did, but confronted with the opportunity so soon—

"This thing has a mind of its own, I swear." Lia balked. "I only meant—"

"What, exactly?" Kayce asked shrewdly. "That 'preparation' meant going to the bookstore and researching?"

Crap.

Lia swore the blade sharpened itself as she whirled on him. "Finding out Papa's projects is part of knowing the enemy, isn't it? Besides, we have an entire castle and kingdom to search in the meantime. Papa could have hidden this information anywhere, not just with the Lions."

"That's true." Terranth strolled around his younger brother, boots tapping on the stone. "But preparation is not only for the mind."

He drew his sword. And he clearly had no intention of sheathing it a second time.

There was no avoiding this.

Lia's palm sweated, but she tightened her grip. *Fine.* No time like the present to master this. To be what they—her friends, the Order, Mom and Marcus, Norenth—needed.

She could balance it all. She had to.

When light and metal clashed, sparks flew.

CHAPTER TWENTY-SEVEN

I t didn't matter that Lia had only just been inducted into the Order.

That she had endured major, intensive therapy with a Sci-Fi blacksmith for a counselor.

That she had been on a cosmic roller coaster she did *not* consent to ride.

That she had a "sparkly new toy" as Kayce liked to quip, considering he was benched with a stitched-up chest.

Oh, or the sheer fact that this all had happened *in a single night*.

Nope. Not one of those things mattered. Not when under direct tutelage from the commander of Norenth's armies.

Terranth only made her train for a few hours, mainly to analyze how the pen-sword differed from a Norenthian blade. Looking back, that was a gift. When Fee declared it was time to coach Lia back to Earth, she practically lectured Terranth's ear off regarding the hazards of working when overstimulated and exhausted, both mentally and physically.

Jace, who had stepped in to help with elbow positioning, at least had the nerve to look sheepish. But Lia knew she was like a sister to him. He wanted her to be prepared, pushed and trained at her most malleable, and she *was* grateful for it. Even if her body hated her the next morning.

Especially when her mom broke the news: it was time to go back to school.

Lia spent the next week catching up on her studies during the day while working with the Weatherstone boys at night under Fee's prudent eye. Terranth made sure to strain every muscle as they sparred. Even the ones in Lia's ears hurt. Kayce traveled with her throughout the kingdom when he didn't have duties with the Ranger's Guild. He had some cleaning up to do after their absence, but as soon as she stepped through the portal, they were off in search of anything her papa might have left about the Seekers and their plot. It was a perfect distraction from their own problems, the shift in their dynamic.

Neither of them brought up their fight.

They looked everywhere. The bookstore where Lia rented a room saw each book flipped through and upended. Every servant in the castle knew their faces as they combed the halls, every nook and cranny. But nothing availed itself. Not even in the infirmary, where Kayce spent a good chunk of time getting his stitches removed. And the Lions, it seemed, were harder to chance upon than Lia originally thought.

It was time for their next lead.

"Just try," Kayce insisted, standing in a small hallway of Castle Finerda's west wing. For the past twenty minutes, he had been trying to get her to open a portal to pay Adrian's bookshop a visit. The trouble was, Lia had yet to consciously bring a creation with her, even one she knew as well as Kayce.

"I don't even know how it works," she huffed, glaring at his boots. "Blood worked with the gremlin to send it back, but you came through while I slept. Maybe I should go to Adrian's myself. No one's supposed to know I can do this, anyway." Besides, how Veera alluded to Kayce's potential harm in the process hadn't sat well with Lia.

Kayce let out a breath, considering her. "What were you feeling?"

"When?"

"That night in our alcove." He raked a hand through his hair. "When we fell asleep."

Lia flushed, refusing to raise her gaze. The grief since then had been manageable. But opening up to him, it loosened something in her. She was always bottled up, wound so tight to keep everyone happy. That night, she'd slept without a care in the world. She couldn't linger on his warmth, the strength in his body as he held her.

"I was relaxed," she muttered. "Comfortable."

Nodding, he took her hand. "Then focus on that again. Get out of your head."

Her focus went entirely to the way their calluses aligned. His hand was warm, secure in its grip. Lia's gaze rose to find him staring down at her. Her stomach tightened, her body reacting in a way totally unproductive to relaxation. And it had nothing to do with their disagreements.

Kayce's gaze didn't waver. "Close your eyes."

Lia did. It was easier this way. She didn't want to dwell on how different he had made her feel lately. How every brush of his skin was a whisper that made her want to lean in closer. How the facets of his amber eyes burned at times when she caught his stare. How few his smiles were. Too much information was crammed into her head as it was. What if they found nothing at Adrian's? What if the Lions had no knowledge of Papa and they'd wasted their time?

"Aurelia, you're going to cut off circulation in my hand."

Her cheeks heated. "Sorry."

"Breathe. Think of flying. The wind in your hair, Paxia's strong frame beneath you." His voice was a gentle ebb and flow, lulling her from a rocky shore. "How light, how effortless it is when her wings glide over the currents. The surrounding seas, salt kissing your skin."

Her lungs loosened, her shoulders eased. Kayce brushed a thumb over her knuckles. She fell into that familiar breathing pattern, but this time, her mind turned inward, tunneling someplace warm and quiet.

A safe place, where it was just her and the soft cadence of Kayce's voice painting images in her mind. After another moment, she opened her eyes. Lia hadn't needed anything last time, but she wasn't going to take any chances. With a hand still holding Kayce's, she fished out her pen. Her mind emptied before drawing up a vision of Earth, the downtown she had walked through, an alley close to the bookshop.

An alley that would forever be burned into her mind.

She summoned every detail of that fateful day, removing the gremlin and her fear. The peace remained as she drew, and the light burned when the portal hung in the air.

"I don't know what will happen," Lia said. "So don't let go."

"Never," Kayce replied, and the two stepped into the portal.

It was a flash of light, a pervading warmth like Lia had laid out in the sun on a late spring afternoon. Then came the cars honking. Opening her eyes, Lia found herself standing inside the alleyway's entrance. Their hands remained locked.

"I did it!" she squealed, jumping to throw her arms around Kayce. He caught her, his hold tight. She could feel him smile into her hair.

"I knew you could."

Their hearts pounded as though to meet each other. It took another beat to realize their closeness before springing apart. A blush mirrored on their cheeks, smiles quick to fade. Lia forced her gaze away. They were friends. *Best friends*, she reminded herself. Not to mention he was from another realm, she was from here...she had to be over-analyzing this.

"The bookstore's this way," Lia managed before heading to the sidewalk. She swayed slightly, a rush of lightheadedness catching her off guard. Perhaps Kayce's additional weight had added some strain to the jump. It wasn't this bad every time she walked between worlds, a skill that came more easily to her with each trip. Shaking it away, Lia reoriented herself and continued.

Downtown bustled with activity. Couples and families meandered to dinner, while local restaurants with patios boasting outdoor heaters burned brightly despite the mild temperature. Lia and Kayce blended in, the latter having worn his Earth wardrobe.

The shop came into view. It was a small establishment, a whitewashed brick facade with black awnings. The name, Parchment and Leather, was inscribed in gold lettering on the window.

"If he asks how you got here, say you popped in during my sleep again."

"You're going to make it sound like I'm some lewd stalker if you keep up this excuse," Kayce said in a sour tone.

The door chimed when he opened it for her. Warm leather greeted Lia's senses, a scent of old and new books mingling together. As she took a big whiff, a satisfied smile graced her lips. No one was in the shop, at least not that she could see from the various shelves and display tables. Lia approached the antique desk, ringing the bell beside the cash register.

"Yes, yes! Apologies, I'm coming!" came the hiccupping voice. Adrian hustled from the back room, several stacks of the newest thriller in his spindly arms. "Lia—and Kacerion! I thought you had returned to Norenth."

The two shared a glance. Kayce's smile was strained. "It would seem I'm susceptible to some, ah, late-night wanderings. Weak boundaries and all."

Adrian bobbed his head and dropped the books on the desk. "Right, quite right. What can I do for you?" He seemed more comfortable here in his element than in Lia's previous encounters with him.

"I wanted to ask if you knew what Papa—um, Julian—was working on before his accident," Lia said, the smile she wore for her teachers slipping into place despite the hitch in her voice. It was hard to discuss her papa, especially since suspicions of his murder weren't common knowledge. But the floodwaters didn't rise, her chest remained calm. "I'm hoping that it might help me understand this Flameheart stuff."

"There's some, but I'm not sure how helpful it will be." Adrian pushed his glasses up, lank strands of brown hair falling forward. "Did he leave anything for you? Notes and such?"

She wasn't about to expose Papa's secret study, even if he did work closely with Adrian. Leo hadn't seemed shocked by its existence, but that didn't go for everyone else. Whatever Papa was looking into, he didn't want everyone to know. And her mom hadn't voiced anything about sharing her suspicions, either.

"He kept things cryptic about this family business. My mom is pretty strict." Lia tilted her head, deflecting. "Have there been other creations spotted since the Order meeting?"

"No more Transcriptions here since the dragon, thankfully. But, who knows what other little things we've missed?"

A shudder ran down Lia's spine. Who knows what else could be lurking on Earth, unbeknownst to the general population, for the last three years since ImaginX was established? Order secrets or not, Lia was disconcerted to hear they weren't taking their job to the level of care she would have expected. One would think they'd be on the hunt. Even Kayce wore a disappointed frown. She knew he'd be searching in a heartbeat if they weren't otherwise occupied.

Adrian looked between them, twisting his hands like he debated something before finally waving them forward. "Come this way. I can show you the last records he was going through."

Lia thanked him, her and Kayce following Adrian to the backroom. It seemed like a storage closet one would find in a bookshop, but like her papa's study, it had a secret. Adrian went to a box of dusting cloths, revealing a hidden door.

"Clever," Lia complimented. Adrian shot her a small smile before ushering them inside.

A matrix of cubes on one wall held reams of paper, scrolls that ranged from a heavy brown tone to pale yellow. The space was twice the size of her papa's secret study, leather tomes filling most of the ceiling-high shelves. Adrian moved with long strides, his narrow fingers darting for various scrolls and parchments and gathering them in his arms.

"Ever think of going digital?" Lia asked, noting an easel displaying spherical maps in a far more organized fashion than her papa's table had. "Save space, not to mention safer from damage."

And theft, she thought.

Adrian paled, the words apparently blasphemous. "These relics are treasures of our past! I would never defile them in such a manner." Shaking his head, he lowered the papers onto a cleared desk. "Most of these are on loan from the Celestium Librus, anyway."

"The Celest—what?" Lia asked, Kayce's frown echoing her confusion.

"The Celestium Librus Sphere. It's essentially a library for the Order, but only the record keepers and several leaders can check texts out. *These* are centuries old, predating even the Greek Empire."

Already Lia was itching to go. She was always most content when lost in the stacks, time disappearing. Expectations ebbing away.

As though sensing the eagerness bubbling inside her, Kayce patted her head. "Simmer down. Maybe we can get you that special membership."

She glowered while Adrian shook his head. "Those are highly improbable to get, only given out in special circumstances. The training alone to handle these records outside of the sphere—"

Kayce raised a brow. "It was a joke."

Adrian flushed at the missed social cue. Lia felt a flare of sympathy, and trying to spare him the embarrassment, she started to sift through the pages. "Papa was reading these?"

"Yes, he'd gotten that special permission I mentioned. He returned most of them about a week before his passing. Claimed it was a dead-end."

"That's a bit odd, no?" Kayce questioned. "The timing? Perhaps he found something he did not want anyone else noticing."

Subtle. Lia forced herself not to react.

The Flameheart swallowed noticeably, his fair skin turning sallow. "You say it like his death was not an accident, but measured."

Lia closed her eyes, smothering a groan. There was no taking back those words, the inference to be made. Her mom would throttle Kayce if Lia didn't do it first.

Adrian watched them from behind his thick glasses as the silence lengthened. "You *do* suspect foul play."

"We do," Lia admitted after a weighted breath. "He called my mom about some proof before he died. There are also inconsistencies with his accident. And his study was trashed after. We think he found something about *how* Seekers are thinning the barriers."

So much for keeping this to themselves.

Adrian placed a hand on the table, swaying slightly. "This...this is significant."

It was a bit of an understatement, but Lia was nervous the poor man was going to drop any second.

Adrian remained standing, looking back at the papers with clear eyes. "Your theory makes sense. Especially when aligned with these. I'd only thought he was looking into this for curiosity's sake. More of a treasure hunt of fun than anything substantial."

After shuffling through several pages, Adrian found a vellum one, far older than the rest. There were several images in reds and browns depicting an old book, rays of light pouring out. In one, the book was torn into three pieces: two halves and the spine.

The words were in Latin.

"I can't read this," Lia said lamely.

"Julian didn't insist you take Latin in school?" Adrian said, shock coloring his words.

"Mom wanted me to learn Spanish." It had been more of a fight than it should have been, until Lia acquiesced to appease her. Now, it made much more sense. Latin was the Order's language—a world Mom had wanted Lia as far from as possible.

Adrian shrugged, summarizing the text. "It's a myth, even to us. Most of our records are from after the First Rift, and having been copied several times over, details were lost. Only a few recall the Initiis."

"Your mother never mentioned that," Kayce said.

"She wouldn't have. Many Flamehearts don't believe it exists, especially in recent years," Adrian said. "But this record from one of the earlier Flamehearts tells of a book used to create all there was. That the Devourer stole it to create his world, then tear the veil."

Lia's eyes widened, recalling the story. "And then he was banished."

"Precisely."

"But what happened to this book?" Kayce asked, pointing to the image.

"According to this source, the process ripped the Initiis into three pieces," Adrian replied, adopting the tone of a lecturer before a class. "Two were lost during the First Rift. But some records mention another guardian used the remaining piece to create the Flamehearts before hiding it. There's also a theory that the piece fragmented even further, flying into the nearest hosts—the ember we all possess. Another yet is that it was the seal on the First Rift entirely—see, so many stories, yet none of us know the right one. Hence, why many believe the Book of Beginnings simply met its end. Or that even this mighty tome was pure fable. The only one, ironically."

It made sense. A tool used to create new life; a tool used to tear down the fabric of the universe. It was dangerous, powerful.

A darkness coming, Fee had told them. Perhaps this was it.

Lia ran a hand through her curls, working out several knots while speaking her thoughts aloud. "If Papa found this, could he have theorized that a piece of the Initiis is being used to reopen the First Rift?"

"If this thing is even real, it was lost several times over," Kayce countered. "How would the Seekers find it when they can't even walk the Emperium freely?"

Breathing a sigh through her nose, Lia glared at the page in demand of answers. None availed themselves.

Adrian shifted. "If you believe Seekers killed Julian shortly after coming across this information," he hedged, "perhaps there is more validity here than anyone thought."

"He would have tried to locate this book himself," Lia surmised. "To prove it exists, but also to prove that the Seekers managed to get their hands on a piece. Maybe even to protect it from them."

"We should look through his study again," Kayce said. "But later. Terranth is expecting us for training."

She wanted to rush over to the old Victorian home now, to find any scrap or sticky note mentioning the Initiis. But she wasn't about to stand up Terranth. He would make her run for the infraction, and she was still *not* a fan of cardio.

She caught Adrian's eye. "Please keep this between us, okay? I'll tell my mom, see what she thinks."

The Flameheart nodded, walking them out to the shop. "Julian was smart. He wouldn't have left such information where you or his daughter couldn't find it."

The thought should have comforted Lia, but all it did was resurrect the tide inside her—a reminder that her papa was no longer there.

CHAPTER TWENTY-EIGHT

Sensing the struggle in her, Kayce steered Lia toward a glen in the western forests once they returned to Norenth. He coached her the entire way to pour those emotions into something more productive: learning her pen.

Sword. Shield. Ax. Hammer. Bow.

All weapons familiar to Norenth, the pen could become. It had been a jolt, at first. One passing thought, and the thing would flare and shift. It was a headache focusing on a single form so it wouldn't transform mid-strike—especially when questions about the Initiis flitted like sparrows in her mind. But luckily, Lia's body hadn't merely adopted Aurelia's eyesight. She dove and struck and jumped as the ranger had trained to do since childhood.

Her body knew what to do; if only her mind would accept it.

"Stop letting your thoughts wander," Terranth instructed calmly from the side. "Let your body react."

Blowing a damp curl from her face, Lia glared across the field. She already had Kayce telling her to get out of her head—she didn't need another Weatherstone boy doing it.

"Agreed," Kayce grunted. He pushed hard, his sword swinging their crossed blades to the dirt before lunging toward her.

Lia yelped, flinching as she swung the pen and light peeled away to form a shield. Sparks rained on her sneakers until he jumped back.

"The enemy will use any distraction." Kayce adjusted his shirt, the cream cotton dark with sweat below his throat. Grabbing the hem, he pulled it up to wipe the sweat from his brow, exposing the abdominal muscles carved below tanned skin. Lia's mouth dried. Black breeches hung low on his hips, replacing his jeans—which weren't conducive to swordplay, apparently.

Lia mentally shook herself. *He* was the distraction.

"I don't want to tear your chest open!" And that was truly her hesitation. Besides, what was *with* him? It seemed with each training session he pushed her harder. So much for that moment before their Earth trip, the tenderness gone. Not to mention letting it slip to Adrian about Papa's death. Irritation powered her next strike, using the shield as a battering-ram. He swerved to miss it.

"The healer gave me the all clear for light work," he said coolly.

Lia glowered. "This is light?"

The prince shot her a grin, but it was missing its trademark wink. Something was off. And it was getting to her.

Lia leapt, swinging her shield up to hammer it against his side. Brandishing his sword, Kayce outstepped the maneuvering. She came at him again with a frustrated cry, only for him to block with the flat face of his sword, pushing against her. Her toes dug into the earth, slipping back across the grass. Sweat trickled down her temple, a damp curl falling into her eyes. Her arms strained, muscles burning until she finally dropped her shield, Kayce coming into her space instead of away. His chest pressed against her, heaving from the exertion.

His eyes were molten, lips parted as he took breath from the air between them. Any irritation she felt burned away under that stare. What was she even mad about? What were they even doing here? That shift between them hummed—

"Aurelia, you have to use your core more," Terranth chastised. "I know you have abs in there somewhere."

—and the irritation was back.

Lia took several steps from Kayce, her shield dissolving. "We've been at this for—"

"Three hours and forty-seven minutes!" Fee called from her seat on a rock beside Terranth, her powder-blue skirts arranged like cresting waves. She slipped her pocket watch away. "Which means you have at most an hour before we need to skedaddle for your beauty sleep."

"What are you, my inspirational coach?" Lia huffed.

"More like your conscience."

Kayce barked a laugh. "She has too much of her own to require two."

"You'll eat that remark." Lia glared over her shoulder. "And what's with running your mouth at the bookstore?"

Kayce sheathed his sword, avoiding her stare. "I don't know what you're talking about."

"That's wyrm crap, and you know it."

He ignored her, thoroughly intent on massaging his hand. "Ever think perhaps someone like Adrian could be useful? Sure, he's a nervous wreck, but even Leo said he worked closely with Sir Julian."

"But you didn't ask me," she countered. "Something that important involves a conversation, don't you think?"

His thumb continued to sweep back and forth over his palm. "Haven't had many of those, have we?"

Her temples pulsed; her mouth went dry. Frustration trembled in her hands. She'd thought training like this, like Aurelia, would make him move beyond their fight—she'd thought since the meeting, since the Forge, they'd been all right.

Maybe they needed to have that talk soon.

But honestly, Lia preferred hard labor for another three hours.

"As much as I would love to see you chew Kayce out," Fee said, making her way over. "Let's take a walk."

Lia scowled, earning an arched brow from Terranth before Fee guided her through the pine trees. They strolled silently, Lia's heart calming the more distance grew between her and Kayce. He hadn't even looked her way as they left. Terranth, however, let his gaze linger on the guardian.

Insufferable Weatherstones.

She kicked a branch, sending it skittering into the underbrush.

Fee arched a silver brow. "Wishing that was Kayce's shin?"

"More or less."

Fee hummed in thought, and Lia's annoyance began to dissipate. The guardian had proven to be an amusing addition. She was outspoken, to say the least. Never afraid to say the truth. Lia appreciated that.

When they came to a small creek bending through the woods, Lia turned to her. "Let me have it."

"Let's put your rightful irritation with Kayce aside for a moment." Fee assessed her with swirling, purple eyes. "You doubt yourself too much. But you already knew that."

"Of course I did," Lia muttered, watching her friend stoop to examine a school of silverfish dart by. "It's a chronic character flaw."

"Ha-ha," Fee mocked. "Don't *do* that."

"What?"

"Belittle yourself. It does nothing but make people pity you."

Lia flinched. Perhaps she should treasure Fee's bluntness a little less.

Because the guardian wasn't done. "When you do that, it makes it easier for others to keep you down in a fight. You don't want to give them any opportunity, especially if you're distracted by giving yourself a pity party." She stood, her manicured hands gripping Lia's arms. "You are capable, Lia. Why do you insist you're not to the point that you're psyching yourself out?"

She chewed on her lip. Lia hated being called out, but she couldn't say Fee was wrong. "I guess because all my life, I've never been *this*—a fighter. Just a reader. I don't even do cardio."

Not that Mom never tried. Nope. Lia had been perfectly content, sitting in bed with a book until a permanent indentation formed. Her mom could run around the neighborhood as many times as she wanted. Running, but never really going anywhere. How pointless.

"At least it's not drugs," her mom would lament when she was denied in favor of literature.

Great priorities.

"Why do you read?" Fee asked.

"Because I want to escape," Lia answered. No deep thinking required there. Reading was her getaway from the anxiety, from the pressures to ease everyone else's burden. "It makes me feel...anchored."

"Anchored," Fee echoed, nodding. "And why would getting lost in your head do that?"

Why would it? Perhaps because she wasn't lost. Not when she was racing through skies, sailing on ships, swooning over romances. When the stakes were high, a fantasy world at stake, her heart raced, but it *settled*. She settled into her skin when she read, when she explored. Fought alongside found families. Championed those suffering. Solved mysteries and ancient curses.

She wasn't getting lost in her head.

She was being found.

"I don't have to be anything but what I choose to be," Lia realized.

Fee smiled. "Exactly. You choose. Choose to believe in what your body knows. Choose to be more than who you think you're limited to being. Just like you chose that memory to give into forging your pen."

Lia wanted to grip those words in her heart and step into Aurelia's shoes completely. But they still felt too big. And the issues Lia had to grapple with couldn't be left behind, not when doubts circled her mind like vicious, starving vultures.

Doubts about her place in an Order that had continued to monitor her progress. The Seekers. The nightmares on Earth. About Mom and that silent, wary gaze etched on her face when she thought Lia wasn't looking. About Marcus, who pestered Lia for stories about her training, about what the other starlit plane was like. Kayce's words, implying that she could just *be Aurelia* like it was a flip of a switch. As real as he was. His silence on the matter since hadn't helped.

Then there was her papa. His death.

As though sensing Lia's mounting anxieties, Fee caught her attention. "Remember when you were falling through the spheres?"

"How could I forget?"

The guardian gave her a deadpan glare. Lia dropped the sarcasm, nodding for her to continue.

"Chaos was all around you, and you were able to find peace," Fee said. "What did you think of?"

Lia scuffed the ground with her toe. It had been terrifying—falling with no control. She had been utterly helpless. Except, she really hadn't been. She'd thought of home. Of Norenth. The one place that was always with her. But even beyond the kingdom, the crisp pine to her nose and mist on her cheeks that she could recall, it was the feeling it drew. The comfort of home, of belonging. It was like when she brought Kayce through to Earth.

"Here," Lia answered. "And how I feel when I am here."

"That peace can always be found. You can be still—even in freefall." Fee softened before pulling Lia in tight, the pressure of the hug smoothing the knotted thoughts in Lia's head.

The predators retreated, doubts snarling off into the dark. But there was still that uneasiness, the pricking of her skin. Looking over Fee's shoulder, Lia scanned the branches. A shadow flickered before fluttering out of sight.

"You don't need everything around you to go right for you to *feel* right," Fee assured. "You don't need everything to be resolved."

Lia squeezed back, nodding into her shoulder. She would try. She wanted to, she really did. But here was the thing about anxiety. Just when you thought you had eluded it, it was there, lurking—waiting—in the shadows of your mind.

And it was always hungry.

Voices filtered through the floorboards when Lia stepped through the portal into her bedroom late that evening. It was well past dinnertime, and Fiore ran in, paws slipping like she couldn't get under the bed fast enough.

Someone was here. The poor thing hated strangers.

The voices grew clearer as Lia tiptoed out to the stairwell.

"Where are his notes, Leo?" her mom hissed low. "I know there are more."

"You saw what Julian had," Leo stated, his voice low and level.

"That's not true, and you know it. I hadn't been in that room for a while, but I know him. Papa would have had dozens of notes and ideas beyond the few pinned to his corkboard."

Mom must have meant the hidden study. The corkboard had been an intricate web of newspaper clippings and notes filled with questions. Now, it sounded like it was nearly empty. Lia edged several steps on the balls of her feet before sinking onto the top step. Her hands fidgeted. Straightened her leggings.

"Seeker research was not his job. Why would he have pieces of it on display for all to see?" Leo implored.

"Only you and I knew about that room."

Silence before Leo's voice rumbled. "What are you implying, Cordelia?"

Lia gripped the banister.

"He called me that night," her mom said. "He was coming here, he'd found proof. *Actual* proof on the thinning veil beyond his theories."

"Then why not share it with the rest of us?" A muffled thud sounded, like someone threw their hands up in exasperation.

"Because he was killed for it!" her mom shrilled in a terse whisper. "He didn't trust *anyone*! So where—are—his—notes?" Each enunciated word was a punch for Leo's throat.

Lia didn't dare breathe.

"I want to know how the rifts are worsening," Leo uttered. "I hate that Julian didn't trust me. But I didn't overturn his study before your daughter came over." A ragged breath sawed up the stairs. "I didn't *kill* him."

Closing her eyes, Lia rubbed her face. The grief in Leo's tone mirrored her own. Mom's. Everyone in the Order's. Her papa's absence was a festering wound to so many.

Her mom's voice lowered. "I respect you, but I knew my father a great deal. He was worried, he—"

A pause. Lia held her breath.

"He what, Cordelia?"

Another beat. Lia's lungs burned.

"There was something else on his voicemail. Besides mentioning he'd found proof. He said he was concerned about how Imag-inX advanced their technology so fast. How their tech went from cheap plastic to genuine products that sent the company's stock skyrocketing." Her mom's voice trembled on her next breath. "He said they would need intimate knowledge of the Emperium, how traveling through portals to the different spheres works."

Lia's stomach flipped. Mom had left this out entirely. But she hadn't mentioned a lot of things.

"What are you suggesting?"

"*He* was suggesting a Flameheart helps them."

Lia bit back another gasp, curling her knees into her chest.

But Leo laughed. "A traitor to the Order? Impossible."

"Is it, though?" Mom rushed. "Leo, it's the only thing that makes sense. They've been trying for centuries. Seekers cannot access that plane except in their dreams, and only single spheres at that. Who better to recruit than one who isn't so limited?"

"It goes against our oath."

She scoffed. "As if that's ever stopped anyone. Just look at our government. History!"

Silence ticked on before Leo spoke again. "You think Julian was looking into a potential traitor?"

"One, multiple. Who knows how deep this might go? They could be in our own chapter."

"None of us have been well since his passing. How can you say such a thing?"

"I've been looking in the wrong place, unwilling to see the truth for what it is. What he tried to warn me of before he—" Mom choked, emotion gripping her.

Light flared in Lia's pocket. She pressed a hand to her mouth, bending over her knees. A traitor? Someone she may have even *met* killed her papa, or organized it at the very least?

Breathe. Focus. Breathe.

She steadied her breath, the pen's light dimming. Disbelief muddied her thoughts, so much that she almost missed Leo's response.

"Cordelia, I..." A pause, his voice hoarser. "You truly think so?"

"I feel it in my bones," she managed, barely suppressing her emotions. "To come to me when he was on the verge of something? Someone knew, someone close, and they didn't want him telling. They *knew* and scrapped whatever evidence was in his study."

"Julian..." Leo's voice cracked, and it was several breaths before he spoke, his voice struggling for calm. "Perhaps you just haven't found it yet. If Julian suspected one of our own, he wouldn't leave such information lying about. He would ensure it would survive beyond him. That it would be found by the right people."

Adrian had voiced the same. But like Leo, he didn't seem to consider one of their own.

Her mom laughed, breaking into a hitch she failed to smother. "Papa always had contingency plans."

Lia's heart raced. Contingency plans. If someone was betraying the Order to destroy the barriers with the Seekers, her papa would have put that information and anything about the Initiis somewhere safer than his study. Norenth was the obvious answer, but they'd been searching for a week with no luck. Maybe she had been looking in the wrong place this whole time. The thought made her sick.

"I'll do what I can on my end." Leo said as footsteps echoed toward the door. "His study will need to be combed through more thoroughly. I can tell you what I find."

"I can help. The rest of the chapter doesn't need to know. I'll say I'm packing."

The door creaked before a pause filled the air. "Does Aurelia know?"

Lia leaned forward, unwinding herself.

"She knows he was murdered. But I can't bring myself to tell her my suspicions about the Order. Not until we find Papa's proof.

She has enough to deal with right now, and I can't burden her with more."

"She is stronger than even she believes," Leo replied. "You need to give her the chance to be."

"Trust me," her mom said in a low voice. "Some truths shouldn't be shared so quickly. If I can shield her, at least for a little while, I will."

Leo hummed. Lia couldn't tell if it was in agreement or disappointment. "Be well, 'Delia."

Lia didn't want to hear anymore. She eased out of the stairwell on trembling legs, like she couldn't support the weight of all she heard. But she didn't retreat to her bedroom. Not this time.

The steps creaked as she came down, meeting her mom's wide eyes when the foyer came into view. Lia stopped on the last step.

"Lia," her mom said, mustering a thin smile. "I didn't realize you were back—"

"Do you really think Papa was killed by someone we know? A Flameheart gone to the dark side?" No minced words, no dancing around what was uncomfortable.

Her mom's shoulders sagged. "No doubt you heard my reasoning."

Lia didn't bother looking guilty. "It makes sense. I'm trying not to kick myself in the teeth for not realizing it sooner." It wasn't hard to understand why Mom would keep this from her. But the old betrayal flared, a dull sting. "Mom, you and Leo can't take this on by yourselves."

Her mom's jaw slackened. Clearly, she had been expecting something far more emotional instead of her collected demeanor. Even if Lia forced it.

"This isn't your burden to carry. It's too much, yes, but I cannot bring myself to put it on you. Focus on your training." She paused, reaching out to cup her daughter's cheek. Her smile was pained. "You think I don't see what you do? Trying so hard to make life easier on everyone else, forsaking your own limits to do it?"

Lia reached out, hugging her mom hard so that she couldn't see the exposed panic flash across her eyes. "Where do you think I learned it from?"

"Fair enough." Her body shook with bitter laughter. "It took me a long time to learn this, so I hope you'll take my advice. Sometimes, true strength lies in knowing when to step back."

Lia had done a fair amount of stepping away in her life. She wasn't certain this was one of those times. Not when Mom had kept yet another revelation from her. And shared it with someone else, before her.

They pulled apart. "Please," Mom implored. "Leave this to Leo and I. To avoid the traitor's suspicion, the less poking about, the better."

Because if he or she was willing to kill her papa, Lia knew anyone was fair game. Which is why she couldn't tell her mom about the Initiis. Not yet.

Lia donned the mask of the dutiful daughter again, but she would help her, whether her mom knew it or not. Just like she always had. But this time, Lia would need help, too.

Because, she realized, Leo had never denied taking research from her papa's study.

Nor did he react in surprise to the true circumstances of his death.

CHAPTER TWENTY-NINE

Snow was falling. It hardly ever snowed here. Given the fact it was autumn... Lia wasn't in Seattle anymore. She didn't bother clicking her heels three times.

Not as a hush fell over the world, like every living thing had burrowed deep and gone to sleep. The muddied ground muffled her steps as a path wound into the forest. Dark silhouettes of pine trees pierced through the heavy fog. They towered over her, giant spears to the dying sky.

Each breath clouded the air. Lia shivered, still in the soft cotton shorts and shirt she had gone to sleep in. Her last memory was tucking into bed, thankful for a weekend ahead without alarm clocks.

But she was more than ready to wake up now. The cold pierced her skin like tiny knives. The Order had told her dreams would still happen, that she might have an additional awareness of them; a lucid sort of dreaming. Hugging herself, she continued through this unknown world. Her heartbeat was a drum, too loud in the eerie quiet. Chills increased the further she went. Her ears and nose stung.

It unsettled her, the reality of the cold, the way her socks soaked with mud and snow, clinging to her toes. Why wasn't she waking up?

Maybe if Lia closed her eyes and focused, like when she summoned a portal, she could get herself awake. She glanced around, the darkness thickening in the wooded depths. Her skin prickled, a ringing in her ears as she strained to listen past the silence of falling snow.

All was still.

Stopping, Lia screwed her eyes shut. Okay, think of her bed: queen-sized, sage green sheets tucked in at the footboard. Her bookshelf, now arranged neatly by hardcovers and paperbacks and descending in size. The desk—

A twig snapped, like a bone breaking.

Heart palpitating, muscles tensing, Lia spun to face the sound.

Nothing moved. Not even her, as she scanned every trunk and bush. Her throat bobbed. She closed her eyes again, so hard dots danced over the darkness. Her desk had become a little more chaotic, homework waiting—

Branches shuddered, like teeth chattering.

Aurelia. Her name was a hoarse whisper.

Lia opened her eyes, but this time, she held herself frozen. A hare caught under a wolf's hungry stare. Such wolves were not asleep here. Not anymore.

Lia knew then that this was not a dream she could easily wake from—*if* she could wake at all. And she didn't need to pat herself down to know her pen hadn't made the trek.

Aurelia.

A second call made her spin once more. Yet the owner was nowhere to be found in the misty snowfall.

Aurelia.

Lia realized with sickening clarity that the voice called from *inside* her mind. Any recollection of her bedroom vanished. She stepped forward, peering around the trees.

And then the humming began. A young girl's voice carried on the wind. The lilting melody chilled Lia to the bone.

"Hello?" Lia called.

The humming continued, louder this time. Searching for the voice, Lia's focus flew to the trees. In the midst of skeletal branches and pine boughs, a pair of icy blue eyes cracked open.

From the shadows they glowed, meeting Lia's stare with a preternatural calm. The owner hugged the tree, limbs wrapped around the trunk like an ape's. After a moment, the creature began to slink down. It was too dark to fully make out, tendrils of fog and larger snowflakes blurring the creature. But one thing was evident.

It was no little girl.

Its eyes never left her. Its song never stopped. It morphed into words, that girlish voice, sweet and melodic. Sinister words.

Stench of gentleness,

Rot of love.

Peaceful destruction.

Kind degeneration.

A tail unfurled, gripping branches like an extra limb as it reached the ground. A single pawed foot stretched down to the freezing mud. Long, horn-like claws jutted from its back legs. It paused, watching Lia before the other leg lowered. The feathered tail flicked, eyes fixated.

Aurelia, came that dark timbre, reverberating in her mind.

Lia couldn't even flinch against it. Numb. Fear consumed her.

Finally releasing the tree, the creature took several steps toward her before dropping to all fours. Lia always knew nightmares were fears given claws and teeth. Doubts snarling in the dark of her mind. But nothing could have prepared her for the horror that inched closer. That froze her body more than the plummeting temperature with each step it took. That made her aware of each loud pulse of her heart, hammering against her rib cage as if desperate to flee.

It sang again.

> *Drawing the weak into its grip,*
> *Joy is all's graveyard.*
> *Hope decays the soul,*
> *Strength sapped until it is gone.*

Lia noted its limbs were hairless, but the body was covered in white feathers. Its head rotated unnaturally the opposite way as it framed her in its vision. Such a head might have looked like a wolf but tilted like an owl, those glowing eyes sunken and ringed.

Like a barred owl, she realized. The very same that had haunted her since the day her papa died. Even the snow seemed to pause, flakes hovering for a breath to see who dared move first. Lia didn't look away.

Aurelia, the voice growled in her mind. *The girl who knows not who or what she is.*

The creature loomed over her. Twin tongues shot out to taste her scent—her fear.

Tears of blood
And rivers of sorrow
Wash away the sins of faithfulness,
Cleanse the land of mercy's lies.

Glowing eyes regarded her. Lia trembled.

Do you like it? the dark voice asked inside her. *It is a pretty voice. I just* had *to keep it.*

Lia didn't bother replying. She ran. Whipping around, she slipped in the icy muck. Dodging trees, branches struck as she tried to navigate through the growing dark. The snow provided some light, the whiteness of it casting the world in a ghostly blue tone.

Feathers rustled behind her.

Come on, think. Wake up! Portal to her bedroom: bed, bookshelf, desk, Fiore—

She stumbled, flinging herself behind a tree and pressing against it in an effort to disappear. Straining to listen, Lia couldn't make out much past the blood roaring in her ears. Nostrils flared, she forced measured breaths to calm herself.

What would Kayce do? Aurelia? With no weapon, she highly doubted much.

So make one, prompted a thought that sounded like Kayce.

Lia scoured the ground—a broken branch. The bark dug splinters into her hands as she snatched it. Not like she could feel it, cold numbing to the elbows.

She inched around the tree. Nothing but snow fell. She looked back, but again, nothing. No monstrous creature that she couldn't believe someone created. Suddenly, snow fell heavily as if dusted off from above. Lia's heart sank. She raised her head.

Why do you run? Blue eyes bore down on her in an impossibly upturned face. *You and I can have much fun together.*

Its tail gripped a branch. Nimbly, the creature climbed down. Its head tilted back and around to gaze into her eyes.

I want to hear you sing—perhaps your voice sounds better than what I already have.

Lia spun off the tree, her branch upraised. "I promise, I don't even sound good in the shower." Her voice wavered as she inched back.

Her hopes were decadent, the despair delicious. Its voice slithered in her head like a serpent. *It smelled so sweet—like your own.*

The creature dropped to the ground.

Lia's whole body clenched, waiting for it to strike, to snatch her up—like those vicious doubts that had circled back from her training. Part of her hoped it would just do it already, to save her from the madness of anticipation.

But I also smell smoke, flames—the ember inside you. Circling her, the beast cocked its head. *It would seem you are the one Father is so intrigued by. How pleased he will be—*

"Your father?" Lia was unnerved that it may have read her mind, never allowing it to leave her sight. "He'll have to be disappointed. Common expectation for parenthood."

She didn't think—she couldn't anymore, muscles wound too tight, heart pumping so hard and fast that her bones practically vibrated. Lia lunged, jagged splinters swinging toward the creature's lupine head. The creature twitched to avoid the strike, but the stick caught part of its head, splinters digging into its eye.

Tarry blood spurted forth, and it screeched in a voice that tore the very air apart. A discordant harmony between male and female, ear-splitting highs and thundering lows. It would chill the blood of any hardened warrior. Even Terranth would have found himself hard pressed to remain calm.

The male voice raged in Lia's head, hissing in anger and pain. *You will pay dearly for that, daughter of flame!*

Lia regained her footing and pulled back to swing again. But not fast enough.

Lashing out just as quickly, the creature's claws carved deep into Lia's waist. Skin split, creating gullies. Blood seeped from the wound as the monster hissed and lashed out once more.

Lia screamed, voice catching on a sob. The pain snatched her breath. Why couldn't she wake up? Lia nearly sobbed the thought aloud, stumbling back.

Your soul is ours, young Flameheart!

"No!" Lia cried, despite her hip burning, pain searing, heart bursting—

She bolted upright, damp shirt clinging to her skin. Scrambling, she beat against the mattress, the sheets tangled around her legs.

Home. She was home, in bed—awake.

Lia laughed out a shaky breath, a sound delirious with relief. She collapsed against the pillow, shivering despite the warmth.

No splinters in her hands. No painful gash in her hip. Just a dream. A frighteningly real one. She needed to have a serious sit-down with the Order about some sleeping medication. Perhaps even therapy. Lia would prefer the latter, considering the roller-coaster that had been her life this past month. Maybe she could pay Smithy another visit.

As Lia shifted, a twinge pulled on her side. Clenching her teeth, she lifted her shirt. Through the dim light filtering through the window, Lia could make out four ridges of puckered pink.

Lia whimpered and traced them, the stinging nearly engulfing her side. Seeking comfort, she reached for Fiore—only to find the bed empty.

The prissy thing *always* slept with her.

The shadows in her room seemed to pulse. Her muscles froze as she analyzed each one. The sense of foreboding only writhed deeper inside her gut. The hairs on her arm stood on end. Lia held her breath.

Until the humming came.

CHAPTER THIRTY

No. No, not here.

But there was no mistaking that voice—it would haunt her for the rest of her life. Gooseflesh broke over Lia's skin as terror seized her throat. Her eyes drifted to where the voice had called, the sickeningly sweet melody cloying at her.

> *Discipline binds the heart,*
> *Patience festers like mold.*
> *To give is to take,*
> *To take is to give,*
> *A world reborn through suffering.*

One blue orb glowed from the ceiling, the other filled with ruined, black-bloodied flesh. The beast had dug its claws into the sheetrock.

This is a pleasant surprise. It tilted its head. *I must thank you for bringing me here.*

Her blood. Just as her blood alone had sent the gremlin away, it had brought this nightmare back to Earth when mixed in the fray.

A gift, twisted into a curse.

I have always wanted to see Earth, the creature continued in her mind. *Father had told me such wonderful stories. Though much seems to have changed.*

Dread pooled like oil, sticking to every thought to paint her with guilt and shame. But there wasn't time for that. Not when claws dragged over the ceiling. When heavy breathing broke the silence.

When her family slumbered down the hall.

Stop thinking, Terranth and Kayce had said. *Let your body react.*

How could she not think about her cat missing, her brother down the hall—

Lia dove for the bedside table and rolled to stand. Light flourished, the pen shifting into a blade and casting the room in a prism of colors. Unearthly, the creature's eyes reflected it, narrowing with a growl.

"This world isn't yours," she said, far braver than she felt. "You'll have to fight me for it." Perhaps if she faked it, she would make it true. But the words rang hollow, even to her.

Light, girlish laughter filled the room. *You can't be so naïve, little Lia.*

Such a sneer on her preferred name made her want to run into the closet. The creature's claws retracted, its body flowing like a cat's to land on its feet. Lia tried not to dwell on the disquieting knowledge that it knew her—knew her well. And failed.

He will soon destroy the barriers between Earth and the Emperium. He will release power, allow creation and destruction even here. All stories will become one. The Emperium, the precious spheres—he will glutton himself on the endless stores of creativity.

Its father, its family. Realization hit Lia like a towering wave, dread sweeping to consume her. It belonged to Malum.

"That's a lie," Lia spat. "The Devourer is gone, and his Seekers would destroy this world, all worlds, for their own gain."

These people who followed Malum's ghost—workers for ImaginX and backstabbers like the Flameheart who murdered her papa—didn't care who they cut down in their path. So long as they absolved their own greed.

Widening her stance, Lia shifted the sword. "You would devour *everything*."

The nightmare crouched, its tail flicking slowly. Sizing her up. *It is unfortunate you will not see it.*

A bone-chilling scream sliced the air before the beast launched at Lia, careful to avoid the sword. It slashed and snapped within inches of her face, but she dipped to the side. The two tumbled to the floor.

Pain barked up her spine, her limbs twisting. Light flared, and Lia pushed against the creature, its claw snatching at the air. It grabbed a fistful of hair and yanked. She yelped, tears springing to her eyes as she tore free. Several copper curls remained in its grip.

The creature snarled, tossing the strands aside, and watched while Lia scrambled up, parrying its next strike with her sword.

"Lia?" a voice called from the hall.

"Marcus, stay out!" Lia screamed before dodging another swipe. She prayed he'd listen this time.

Her pen flared once more, shifting into an axe, the pick at the back as sharp as the edge on the front. Kayce would have been proud. She swung, the light of stars whistling through the air toward the creature's head.

It hissed and grabbed her arm, halting the swing before yanking Lia to the side. She careened into a bookcase, shelves breaking and books raining.

Oh, this thing was *definitely* dead.

Before Lia could drag herself out of the mess, the nightmare lunged—and its teeth sunk into her thigh. She screamed, muscle and tissue ripping apart. Blood spilled.

You are mine. Its eye glowed as scarlet welled over yellowed daggers. *I will take everything!*

Lia screeched against the pain, swinging the pick of the axe down into the beast's hunched back. It wailed, releasing her leg. Black blood ran over its shoulders. It coated the axe, which shifted at the next thought into a pen again. Leo had needed to write with the dragon's blood to Transcribe it back to its sphere. She had no idea what words he'd written to do it—

But Lia did not need to.

She slammed the pen into the gushing wound at her thigh, the black blood burning as it met her own. Light enveloped the room, the creature twisting as the fringes of its being started to smolder and curl and shrink like burning paper.

When the barriers crumble and Malum is freed, daughter of flame, it cried with chaotic dissonance, torn between male and female, old and young, *there will be no place in all the realms you can hide. The hunter is coming.*

Flames engulfed the nightmare until only smoke lingered. Even the blood on Lia's pen and in her wound sizzled out of existence. If only the same could be said of her fear.

The Seekers were not only hungry for power; they wanted a leader. Not one to be *like* Malum. But to return him from exile.

"Lia?" Marcus's voice was soft, unsettled. "Are you all right?"

She took a shuddering breath, wincing. There was no making light of this. No way to spin it so it seemed like she was fine. Lia bit back a whimper at her leg, blood flowing steadily from the bite. She was growing tired of almost being made a meal.

Raising her head, she took in the books and broken shelves strewn across the floor. The nightstand lay in ruins, crushed during the fight. The lamp lay shattered next to it. Sheetrock hung from the ceiling in splintered chunks. Claw marks gouged the floor.

At Lia's prolonged silence, Marcus opened the door. His eyes darted over the wreckage before landing on his sister. He paled at the sight of her. "What happened?"

The next words burned like bile. But they needed to be said—the small, vulnerable piece of her that was that little girl alone at her birthday was desperate for it.

Tears stung her eyes. "I don't know, exactly," Lia said, forcing her voice to stay even. "But I need you to call Mom. Tell her to come home."

He jerked a terse nod before disappearing. The fear in his boyish face unsettled Lia more than her injuries.

Gritting her teeth, Lia held back curses as she hobbled to the bathroom, the pen locked in her grip. She wasn't getting her room in order before her mom returned from the hospital. But the least Lia could do was make herself look like less of a mess. Even if that small piece inside her demanded she sink to the tile floor and sob, waiting for her mom to come take care of her.

Mom has troubles of her own. Dig deep. Don't scare Marcus. The thoughts trickled in, as they always did. Eager to please. Eager to soothe. Eager to push Lia aside.

For the first time in a long while, she had asked for help. But here she was, stumbling two steps back. The energy to fight those old habits was gone. She was too tired, too hurt, to even muster a spark.

Grabbing the first aid kit, Lia got to work. But not without the thoughts slithering through her mind. If that creature could be brought here. If the gremlin had gotten here. Was Norenth's barriers not far behind Earth's weakened ones?

Those ringed eyes haunted her.

Or were nightmares already there?

CHAPTER THIRTY-ONE

Even at seventeen, there was still comfort in curling up in the center of her mom's bed, wrapped in one of her towels. The floral scent of her perfume clung to the fabric as it enveloped Lia, water dripping from her curls. It was a familiar scene of years past, though no one said it—Lia instead of Marcus trembling on the bed from night terrors.

But these weren't phantom wounds. These were real.

Minute, pink streams ran down the swell of her thigh, staining the gray terrycloth underneath. Better than the scarlet rivers that had roared down the drain. Lia traced the indents burrowed into her palm where she'd bitten down to stop herself from screaming. Marcus didn't need to hear that again.

She pinched them anew as her mom doused the divots in her thigh with alcohol.

Lia didn't even whimper. Granted, she had done it to herself twice already before her mom had rushed in, a maternal hurricane tempered only by the medical situation at hand. With no questions asked, she'd dove right into action. Into mending. Lia hadn't resisted being ushered away from her destroyed bedroom down to where their mom slept.

Now, Mom dabbed at the gouges with a gauze pad. The nightmare's teeth were larger than the gremlin's had been, but shallow enough that butterfly bandages were enough to pull the gashes closed.

An uneasy Marcus hovered in the doorway, grocery bag in hand already half-filled with soiled supplies. The joke on how at least they didn't need another bag of fluids in the living room hung on Lia's tongue, but exhaustion held it. Weariness darkened soft circles beneath their mom's eyes. Lia was certain she had some of her own.

As her mom had taken inventory of the nicks and scratches, the bite wound in her thigh, the soreness of her back that would bruise by morning, Lia spoke softly of the nightmare. The snow-quiet forest. The horrid song. The creature that sang it. The fight Lia mustered.

The mistake she made. The pen-less Transcription.

It was the gremlin all over again. Except now Lia knew she wasn't losing her mind. Now, it was much worse.

Only when finished wrapping the gauze around her leg did her mom sit back to regard her and speak. "This creature. Did it say anything to you?"

Lia stared at the comforter. Her mouth was cotton, her throat sand. Never would she forget that voice. She swore she could hear it even now, as the wind whistled against the windowpane. "It mentioned Malum," she whispered, voice cracking. She cleared her throat. "It kept referring to him as its father. That he was active, somewhere. That he would destroy the barriers and release the Emperium's power so people could create here."

Mom balled her hand into a fist. "Those foolish Seekers want power, so what makes them think the Devourer wants more than utter destruction?"

"What if he doesn't?" Marcus blurted out, joining them on the bed as they stared dumbly at him. "If the barriers are destroyed, Seekers would be able to do whatever they wanted in reality. But they wouldn't release the biggest bad of the multiverse if he was going to end everything. It's counterproductive. Malum wouldn't simply devour everything; he'd remake it into what they want. They could enslave humanity, and Malum would consume anyone or anything that stood in their way."

"How does that make sense?" Mom inquired. "That's not what the legend says. He wants to consume all, destroy it."

"That's just it. 'The legend says'. But what if what the Order has been telling the Flamehearts for centuries isn't the *full* truth? Maybe it's the victor's version."

Lia had promised to tell her brother all she knew. But now he was putting the pieces together faster than her.

"*Why* would he only want to destroy everything?" he repeated, looking at both of them expectantly. "*Why* would the Seekers want to free Malum only to watch him destroy everything, including them? Does that really make sense?"

It wasn't the apprehensive ramble like when Marcus had first heard the Devourer's name. It was cold clarity, a list of facts. A resignation beyond his years.

Every villain needs a sympathetic motive.

Lia's jaw slackened. Papa's knowing smile emerged on Marcus's face as he watched the realization dawn. She thought back to the imagination story. What if it wasn't only to let her know about her identity and the weakening barriers?

What if it was a clue about why Malum had done this in the first place?

Their mom reached out to smooth Marcus's hair. "I see your point. But regardless of the whys, what matters is that it's happening. And that creatures like Lia's nightmare are only a glimpse at what would ruin this world if the barriers fall."

A chill ran down Lia's spine. She hated how there was no hiding from this. Hated the blood staining another one of Mom's towels. Hated not being in control.

"I'm sorry." The words squeezed out, her voice cracking once more.

Mom and Marcus frowned, their mom speaking first. "Whatever for?"

Disappointing you. Worrying you. Causing you to miss work on top of everything else we're dealing with. Having abilities no other Flameheart has—ones that put a target on my back.

But Lia didn't say any of those things. She shrugged, looking down at the bandage. She pulled the hem of her cotton shorts to cover it. "I didn't mean to bring that thing here."

Her mom's face softened, and she reached for her arm. "You didn't learn to ride a bike in a day, or drive a car. This ability you have, it'll take time to master." Tension chiseled new creases in her brow. "But time is not a luxury we have. Not anymore."

Lia closed her eyes. Failure was nearly as suffocating as grief.

Because even though she'd held her own against that hellish creation, it ended in burdening those she loved. Something she pushed herself never to do. Despite the triumph, that failure had become a familiar, loathsome aftertaste burning the back of her mouth.

"It also mentioned the hunter is coming." Lia recalled before opening her eyes. "Is that another name for Malum?"

Mom stiffened, the blood draining from her face. Silence filled the room for a moment before she finally spoke. "You need to train your mind, Lia," she implored. "More than pen exercises."

"What do you mean?" Lia sat straighter, anxiety the puppeteer to her strings.

Their mom stood, packing the first aid kit and collecting the bloodied rags. She didn't speak, taking the trash bag from Marcus.

"Mom?" Lia's heart pounded as she watched. She hated the withdrawn silence, seeing Mom tunnel within herself as she no doubt worked through several thoughts simultaneously. Leaving Lia and Marcus on the outside, with no chance of peering within. Was it as tumultuous as the seas that raged in Lia, the squalls she was desperate to quell?

Finally, their mom stopped and turned to Lia. "I'm sorry. I just—" She hesitated and took a deep breath. "This is so much bigger than you realize. It seems you can access spheres that don't belong to you when you sleep. Even bring things back to the waking world. You need to learn how to discipline your mind—before you find yourself in a situation you cannot escape from." She paused, taking Lia's face in her hands. "You have done so well with this. No one's mad at you. But I can't bear the thought of something else coming here and hurting you."

Lia frowned, unable to reign in the sarcastic bite to her tone. "What's bigger than I realize? Nightmares roaming the earth seems pretty big."

Dropping her hands, their mom stared out the window. "There's more I have to tell you. It's important, but it can wait until you've mastered this gift."

Irritation broke through the fog that fear and failure had clouded in Lia's mind. Again with the secrets. She was already keeping this gift a secret from the Order. There was no control left in her to be quiet and accept this. "Just tell me—"

"Not yet!" The words were a bite into Lia's resolve, her mom's tone a slap that left her spinning. And in her mom's eyes, a rawness Lia had never seen. They stared at each other, everything left spoken and unspoken to hang in the air.

And Lia saw. They were *all* fraying at the seams.

Lia pulled at her fingers, picking at the thin skin of her pinky. Her mom's hands fisted, relaxed, fisted, relaxed...

And it was Lia who broke the fraught silence first, Marcus's presence nearly pulling the air from her lungs. She nodded, looking away from her mom. She'd listen. She'd train her mind. She'd make it safe for them.

And her mom would tell her everything.

"Soon?" she managed.

"Soon," came the whispered reply.

Shoulders bowing, their mom tossed the medical debris to the top of her dresser. She motioned for all of them to climb beneath the covers. Despite everything, it was the familiarity Lia needed to find comfort.

Their mom's copper hair slipped free of its clip as she reached for the lamp. "The Devourer is where he belongs. It's the Order's duty to ensure of that."

The reassurance was soft, as if their mom didn't quite believe it; said it for the comfort of the room, though no goodnight murmuring could make it so. And from what Lia had seen of the Order, the legend they maintained, she struggled to have confidence in them also.

As their mom turned off the light, the crystal nib of her pen shone dully on the sheets.

CHAPTER THIRTY-TWO

It felt like walking through tar, like the very air itself was thickening to prevent her next step. Lia pushed through, gritting her teeth against the screeching that filled her head. The ringing that reverberated in her skull—until it all stopped.

The hand that gripped Lia's squeezed.

Lia took a ragged breath as her companion looked cautiously about the destroyed bedroom, holding Lia's clammy hand as they finished stepping through the portal. The sudden quiet was too loud. Too familiar to that snowy wood, despite the traffic that blared down the street. The Emperium's light faded behind them. Even with the sunlight streaming through the window, Lia over-analyzed every shadow. She hadn't been in here since last night. The bruised muscles in her back were taunt, pulled so tight she was surprised they hadn't snapped over her spine. She blinked hard as the room swayed, vertigo overwhelming her senses.

Bringing a guardian to earth was far more draining than bringing Kayce.

After several slow inhales, Lia's vision stopped swimming.

"This feels so wrong. I really shouldn't be here," Fee reminded her once more. She smoothed the invisible wrinkles of her designer blouse, which melted to transform into a simple white tee, denim coveralls forming into place.

But Lia couldn't think, couldn't see anything but the monster bearing down on her, her thigh aching—

Words tumbled free of her chapped lips with a deep exhale. "I have these unique powers that no Flameheart can really teach me to use. I was chased into reality by a nightmare claiming to be Malum's child, singing about how his daddy wants me for some reason before biting a chunk out of my leg—while also claiming that what the Order says about the Devourer isn't quite true, that he doesn't want to destroy but to enslave everything. My mom is holding more secrets from me, staying all cryptic and won't tell me why. Meanwhile, Kayce keeps *spilling* secrets and yet won't look me in the eye. And it's not like I can tell Suzy-Ann from my favorite coffee shop about my problems!"

The room was still. Lia took another breath. "So, no. You being here isn't at the top of my list. In fact, as my mom suggested, you're the only one who can really help me with the first one. Therefore"—Lia waved to where the portal had disappeared, then back to the shambles around them—"here we are. Can you use a dustpan?"

Fee stared at Lia a moment before closing the distance between them and enveloping her in a tight hug. Lia stiffened at first with a hiss, bruises throbbing, but the longer Fee held on to her, the more she relaxed into the embrace. After verbally vomiting all over someone, a hug was expected. She could take the comfort—but she couldn't let her walls crumble. She had to be stronger.

Lia exhaled deeply, allowing herself to lean into Fee just enough for the waters to recede and pull the tension from her body like sand to the depths. To have a friend to confide in, it kept the tide at bay. Blink by blink, brick by brick, Lia refortified the walls inside her.

Pulling away with concern giving way to a wry smile, Fee snapped the straps of her coveralls. "I wouldn't have swapped for these if I couldn't."

The pure selflessness of Fee's attire loosened the knot in Lia's throat—especially when she didn't push further on Lia's tirade. It was enough vomiting for one afternoon. When she had awoken that morning to a text from her mom about work and getting Marcus to school, she hadn't minded the quiet house. Fiore had been curled into her side, the feline unscathed. But that relief had been short-lived, the clock's ticking in the hall too loud, the toaster popping burnt waffles bringing a scream that itched her throat.

She had wanted Kayce.

But he had been so *off* lately, not to mention she was still a little pissed at him. Her mom's mention of the guardian was appreciated. Besides, having someone so outside of her problems was refreshing. Figuring that Fee could deduce something Lia had missed, she told her everything as they set about cleaning her bedroom. What her and Kayce discovered about the Initiis. Her mom's suspicions about a Flameheart gone dark and Papa's murder. Her powers, from the gremlin to now. Then of course, the nightshriek—a name invented by Marcus to make the creature feel less ominous.

Clearing the lump in her throat, Lia straightened a pile of books she'd stacked. "Do you think the Order needs to know about the Transcription?"

"They already do," Fee said as she swept sheetrock dust into a pile. "From what I've been told, Flamehearts in the vicinity feel something like a knot loosening in the chest each time a creation is sent back. It was a defense mechanism, back when creations ran rampant and Flamehearts needed help from others nearby."

"Would they know it was me?" Lia asked, thinking of the gremlin as well.

"Likely not. But they will suspect, given everything with creations in this area involves you." Lia glared at Fee, the guardian's bluntness chipping at the meager mask she'd thrown on. Fee arched a silver brow. "It's basic probability, Lia. Not much to like about it, but it's the truth."

Speaking of truth, Mom had probably told Leo. The thought turned Lia's stomach. She didn't know who to trust, even if Mom did. Lia busied herself with straightening the stack so the spines aligned. Again. "If we're talking 'truth', what about the Flameheart helping the Seekers? Do you have any guesses on who it is?"

"The Flameheart responsible for your papa's death is no friend to guardians, that much I can say." Fee's tone had shifted. It wasn't the glittering dryness of her laughter and or the cold ferocity of her truths. It was the intense burning in stars—and the darkness between them. Even the stars in her eyes guttered, eclipsed before flaring once more. "But I don't know any of this chapter's Flamehearts personally enough to guess."

It registered for Lia then how much she didn't want to get on a guardian's bad side. Thank the skies and seas this anger was in response to Papa's murder. A powerful ally, even with her small stature. Not that she would even ridicule Fee for *that*—at least not now.

"Papa hid everything because he didn't know who to trust in his own secret society," Lia grumbled, starting a new stack of paperbacks. "Yeah, there's only six of them here, but what about the whole Order? Maybe it was someone he crossed paths with in another chapter, set in another country. Skies, it could be another *guardian* gone bad—"

"Breathe, Lia. Mere speculations aren't going to avail an answer." Fee set the broom aside, reaching for Lia's arm. "You need to give yourself a break. You keep trying to tackle all of this by yourself. Take a step back and let others help you."

Shame burned Lia's cheeks, but it was like her tongue had a mind of its own. Her conflicting emotions were eroding the wall she'd only *just* repaired.

The desire to figure things out with Kayce.

The need to watch out for her family.

The fear of knowing Malum's creatures marked her.

The frustration at the lack of justice for her papa.

And the last mirrored in her mom's face last night, the lines at her eyes deeper than they had been a month ago. Lia couldn't afford to take a break.

Huffing a sigh, Lia strode to an upended box, the one she had brought from her papa's attic. Papers and drawings scattered over the floor, and she hid her frustrations by collecting the papers to be returned to their rightful home. She wasn't even seeing what was on them until a sticky note with painfully familiar handwriting snagged her attention.

It wasn't much. It was only a sentence. But it was enough. Because it was for her.

Little Lion,

You don't have to smell like the fire you walked through.

Papa

Lia's throat tightened. The note trembled in her grip—and hardly made much sense at all.

It filled her with equal parts elation and dismay. This was a clue. But what in skies and seas did it mean? She rifled through the rest of the papers, hunting through the crayon drawings and regressions of handwriting from her youth for what the note had been stuck to.

A page of printer paper, still crisp, was at the bottom. She had never seen it before. It was a photocopy of the vellum page Adrian had shown her and Kayce. So much for a "dead end".

Papa had set this aside for her. The note proved it. Only he ever called her "little lion". He wanted her to see he knew the Initiis was at play. That its pieces were no longer scattered to unknown corners of the Emperium. Lia stared at the note. *Walking through fire.* It might have something to do with being a Flameheart. But what? It didn't make any sense.

But here was proof. She had no idea how it got there, what it all meant. And it was likely no coincidence that the imagination story had come from this box as well.

Fee frowned as Lia handed the paper over to her, eyes roving over the Latin words. "This is about the Initiis. Didn't you say that you and Kayce discussed this with Adrian?"

Lia nodded. "Yeah, as a theory, but I packed *this* from Papa's attic during the funeral. It was with my old Norenth stuff." She had completely forgotten about it in the midst of everything.

Stupid, this should have been the first place you looked. How much time would you have saved? Wasted, precious time wasted—

"I didn't think this was real," Fee interrupted Lia's relentless self-talk. "I'm relatively young by guardian standards. No one talks about it, or the First Rift. Too taboo."

"Think it's something worth killing over?" Lia dared to ask.

Fee perched on the bed, gazing at the paper with a studious eye. "It may indeed be part of it. If half of what it says about the Initiis is true and your grandfather found the location of a piece, then yes. It's motivation for murder."

Lia took the page back. "Papa's attic may be where he hid everything. Kayce and I suspected as much before…"

It's too much.

Lia squashed the tiny, pathetic piece of her. She didn't need those loathsome thoughts, not right now. Not when she felt she stood on the precipice of figuring this all out.

As the text said, perhaps this truly was part of how Malum consumed a sphere in the first place. More secrets, more stones to the mound of her papa's grave.

Lia couldn't dwell on that—not when she had a lead.

There were at least a dozen trunks full of paperwork that couldn't fit in his office. Norenth histories, character profiles, political mappings. Not to mention some of Lia's notebooks and art projects from grade school. The box she had thrown together was only a fraction. But what better place to hide information on a cosmic artifact than an old man's packrat paradise?

"That's a lot to go through," Lia said. "Papa was old school, that's for certain. But we need to get those trunks out of there until we can comb through everything. Whoever broke in last time could return, despite the additional security measures my mom installed."

"Where would be safe?"

Lia chewed her lip, a pained look to her eye. "Could you ask Kayce if we could store them in the castle?" she asked. "It's the only other place I would trust."

Fee frowned. "Couldn't you?"

Lia didn't want Kayce to see her like this, limping and bruised. Not until she stopped jumping at every shadow. She already knew he would have a mouthful to say about it. Thankfully after a long look, Fee didn't press.

Norenth was more fortified than anything. But Lia's fear rose. If she brought sensitive material to Norenth, was she inviting trouble to their doorstep? Creepy owls, they could handle. No doubt Terranth would see them stuffed and mounted throughout Castle Finerda.

Gremlins, dragons, and nightmares were a different story.

Lia hated the risk, but she knew the boys would agree it was the best place.

Fee cocked her head, the clear beads at the ends of her braids clicking together. "You know, those trunks aren't light. It would be nice to have a few extra arms to haul those boxes back into Finerda. I'll get the Weatherstone boys to help us. Besides, with everything that transpired, some handsome, muscular boys to ogle would be a nice distraction."

Lia's neck heated. "I can't believe you said that."

"It pays to be honest."

"You're not getting paid at all."

"Shame. We really need to set up an Emperium Workers Union." Fee crossed her legs as demurely as though she wore a gown of fine silk. "Training exercise: bring the boys here."

All four of them? Sure, Lia needed the help and it would be good for honing her abilities, but her mom would kill her. Though securing research that got Papa into this mess might take precedence.

"No one can know what I can do," Lia warned. "They're to stay inside the entire time. It would be too suspicious if any of the Order saw them walking about. The same goes for you."

"Think you could get Terranth a pair of jeans?" Fee grinned as though the desert buffet had just opened their doors.

Lia's exasperated groan turned into a full-bodied laugh. "An admirer indeed, hm?"

Fee shrugged, smile still in place.

Lia laughed again, the sound so light and airy, it was like the gentle lap of the sea against her toes. It tickled her, and as it receded, it drew some of the sand's abrasive tension with it.

After being berated for her priorities, Fee made amends by helping Lia pack the rest of the box. A handyman had already been called to come fix the remaining damage. What he would make of the claw marks, Lia couldn't guess. Only when Lia was alone did she pull Papa's note out once more.

She read it over and over until it was engraved on her mind—burned in her heart.

CHAPTER THIRTY-THREE

It wasn't as much of a strain, bringing Fee back to Norenth. But Lia felt the pull, the heaviness, and the ringing. Earlier, it was as though the very fabric of her being was at war with the Emperium, like it clung to whatever she tried to bring through. And in returning Fee, it relented, the return of its guardian a victory.

Fee asked the Weatherstone brothers herself about using the castle's fortification for Papa's trunks. Like Lia had thought, Jace—since his parents were locked up in meetings, *literally* according to Terranth—agreed to bring her papa's storage to Norenth until they could comb them for clues on the Seekers' status with the Initiis. When asked about coming to Earth to help, Jace and Terranth were curious, eager even, for the chance. Kristof opted to stay back and organize the boxes in the castle, but appreciated the offer.

Kayce ignored her.

Well, he was *distant.* Quick responses. Wouldn't look her in the eye.

Worse than right after the dragon attack.

Lia didn't know what to do.

Before all this Flameheart business, they'd hardly ever fought. There were small tiffs and spats over the years, especially when the first bout of hormones went raging. The whole bit over his lost pendant and the pastries. Since he'd arrived in her reality, they'd had two major blow-outs, one rolling right into the next. It was a matter of time before the avalanche came crashing down around them.

He'd weathered everything with her so far. The mall attack. The meeting. The Forge. But this fraught tension had been growing steadily, like Kayce didn't know what to say, how to act. Now, he avoided her. Didn't even ask about her limp when the other brothers had reached for her with concern, willing and able to do all the heavy lifting for her.

So Lia did what she did best: try to be proactive. Pretend like it didn't hurt. She put the smile on for Terranth and Jace, escorting one and then the other through the portal after Fee. But it was challenging, channeling those feelings of comfort and peace from her last attempt.

But coming back for Kayce, Lia nearly stumbled. Her boots scuffed the carpet of Jace's room where they'd all met, the navy filigree rushing to crush her face before Kayce's arm banded around her waist.

"Don't you normally warn against rushing into things?" Kayce muttered, his arm leaving her so fast it was as though she were a pyre.

"I didn't mean *carpets*."

The ringing in her ears was deafening, a keening shrill that could burst an eardrum. Lia rubbed her temple, ignoring how much it twisted like a knife in her chest to have Kayce turn from her, palm up. She could have been a volatequis he was readying to ride for how much he cared—no, he showed far more care for those winged horses than her in this moment.

Shaking her head of the ringing that had faded to a rung bell's hum, Lia took his hand. Their fingers laced together, her fingertips brushing his knuckles, the swell of his oath scar nestled into her palm. Eyes closed, Lia grappled for peace. There was so much chaos to sift through, and she felt like she was falling through the spheres all over again.

It took several heartbeats, and she swore she heard Kayce take a breath to ask, but she tugged him forward.

The world *tore*—

Ripped—

Resisted—

Lia wrenched her hand free to cover her ears, the ringing a scream carving its way deep into her marrow. Her teeth vibrated with it, nearly cracking a molar as she clenched them shut to keep from crying out.

"Aurelia—" An emotion *finally* pinched Kayce's voice as they stumbled into her papa's study.

"Give me a minute—"

"Wyrm *crap*—"

Breathing through her nose, each one loosened the tension in her jaw, the noise in her head. Her stomach settled, her heart slowing from a gallop to a trot. Forcing herself upright, Lia caught a glimpse of her reflection in a mirror hanging opposite the desk. Her skin had paled, and her lips cracked like she was dehydrated from fever. Touching her hair, she saw that the curls had lost their luster. Like bringing a creation to Earth took something from her.

But there was Kayce, looming over her from behind. His broad, callused hands came to her arms, steadying her. This time, he didn't let go. She met his gaze. Something burned in those amber depths.

"This wears on you worse than when you fell through all the spheres." His voice was a rumble of waves. "You need to eat something."

"I need to master this power. Headaches are why we have Tylenol." Lia licked her dry lips, Kayce's gaze dipping. "I'll have my mom order Chinese."

His hold tightened, and Lia's pounding heart had nothing to do with her recovery. Kayce's brow lowered, casting shadows over his eyes. "Why do you insist on shouldering this all by yourself?" he asked. His breath whispered against her hair, the shell of her ear.

Fee had asked the same thing. Lia wanted to erase the worry, but more so, she wanted to remove the tension between them. But this intensity that suddenly came with it, she didn't know *what* to do with. She turned her back on her reflection, forcing him to let her go. "Look, I'm sorry I didn't tell you about the nightshriek right after it happened."

His jaw flexed, the burn in his eyes extinguished. "That's not the point."

"Then, what is?" She reached for him, but he stepped back from her. The pain that sliced through her was a barely suppressed flinch. Her hand dropped.

"Eat something before we head back," was all he said before heading to the attic where Fee and his brothers worked.

Agitation twitched in Lia's body, ready to move into action despite the bruises that tightened her back. Everything was spiraling out of her control. And her papa's note, clearly placed for her to find after he was gone, sank a slice of pain deeper into her being.

How could she no longer smell like fire when she felt like she was constantly burning?

Chinese food was becoming a favorite for all the Weatherstones. Terrenth had to be shooed from the door when the delivery guy arrived, wanting to see more of Earth. It was innocent enough, but Mom had freaked. Lia decided not to comment on the overly generous tip she gave, or the pedestrian minding their own business walking a dog.

And even after eating a generous helping of chicken lo mein, Lia felt weak. But what would Aurelia have done? There was a job to do. It didn't matter if she had to break her back doing it.

After dinner, they condensed the trunks to about half a dozen after realizing many held old photo albums or other mementos unrelated to Norenth or the Order. Jace and Terranth did well to fill the silence as they worked, Fee ordering them about in her own way, especially Terranth. Marcus peppered the Weatherstones with questions, in awe of their attire and asking all about the kingdom. They were kind enough to humor him, Kayce as well. Lia tried to catch Kayce's eye, but he refused to look at her—though she swore she'd felt his stare like a weight settled between her shoulder blades.

Bringing Fee back to organize with Kristof, Lia managed three more trips with the brothers, a trunk in hand. It was hard to mask the exertion it took, her lungs burning like she ran the steep face of Mount Fealtek. It was easier to ignore the ringing with the pounding of her heart.

Lia waited for Kayce to reach out as he had last time. The first trip, he was intent on wiping the dust and grime off one of the trunks. The second, his gaze snagged hers, words hovering between them, before he swallowed them with a drink of soda Marcus had goaded him into trying. The third, he stood, took several paces away as she stumbled on the landing back into the attic—then froze, rubbing the back of his neck as he looked out the gabled window into the night.

The little stubbornness Lia had to keep it all together was thinner than a volatequis hair.

Her mom was by her side as the portal faded behind them, her lips a pinched line. "How about we stop here? Lia can bring you boys back to Norenth in the morning with the rest."

"I can do it, Mom, I just need—"

"No," Kayce interjected. "She said it could wait until morning. Rest."

Lia's eyes burned, but not with fatigue. "But she needs these out of here in case—"

"Nothing will happen tonight," Jace said, a wary glance shot toward his youngest brother. "We'll make sure of it."

Kayce grunted in agreement, studying her with a furrowed brow before he turned on his heel and disappeared down the stairs.

So much for proving you were strong enough. Can't even do what Mom needs, either.

The discordant ring faded, but Lia's temples continued to throb. Her shoulders dropped as she followed everyone downstairs.

Kayce's distance was more than the bookstore blunder or training agitation. Refusing to touch her one moment, nearly cradling her the next. Their tentative peace was gone—she couldn't understand what changed.

Lia's night was nothing more than twisting sheets around her legs and staring at the ceiling. Every time she shut her eyes, girlish humming and her own screams echoed in her mind. She heard it in the wind against the windowpane. The creaks of the floorboards as one of the others went to the bathroom. The drum of her heartbeat, an increasing staccato in her ears. Her chest ached, the loneliness a creature nestling its burrow between her ribs.

Kayce was a wall away, but he might as well have been back in her pages. She desperately wanted to go back to their alcove, back to before they woke in her bed. She only wanted her best friend back. Nothing more. Her eyes burned, but the longer she kept them open, the more of an excuse she could use that it was because they were dry. *Nothing more.*

Rubbing the scar in her hand, Lia stared at the ceiling until the window threw a dawn silhouette across its expanse.

True to pattern, Kayce avoided her until they arrived back at Castle Finerda, stowing the remaining trunks in a nondescript closet in Jace's rooms to pilfer through later. Her leg burned, but she'd assured her mom she would stop at the infirmary for a poultice that would help speed the healing. Cheeks wan from the multiple trips plus the additional heavy loads, Lia huffed a limp curl from her face as she pushed in the final trunk. Kayce brushed past her, hardly sparing her a glance. Lia gritted her teeth. Never did she think she would lose so much sleep over a guy who was *supposed* to be fictional.

Enough with the silence.

Enough with the one-word responses.

Enough with the lingering stares when she wasn't looking.

Enough.

Whipping around, the verbal tongue-lashing poised, Lia poisoned the words with the loneliness and agitation burning in her belly—

—only to find him gone. Again.

Fury splotched life back into her face. "Where is he?"

Terranth and Jace, leftover take-out in hand for the royal chefs to replicate, shared a glance. "The woods," Terranth said. "He mentioned something about Fee."

Biting out a terse "thank you", Lia turned to leave.

Jace caught her arm. "Aurelia?" he asked, eyeing her from head to toe, "are you well?"

"Yep!" Lia smiled, stepping back. "I'm fine." Because she had to be. No one needed her flailing about when they had so much else to contend with. Her mask was slipping, her wall crumbling, bringing the boys back and forth across the barrier destroying what little energy she had to put on her best face.

Was that why Kayce was so distant? Because Lia couldn't prove that Aurelia existed as much as he did? He had spoken like she could be both. Did he not see she was trying to flip between the two as best she could?

Lia felt Jace's stare on her back as she left.

The mist was thick, sunlight barely piercing through what had become their normal training spot in the forest. But not even the crisp pine and seawater scent could ease the tightness in her lungs. Despite a slight limp, Lia's steps were soft, the quiet gusts preluding a storm.

She was so lost in her thoughts, she didn't hear the subtle *hoot* carried on the wind. She didn't see the bird until its shadow eclipsed what little light shone through the trees. The hairs on the back of her neck rose, that awareness that only came with being watched. Since the nightshriek's attack, it wasn't a feeling she would forget any time soon.

But it wasn't the first time she had felt it in this forest.

Lia stopped, her hand deceptively lax at her side. Only her eyes moved as they flickered up to the canopy. There, cupped in a skeletal palm of bare branches, was an owl. Six eyes beheld her, skewering her to the forest floor with their stare.

She had seen one on Luddeck's ship. Heard one outside Castle Finerda. Felt its presence as they trained here. Her anger snuffed out, a flame extinguished. A tear was in Norenth. But she had seen this creature before.

Before she could utter the name, the barred owl stretched its gray wings, those ringed eyes narrowing, and took flight for the darker part of the wood. She didn't have time to pull out her pen, send the infernal bird back from whatever hellscape it had clawed its way out of. Though from those eyes, ringed like the nightshriek's with a glazed obscurity devoid of life, the two could have only come from one sphere, a sphere supposedly lost and imprisoning all within.

She had unknowingly broken into Malum's prison.

CHAPTER THIRTY-FOUR

Lia had barely held her own against the nightshriek. If Malum used the tears to send out his messenger birds, it was only a matter of time before he sent more lethal creatures—*without* her accidental assistance.

The nightshriek was gone, she reminded herself. There was no way of knowing it came from the sphere Malum had created. Same with the owls. And who's to say the owl in Norenth was the same as the one in her papa's yard?

Stop deluding yourself. It's all connected. And you're not equipped to handle it.

She struggled to continue onward in the woods. Her training now seemed pointless. Her shoulders bowed inward as she held her elbows. Norenth was in danger, but who was she to stand up against the darkness? She could barely keep her own dark thoughts at bay. And she didn't exactly survive the nightshriek's attack unscathed.

She wasn't ready. And if no one knew about the tear, perhaps it could wait until she was. It was selfish, but she was so tired of being a disappointment. She couldn't handle letting Kayce down again, having him ice her out further—

A sharp snort filled the air. "You aren't hearing me." Kayce's voice was crisp.

Lia stopped, pressing against a pine's rough trunk to listen.

"I can't always be there when she freezes." A beat, his voice straining. "She *has* to unlock the skills she already has by accepting all that she is."

"You don't think she does?" Fee replied. "She handled that nightshriek well enough."

"Well enough? She's limping! And her back—" His voice caught.

Lia was painfully aware of the mottled coloring over her back, the purples and blues and sickly yellows blooming along her shoulder blades down to her hips. But when had Kayce seen that? She flushed, wondering if he had seen her as they readied for bed last night, her mom checking her back and fussing. But if he was so concerned about her welfare, why ice her out?

Because you can't handle this. You freeze every time—

"She's a Flameheart...and a gentle soul." His voice faltered a fraction before pushing on, forcing Lia's thoughts to a halt. "But she already *is* a Norenthian soldier. She's trained with us all her life. She knows what to do, her instincts are sharp. But she hesitated—she wouldn't have been hurt like that if she hadn't."

"Maybe you underestimate how fearsome that nightshriek was," Fee contended.

"Or maybe she's holding herself back because she's too caught up in pleasing everyone."

Lia flinched. Did he really see right through her? Ignoring the sting, she peered around the tree to find him and Fee in the clearing, the latter crossing her arms and opening her mouth.

But Kayce held up a hand. "I'm not saying I want her entirely as a soldier. But her life is at risk in a way she's never known. She needs to train so that it forces her to think of only herself—*all* of herself."

A hum of thought came from the guardian. "The Vilentian Sphere can help. These crumbling barriers won't wait. You saw her at the Forge—this runs deep inside her. She's processing. But this acceptance of all she is, I fear Lia won't see it that way. At least not soon. Unless—" Fee assessed him in that pragmatic way of hers. "You know her better than anyone. Maybe even herself. She would listen to you more than I."

There was a long pause. Even the gentle breeze stilled, holding its breath with Lia.

"Please, Fiducia, she won't listen to me," Kayce said in a soft, genuine plea. "You have to talk to her."

Lia had never heard him speak like this. Not even when he first landed on Earth. Her earlier irritation waned completely, even her insecurities shrinking. All thoughts of Malum, the owl, a tear in Norenth—they rippled away, Kayce's words a stone in the pool of her.

"She does what she believes others want. She thinks I'm this reckless, adventure-hungry boy to babysit. All she sees is me pushing her." He shook his head. "It can't be me. She'll only push back."

The words rocked Lia. Her cheeks heated, nails digging into the bark.

"She can't change her thoughts if she doesn't know they're wrong," Fee said. "You need to tell her. She'd never turn from you or retreat like she does with everyone else. So what if she pushes back? Push harder. Isn't that what friends do?"

Lia strained to hear, to see, but only saw Kayce's back, the muscles taut.

"Oh," Fee breathed. Her nebulous eyes darted over his face, reacting to something there. The changed pitch in Fee's tone, normally so controlled, had Lia leaning forward. In trying to determine the shift, she stepped on a twig, which cracked under her foot.

Both of them turned, and Lia stepped out from behind the tree. Words fled when her gaze collided with Kayce's, uncertain of the emotion she read there. He looked like he was rooted where he stood, his skin pale, lips a firm, bloodless line. A tremor ran through his hands. He fisted them, a muscle feathered along his neck. Then he turned on his heel and left.

Watching Kayce turn his back on her cleaved Lia's chest in two. Her heart could have tumbled out right there. In trying to be who she thought he wanted, Lia had lost sight of who Kayce was. The irony made her sick.

Stricken, she turned to Fee. "I didn't mean—I never wanted to hurt him." Lia curled her hands. "Never him."

"Of course you didn't." Fee was solemn in her assessment. After several heartbeats, she caught Lia's eye and nodded to where Kayce had disappeared through the thicket. Her usual bluntness wasn't needed—nor her encouragement.

It wasn't difficult to follow his path to the creek. Lia found Kayce splashing water over his face, which had returned to its tanned complexion. "It seems like this is the place for deep conversations," Lia said quietly, trying to ease the tension. To deflect the pain. Anything to loosen the rigid set of his shoulders.

Kayce tilted his head to her. Water dripped from his clenched jaw. "You almost died."

"But I didn't. You and Terranth have been re-training me. Besides, I thought you wanted me to hold my ground. Help people." Was this how they finally went about it? Their fight after the dragon attack stewed inside her. Lia pulled herself straighter. The practiced words bubbled up before she could stop them. "I'm fine."

Liar.

She wasn't fine. She was bleeding out, as Lioness Silva had forewarned. But Kayce was hurting, and she couldn't drag in more of her mess. No matter how true his words to Fee were. How the exposure made her want to turn and run back to her bedroom.

Even though this was *him.*

"You aren't fine." He surged to stand, facing her. "That was too close. You shouldn't have to work with Terranth and me. I've heard how fluid Flamehearts are with their pens, but you're too busy fighting yourself."

There it was again. He wasn't going to let it go. But Lia shook her head, unwilling to face it. "I'm not fighting—"

"Stop lying to yourself!" he beseeched. "You are...so much. A warrior. A writer, a thinker. My *best friend*. You believe people expect you to always have it figured out. But you don't—it's okay to let go. To stop thinking about how to act and just be you. Thinking is making you hesitate—*that* is going to get you killed." His voice choked around that last word.

It broke something in Lia so fundamental, so intrinsic, that there was no holding back the emotional deluge. "Let go? You don't think I'm trying?" Lia stepped back. The illusion of being fine was stripped, his words leaving her bare. She held her hands to her chest as if to protect the fragile beat within. "I am trying. Every. Single. Day. Do you realize that some days I have to fight to wake up? Or that I fight to go to sleep? To do even simple things like talk to the Order members?" She choked out a laugh, incredulous with the frustration. "Just be me? I want friends, but I can't stand socializing. Sometimes, I want to be alone, but I can't bear being lonely. It's like I feel everything at once and then I'm just...numb. Paralyzed. But I can't let anyone know, not when they depend on me."

Kayce moved in, towering over her. Lia's eyes were made of glass as she flung out her hands, retreating again. Flashes of her adolescence surged in her mind's eye. "They see the girl I give them, the one who can handle it all and she is thriving—but I'm not thriving!

I'm *surviving*—and I'm exhausted." Her voice cracked, but the words didn't stop. "You're right—all I do is fight for everyone else's comfort. But I can't *not* do that. If I don't—" Her throat seized. The walls she had built to protect others had become her cell.

Kayce had hung on every word, eyes never straying as she bared her long-hidden soul. What she'd revealed in the Forge had nothing on this. Kayce inched closer, like she was a doe to bolt any moment. His rough palms whispered over her skin when he took hold of her arms. He slid his hands down to hers. The worn pad of his thumb ran back and forth across the torn skin beside her nail, in tandem with their breaths that filled the small space between them.

"If you stop trying to be there for everyone else," he asked, "what will happen?"

Lia flinched, but Kayce held fast. She couldn't say it. She couldn't expose that—

Leaning in to get her attention, Kayce's words were soft. "The world would fall apart? Your brother wouldn't be cared for? Your mother would falter?"

"I had to. When he left." Heat burned her cheeks. It seemed so silly, years later. But she had never stopped. She couldn't. Not even after the Forge.

"You stepped up when their world fell apart." He tightened his hold. "But it's not your role to be the backbone of your family. Not anymore. They can't grow stronger if you won't let them."

Kayce will never understand—

No. He actually might.

The raging doubts had slowed under his touch. But one remained.

"Aurelia—"

"I just want to be good enough," Lia rushed, finally giving those badgering thoughts a voice. "A good sister, daughter—a good friend. I'm scared that if I truly accept Norenthian Aurelia as part of myself, I'm going to disappoint people. Because Aurelia, she—*I*—wouldn't be afraid to say no. To do what *I* want for a change. But what do people do when they don't get what they want? When they're unhappy or disappointed?" Tears blurred her vision. But she forced the words out despite her closing throat, knowing if she didn't say them now, she never would. "They leave."

Her father. Papa. Even Kayce, every time she had woken up or closed the journal.

Everyone leaves.

"Aurelia—" His voice roughened over her name. Glancing up, Lia watched Kayce's gaze dip over her face before speaking. "Are those really the relationships you want? Do you *truly* believe we will leave if you stop?"

Lia chewed her lip. What *did* she want? More than anything, she had wanted to be seen. To be wholly understood and read like a book. Not a single word skimmed over, each page of her being. But what if no one liked the story they found inside. What was a story if it cowered on a shelf? Was it really a story—a world created—if no one opened it?

But...Kayce saw her, Lia realized. He had always seen her.

Looking at her now, the intensity of his gaze made her feel like he read all that she was. Like the spine of a treasured book, he had broken into her with tenderness. Spread open the very pages of her soul. Scoured the words written in her heart. Lia was open to him, and Kayce did not flinch.

He reached out, brushing a strand of her hair back into place. His fingertips lingered on her cheek. "If people leave because you stop putting them first, you don't need them anyway. But you're enough." His voice shook. "You're more than enough."

Lia's breath hitched. She was tired of being shoved away, unread. Unseen.

Their gazes locked, their bodies pulling together by a magnetism Lia couldn't ignore any more. They moved in the same instant—Kayce cupping the back of her head as Lia ducked under his chin. The wind's salted-pine clung to Kayce as she buried her face in his chest.

"How?" Lia whispered, her voice a vulnerable tremor. "How do I do it?"

He took a deep breath, his body bowing over her own, pressing his face to her curls as though he found her scent as steadying as she did his. Several heartbeats passed until he slid his hand from her hair, down her back.

"Fee and I have an idea," Kayce murmured.

She sank into the surety of his tone, its strength there in the arms holding her, the heart pumping beneath her cheek. The Norenthian soil at her feet.

This is real.

And Lia gave into it at last.

CHAPTER THIRTY-FIVE

Hiding away in Norenth was over. From her conversation with Kayce, that was truly what this past week had been. What her life since she was a child had been. He was right—there wouldn't always be someone to help her, or someone else to rally for. She had to choose herself. Listen to her own instincts, if she could ever find them.

She just didn't think backpacking in a storied wilderness like some hobbit was the way to do it. Not when they had a murder to solve, a piece to an ancient book to track down—

"Look, I said I would work on it," Lia said to Fee in their clearing later on, as the guardian handed her a bag that looked suspiciously similar to the one stashed with her ranger gear. "That didn't mean I was about to sign up for 'Girl Scouts of Mordor'."

"You're stepping on some serious copyright issues," Fee chided. "The Vilentian Sphere is full of orcs, trolls, and goblins, but it doesn't give you the right to snub one of the greatest Flamehearts we knew. It doesn't even come *close* to his sphere."

Lia's mouth popped open. "Are you actually insinuating—"

Kayce cleared his throat, eyeing her sneakers. "Are you certain you want to wear *that*?"

Lia glared at the interruption. "I have all the comfort of Earth athleisure and Norenthian practicality. I'm not changing."

The brown cloak would give her the warmth and camouflage she would need in whatever climate Vilentia offered. But a cotton shirt gave her the freedom of movement she found lacking in Norenthian fashion. Not to mention, the leggings had *pockets*. Lia's hand went to the one holding her pen.

Fee tracked the movement. "While you're there, you can only use the pen to form tools found in a feudal-fantasy setting. You know the rules by now."

She did. Lia had been told after the Forge that her pen should only transform into items found in that sphere. Not that she would ever wave a gun around in Norenth. Not only would it unsettle the locals, but she had no idea how to use it. From what she gathered, Earth was fair game. Any tool could be used there to Transcribe a creation back to where it belonged.

"Your mother knows to expect you to be gone for a few days?" Kayce prompted.

Lia winced. It wasn't hard to recall the vein pulsing in her mom's temple when Lia said the guardian had insisted on this trip—vital for her training, Fee assured. The nightshriek's attack alone proved that time was of the essence for Lia to learn control. Afterward, her mom's face was stoic, words minimal as her daughter prepared to leave.

Lia had hated it, but she hated what she'd done to herself more. "She knows. Though it's no wonder writers hardly set fantasies in the modern world. They seriously hinder a person's education."

Lia had needed to promise to make up her studies and do household chores for a week straight. Thankfully, Marcus only asked for an orc horn. If she could do anything good with her strange barrier-hopping abilities, she would leap at the chance for a souvenir. Anything to soothe the disappointment on his face every time she left.

"Lia," Fee said, her cosmic wings unfurling. "I'll return for you in two days."

Two days to focus on herself. To find the Flameheart—the writer *and* the warrior—on the inside. Their hunt for answers could spare two days, even though Lia's stomach rioted at the thought. But she knew her papa would want her to do this. He always had.

"What about Papa's trunks? His research on the Initiis?" It tore at her to leave them behind, feeling as though they were on the cusp of solving this. She flipped again. Maybe taking time to figure herself out wasn't a good idea right now.

Especially with the tear. She hadn't told either of them about it. But it was only an owl, one she didn't know for certain *was* connected to Malum. She had to do this first. When she came back, she would be able to confront whatever was going on with her kingdom. She couldn't saddle another hunt on her friends while she was gone.

"Fee and I will handle it," Kayce responded. "I know what to look for. Besides, it'll be like taking a trip down memory lane."

"Can we trade trips?" Lia tried, earning her a weathered glare from both of them. She held up her hands in mock surrender. She was ready as she'd ever be. Because as tired as she was of holding onto everything she'd thought others wanted, a new emotion sparked deep inside: longing, a flame of anticipation. All to see what she was truly capable of.

Yes. She needed this. Again, what would two days hurt?

That spark simmered in the gray depths of her eyes when she grinned at Kayce. She knew, for his own lit up when their gazes met. "If I come back with poison ivy or reeking of troll, I'm forcing you to launder my clothes."

"I'll pick up your tavern tab for a month," he countered.

"Deal."

Their scarred hands shook and held.

"Trust in yourself." There was an intensity in Kayce's eyes, a wistfulness she couldn't understand. "You can do this."

Lia supposed he hated to be left behind, to miss out on the adventure—no, it was more than that. Had she learned *nothing* from their conversation? She was certainly conscious of each time their eyes had met, their hands had brushed. He stood nearer, answered more readily. It tied Lia's tongue. So why did he look at her like he was...missing something?

It seemed to linger as Kayce traced her features with his gaze. The study made her body tense. Letting go of his hand, Lia stepped back for Fee's.

"Don't worry," Fee said with a wink. "Julian told me not long ago that Vilentia is lovely this time of year." The guardian's wings were a soundless pulse, and they were gone.

Her papa had lied. Vilentia *sucked*.

Thanks to the healing tonic she had taken, the limp was nearly gone apart from a slight twinge and an angry lattice of scars. Lia's legs were by no means little, but she couldn't understand how four halflings had crossed miles of hills, forests, and mountains without much complaint. Then again, this place was swampier. She had been in Vilentia's dense woods for several hours, and she cursed just about every upended root and stone.

She knew she was supposed to use this time to "find her inner Flameheart", but Lia wasn't happy. Couldn't Fee have taken her to a tranquil meadow? Or a hot spring? Lia guessed neither of those were character-building enough. And this was the crash course. She needed to find herself again—she only wished hiking with her body bent out of shape from the nightshriek's attack hadn't been on the agenda.

Night quickly rolled in as twin suns set and double moons rose. Lia wasn't deterred in looking for shelter, the pale orbs illuminating the way. Crickets chirped a summer symphony despite the cool breeze. Vines dipped over tree boughs, the stringy moss reminding Lia of a muggy climate similar to the American South. Every so often, the canopy broke to reveal hills blocking out the starry sky. The trees eventually thinned, opening to a small, water-logged field. She regretted bringing her sneakers, already soaked—not that she would ever admit it to Kayce. However, her leather boots wouldn't fare much better in this swamp.

Lia wasn't dim enough to walk out into the open field. She was about to circle around it instead when a light flickered across the tall grasses.

The crickets quieted.

The light splintered into three. Then five.

"Crap," Lia breathed at the sight of torches approaching.

She would fend for herself, but that also meant knowing when to pick her battles. As sore and weary as she was, she didn't think twice before retreating. She banked to the right, away from the hills, and didn't stop until the crickets resumed their song. Only then did she climb into a tree with enough moss to conceal herself. She fished a belt from her bag and secured herself to a sturdy branch for the night, pen in hand.

Sleeping in a tree had seemed like a smart idea. It kept Lia from whatever horde hunted these woods. Plus, she had read about it in a book once. But the crick in her spine followed her as she continued to search for better shelter.

Lia had another thirty-six hours in this world, give or take. She didn't want to spend another hour of it tied to a tree.

It was an effort to pick up the pace, despite the sunlight illuminating the dark green world. Gnats flew in her face, humidity frizzing her curls no matter how tight she pulled them back. By the time the dual suns peaked, Lia had ditched her cloak.

At least it wasn't Malletor. That was a heat so intense, it burned cold.

Praise the skies and seas, it wasn't much longer before Lia found an outcropping formed from a fallen tree, the burrow beneath deep enough for her to duck inside. Gnarled roots wove a ceiling, the ground drier than anything else she had seen. The shade was a cool relief, along with a quick search that proved no other living thing called this burrow home.

Her shoulders uncoiled almost too fast under the yellowing bruises as she released her pack. She winced, rolling them to ease the tension before taking out her canteen. Despite measured sips, the water did little to quench her thirst. She would have to find a source of clean water soon. Especially now that she'd found shelter.

She'd come into the sphere with a few full canteens and several provisions—it was part of a list she'd been forced to memorize alongside Kayce in the Ranger's Guild. The rediscovered knowledge had startled Lia at first. She wasn't a survivalist by nature on Earth, yet in Norenth, she had been to a degree.

Knowledge or no knowledge, her aching body protested. Just a few moments rest wouldn't hurt. Lia fished out her notebook and a sandwich sent courtesy of Marcus. He'd been adamant about making several for the trip.

"Think of it like a retreat," he'd said, laying banana slices over the peanut butter and jelly. "I'm sure there won't be any light pollution, from the sounds of it. The stars will be spectacular."

Considering how dense the canopy was, Lia could only muse the same. However, what she had glimpsed the night before *was* quite magnificent.

Yet nothing could top the Emperium. She hoped she would be there with Marcus the day he Sparked and saw it all for the first time. A smile traced Lia's lips. She was grateful it had been Kayce by her side. She couldn't think of anyone else she would have wanted there.

Despite his distant demeanor at the time, Lia had told Kayce and his brothers about the dark Flameheart while at her papa's—that a traitor was helping the Seekers find the Initiis. Or worse, that person had already given them one of the three pieces.

Opening the journal, Lia leafed through the pages until she found her notes.

<u>*The Murder of Julian Corvine*</u>

How: Hit by a car in front of his house

☒ *Where was he going?*

☒ *Who was he seeing?*

Who: Seekers–Dark Flameheart

Why: Problematic veil — more creations escaping

☒ *What did Papa find?*

☒ *Are the Seekers to blame or just taking advantage?*

She added "Dark Flameheart" beside the Seekers. Somehow, they'd converted this Flameheart to their cause. How, Lia couldn't guess. It twisted her stomach, ruining the sandwich. Flameheart oath notwithstanding, the betrayal was a low blow. The two groups had been at odds since the beginning. The Seekers wanted the power found in the Emperium, power their ancestors witnessed during the First Rift and they could no longer access.

What would a Flameheart get from helping them?

Unless they didn't want a *what*, but a *who*.

When the barriers crumble and Malum is freed, daughter of flame, there will be no place in all the realms you can hide.

The creature's words made her shiver despite the muggy air, but Lia focused not on her own jeopardy, but on the admission. Malum would be freed once the barriers fell entirely. What Flameheart wanted that?

Lia didn't know for certain that it was someone in their chapter of the Order, but as disconcerting as it was, it made sense. It needed to be someone close to her papa, one who knew his work. She would wager a guess his role had been more than just mapmaking, but had also included the search for tears in the worlds.

Fishing out a pen, she wrote the members' names in her chapter, starting with the ones she knew had been closest to Papa.

Obviously, there was Leo. Lia recalled his warmth and concern in a manner so similar to her papa's that it swelled the grief in her chest. He had helped her each step of the way. He'd advocated for Kayce. And Mom trusted him. Even if he seemed to know more than he was letting on. And he didn't deny taking some of Papa's research.

Then there was Adrian and Mirel. The squirrel, while working closest with her papa as the record keeper, didn't seem to have a murderous bone in his body. Plus, he'd given her and Kayce the information about the Initiis. Then again, he seemed to be one who'd known most about Papa's work. They would be nowhere without him.

Mirel, on the other hand, was apparently good at cover-ups. She'd been there when the gremlin attacked her, but she was playing ignorant of the fact. Lia wasn't sure if the ignorance was genuine or not.

She continued to bounce names around, analyzing motives until a steady ache pulsed between her brows. This wasn't exactly what Kayce meant by putting herself first. However, being in a realm apart from her own helped untangle her thoughts. Away from everything, Lia knew she needed this space to figure out what she really wanted.

Who she truly was.

While lost in introspection, the headache grew in tandem with the dryness of her mouth.

Pen in pocket and canteen in hand, Lia noted her shelter before walking toward what little she could see of the suns. She had only made it several paces past a particularly mossy tree when, out of the corner of her eye, the air shimmered.

She blinked hard, doing a double take. The dehydration had to be getting to her. But when she looked again, the air continued to shift, to waver between the boughs of a weeping willow. A small lake beckoned with a mirror-like surface, but the water didn't call to her.

There was a steady hum—small, so faint it was like a ringing in the ears—that pulled at Lia. Mindful of her step, she parted the wispy, ground-sweeping branches, paying no mind to the slender leaves tickling her bare arms. Between two arching boughs, no bigger than a window, the air fluttered like gauze on a breeze.

Lia shifted, catching it from different angles. Within, she could see stars flickering in and out of existence. No, not stars. *Worlds.*

Her throat tightened. This realm's boundaries were about to rip apart.

CHAPTER THIRTY-SIX

The Order had mentioned the rifts were worsening. Her papa clearly pursued them across the Emperium, but it was another thing to see it for herself. That gremlin didn't just *poof* in the middle of Seattle. It needed a door to begin with. It had crossed through a tear like this one.

"So, ye found one."

Pen flaring into a sword, Lia spun to face the speaker—only to find nothing but whispering leaves.

"Show yourself," she demanded, heart pounding.

"Aye, I will. Put the light out. I hate being out during the day as it stands."

Warily assessing her surroundings, Lia willed the sword back into a pen. As the light dimmed, the leaves bent and gave form—no, a creature had stepped out, his green skin blending with the foliage. How long had he—Lia assumed it was "he" by the voice—been watching her?

He was like the gremlin, with large bat-like ears so thin sunlight shone through the membrane. But he was taller, half her height, with a significant under-bite and bulbous eyes to match.

A troll, no doubt. Albeit a small, goblin-like one.

"What did I find?" Lia asked, seeking confirmation. Who would know she would be here, stumble upon something like this? Then, it clicked. "Fee sent you."

"Aye, the pretty-eyed one. No-nonsense too, made sure I stayed here until I found ye. Well, until ye found me." The troll wiped his hooked nose on the brown smock he wore. He held out his hand. "Call me Murdoc."

Lia tried not to gag at the sulfuric odor of rotten eggs as she shook his hand. "Lia. So, I got dropped here for more than just a solo trip." Why wasn't she surprised? Fee had probably plopped Lia so far away to encourage her sense of self-preservation. Lia didn't know if she wanted to thank the guardian or throttle her. "Why *are* you here?" Lia raised a brow. "No offense."

"She wanted me to show ye that this is not the beginning," the troll replied. "It's been happening—"

"I knew this. Why couldn't she tell me this herself?"

"Because the Order didna want ye to know. These little rips are popping up and not just here—it's only a matter o' time before they're ev'rywhere." The troll eyed her shrewdly. "I dinna think ye understand. This here hidey-hole appeared here when me mam was a girl."

Lia suppressed the urge to roll her eyes. "And how old is your mother?" These trolls could breed like rabbits for all she knew.

A smug grin splintered his warty face. "She only looks five and thirty, but is nearing her fiftieth season."

Fifty years.

A sinking feeling filled her gut. If she had to go through some backwoods troll to show Lia the tears, it was because Fee didn't feel it was safe to tell Lia herself. Not that Lia blamed her. It wasn't the past three years at all, but *decades*. And the old tears were not only getting worse, new ones were ripping open.

"Has anything ever come through?"

Thankfully, the troll shook his head. "Me mam said she remembers when it was no bigger than her fist. A sparkly turn of the light was all it was. We paid it little mind. But then more appeared in the trees, in the hills. And this one, o'er the last few summers, has gotten bigger at a far faster pace. We do well to steer clear, but more of the land is falling to 'em."

The hum from the tear reverberated in her ears. It sang to her. "Come," it seemed to whisper.

Lia shook herself, managing a strained smile. "Please consider your message received."

Bowing so his nose whispered against the grass, the troll straightened. He was partly through the leaves when he turned back, assessing her. "Ye remind me of someone I saw not too long ago. He had yer eyes. Bit o' the hair, too, albeit more silver."

Lia's breath caught.

Julian told me not long ago that Vilentia is lovely this time of year, Fee had said.

"Tried to get us all to migrate away from the worst of the tears. Helped another troll not even a moon ago," he continued on. "Stuck his finger in the shimmer—singed it clean off! The old geezer whisked him away, and when Snerglick returned, he had a fancy wooden digit instead. Kept blathering about oceans with stars and a giant, none like found in these parts." The troll sighed, shrugging his shoulders. "I'd hate to see the blithering mess he'd become if he'd lost anything *important*!" With a saucy wink, he disappeared.

Lia sank onto an exposed root, the knowledge pressing on her.

Papa had been here. Not a moon ago—a month? That would make his visit here *just* before he died. And if he'd spoken to Murdoc, her papa had learned the truth. The rifts had been growing for at least fifty years. And not just growing—multiplying.

Murdoc had said the land was...falling to them. Would there be a point where these tears ripped worlds apart in their entirety?

But her papa had helped, been here.

Been here, breathing this air, just before his death.

Something else clicked into place. Murdoc's story of his injured friend reminded Lia of Veera's comment at the Order meeting about Kayce being in one piece. Adrian had explained that creations got burned—*maimed*—when they touched a tear after the First Rift. It made her sick to wonder what could have happened to Kayce if he had stumbled through one without her.

But how were creations like the gremlin and the dragon coming to Earth unscathed? She wracked her brain, recalling each in unsettling detail. Neither had born an injury, both frighteningly whole like—

Lia choked on a gasp. The owl at her papa's. Mom hadn't confirmed it before the Order meeting, but the burning parchment, the flare of light—Papa *had* Transcribed it back to the spheres. Lia knew it in her bones. And in her memory, the owl then and in Norenth hadn't been missing anything, hurt in any way. Just quiet. Watchful. She couldn't stop her shudder, the way she looked to every shadow like its claws could snatch out and grab her.

But her papa had seen the owl. Known it was unscathed, a nightmare on Earth—like the gremlin and the dragon.

And then not even a day later, Papa was killed.

Because he knew with certainty, Seekers possessed part of the Initiis.

A small fire was all Lia would risk when night set in for a second time. The lake had offered enough water to fill her metal canteen. It cooled beside her, having boiled in the flames. Lia wasn't about to risk getting ill on top of everything else. But her stomach was eating itself, the last of her protein bars gone.

After Murdoc left, Lia had doubled back to her shelter. The steady ache hadn't eased. Not after the information she learned.

Why would Fee orchestrate this convoluted show-and-tell with that troll? Unless this was another of papa's clues. This time, not through a note, but a message from their guardian. Her head pulsed, forcing Lia to file the questions away. If she didn't get her wits about her, she wouldn't walk out of this swamp any better than when she entered.

She was grateful the rangers had taught her to trap several years ago, the small snare she set up successfully capturing a rabbit. It was nice to see that it was similar to those on Earth. After skinning and gutting her meal, Lia set about roasting the meat when a similar dinner came to mind.

It was the first night Kayce had stayed with them, before the mall fiasco.

Out of respect, Kayce had taken his leave once seeing the family needed more time to process. However, he did not remain idle. When the three had finally remembered they had a guest, the Corvines headed to the dining room only to find a meal ready with Kayce waiting.

Her mom had looked over the chicken with carrots and broccoli steaming on the plates, relaxing at the pleasant surprise.

"After the day we all had, a warm meal seemed the best course of action." Kayce had beamed.

Lia snorted. Of course he would. Kayce could hardly go an hour without thinking about the next meal.

"Well, if I had smelled anything cooking I would've helped." Her mom had smiled as they all took their places.

"I couldn't figure out how the oven in your kitchen worked, so I used the firepit out back," Kayce commented cheerfully.

"We have a firepit?" her mom replied.

"You do now."

Her mom sent a worried eye toward the backyard, causing Lia to chuckle before saying, "Don't worry, Mom, he knows what he's doing."

After a few bites, her mom looked up at Kayce. "This is fantastic! How did you keep the chicken from getting dry with an open flame?"

But Kayce shook his head while clearing his mouth. "It's rabbit, not chicken."

Everyone had paused.

"What?" asked a wide-eyed Marcus, his face a shade paler.

"Rabbit. I found a couple in your yard and was able to—"

"I'm eating Fluffles and Floppy Ear?" Marcus spat out a mouthful, clamoring for his water.

Kayce paused at looks of horror around him. "Uh, these weren't wild rabbits, were they?"

The rabbits in question had been regulars that Marcus had started to feed, which they had enjoyed watching in the evenings. The prince looked over at Marcus apologetically, his face solemn and uncertain. An awkward silence had filled the room before Lia made the first move in suggesting take-out.

Lia laughed now as her own rabbit finished cooking, removing it from the flames. The relief on Kayce's face was easy to recall, the take-out an instant winner. Thankfully, Marcus didn't hold it against Kayce for too long.

She supposed nearly being roasted by a dragon evened the scales.

Halfway through her gamey dinner, Lia was in a reverie when the bushes rustled. She paused mid-chew. Only her eyes moved, darting over the shadows, looking for a solid darkness, a highlight from the small flames.

Flames she had foolishly forgotten to stamp out as soon as her dinner cooked.

Rookie mistake.

A snort echoed as the brush parted, cloven hoofs sinking into the damp earth. Tusks, the yellowed bone blade-sharp, parted the leaves to reveal a boar.

The rabbit might have been of Earth, but this beast was not.

Lia slowly lowered her meal, not daring a full breath. Beady white eyes met hers, ringed with sagging pink skin. The coarse hairs blended with the dark. Antlers, six total, mirrored the pale branches of dead trees littered in this area.

Her pen was an inch before her.

The boar toed the ground.

Both moved simultaneously. Light flared as the pen morphed into a spear, the boar charging over the open flame. Embers sputtered, the light dying. But Lia didn't need it.

Trusting all the years Kayce had goaded her into tracking after dark, Lia darted back on the balls of her feet as the boar barreled past her. What little light the pen provided caught the beast's eyes, narrowed in rage.

This was no friendly troll or unknown horde tracking her down. But Lia wasn't going to give anyone the satisfaction of knowing she was skewered by an overgrown pig with anger-management issues.

Steam clouded the air before its nostrils, and the boar charged again, central horn raised.

Trust your instincts. Stop thinking.

Lia rolled to meet it, springing with sudden force from the momentum she had gathered. Her spear ran through the boar's jaw, the soft underside giving way to sizzling heat. Those pearlescent eyes rolled back, the ground shaking when it dropped.

A breath shuddered through her, the spear dimming and retracting to become a pen once more. The horn had scraped her cheek, a thin welt stinging but barely larger than a cat scratch. Far too close. But the voice that urged her on was her own. That was a victory.

Marcus would have to settle for a boar's horn. She would do her absolute best to steer clear of any others on her tail until she was off this sphere, souvenir or not.

Lia was ready to go home. Earth, Norenth, it didn't matter.

She wanted a bed. She wanted a shower. She wanted her friends. She wanted Kayce.

She needed to tell them about the increase in tears. The owls on Earth—*and* the one in Norenth. It didn't matter if she was ready or not. Lia couldn't do this alone.

The suns were dipping, the shadows lengthening as Lia left her shelter. Fee had instructed Lia to return to an open clearing once the second day ended. Hopefully whatever—or whoever—held the torches Lia had seen on that first night were long gone.

This excursion, while disconcerting with its revelation on the rifts, had been oddly relaxing. Focusing on basic needs for food and shelter, caring for herself. The boar horn was a heavy weight in her pack, but it reminded her that she'd faced it. Defeated it. All without hesitation.

She couldn't wait to tell Kayce.

Last night, she had found herself thinking of him more, especially the way he'd held her after she opened up to him. His touch unmade her; it anchored her. And when they'd parted, it was like a piece of him had embedded itself into a soft, vulnerable place she seldom wondered about—had never *allowed* herself to. In his absence, that piece tugged at her with its own current. Not an undertow, but a beckoning toward shore.

Traipsing through the swamp, curiosity over the feeling nagged at Lia. Was she reading too much into it? She likely was. The Weatherstone boys had always seen her as a sister—until the inaugural ball.

Lia pulled up short of the clearing.

Terranth had asked her to dance and the look on Kayce's face...was that jealousy? She hadn't been able to read it then. But now, in light of everything, she couldn't help but wonder if perhaps there really *was* something he'd been trying to say before her head split open and her world tore apart.

She couldn't think much more of it—the breeze had died. Insects ceased their song.

A chuckle chased over the field. "We had hoped ye would find a way back to us, little fox," the voice said. Several grunts rose to meet it. "Our dinner has been a long time coming."

Lia pressed against a tree, heart clanging. It was as if this horde knew her route, knew her plans. Knowing Fee, this was the last test. A final part of her training here. Not that it would ever be over... Lia sensed this was all just the beginning.

Steeling herself, Lia's pen unleashed into a broadsword, the weight comfortable in her hands. There was no point in running. No point in hiding. Dropping her pack, Lia forced an ease she did not feel into her limbs before trekking out to the field. She just prayed she lasted until Fee arrived.

Trees rustled and shadows parted. There were five of them, like the earlier torches had suggested. Orcs, heads bald and ears pointed. Bodies stocked with muscle and bare apart from scrappy leather jerkins and torn breeches. Small skulls adorned the belts at their waists.

Lia stopped in the center, the horde several paces away. It was an effort to tilt her head up, to meet the leader's hooded, yellow stare.

He arched a wiry brow. "Care to dance, little fox? Ye will find no city men here."

Lia's eyes narrowed. "I didn't come here to dance with men."

The pen shifted into a flail, the metal ball embedding itself into the orc to the leader's right as Lia spun low. Dark blood flowed when she pulled the spikes free, the illuminated chain swinging in a vicious circle. That orc dropped, and she dove under the retaliating axe of another, its chipped blade singing through the air where her head had been.

Five—well, four—on one. Not good odds.

She gritted her teeth against the traitorous thought, narrowly missing a sword. Light pulsed, and the flail morphed into a bolas. Lia, her stature smaller compared to these giants, wove around their thundering legs. Muscles coiled, she swung the throwing weapon. It was a risk to release her pen, but she had to get these numbers down.

She collided with the ground, watching the interconnected cords expand and entangle several orcs. The weights locked, the group falling with a thud and rattle of axes.

The leader watched with interest, stepping on her pen as it dimmed and shrank back on itself. "Sorcery," he mused, grinning savagely as he tested it with his weight.

Lia's heart faltered.

But the pen didn't break.

The orc frowned, snarling before stomping on it. The pen remained unscathed.

It strengthened Lia's resolve. With a cry, she tore up and tackled the orc's legs. The shock, not her weight, took him off guard, making him falter. Lia snatched the pen, a sword bursting from the crystal nib.

She didn't anticipate the meaty backhand to her cheek, the impact knocking her to the ground. Stars burst in her vision, her tongue burning when she bit it.

The orc laughed. "Feisty little fox! Perhaps we keep her for sport."

The others stood and joined in his mockery, drifting back to let their leader deal with her. She spat blood from her mouth, chest heaving. Their laughter rained like stones, each one a chip at her resolve. The thoughts swirled, predators all their own.

You can't do it. Kayce will see who you really are and find it weak—

No, he wouldn't.

Fighting monsters? The nightshriek was defeated by pure luck—

Please...

You can't put yourself at risk. Who would be there for Marcus, Mom—

Stop it—

You're not good enough to be in Norenth, so settle to be—

SHUT. UP!

It seemed like the more Lia stepped into herself, into the life *she* wanted, the more her mind was intent on sabotage, on sucking her back into its murky depths. Not that she wanted a life as an orc punching bag. But one that was at least *hers*, one where she was strong enough to fight for herself. There was no one on this world to tell Lia that she couldn't, that she shouldn't.

You're not ready, that traitorous voice of hers whispered.

Spitting another wad of blood and saliva, Lia acknowledged the thought. The current tugged, wanting to pull her under. But unlike before, she paused. Allowed it to sit for a moment. And then, like a leaf on a river, let the thought flow past her.

Because she was ready. She chose to be.

Lia wasn't interested in the record-keeping of the Order, or the politics involved with the Seekers, or cover-ups. Her role—her core—was an explorer, a defender of these realms.

Like her papa had been.

Some days, she could be a warrior. Others, an anxious mess. Most days she was a bit of both. But every day, beginning with this one, she would be there standing. Trying. Fighting.

Because she was all of herself. All that was Lia of Earth. All that was Norenthian Aurelia. Compiled into simply...her. Aurelia Corvine. The introverted bookworm. The justified smuggler. Daughter, sister. Best friend.

Anxious courage, ordered chaos.

And she chose everything.

Lia rose to her feet, sword of light in hand, and ran toward the roar.

CHAPTER THIRTY-SEVEN

"To my dearest friend!" Kayce hollered with a tankard raised. "She conquered her fears and a few orcs, and looked absolutely wondrous doing it."

In the small Norenthian tavern, several strangers rallied for the sake of cheering. The crowd was full of faces leathered from working ship decks. The exposed wooden beams along the ceiling echoed their voices, plates laden with cooked fish and vegetables. Not to mention the fluffiest rolls in the kingdom. It was a common haunt of Kayce and Lia's, best for eavesdropping about various smugglings. But they weren't here for work. The bread had been on Lia's list of demands upon returning home.

Lia flushed when Kayce's gaze returned to hers, the amber like pools of honey unhindered with his dark hair partly tied back, the loose half settled on his shoulders. She didn't remember this tavern being so hot, the air so difficult to breathe. "You weren't even there to see it."

"Actually, we watched from afar nearly the whole time," Fee said, sniffing her cup. "And you *did* look pretty marvelous."

"My point stands." Kayce drank deeply before wiping his mouth with the back of his hand. "I showed you more than half of those techniques, so of course it's going to be equal parts effective and awe-inspiring."

Terranth snorted beside Fee, surveying the packed tavern. "The only thing you inspire, Kacerion, is rebellion."

Kayce's teeth shown within a wide grin. "That, brother, is perhaps the kindest thing you've said to me."

Lia chuckled, basking in the warmth. Facing off against the orc horde had been harrowing—an honest understatement. She had a busted lip and bruising to show for it. But knowing she hadn't been alone, that her friends were there even when she couldn't see them, gave Lia comfort. And part of her, the one that was louder than her fears, saw the marks as badges of honor. The gremlin and nightshriek had tried to take a piece of her, too. But each scar was proof that she was more than she ever dreamed she could be.

Not to mention, her nails had never looked better.

Lia tried to catch Fee's eye. She needed to question her about the troll, what he'd revealed—but the guardian avoided her gaze. Lia knew it wasn't her split lip or how she smelled, having bathed immediately upon their return.

Kayce had even done her laundry, despite the new additions reeking of troll and orc and mud. He'd found time to read the first of her papa's books—and had several things to say about the depiction of his fight with the Widow's Whale. Her friends had also stuck true to their word, and looked through her papa's trunks. More photocopies of various texts referencing the Initiis were mixed in with old stories Lia had written. It turned out that the Initiis could work in pieces, according to one theory. Putting them together crafted a tool to begin a whole new story—a new realm. Or to end one.

It was more solid evidence than her papa's cryptic note.

But once Lia had donned fresh clothes, Kayce had surprised her—their other friends waited with greasy tavern fare. He knew her well. Couldn't plot on an empty stomach, last night's rabbit long forgotten. She would tell them about the owls, too. But the way that topic darkened the doorstep of her mind could hold out another hour or so. The lightness within her now had been hard-won.

Surrounded by Norenthians, Lia's smiles were relaxed, easy-coming as Fee and Terranth bickered. He'd warmed up to her, but the two were still like oil and water. It was nearly as fun to watch as Fee with the Smith. But Lia noticed a curve to Fee's lips, her smiles more frequent than they were for other people. Lia hid her own grin in a sip from her tankard. Only for Kayce's eyes to slide toward her, a softness there as if he, too, noticed the shift.

It was an effort to swallow. Just like it was an effort not to notice how much of a pair they looked in the glass window beside them. Both in navy-blue coats that draped to mid-thigh, belted at the waist with bronze. Hers fit more like a small corset, his gloved hand fitting snugly in the dip of her waist as he escorted her into the packed tavern. She couldn't even find the words to reprimand him that she was perfectly capable of getting to Terranth's table unescorted. It was an effort then just to breathe. And it wasn't the corseted belt's fault.

Lia took another deep drink before smoothing the bronze-edged lapels of her coat. She needed a distraction. They were partway through a fourth round of sparkling honey-water—the sugar having made them all giddy—when Lia smacked the table. "We need a song!" she cried.

Several cheers rang out again.

Terranth groaned. "Since when do *you* make such a request?"

"Since I almost died several times," Lia rebuked, raising her drink. "And I'm on a sugar kick."

Kayce wagged his eyebrows before shouldering his way to the minstrel near the hearth. A fiddle's melody rang over the crowd. It was a lively jaunt that broke the tavern noise apart like children running through a market square on a summer evening. Random trills and slides slipped up and down in pitch before settling into a melody. Everyone knew the tune, singing along and stomping their feet.

> *Skies above, gray to the mast*
> *Set sail o'er the mist, sailors hold fast!*
> *Seas be a'callin'*
> *Our women be hollerin'*
> *"Be home 'fore the mist floods the shore!"*

Laughing, Lia grabbed Fee's hand. The guardian glared, her cheeks darkening to a purple flush, before relenting. The girls wound through the crowd to where several patrons danced in time with the beat.

"You loathe dancing," Fee accused, raising her arm for Lia to slip under.

"You're right." Lia mimicked the movement, her coat flaring around her hips on a turn. "And you don't?"

"Hardly. Sneaking into balls across Norenth is one of my favorite things to do. The drum circles of the Southern Seas are especially fun." There was a steady rhythm to Fee's movements, a gracefulness.

"I haven't been south in years," Lia lamented. "Perhaps a girls' trip is in order."

The music continued, Terranth's voice ringing louder than anyone else's.

> *Seas above, bob to and fro*
> *Tis not fields we sow, but waters we ho!*
> *Sails be a singin'*
> *Our spirits be ringin'*
> *"We're home as the mist floods the shore!"*

Fee smiled radiantly, adding a skip to the simple tavern dance. A shrewdness glinted in her eye. "Do you really want to dance?"

"Not particularly."

Understanding narrowed Fee's gaze. "Be brief."

The melody built as they clasped hands, stepping lightly together and then apart.

"You sent me there on purpose," Lia accused. There was no need to elaborate.

Fee did her the honor of not acting oblivious. "Everything can be used for a purpose."

Her papa wanted Lia there. Thought far enough ahead to make sure Fee knew to send her when she needed it most. Wanted her to meet the troll. See the tears for what they truly were.

He really knew he was going to die.

It hollowed her. And reminded her. She needed to tell everyone everything.

"Who do you suspect knew? Knew and killed him for it?"

Fee's face contorted. "I don't know. Just that Julian was on edge, distancing himself from the others. Vilentia was the last sphere Julian was known to visit before his death. Sending you there under this pretense was the only thing I could think of without alarming people who didn't need to know."

It would make sense if he'd found proof of a traitor's involvement with the Seekers.

"The barriers have been worsening for fifty years, at least. Why would the Order make it seem like a recent problem? Did they not realize what was happening?"

Fee lifted a shoulder, shifting the tight sleeves to her copper tunic. "It's not that they're inherently bad. They're also not inherently good. They're humans, trying to do the best with what they have. Caution is expected with newcomers. No one would show their full hand at the start of the game."

Yet, a dark look came over her face at the statement.

"What?" Lia prompted, weaving through the crowd as the melody crescendoed, rhythmic patterns of a leather-skinned drum joining in. If this was a game, Lia didn't want to lose. But she was a step closer, the pieces falling into place.

"Because some guardians chose Malum's side, we've had to stick to our own spheres, or those deemed neutral to the Flameheart Order. I learned about Vilentia through Julian. It was odd when he mentioned it so suddenly." Fee's smile was sad. "Even odder when he commented on how you would enjoy its climate. I figured this training was the only way to show you the truth."

He was a conniving old man, Lia's papa. Rivaled another elderly sage she'd read about. But there was no bitterness in her heart. The troll's parting words about his injured friend—and her papa's aid—rushed through Lia's mind.

"I think they have a piece of the Initiis," Lia speculated, not daring to raise her voice. "That's how the Seekers are getting new creations to Earth. How ImaginX is getting the MemoryBank to work. Like the First Rift, it's the only way without them getting hurt in the process."

Besides her, that is.

The starlight dimmed in Fee's eyes. It was all the confirmation Lia needed.

"And if they want Malum freed—" Fee looked over Lia's shoulder, her expression shifting with the interruption. "It would seem someone wants to cut in."

Lia turned to find Kayce staring down at her. Heat radiated from him, standing so close she could see the pink scar through his eyebrow. A flush crept over her cheeks.

"I need to make up for that terrible dance at the inaugural ball," he said.

Even though the crowd sang along, Lia could have picked his voice out like it was the only sound in the tavern. "To be fair, I was under the weather," she murmured.

His mouth quirked up at the corner. "Just a tad."

Lia clasped his upturned hand. She didn't want to squander this. She wanted her joy, this warmth that had been blossoming with him to quicken. But speaking with Fee, who had now disappeared back to their table, had sobered her.

He pulled her close, poised to dip her into the next turn around the tavern floor.

"Kayce," she breathed, "there's something I have to tell you—"

"Hate to cut in, but you won't be getting this dance," a cloaked figure said before lowering his hood. Jace winked an amber eye, wry amusement curling his lips. "Not with what I've got to tell you."

A rumble built in Kayce's throat, the sound curling around Lia's midsection despite the disappointment in it.

She glared at Jace. What she had was far more important. But the way Kayce gripped the swell of her hip, the possessive timber in his exasperated growl, all thoughts of irritation at his eldest brother scattered like gulls from ship rigging.

"Why the cloak-and-dagger, brother?" Terranth asked on his approach, likely having tracked Jace from the moment he stepped into this establishment. "Sorry to say, the lion pommel on your sword is a dead giveaway."

"Someone needs a lesson or two in stealth," Lia agreed, mastering herself with an elbow in Kayce's side. "Perhaps we can oblige him sometime."

Finally releasing her, Kayce's frown deepened. "He'll have to pay a year's supply of honey-water for this infraction."

"Enough." Authority echoed in Jace's tone. "There's not much time. Ma and Da are retiring to their chambers before the council dinner. It's the best chance you'll have to get those answers about Sir Julian."

CHAPTER THIRTY-EIGHT

One would assume that being a son of the Lions would make it easy enough to visit their chambers. Not so much. Every year, the Lions met with the council representing the various guilds that made up the floating continent. And during that time, they did not allow for distractions—not even from their sons. The guards were under orders to turn them away unless, as Lion Magnar so eloquently put it, they were maimed or in mortal danger.

Which was why Lia and Kayce now dangled precariously from the balcony outside the royal suite.

The kingdom sprawled out below them, a network of cobblestoned roads and buildings carved from the ravine walls, their roofs of copper muted green like the castle turrets. Mist kissed Lia's cheeks, making the limestone slick under her palms. The stone was carved with a lattice up the towers, including the one housing the royal suites.

"Remind me again why flying was out of the question?" Lia grunted, her leather gloves slipping as she pulled herself up.

Kayce looked down over his shoulder at her. "Because the guards would have spotted us a mile away, *obviously*." With a shake of his head, he resumed his climb until he could swing himself over the balcony's railing.

"And none of them have spotted two figures climbing this tower?" Praise the skies they were at the top. Her arms were quivering.

A gloved hand appeared before her. She took it, Kayce hoisting her up and over. "It's more inconspicuous."

"It's nearly dusk."

"We're wearing gray cloaks. You covered your hair. We blend in!"

Lia checked the scarf tied around her head to be sure it was secure. "Sometimes I wonder if half the luck we had with these disguises is because I was too charitable a writer."

"Don't make me question my abilities with some existential nonsense," he said, picking the lock on the balcony doors. "We've moved past that."

"Just be grateful your scars haven't ripped open."

"With your leg, I could say the same about you."

Lia didn't want to be reminded how much it sucked hiking with an injured leg, healing tonic or not. At least the limp was gone.

The gilded glass doors clicked before Kayce eased them open. Gauzy white curtains fluttered as the pair slipped inside. The royal chambers were outfitted in Norenthian colors. Lion sigil emblazoned in copper and gold, banners of navy blue hung over silk-lined walls. The bed dwarfed a platform, sky-blue sheets folded neatly across its expanse. Armchairs faced a fireplace, flames flickering to chase the damp of the mist.

Lioness Silva's voice filtered through the open doors that led to their sitting room. "Honestly, Magnar. If Luddeck continues to air his grievances about tariffs on fishing, we are going to have some serious issues on our hands."

Kayce and Lia clung to the bedroom perimeter as they drew closer.

The Lion sighed. "Not much can be done. More ships are drawing fewer fish."

"Why?"

"I know not. Our scholars and builders are working out the kinks of these underwater ships."

"Well, they need to move faster. For the past couple of years, catches have been steadily declining. We cannot avoid raising the prices any longer. The people will know. Start worrying."

"They already are, Silva."

Lia stopped short of the door. The fish were disappearing?

Kayce shot her a questioning look, to which she could only shrug her shoulders. Norenth had grown beyond her. Many spheres did at a certain point, according to the Order and her conversations with Fee. But a pit grew in Lia's stomach. This had been going on for years, and they didn't know? In all their adventures and crosshairs with Captain Luddeck, they didn't once stumble upon this?

It unnerved her. And the timing lined up with the increased activity in the rifts. With the owl she had seen.

But a phrase nagged at Lia's attention more. *Underwater ships.*

She had mentioned submarines to Kayce at the mall and he'd been impressed by the idea, thinking it all to be a dream of another world. Lia had thought so as well. The only other person she'd mused with about exploring Norenth's seas was...

Her papa.

He must have given the Lions this idea. Meaning he'd also known about the fishing issue. Why hadn't he told her, in all their writing conversations?

Lia was so wrapped up in her head that she didn't notice silence fell in the sitting room. When she did, all she had time for was an exchange of panicked glances with Kayce before a feminine sigh of exasperation sounded. "Come out, you two."

Should we hide? Kayce mouthed.

Rolling her eyes, Lia grabbed his arm and stepped into the sitting room.

Lion Magnar sat before the second fireplace, his brocade tunic silver over blue. The top two buttons were undone, the scarf untucked. The Lioness held herself at the elbows, her gown liquid mercury and pristine. Even her circlet was in place, albeit a simpler one than she'd worn at the inaugural ball.

When Lia and Kayce inched before them, both dipped their heads in respect. Despite the total lack of such in their entry and eavesdropping.

"Kacerion, do not slouch, if you please," the Lioness said. "And Aurelia, take that rag off your head or you will ruin those lovely curls."

Both instantly did as they were told. From the queen's tone, now wasn't the time to argue, nor get indignant that they were both closer to eighteen than eight.

"Who is bleeding?" Magnar asked, rubbing his brow.

"No one," the teens muttered in unison. Their recent wounds were intact.

"Is anyone dying?" Silva prompted.

"Technically..." Kayce started, but Lia glared at him. While she hadn't exactly envisioned how she'd wanted this conversation to go, "technically" was certainly not it.

The Lion and Lioness exchanged a glance. The latter dropped her shoulders a fraction before lowering herself to the settee across from her husband.

"We were wondering when you would pluck up the nerve to approach us," the king said with a tired smile. "Julian said it may take some time, given the circumstances with Aurelia's mother."

"You didn't exactly make it easy," Lia said with a frown, forgetting for a moment to whom she spoke. "And your lack of surprise isn't comforting."

"We have a kingdom to run," Silva said. "And Julian gave us explicit instructions that *you* were to approach *us*."

"Why?"

"Because then you would be ready. And you must be, for what is coming."

Lia's chest tightened, but she fought against the urge to fidget. Instead, she took off her cloak, already overheating with her coat on underneath. She would not bend to her fears and uncertainties, not when she was so close to finding out the truth.

"What happened to my grandfather?" Lia asked the royals. "What information did he find that got him killed?"

The Lioness studied her before looking at her youngest son. As though coming to some shared conclusion, the king and queen nodded at one another. Then she said, "We know Julian was a Flameheart. We know how Norenth came to be, how our world stands as a sphere in the Emperium." A small smile graced her red-painted lips. "For that, we will always be grateful to you, Aurelia. You and Julian both."

A blush crept up Lia's neck. Never had she been thanked for this, and she wasn't sure what to do with the pride that filled her.

"But we are also aware of dangers outside our world," Magnar said. "That dark forces gather to break down the borders between us and others. Our world and yours. And those far more sinister."

"The Devourer," Kayce clarified, stepping closer to Lia. "And the ones who seek him."

His mother nodded. "Precisely. Julian came across various beings in his mapping of the Emperium. Several were injured and in desperate need of intervention due to the deterioration of their home spheres. It is through them that he discovered a Flameheart was working against the Order, helping Seekers in their quest for power."

There it was again, the aiding of injured creations. How did he get them off-world? What sphere was capable of acting like some infirmary? The questions bounced in Lia's mind, but there was one far more pressing than the rest.

"Who is it?" Lia asked. She couldn't hold it back anymore. "The traitor killed my papa for what he knew."

"All he told us was that it was someone in his chapter."

Kayce glowered, the leather glove groaning as he fisted his hand. "Leo."

Lia spun, her thick braid flinging over her shoulder with the force of it. "What makes you so certain?"

"Think about it," he said, warm amber eyes cold. "He was there when we first found Julian's study—*very* inquisitive on how you pulled me through to Earth. He was there at the mall when the dragon appeared. Not to mention, he has your mother's confidence. He knew she would be poking around Julian's death. A wise person would stay a step ahead. What better way than to befriend the investigator and embed himself in the search?"

She shook her head. Leo had been so kind, helpful even, as she adjusted into her new life. He'd always answered her questions and was honest when he couldn't. But she couldn't deny that Kayce's speculations made a lot of sense. Maybe she had been blinded by the similarities to the one she missed most. "But he advocated for you to stay with me. He wanted us to work together to fix the barriers."

"And has he actually told us, or anyone for that matter, how to do it?" Kayce retorted. "Because all there has been is talk and no action."

"Of course you would say that! Need I remind you I've been in basic Flameheart training?" Her mind raced faster than her pounding heart. "Mirel was also there that day the gremlin attacked me. She's close to my mom. And let's not forget how *charming* Mikayla is—"

"Enough!" the Lion boomed, his voice causing both teens to lower their heads. He studied them, nostrils flaring. "This is exactly why Julian kept the knowledge to himself. Accusation is deadly when misfired. It is a weapon that must be handled with care, used only at the right time and place with proper support. You of all people, Kayce, should know this." A muscle feathered in his jaw, an exact mirror to the one in Kayce's.

Silence fell, the fire crackling softly to fill it.

Lia didn't want it to be Leo. He believed in her, thought she was one to trust. But then, there was the truth about how long these barriers had been thinning and new ones appearing. Fifty years, at least. Leo had to have known that, old as he was. And he'd kept it from her.

Doubt wormed through Lia's mind. "Did Papa mention anything about a Book of Beginnings? The Initiis?" Lia asked. "Something powerful enough to fix rifts and mend what binds the worlds?"

Magnar nodded. "He did. And he said you have everything you need to find it."

No way had Lia heard him right. "I'm sorry—find it? The Seekers already have one piece, at least. It's how they're getting creations through, causing the tears in other spheres—"

"You have," Magnar interrupted, enunciating each word carefully as he leveled his gaze at Lia, "everything you need to find it."

Lia focused. Her papa chose his words carefully. If she had everything she needed...

"Aurelia," Kayce broke through her thoughts, gripping her shoulder. "The Initiis was broken into three. That means he found at least one of them."

Understanding dawned, Lia's jaw slackening. "This research isn't just on the Seekers' piece—"

"—but on one Julian found," Kayce finished, "and left for you."

A tool so powerful, one would kill for it.

The Lioness observed Lia, her features softening. "Aurelia—"

"I'm sorry," Lia interrupted breathlessly, "you all need to know—"

Bells clanged in the distance as the doors were shoved open with a bang, ricocheting off the walls as Kristof rushed in, eyes like a darkening sky. "We're under attack."

CHAPTER THIRTY-NINE

Lia was too late. Dread filled her as she tore for the balcony, Kayce hot on her heels.

They heard the screaming first. Wails and snarls bounced off the stone, the streets below a network of chaos. Inhuman screeches pierced her ears. Smoke bloomed in the distance. Lia scanned the misty twilight sky, but no owls blotted its surface.

Still, creatures not of Norenth were here. She'd run out of time.

"You both need to remain here," Kristof demanded of his parents, his sword drawn.

Red splotched the Lion's cheeks. "Listen, boy—"

"Da." Tension bracketed Kristof's mouth. "Please. Let us see to this."

The Lion and cub—really a lion of his own right—regarded each other. The sword glinted. It was the only piece about Kristof that looked battle-ready, his fingertips blackened with ink and several splotches along his billowing white sleeves. But Lia knew as much as he looked like a scholar, Kristof was as well-versed in battle training as his brothers.

As if recalling this, the king's passion simmered.

Silva blanched. "Magnar, you cannot—"

"Go."

With a nod, Kristof jerked his chin for Lia and Kayce to follow.

"What is it, exactly?" Lia bit out.

Kristof ground his teeth. "A living nightmare."

No.

Her worst fear had come to life. She ran harder than she ever had. Each step was a beat of her heart. Her home was attacked. Her home was *hurting*. She wouldn't let the Seekers, Malum, or whatever had sneaked through touch one person in Norenth if she could help it. It didn't even matter how it had happened; she would not be afraid.

"There's a tear," Lia huffed as they ran down staircase after staircase. "I was going to tell you at the tavern—I should have told you before I left, as soon as I knew—"

"Save the regrets," Kristof bit out. "Highguard will *not* fall."

"Though the warning would have been nice." Kayce's words held no spite. The crystalline lanterns shadowed the hard, determined lines of his face. He was not a boy practicing war games in the woods. He was not a ranger off to scout for the kingdom. Nor was he a vigilante against the crimes of the high seas. He was a prince of Norenth, ready to lay his body down for his land and his people.

Kayce's sword was out and Lia's pen mimicked it as they emerged into the courtyard. Beyond the walls was chaos. Nightmares stalked the streets outside Castle Finerda, warning bells ringing over the night-veiled mist. The three of them wasted no time rushing through the gate that was being drawn closed to fortify the castle.

"Keep these gates shut!" Kristof shouted to the guards before the bars closed behind them.

People ran for shops and homes, falling over themselves to get inside. Darkness pursued them, shadows peeling from crates and wagons. Obsidian creatures snarled, their gargoyle forms polished like stone with claws glinting in torchlight. Bone-chilling shrieks ripped the night apart—human *and* monster. Smoke rose, burning Lia's nose as she tracked black trails down the skyline to the Market Guild's square.

Lia couldn't allow her mind to trample over thoughts of "what if". Her mind emptied, adrenaline pumping blood to her body. A body that had been trained for such a time as this.

She didn't hesitate. Lia spun toward one gargoyle clawing after a local businesswoman. It pulled at her skirts, teeth gnashing. The woman screamed, and Lia was there. Pricking her thumb, she imbued the blade with her blood. The idea was as natural as breathing. It had worked on the gremlin, the nightmare in her room. She didn't know how to Transcribe yet. But she knew how to do this.

With a cry, Lia swung her sword, her pen searing through the gargoyle's moving stone flesh. It howled, then burned before their eyes into nonexistence. *It worked.*

The woman scampered against a shop door, trembling. "Th-thank you, my lady!"

"Get whoever you can to safety!" Lia ordered, already turning for the next beast.

But she glimpsed Kayce, whose eyes tracked over her with a heat she'd never—

Another monster, an insect scuttling along thousands of small legs, roared up with giant pincers at his right. Without missing a beat, Kayce whirled and sliced through its head. It rolled to his feet, black lifeblood oozing in a pool.

Chest heaving, he looked back at her, blood splattered over his face. The heat was still there. Her heart pounded beyond adrenaline. He took a step toward her.

Lia inhaled sharply, trying to ignore the responding sensation inside her. "Get to work, Trident. This is what we do."

This was not a time for teasing, responding to their shared magnetism—whatever this recent shift was between them. Soldiers from the castle had joined the fray immediately, though most dispersed themselves along the castle wall. Their copper breastplates shone almost silver under the crystalline's lantern light. Their arrows glinted, notched and loosened against the fleshly creatures. Lia and Kayce doubled their efforts, working to get the beasts away from the civilians trying to find shelter. It wore on her body, fatiguing her quicker than she thought.

Her arm burned. Her thighs quivered. Her joints strained. Her heart roared.

Lia would not let Norenth fall into darkness.

This is only a taste of what is to come.

The thought was not her own.

Her sword paused, a gargoyle's claws obsidian shards aiming for her throat before Kayce shoved into it. Shaking her head, Lia leapt onto the creature, piercing through its midsection for it to burn away with an earthshaking howl. It overwhelmed her senses—but not the distant hoot of an owl.

Kayce shot her a worried glance, his brow shadowed. But Lia waved him off.

Focus. Breathe. Fight.

The earlier thought had been so like her intrusive tics, but it held a darker tone than Lia's own. She scanned the rooftops, several occupied by rangers in gray cloaks, locked with swords and crossbows against nightmares of their own.

No owls in sight.

Clicking slithered up the Market Guild's streets, Kayce hollering to Kristof to advance. Lia couldn't divert her focus. Owl taxidermy had to wait.

She was decapitating another insect-like hellion when Terranth whirled into view, Jace beside him as the two tag-teamed against more stone monsters. Metal reverberated off them with each strike. Terranth barked an order, Jace pressed against his back. They were able to face the ends of the street, holding the intersection.

Jace whistled loud. The light blue of his tunic was dark with blood and sweat. Terranth cursed, his knee buckling as a nightmarish insect snapped at his thigh. There was no reprieve until Fee dropped from the sky, wings iridescent, with a shock wave that knocked the creatures and two princes off their feet. One of the beasts snapped back up and Fee flew toward it, striking an open palm to its chest.

Light flared, accompanied by an unholy screech, before the creature disappeared.

A gobsmacked Terranth watched the guardian engage the two that took the creature's place. "I don't care how," he muttered, surging to his feet as Lia, Kristof, and Kayce rushed over. "But I'm going to marry her."

"Battle first, proposals later," Jace urged.

"She isn't able to keep that up for long," Lia said, keenly aware that her own abilities were finite. Everything—everyone—had their limits. "We need to flank her."

The princes nodded, the five of them circling Fee with their swords toward the encroaching streets. More of the obsidian gargoyles rushed them, but they allowed those to run past to Fee in what measured waves they could manage.

Because there were more than these gargoyles and insects. Gremlins like the one Lia fought in the alleyway ran around their knees, tiny teeth chomping at the air. Lia didn't hesitate to plunge her sword into each one that crossed her path.

"I see why you hate these things!" Kayce yelled beside her, slicing through two of his own.

"Aurelia, duck!" shouted Jace.

Lia dropped to the cobblestones. Jace threw his sword like a javelin into an overgrown wolf, red eyes bright, as it bolted from behind a tailor shop. The blade pierced its chest, and the ground shook when it fell, sliding to a stop at Lia's feet. She pulled the sword free, tossing it back to Jace. He grabbed it by the hilt, swinging in a low, fluid motion to maim the gremlins nipping his knees.

Then Fallon was there, answering his master's earlier whistle. He snarled as his large paws hit the cobblestones, leaping against another monstrous wolf twice his size that had pounced for Jace's back. The wolf-dog's sandy coat turned black as he ripped into the nightmare's throat with bared teeth.

It was a never-ending sea, like a leak sprung from some—Lia pulled up short, tossing loosened curls from her face. That's right—a tear. In Norenth.

"Fee!" Lia rasped. The guardian jerked toward her, eyes white like beacons. Twin stars burning toward full power. "Get the Order! We need their help!"

"But what about—"

"Go!" Lia pushed, her pen flaring into a bow, arrow notched.

Fee nodded, wings lifting before pushing down. The mighty downdraft sent several gremlins scattering across the cobblestones. Taking Fee's place in the center, the boys easily fell in step defending Lia. She took aim and shot arrow after arrow, flying like shooting stars at the nightmares ravaging her home.

So many, such a variety it was almost like it was meant to—

Terranth shouted before she could finish the thought. "It's a diversion! They're pulling us away from the castle."

"Whatever for?" Kristof bellowed, slicing into a smaller wolf.

Kayce looked over at Lia, scarlet and black smeared over his face. She knew their thoughts were in tandem. They didn't know if her papa's Initiis piece was hidden in the castle, but the one who killed him—likely the same who caused this diversion—didn't either. But they would need the castle cleared, its forces occupied, to find out.

"Go!" Jace urged, grabbing Kayce's sleeve to push him toward the gate.

Lia followed Kayce, the two of them slipping into the courtyard and racing inside. With every step, Lia felt an urge pulling her, inching her closer to the one who'd taken someone precious from her. A snarl formed on her lips, her arms pumping to sprint faster.

The halls were deserted and sealed until open doors greeted them in the wing of royal chambers, those set apart from the Lions' tower. Glimpses into Kayce's and Terranth's rooms offered nothing. Kayce darted into Kristof's, also finding it empty. All were in a state of disarray, like a tornado had whipped through in a desperate search.

Jace's door was open, and Lia ran toward it—another figure colliding with her. Stars burst in her vision after their skulls clocked together, Lia unable to keep the curse from her breath.

"L-Lia! Kayce! Th-thank heavens," the figure stammered. "The Order sent me when we got word. Terrible, just terrible—"

Rubbing the pain from her face, Lia found Adrian rambling in front of her, cloaked in black.

"Wha—Adrian?" She looked at Kayce, who hadn't lowered his sword. Lia turned back to Adrian, who refused to meet her gaze. "What are you doing here?"

He tried to speak several times, shifting to put the door to his back. "I-I told you I came to help—"

"You're lying," Kayce said in a low voice that promised violence. "Fee only just left for the Order. You've come to find out if Julian has a piece of the Initiis. A piece to match the one you gave the Seekers. Isn't that right?"

Lia fought to keep her composure, but her skin, slick with gore, had turned clammy, her breathing shallow. Looking at Adrian now, she realized the dark clothing was medieval in style. There was no way he would have thought to change before coming. And the crumpled paper behind him, coming out of Jace's room, the others already ravaged...Lia knew.

She was staring at her papa's murderer.

"Why?" Lia croaked, blinking hard against tears gathering of their own accord. "You said—you said it was a *shame*. That Papa was a good person!" The light of her sword burned brighter. "You helped us!"

It hardly made sense. Adrian, of all people?

"I-I didn't mean for Julian to die!" Adrian balked at the swords before him. "But he was sticking his nose where it didn't belong! He knew what I had discovered, that I was—"

"You trashed his study," Lia seethed. "But you weren't looking for his Emperium story, his information on the Seekers—you were looking for his piece of the Initiis."

"You were supposed to be at school," he muttered. "I had no choice but to leave it like that."

And she had revealed as much when she and Kayce had visited his bookshop. Lia wanted to berate herself, but there was no time as snarls and shouts echoed from the streets below.

"Adrian—"

The man paled further. "You don't understand, he didn't understand—they'll kill me if I don't find the second piece!"

"Who?" Kayce demanded, his blade level with Adrian's sternum. "Spit it out."

"The Seekers, the ones running ImaginX! I-I helped them find the first piece three years ago. It's how they got their MemoryBank to work, but I-I just thought they wanted creations back on Earth, like I did!"

Fool. He didn't realize Malum was puppeteering them, or he didn't care.

"How did you know we moved Papa's things here?" Lia questioned. Then it dawned on her. "You were watching the house."

"I have been since Julian started poking around the myths on the Initiis months ago." Adrian's throat convulsed. "I saw Kayce's brother. Knew you'd move what you found to the safest place you could."

"Why would you do this?" Lia shook her head, disgusted. "They don't care about you!" It was harsh, but it was the truth. Seekers only cared for their greed, their thirst to be above all else. A way to get what they foolishly believed they'd been owed, but passed over for, millennia ago.

"Because I'm tired!"

Lia hesitated. The familiarity of Adrian's words, the desperate plea misting in his eyes, ensnared her.

"Don't you ever want to be more? Be who you are in your wildest dreams? They offered me that." Wiping his nose, Adrian straightened. "Wouldn't you want the chance to have more than the hand dealt to you on Earth, Lia?"

Lia studied the anxious, fraught man before her. There was a time she would have given anything to be in Norenth, to see Kayce like she could anyone on Earth. To sail the skies with him. Eat take-out with him and his brothers. Laugh with him. Be held by him. But more than those things, Lia had wanted to be who she dreamed she could be. She'd thought she could only be this way in Norenth. But what was reality but what they chose to make it?

In Adrian's glasses, the reflection that stared back was a girl who'd once longed for the exact things he did. But the young woman she was now opened her mouth, saying, "My *name* is Aurelia."

A spasm pinched Adrian's face. He raised his arm, glowing pen in hand—

She struck, knocking his arm back. Breath left Adrian, the man stumbling as her papa's papers fluttered to the ground. Her own pen was ready, already flaring to life. And there, tucked in his cloak, the half of a book—

Kayce was about to grab hold of the Flameheart when the walls vibrated, chandeliers clicking. The crystal beads trembled. Each vibration, like a steady pulse, made them sway, each louder than the last. They looked down the corridor.

A minotaur consumed the archway. His snout flared, twin axes dragging over the marble floor, screeching like nails raking over glass.

She looked back at Adrian only to find the space empty. The rebel Flameheart rushed through Jace's room to the balcony before a portal of light swallowed him, whisking him away.

CHAPTER FORTY

Kayce glared where Adrian disappeared before turning to Aurelia, a look of pride softening his face. Under his gaze, she couldn't even be disappointed at Adrian's escape. Aurelia hadn't done this for his approval, but skies, to see it in his eyes made her burn in a way she never had. Flickers had been there before, but now it was like an inferno raged in her chest each time he looked at her.

Before he could say anything, the minotaur's hoof scraped the ground. Over the whistling wind from Jace's balcony, battle raged outside. She knew then the gates held fast; Adrian had brought the monster for this exact purpose. Spineless coward. And yet, she couldn't quite shake the fact that she had seen a piece of herself in his plea.

"Looks like we get that redo from the mall," Kayce said.

"Was this what you had in mind?" Aurelia grimaced before the minotaur snarled.

"No, he's going to be a very annoying pain." Kayce stalked to the other side of the corridor, his attention on the minotaur. "Some ugly beast you are!"

Huffing, the minotaur leveled his bull-like head. Kayce caught Aurelia's eye, jerking his chin to signal her to circle. She was already moving, the pen's light morphing into a lasso. The beast snarled at the magic, eyes narrowing to watch Aurelia.

"Should I even ask about your parents?" Kayce wore a diabolical smirk, tossing his sword idly from one hand to the other. "Though, I am curious: was your father or mother the cow in the equation?"

She snorted and rolled her eyes, despite a twinge of mounting anxiety. That gargantuan head swung toward Kayce with a grunt. Aurelia twirled the rope, the circle swinging beside her.

Kayce's brow rose. "Oh, so you *are* intelligent. You had me fooled."

That did it. The minotaur roared, running full-tilt toward Kayce. The floor trembled, marble cracking under each step as the beast thundered toward them. The minotaur raised one of his axes, swinging hard and towering over Kayce.

Kayce ducked, the blade brushing his hair and back. Aurelia grit her teeth—that was *too* close. But Kayce was already bouncing back, sword swinging to claim its own mark. The blade bit into the beast's hide, splitting its midsection. The minotaur growled, knocking the prince backward as though he were no more bothersome than a gnat.

Aurelia's heart leapt into her throat when Kayce collided with the wall, face contorted in pain. But he scrambled to his feet as the minotaur stalked forward.

This wasn't going to be the mall again.

Running, she twirled the rope, the circle swinging wide overhead before she threw it from behind. A loop settled around the bull horns and wrenched the beast's head back as Aurelia hauled with all her strength. The minotaur jerked, dropping an axe to grab at the light tangled about his head. He snarled, burning himself. The motion freed Kayce, but the minotaur turned to glare at Aurelia.

She balked. "Oh, crap—"

A roar erupted from the beast, causing crystals to fall from the chandeliers. He flung his head left and right, whipping Aurelia around like a fish on a line. She stumbled over her legs, trying to keep hold, but her pen was slipping. Another twist was all it took for the minotaur to send her tumbling to the left, pen soaring as the light faded. It clattered against the marble floor, rolling down the hall.

Kayce ran to her side. She gasped for breath, the wind knocked out of her. But she shoved to her knees, trying to work through it as the minotaur rounded on them again.

With her pen gone, Aurelia thrust out her hand. "Cut me!"

"What?" Kayce reared back.

"Just do it!" she demanded, the minotaur pawing the ground with his hoof.

Muttering under his breath, Kayce used the edge of his sword to slice neatly across her unblemished palm.

Aurelia refused to flinch, clenching her jaw before standing. "Cover me," she breathed, squaring her shoulders.

Her eyes were hard as flint, staring at the beast, at the cut across his abdomen. Both lunged in the same instant. Crystals from the chandeliers rained under the charge. Kayce was a beat behind her, catching the blow of the axe with his sword as Aurelia slammed into the beast, her hand to his sternum.

Blood met like ink, smeared like words, over flesh like parchment.

The minotaur's arms caged her to his combustion, light searing all around her until smoke and ash lingered instead.

She crumpled back into Kayce, who caught her against his chest. "Aurelia?"

"I'm fine," she muttered, blinking dazedly and trying to catch her breath. "He was bigger than the gremlin."

"You don't say," came a voice from the archway. "Seems like you're well versed in Transcription, Lia. Despite being a bit hands-free."

Turning, they found Mikayla, pearls perfectly placed, standing alongside Fee, Mom, and the rest of the Order. And in the front Leo stood, holding Aurelia's pen out to her.

CHAPTER FORTY-ONE

In the late hours of the night, the Weatherstones and Corvines were in the castle infirmary. Aurelia had watched the Order as they ventured down here. It felt like an uninvited guest had helped themselves in her home. Not like the nightmares, the battle sounds quiet by now, but still. It set Aurelia on edge. She was happy to see them wait outside, only Leo joining her mom as she and Kayce went ahead into the infirmary.

Her mom had resolved to treat every cut and scrape despite Aurelia's insistence that she was fine—genuinely, this time. She was so pale, so tense, Aurelia acquiesced for fear that her mom might crumple.

Where was her strong, resolute mother? It was like it was unbearable for her to be here, despite her mom's best efforts. Though seeing to the princes' injuries seemed to give her purpose.

"I said I'm fine now, Mom." Aurelia pulled her neatly wrapped hand back. "Jace needs your attention more."

The crown prince waved her off from the next cot, despite being in the worst shape of them all. His dog Fallon curled at the foot of the cot, assessing anyone who dared come close to his master with small growls.

"They're all surface wounds," Jace assured, catching the Lioness's glare.

"Which you shouldn't have in the first place," Lioness Silva stated, thumb hooked onto the four pearls at her throat. "You should have let the guard handle it."

"We trained them better than that, love," Lion Magnar said from Terranth's cot, a healer stitching up a bite mark on his son's leg—also at Jace's insistence. "You know they would never stay back."

Color splotched her high cheekbones. "He is the heir—"

"Ma—Mother." Jace's tone held growing authority, but was still full of respect. "I apologize for your worry. But I cannot apologize for defending our people and our home."

"It's I who must apologize."

Everyone turned to Fee. She stood in the doorway, wings out of sight. Her gown was spotless once more, the pale blue darkening her skin yet brightening the beads and shells woven into her braids. Her demeanor was solemn despite the lightness of her attire, her brow lowered.

"I failed as the Norenthian guardian," she said, straightening like a soldier before her commanding officer. "It was my duty to monitor these boundaries. I should have known Adrian's movements, the small rifts he found here. It is an error I will not make again."

Studying Fee, Aurelia knew why she took this so personally. Fee had been at the tavern when the nightmares first broke into Highguard. She was having fun, her guard down. And this could be the moment it snapped back up, permanently.

Terranth moved to stand, waving the last healer to be excused, but Aurelia spoke first. "We can all assign blame to something we did or didn't do. Something to atone for the guilt we feel for what happened today. The damage done, the lives lost." Aurelia's throat tightened. She was speaking more to herself than anyone.

The captain had given the report to the Lions after seeing to his soldiers in the barrack's infirmary. It wasn't as bad as it could have been, but there would be empty beds tonight. And that was enough.

Aurelia cleared her throat. "The only failure here is with the Flameheart who betrayed his calling."

Leo nodded, looking at her mom. "The rest of the Order is waiting in the hall."

"Whatever needs to be said can be done with us present," Kayce said from Aurelia's side, a few stitches on his cleaned forehead.

Her mom, who had been unnervingly pale and withdrawn since her arrival, twisted her lips to the side. "I don't think that's wise. Not with the Order's current climate."

"That's a kind way of putting it," Leo muttered, arms crossed. "We've mucked things up enough. I'm done dancing around matters. Perhaps meeting the Weatherstones will make the others see what's at stake."

Her mom's spine was an unbending rod. "But what about Lia's Transcription—"

"We'll discuss that." Leo's face softened a fraction. "Don't worry."

Aurelia watched her tension ease. Mom had asked her to keep her ability a secret, but there had been no avoiding it with the minotaur. And it wasn't like Aurelia knew the Order would be standing right there, ready to help *after* she had done all the work. But Aurelia was smart enough to try to keep any conversation on her pen-less work to herself.

If Mom was so tense, there had to be a good reason.

Fee went and returned with the rest of the Order after acquiescence from both Leo and the Lions. There was ample space for everyone in the infirmary, which housed twenty beds with only three occupied. Kristof remained standing by Terranth's bed, the Lions flanking Jace. Her mom decided to tend to the crown prince with the infirmary workers excused.

Reynaldo whistled low, eyeing the arched windows and detailed stonework bordering each before easing himself beside Mirel on a cot. She fidgeted with her pen, sleek and bronze with a pearl tip. And then there was Mikayla, eyeing Aurelia when she entered to take her place beside Leo. Aurelia met her stare until Mikayla shifted her gaze. "We shouldn't do this without Veera."

"We shouldn't be doing this at all." Leo sighed with impatience. Gone were the niceties, the soothing of tension. Fatigue lined his face; disappointment furrowed his brow. And sorrow embittered his tone. "Julian knew. He knew *everything*. And he was the only one trying to do right by our creed—our *true* creed. We might as well return our embers for all the good we've done with them."

"He never told us," Mirel defended. "Not about the Seekers getting the Initiis, or that it actually existed!"

"Not like he could when he believed there to be a traitor among us," Leo pointed out. "He didn't know who until it was too late."

"No one knows how the First Rift was sealed, exactly," Reynaldo mumbled.

Aurelia frowned, sharing the expression with Kayce. "For readers, that's pretty poor record keeping."

Leo rubbed the back of his head in thought. "I believe the first Order thought it wise. Less temptation to repeat history if the future, quite simply, didn't know it. It's a theory, since the Initiis has never been seen and mentions of it in the most ancient of Flameheart texts are vague at best. Adrian has access to the Celestium Librus; it makes sense that he would've discovered the truth, bookworm that he is."

Silence filled the room and despite its spaciousness, it felt like it was getting smaller. They all knew who was missing. Aurelia struggled for a full breath, her mind racing as the Order looked at her.

But then she paused. Breathed. Let the thoughts drift, slow. She didn't fight them.

The tightness eased. Aurelia relaxed.

And she told them.

She started from the beginning. Papa had been urging her mom to move back, to help him with the worsening rifts. He saw them throughout the realms, his duties taking him to creations hurt from encountering the rapidly increasing tears. He feared it was only a matter of time until they grew on Earth. For worlds to even succumb entirely to them. Aurelia had spent the most time with her papa leading up to his death. He was increasingly absentminded, worried. Preoccupied. He'd found records of the Initiis, fearing Seekers had access to at least one piece thanks to a Flameheart who found it within the Emperium.

It wasn't until that six-eyed owl appeared in his garden, both a warning and confirmation. He had called her mom that evening, saying he had proof. Then came the accident. Adrian had been watching the house. Knew her papa had Transcribed the owl. Knew he had been compromised.

Aurelia swallowed hard, unable to continue. The others could draw their own conclusions from there. At the beginning of her story, Kayce's hand had slid into hers, and she had yet to let go. She gave it a squeeze.

Leo sighed heavily. "This Order has drifted so far from what it once was. We've gotten lazy, enjoying the beauty and wonder of the Emperium without having to work to protect it."

"Previous generations took care of that," Reynaldo defended. "Are we really at fault?"

"We are when we refuse to look at the signs in front of us," Mirel said in a low tone, her shoulders slumping. "The absence of a choice is still a choice. And our willful blindness was the wrong one."

"Julian saw them." Mist clouded Leo's eyes. "He should have been able to tell us about the tears across the spheres, his suspicions that some would worsen on Earth. When ImaginX marketed their MemoryBank, he voiced how eerily similar it was to our gift. From the whisperings of sightings in the last year alone, he assumed they experimented with tears, getting creations to Earth unharmed. He turned to Cordelia when we"—he hesitated, his voice full of conviction—"when *I* wouldn't take it seriously. And we refused to look into it until Aurelia Sparked."

"We're busy," Mikayla said, arms crossed over her chest. "We all have jobs to do, families to provide for. Did he expect us to just drop all of that to go on some wild chase across the universe? It would have been a waste of time."

"It wasn't a waste of his." Aurelia stood, letting go of Kayce's hand. She was fed up with Mikayla's flippant attitude. "He found injured creations and helped them. He scoured *your* records for anything that might describe how the tears were worsening. He figured out the Initiis must be in play and did what he could to secure it. Before he realized there was a traitor helping the Seekers, he found at least one piece."

"And where is that piece?" Mikayla asked, undeterred.

Elbows braced on his knees, Kayce interceded, "We don't know. Just that Julian placed it somewhere for Aurelia to find."

Mikayla scoffed. "How fitting."

Metal clamored as her mom set scissors onto a tray with force. "I should think so. Who better than someone untainted by our selfishness?"

"Selfishness? That's rich coming from you, Cordelia."

Her mom turned to Mikayla. "No one likes a hypocrite. But Lia is right. My father did what we should have done. And what matters now is that we continue his work."

Everyone nodded, until even Mikayla had the decency to tuck her chin.

"Adrian will have returned to the Seekers," Reynaldo said. "It's likely that ImaginX's CEO is who he reports to."

"Then it's him who has the other book piece." Leo rubbed his forehead. "When it isn't on loan to Adrian."

It was hard for Aurelia not to chastise herself for allowing Adrian to flee, even though she only thought she may have seen the piece of the Initiis during their brief encounter.

"Then there's one more piece to locate, apart from Julian's," Mirel gathered.

Aurelia caught her mom's eye, who nodded. "We need to find them before they do," her mom said. "Bringing creations to Earth is not the only thing they want."

"They want Malum freed," Aurelia finished.

Terranth leaned forward. "Who is he, exactly?"

"He's the worst of the worst." Kayce filled him in. "They call him the Devourer."

Fee nodded. "He was like me once. Meant to guide the dreamers, aid the creations. But he wanted more. He stole the Initiis to do it, and that is a tale forbidden to us, even now. It's how the First Rift began. He was imprisoned in a sphere he tried to make, but the Initiis was broken into three pieces because of what he did.

The legends Julian was piecing together suggested one of the pieces partially mended the First Rift."

"Until now," Mikayla said bitterly. "A piss-poor attempt at a Band-Aid."

"Actually, that 'Band-Aid' has been slipping for fifty years. Another thing you all wanted to ignore," Fee reprimanded, reminding Aurelia of the Vilentian sphere and what she learned there. "It would seem Malum has been growing stronger in his confinement. He has influence, whispering into the Seekers' minds. But he does so in a way even we cannot see."

"So we get all the pieces first," Aurelia summarized. "Once the Initiis is whole, it should mend the tears permanently, hopefully preventing Malum from being freed. Wherever his sphere is."

"That's not exactly true." Mom stepped in, her tone somber. There was an unsettling silence as everyone looked to her with unease. She casted a glance at Aurelia before continuing. "Lia was attacked the other night. By a creature we are certain Malum made."

Leo looked between them with shock turning his skin ashen. "What? You never mentioned this before."

"Because I didn't know who to trust," she shot back.

Aurelia studied her mom in a new light. She had bet Mom told Leo everything. Even though there were secrets that she'd harbored, it comforted Aurelia to know that not *all* of her dirty laundry had been as aired out as she'd feared.

Leo considered this a moment, before leaning back with a look of understanding so her mom could continue.

"Lia's abilities are far beyond what we are capable of. She went to the world where this creature is from in her sleep, and the nightshriek—as we call it—hitched a ride back to Earth. I'm certain that Lia's thoughts of all of this, of Malum and the Seekers, accidentally guided her to Malum's world. His prison."

The words knocked the wind from Aurelia's lungs, leaving her gasping as everyone clamored in reaction. *Malum's prison.* No, she couldn't have—but she did. She'd seen it in the ringed eyes of the nightshriek. Of the owls. She'd known his messenger birds had been stalking her. Resigned herself to it. But to have been pulled into a world no one knew how to access...

She wanted to find the deepest hole beneath Mount Fealtek and bury herself in it. Hide inside it. Dimly, she was aware of the Order's eruption, of how Kayce shifted closer, his heat radiating into her side.

"I'm not sure how it happened," her mom called over the debate, "but it's clear to me that the barriers of even Malum's prison must be weakening. Lia's mind needs to be strengthened so she can master these abilities."

"Absolutely not," Mikayla said, her shrewd focus returning to Aurelia. "We can't trust someone the rules don't apply to."

"What do you mean?" Aurelia demanded, struggling to ignore how her stomach dipped even more after the bomb Mom had dropped on her.

"We saw what you did," Mirel said quietly, as if she regretted siding with Mikayla. "You Transcribed that minotaur without a pen. Likely did the same to the gremlin in the city?" At Aurelia's answering nod, a flash of hurt crossed Mirel's face when she looked at her mom. "You didn't tell us that."

"I thought this very thing would happen!" she insisted. "That you would all look at Lia like she's been helping the Seekers or something worse."

"She's a child," Mirel said, insulted at the insinuation. "Who would ever think a child, recently Sparked, would do such a thing?"

Aurelia figured it wasn't the best time to voice that she was a year shy of adulthood by American government standards.

A scoff erupted from Mikayla. "Stranger things have happened. Just look at Adrian." There was an uncomfortable murmur of agreement before she continued, "Let's not forget that Aurelia brought her prince over. If she can do that, what's stopping her from bringing something worse should the wrong person cross her?"

Aurelia let out an indignant snort. "I have more self-control than that."

That terrible nightshriek notwithstanding.

But the more Mikayla talked, the more appealing a loose gremlin in her home sounded.

"How do you do it?" Mikayla asked. "Do you even need a pen?"

Aurelia opened her mouth to speak, but her mom stood. "Don't answer that."

"Why shouldn't she? We're airing out all the dirty laundry now," Mikayla flung a hand toward the royals present. "Unless you want to spare her precious creations something ugly about the girl they owe their lives to."

"You go too far." Kayce's voice deepened with contempt as all the Weatherstones, even the Lions, wore faces of outrage. They all moved to stand, and Aurelia's eyes burned at their defense.

Leo put a firm hand on Mikayla's shoulder. "Our selfish ignorance has cost Norenth too much. We will not insult them or Aurelia in their home."

Everyone relaxed at that, but Kayce, who had surged to his feet, remained beside her. Aurelia looked at her mom, whose face had gone pale again. Was there something ugly about what she could do?

True to his word, Leo diverted the focus from her. "Aurelia will learn to harness this...additional layer to her Flameheart abilities. Perhaps in the future it will aid us against the Seekers. But it will only be done under direct Order supervision." He glanced at her mom. She gave him a stiff nod. He continued, looking at Aurelia, "Let the Initiis searching be left to us. We have much to atone for, and I know I speak for other chapters as well."

"They have to be told," Reynaldo interjected. "The Legacy Chapter will convene for this, considering Malum is involved."

While the Order murmured agreements, Aurelia glanced at Kayce to find him watching her. A muscle ticked in his jaw, his eyes hard amber shards. He didn't trust them not to mess this up. Aurelia didn't either.

She had been going over everything in her mind, especially what the Lions told her. That message in her Norenth keepsake box, about walking through fire—it all was the key. That clue, if she could figure it out, would help her find the Initiis piece her papa left to her.

"Papa left one piece to me," she said, her voice carrying over the small conversations that had started. "I was told I have everything I need to find it."

Out of the corner of her eye, Aurelia swore the Lioness fought a smile.

But Leo's face was solemn once more. "Then you will tell us what you know."

"No." Aurelia lifted her chin, her tone firm but respectful. "I'm sorry, but no."

"Lia—"

"Mom, I can't," she turned to her mom, heart aching, her mind dissenting. But her soul rallied. "This is what Papa wanted. And this is what I want." Aurelia knew her papa wanted her alone to find this piece. It was bigger than her understanding and what she knew logically. It was faith, a faith in all the good her papa stood for. She could honor him with this.

Her mom's eyes shone as if she knew it too. "I'll officially accept the Corvine seat in this chapter." None of the tension loosened from Mom's stature as she spoke, a look of resigned determination in her gaze. "I'll monitor your progress myself. With both your training and this search."

"Well, we don't always get what we want." Mikayla dropped her arms. "I say we put it to a vote, especially regarding this hunt for the Initiis—"

"Another time," Leo cut her off, a twinkle in his eye like he was also aware—and agreed with the Corvines. "It's been a long day, and we've devoured enough of Their Majesties time. They have a kingdom to run, and we have families waiting."

"Indeed," Lion Magnar said, rising to clasp Leo's hand. "And we all have beds to sleep in. Rest would do us wonders."

It felt like the understatement of the century coming from a king, but it loosened the tension in the room enough. A small mending.

CHAPTER FORTY-TWO

The royal family and Aurelia bunked down in the infirmary after the Order left. Mom had to get back to Marcus, and she didn't seem to have it in her to demand Aurelia's return. Exhaustion had weighed heavily on them all, but Aurelia was awake almost instantly when Kayce lightly shook her shoulder, finger pressed to his lips before nodding to the window and the brightening skies beyond.

It wasn't difficult for two rangers to sneak out. Shades of pink inched over the horizon. Aurelia surveyed the damage from Paxia's back as they flew over the capital. Nightmares had hit the Market Guild around the castle hardest. Glass glittered over cobblestones. Overturned wagons were smashed into walls. Hay was thrown about, goods destroyed. Various homes stood like charred skeletons.

But the gas lanterns were lit, and people were out, soldiers and civilians alike cleaning the streets before another day dawned. The only blood that marred the city was red, a small blessing. The

Order had made sure all nightmares were Transcribed to whatever hell-sphere they called home. But the tear was still there and needed to be monitored so this wouldn't happen again.

Because it could. Likely would. Owls were so easily missed. And none had reported seeing one during the battle.

Aurelia sent a silent thought of gratitude to those who'd bled—and died—defending this beloved world. Tears filled her eyes, melancholy bitter on her tongue, but the wind dried them away as Paxia's wings lifted them higher through the mist and over it, surrounded by a starry sky of seas. Gulls flew with her, weaving between the seas as dawn continued to inch over the horizon. Water broke ahead as a sailfish leapt, its large, shimmering blue fin catching an air current. It speared a bird with its sword-like bill before diving into the next ocean. The volatequis wove around several buoyant oceans, their waters calm despite the earlier chaos on land, until the alcove off Fealtek appeared. Aurelia pulled on the reins, slowing Paxia's flight until her hooves hit the ground, her run turning into a trot before finally slowing to a walk.

Patting her neck, Aurelia dismounted and guided her steed to the small stream that ran down the cliff. She glimpsed her reflection on the wavering surface.

It was her. The coppery hair she had possessed all her life, but with the subtle shifts in darker and lighter tones that she had dreamed for herself here. Her freckles remained to the number, but her face looked a little leaner. The softness of girlhood had slipped away, and not just in a physical sense.

Gray like the mist below, wiser eyes stared back at Aurelia.

And she didn't mind it.

Kayce had slid off Storm with a practiced ease, letting his steed follow as he leaned back against a tree.

"It seems Norenthians aren't in the habit of letting the dust settle for long," she said. "The streets will appear like nothing happened before the sun rises."

"They'll remember, though," he said. His gaze trailed over her sure movements, her straight back. But when she turned to him fully, he averted his eyes. She wrung her hands, uncertain what to make of such stares when accompanied by the smile that tugged at his mouth. "You handled it well. The battle..." He paused, his voice dropping an octave. "And the Order."

Ah. *That.* She couldn't help the smile, nor the flush that spread over her cheeks. "I couldn't very well let Mikayla try to walk about like she owned the place."

His chuckle was dry. "No, but I'm proud of you. You were a true Norenthian lion—without biting her head off. You made your concerns known, but you didn't back down. It's—" He halted, rubbing the back of his neck. "It's nice to see you stand up for yourself."

Kayce hadn't been shy with compliments before, but this time, the way his tone dipped, it tightened Aurelia's stomach, made her hyper-aware of every sensation.

"This is my home." She tried to speak around the desert her mouth had become. "And I may have picked some things up from Jace. He knows a thing or two about tactfulness."

"He's good at that," Kayce agreed, stepping closer. "The best of the four of us."

She smiled, but sobered a moment later, looking out at the expanse of mist cloaking the kingdom. The sun was rising; the seas rippled with its light.

"Vilentia helped a lot," she murmured. "I didn't realize how much I lost of myself, trying to be everything for everyone."

"It looks good on you." Kayce flushed at her raised brow. "The confidence, I mean. It's a good look on you."

"Thanks," she said with snark, but then softened. "Sorry it took me so long."

There was another sideways glance before Kayce looked back toward the horizon with a smirk. They stood quietly, both lost in their own introspection, Aurelia aware of every inch of space between them.

She opened her mouth to speak, but Kayce broke the silence first. "You don't need to apologize to anyone. For anything," he rushed. "You are so much more than you realize."

"A Flameheart with a unique knack for bringing creations where they don't belong would certainly qualify as being 'more'. I think to stay in step with my progress, I should keep dragging you along, no matter what the Order says."

Unable to help herself, she glanced up at him. Kayce was already watching her. The way the growing sunlight caught the angles of his face halted her tongue.

He looked to the seas before turning toward the creek, stepping over the stones to head inside their outpost. "Until you can't."

Aurelia frowned at his retreating back, her steps quick to catch up. "Since when have we bowed to authority before?" she asked as the stone door shut behind her.

Kayce didn't reply as he made for the spiral staircase, taking the steps two at a time.

That wasn't what he meant. Aurelia frowned, following him up to their rooms. "Even when we fix the tears, I can come here. Fancy tricks, remember?" She prattled as he slipped into his room. "Besides, I might not even need the tears to bring you around. Special powers, and all." The lightness was forced, but she didn't care. Old habits died hard, and the thought of being separated from Kayce was a vice clenched around her chest, tightening with each passing second.

Aurelia had to change the subject just to be able to breathe. "Should we look for the third piece and leave whatever section Papa found hidden? Surely he'd put it somewhere safe enough."

Some tension had loosened from Kayce as he reappeared, a small leather pouch in hand. Aurelia liked to think he found relief in the change of subject as well.

"It makes sense," he said, his thumb brushing back and forth over the seam. "If only you can find it, then I truly doubt others can. Even if the Seekers find the third piece before us, they won't be able to free Malum without Sir Julian's."

"Where do we even start? It feels like we'd be searching for a needle in a haystack." She frowned, following *again* when he turned for the final stairs up to the lookout. "I've always hated that metaphor. But as huge as the Emperium is..." Reaching for the end of her ponytail, Aurelia worked out the knots woven from flight. "How did Papa find one? How did Adrian?"

"The same way the rangers trained us." A sly grin slipped over his face as he turned toward her, the window framing the waterfall at his back. "Every animal leaves a trail. Find the trail, follow it to the Initiis. We double back over Sir Julian's research. Perhaps we pay Adrian's shop an impromptu visit, learn how the weasel found his piece—"

"You just want the excuse for some breaking and entering."

"Because I am *oh so good* at it. Besides"—Kayce's tone took an edge to it—"he has it coming."

If the squirrel hasn't packed up and run by now, came the sour thought.

Aurelia steadied her breath, letting it drift by. There was little point in fretting over it. Adrian would likely do what he did best: hide.

"We'll start there, see where the path leads. Then once we get that missing piece, we can get Papa's, and finally, do what we've really been training for." She smirked. "Steal the piece from the Seekers."

And with the Initiis whole, they could repair not only the tear in Norenth, but those all across the Emperium. Hopefully leaving Malum right where he belonged, then she'd never step foot in his frosty world again.

Kayce nodded, but a frown emerged. "They won't stop coming for it, even after you seal the First Rift."

He wasn't wrong. No one births an entire company that's a near-instant success like ImaginX without seedy, underhanded deals. *Malum's influence must be linked to the CEO.* Would finding the Initiis and mending the realms treat the symptoms, but not the actual infection of Malum's darkness?

It was one of those moments that Aurelia desperately wished for her papa's advice.

Her vision blurred. The swells of grief were low, but there. Aurelia's breath shuddered as she steadied against them, blinking rapidly to clear her sight. The urge to rip at her nails needled her, but instead, she pulled out her pen, twirling it between her fingers. "Papa would want them gone. For good."

"So, we're graduating from solving a murder to taking out an entire underground organization with hands in your world's political and economic climate?" Kayce whistled low, a look of danger darkening his gaze as he tossed the pouch between his hands. "Sounds a bit steep, Harpy."

How *would* they even manage that? From the sounds of it, Seekers were as old as the Order. Doubts flitted about her mind, but Aurelia's next breath was smoother. "We start with the Initiis. Tomorrow, clearly, has enough problems. We don't need to be borrowing them when today has plenty to contend with."

He nodded slowly, eyeing her. "For once, you're right."

Her laugh was a choked, bittersweet thing. "Give me another five minutes and some part of my brain will start obsessing over when we'll get into Adrian's shop while another wonders when we can start world-hopping while *another*—" Catching his look,

Aurelia cut herself off with a sheepish smile, finally stilling her pen. Then she blinked, Kayce's words catching up with her. "Wait, did you say I was right for *once*?" Her voice went shrill as she stepped toward him, poking his chest with her pen. "I think that's more my line, Kayce—"

He caught her wrist, the grip halting her tongue. "Are you threatening me, my lady?"

"Potentially." Her tone dipped to match his, and his gaze smoldered in response.

He inclined his head toward her, breath fanning her cheeks. "Is that why this is glowing?"

Glancing down, Aurelia's pen shone. But she wasn't actively utilizing its power. She didn't understand; she wasn't *really* threatening him. Far from it, in fact.

But maybe her pen, like herself, failed to understand the new nuances of their dynamic.

Kayce studied it, the electricity fading to the confusion. "When we found Adrian, he wasn't actively using his pen either," he murmured. "And yet it glowed?"

"Your point? I'm not nearly as skittish as he is." *And there was no magnetic attraction there whatsoever. Ick.*

"My point," Kayce's teeth bit into the enunciation, captivating her focus. "Yours did too. And he had a piece of the Initiis in his presence. The book called to the pens."

The iridescent tip of her pen's crystal continued to glow between them.

"Where did your grandfather hide all of his research?"

His bright gaze ensnared Aurelia, the realization quickening her pulse as much as the tender grip on her wrist. "His attic."

"Where are we now?"

Long ago, when Aurelia was still writing about Norenth's tales in a journal with a Pegasus on the cover, she had jokingly called this alcove the kingdom's attic. Papa argued that Fealtek's crystalline deposit at the summit would actually be considered the attic, but she wouldn't be bothered with semantics.

But here they were. In the kingdom's attic. Crystal nib glowing.

Of one mind, her and Kayce started tapping the walls, tracing the crystalline carvings for anything they may have missed, any secret latches to a hidden compartment. Ultimately, they both converged on the small bookshelf, kneeling side by side and pulling out book after book until nothing remained but a small trunk on the bottom shelf.

The word "Chivet" was embossed in copper script.

Aurelia wrenched the lid open, its hinges groaning. But the game's miniature continent did not float to greet them. Instead, the torn half of a book rested within. Her fingers trembled as she pulled it out. Dark leather, gilded with metal corners on the cover: the back of the Book of Beginnings. Several pages scrawled over in Latin hung from the binding—she really should have taken that instead of Spanish class.

Thoughts collided in Aurelia's mind. Papa's note about walking through fire had nothing to do with locating this piece; he must have at least located the third, the book's spine; her pen was still glowing; and the Initiis? Smaller than she expected.

Kayce broke the stunned silence. "Your grandfather would have been proud."

Aurelia stilled. Because more than anything, she wanted to serve his memory. It was her compass, helping her navigate the storm that would undoubtedly surge. Storms were inevitable. But she wasn't unanchored.

Not anymore, she realized. Small bits of her papa. Training her body, enlivening her imagination. Laughter with friends. This closeness with Kayce, for all that it stole her breath. Discovering this vital piece of the Initiis. All anchors, grounding her in this life.

As though remembering he still clutched it within his fist, Kayce fished something from the pouch he had collected earlier: a thin chain holding an intricate knot, a pendant with a glowing blue emerald in the center.

"I know this pales in comparison to what we just found." A dry chuckle escaped him, a small dimple appearing in his cheek as he studiously avoided her gaze. "But I'm running out of opportunities to give this to you. Apparently, pens of deceased Flamehearts return to the Smith. It wasn't hard to ask Fee how to get it back. Get the Smith to make it into something new. Had to barter with Fee within an inch of my life to act as an intermediary, but it helped that it was a gift for you." He cleared his throat, the curl of his lips softening as he studied her. He gently unfurled her free hand to drop the pendant into her palm. "Now, you can always carry a piece of him with you."

"Kayce..." A breath loosened as she sniffed. All thoughts of the ancient artifact in her lap evaporated. Blinking hard, Aurelia marveled at how the stone caught the light.

Kayce didn't take his eyes off her, like the smile through her tears rivaled the sun rising outside.

"I can't—I can't believe you—it's beautiful." Aurelia's heart stumbled. Not only at the thoughtfulness, but knowing how much he thought of her when she wasn't here. Like how she'd been thinking of him in that swampy wilderness.

She truly was never alone.

"Help me?" She offered it back to him. When Kayce took it, she turned and lifted her bound curls, exposing the pale nape of her neck. His fingertips brushed over her skin, causing Aurelia to shiver as the pendant hung under the hollow of her throat. Several tears clung to her lashes.

"I wanted to honor his memory." He sucked in a quiet breath as his fingers lingered, their heat against her skin. "You deserve—"

Turning to face him, Aurelia didn't think. She rose onto her knees and pressed her lips to his cheek.

Kayce stilled. Blinking, he sat there as she pulled away. Red crept up his neck, and her cheeks burned. She leaned forward a fraction, pulled toward him by a force she couldn't begin to understand.

Aurelia wanted to feel it again. She knew "just friends" didn't look at each other like this. Touch like this. But she couldn't ignore this change inside her—not this time.

Kayce's lips parted. He shifted back onto his heels.

Her cheeks burned hotter as she toyed with the pendant, the Initiis between them. Had she gotten caught up in the moment of discovery? Overanalyzed everything? Seen more where there wasn't anything but years of friendly affection? Uncertainty made her voice waver at his retreat. "Kayce—"

He cut her off. Surging forward, his arms slid around her. His lips found hers.

Questions raced through Aurelia's mind: how, when, and *why* would he ever—

He angled his head, deepening the kiss. He stole her breath and scattered those thoughts like minnows. A stone tossed in the pool of her mind—everything, save him, eddying away.

Her lips moved with his, her hands gripping the lapels of his coat. His own slid up her back, tucking her body against his in a snug embrace. Blood pulsed in her head, tandem with the heart hammering within Kayce's chest. She felt each beat as hard as her own.

When they pulled apart for a breath, Aurelia kept her eyes closed.

"I needed to know what it feels like with you," Kayce rasped against her lips.

He'd wondered about kissing her before? Aurelia shivered. "Just once," she managed. "Just this once."

It wasn't what she'd imagined for a first kiss; she knew him as intimately as she knew herself. And it wasn't like a last kiss, for Aurelia knew her words were utter lies as warmth stoked the flame within her.

Her name rolled off Kayce's tongue as he gripped her hips, brushing his nose along hers.

She didn't want him to explain her apprehension away. Because even as the kiss broke her mind apart and pieced it back together, Aurelia knew these precious moments were all she had to pretend.

Pretend that she wasn't bound by an oath to remain only his friend—the one precept she must obey. He deserved so much better than she could ever offer.

When she opened her eyes, the look in Kayce's set everything she knew ablaze. She rested her forehead against his, releasing his coat to rest her hands lightly on his chest. The still-thundering heartbeat reassured her. Both of them, drawn like moths to something that burned far too bright for them to ignore.

A soft hum came from Kayce as they contemplated each other. "I'll listen to you," his voice rumbled. "For now."

Aurelia's breath caught. Despite the trepidation cloying at her mind, her heart soared at the implication of what he *wouldn't* listen to. But regardless of what was to come, one thing was certain: that night, this morning, was when her life finally began.

Morning light emblazoned the sky and seas as the two rangers exited the hidden outpost. It caught their eyes, bright enough to hide the soft glow emanating from the emerald at Aurelia's throat.

Hope and hesitation thrummed between them, but no matter what stacked against them, they would face it.

Together.

Unbeknownst to them, three pairs of eyes observed from the trees. And in a beat, the owl lifted its wings and left them.

End of Book I of the Flameheart Chronicles

THANKS

Let's be honest and admit that we pulled about a dozen books to read their acknowledgements page. Then we realized there was no way to do it wrong, and that our hearts know exactly what needs to be said. First and foremost, we thank God for the dream planted in our hearts and the talents with which we were blessed. This story would be nothing without the hope in the darkness, the peace in the storm. We are merely the recorders of this story, and we are honored to have been chosen to tell it.

Now, to the fabulous crew at Quill & Flame Publishing House: thank you for taking a chance on this debut. For seeing Aurelia's journey and demanding it be told. To AJ, your enthusiasm and tea spilling gave us life. Brittany, your eye for world building brought this book to a whole new level. Brigitte, thank you for making this novel shine with your attention to detail. And to the other Q & F authors for fighting over the Weatherstone brothers, our chats have been so uplifting when the imposter syndrome was brutal. We wish there was a brother for each of you, but four is plenty.

Our friends and family, thank you for your unwavering support. Your prayers, check-ins, and cheerleading of this journey has helped us in ways you can't understand. It is the love of community that has helped shape this novel. We were never meant to do this life alone. To our sweet sons, thank you for your smiles on the hard days. For reminding us that there are stories you will need as you grow up, stories to arm yourselves with as you face your own monsters. We pray this is one sword of many.

To Emily's students, who read pieces of this first, thank you for being champions and not being afraid to tell Emily when something didn't work. Remember, your words have power, and they helped shaped the young adults in this story more than you know. We also want to thank our amazing critique partners who read this novel in its rougher stages: Alex, Carrie-Ann, Emma, Victoria, and Maria. Your insight was invaluable, from the critiques to the analogies to the unhinged fangirling over these characters. Thank you, thank you, a thousand times thank you. To Aaron, Dan, and Dustin. For the late-night phone calls with Dalton, bouncing ideas and brainstorming together while building the world and deepening plot. You guys were invaluable in more ways than one. Your encouragement and support mean the world to Dalton. Kenton, our conversations, brainstorming, and honest opinions have helped mold this story into something far deeper than we could have expected. Mike, words can't express how grateful we are. You helped Dalton to see the true power of believing in yourself and to chase his dreams no matter what.

And last, to you. Readers are the heart of this story. We pray you found kinship in Aurelia, but also that the desire to escape is truly one to be found. We hope you have discovered in these pages the courage to run toward the roar and face reality head on. Always know, the pages will be there to welcome you back whenever you need. We are so honored that you chose to escape—and be found—within ours. A story is nothing without its reader. Nothing without you.

ABOUT THE AUTHORS

Years ago, Dalton and Emily's love story began over words. Starting as writing partners and delving into friendship, Dalton soon proposed building Emily a library. Needless to say, her heart was won. Since then, they have written countless tales of magic, heists, and romance for their own amusement. When they aren't building stories or marathoning epic franchises, two young sons and a gaggle of animals keep them busy. If additional time is ever found, Dalton enjoys hunting and fishing. Emily would prefer to read while watching him, warm beverage in hand. *Flameheart* is their debut novel.